A gripping and explosive novel of unthinkable acts, inhuman terror, and drastic measures from bestselling author, combat-decorated soldier, correspondent, and American hero,

OLIVER NORTH

Tomorrow in an uncertain world . . .

The free nations of the Earth wake up to devastating news. Islamic Jihadists have struck at multiple targets in Saudi Arabia, nearly wiping out the entire royal family while crippling the kingdom's oil producing machinery. In a terrible instant, everything has changed—as devastating inflation rocks the world's financial markets.

The normal rules no longer apply.

An "Assassination Bill" has been introduced in a closed session of Congress. General Peter Newman has been granted the authority to recruit and train up to 100 specialists for one extreme but necessary purpose: the brutal and permanent elimination of terrorists. It is a task that will take Newman and his team into the heart of the beast to derail an Iranian plot to attack the U.S. And one misstep could bring nuclear destruction to America's greatest cities.

"[North] mixes a few uncomfortable facts
in with his fiction."
New York Times

By Oliver North

THE ASSASSINS
THE JERICHO SANCTION
MISSION COMPROMISED

OLIVER NORTH

AND JOE MUSSER

THE ASSASSINS

AVON BOOKS
An Imprint of HarperCollinsPublishers

Reprinted by arrangement with Broadman and Holman Publishers

AVON BOOKS
An Imprint of HarperCollins*Publishers*
10 East 53rd Street
New York, New York 10022-5299

Copyright © 2005 by Oliver L. North
ISBN-13: 978-0-06-113764-8
ISBN-10: 0-06-113764-2
www.avonbooks.com

First Avon Books paperback printing: October 2006

Avon Trademark Reg. U.S. Pat. Off. and in Other Countries, Marca Registrada, Hecho en U.S.A.
HarperCollins ® is a registered trademark of HarperCollins Publishers Inc.

Printed in the U.S.A.

10 9 8 7 6 5 4 3 2 1

For Betsy
And our adventures: past, present, and future

Contents

Acknowledgments

David Shepherd and his team at Broadman & Holman Publishers have once again proven that patience really is a virtue. I'm grateful for the understanding they have shown for the chaotic life that I lead—and how it tends to sabotage deadlines. The whole B & H team was remarkably tolerant while awaiting completion of this third novel in our series.

Joe Musser, my friend and partner in this effort, made it possible to finish this book. Often, I left him and my indomitable assistant, Marsha Fishbaugh, waiting by a computer while I ran off to cover events in Iraq or Afghanistan for FOX News, where it's tougher than it ought to be to receive or return e-mails—except in the middle of the night. I'm glad that neither have yet seen fit to put out a contract on me.

Because of my several protracted absences, copy editor Amanda Sauer had to read and edit this book a chapter at a time over many months. And on project editor Lisa Parnell's schedule, proofers George Knight, Mary Maddox, and Dean Richardson had to read and pray their way through a belatedly delivered manuscript.

Kudos also go to B & H Author Relations Manager Mary Beth Shaw, Marketing Director Paul Mikos, Sales

Director John Thompson, Publicity Director Heather Hulse, Book Marketing Manager Robin Patterson, Creative Director Jeff Godby, Copywriter David Schrader, and Duane Ward of Premiere Speakers Bureau—all performed "above and beyond the call of duty," for which I'm truly grateful. Thanks, too, for the resourceful maps by David Deis that help readers coordinate the geography about which this story revolves.

Of course there would be no "story" to tell without the encouragement and inspiration of my wife, Betsy, and our children and their mates: Tait and Tom, Stuart and Ellen, Sarah and Martin, and Dornin. Through their faith and affection I am reminded of God's love in my life—for shaping my faith and giving me His guidance for this project.

Semper Fidelis,
Oliver L. North

Alpha radiation. A positively charged particle emitted from the nucleus of an atom during radioactive decay. Heavy dosage of alpha particles can be harmful if they enter the body through inhalation, ingestion, or open wounds.

Amn al-Khass. Iraq's Special Security Service (also SSS)

APU. Auxiliary power unit

ARS. Acute radiation syndrome, or radiation sickness, usually results when a person gets a high dose of radiation in only a few minutes.

ASDS. Advanced SEAL Delivery System, a submarine-mounted mini-sub used for Special Operations

ATF. Alcohol, Tobacco, and Firearms Department

AWACS. Airborne Warning and Control System; aircraft with long-range radars capable of locating and identifying other aircraft in the region and of relaying the information to its own air forces

BDA. Bomb Damage Assessment

Beta. Beta particles are ejected from a radioactive atom during decay. Beta radiation is smaller and faster than alpha radiation and can penetrate human tissue.

BOLO. Be on the lookout

C. The abbreviation for chief of British SIS (see MI6). A green C in the logo of the SIS is an allusion to its founder, the original C, Sir Mansfield Cumming. A tradition of SIS is that all chiefs are known simply as C and sign their documents using green ink.

CENTCOM. Central Command

CinC. Commander in Chief

CNO. Chief of Naval Operations

CO. Commanding Officer

DCI. Director of Central Intelligence

DCM. Deputy Chief of Mission

D-DACT. Dismounted Data Automated Communications Terminal; a computing device weighing thirty-one ounces, built to withstand the most rugged of field conditions and designed to perform key field communications functions, interfaces with GPS—used to provide real-time encrypted reports on troop and threat locations to higher commands and among other units

DEA. Drug Enforcement Agency

DGI. Cuban General Intelligence Directorate

DGSE. *Direction Generale de la Securite Exterieure* (General Directorate for External Security, France)

DHS. Department of Homeland Security

DIA. Defense Intelligence Agency; military intelligence gathering arm of the U.S. Armed Forces and the Department of Defense

DINA. National Intelligence Service (Spain)

Dirty bomb. Whereas nuclear weapons are designed to kill and destroy through a huge blast and heat, a "dirty bomb" uses conventional explosives to spread radioactive material to sicken and kill people.

DNI. Director of National Intelligence

DOD. Department of Defense

Dose. Also, dose equivalent; a general term for the quantity of energy absorbed when exposed to radioactive materials or reactions. Rads represent the energy absorbed from the radiation in a gram of any material. The dose or dose equivalent is a measure of the biological damage to living tissue from the radiation exposure and is measured in REMs or sieverts (also see both).

Dosimeter. A small, portable device used to measure and record the amount of a radiation dose a person has received

Duvdevan. Also Sayaret Duvdevan; an undercover counter-terrorism unit of the IDF

DZ. Drop zone

ECHELON. The name of a global eavesdropping service established by the U.S. National Security Agency in cooperation with Great Britain's GCHQ, Canada, and New Zealand

ELINT. Electronic intelligence

EOD. Explosive ordnance disposal

FAPSI. Federal Agency for Government Communications (Russian Federation)

FARC. Revolutionary Armed Forces of Colombia.

Fatwa. A legal pronouncement of Islamic law issued by a Muslim cleric

FEMA. Federal Emergency Management Agency

FFP. Final firing position (usually refers to a position used by a sniper)

FIR. Flight information region

FMF. Fleet Marine Force

GCHQ. British Signals and Intelligence Agency; similar to U.S. National Security Agency

GOSP. Gas-oil separation plant

GRU. Russian Military Intelligence

HAHO. High-altitude, high-opening parachute deployment

HALO. High-altitude, low-opening parachute deployment

HASC. House Armed Services Committee

HF. High frequency

HUMINT. Human intelligence

IAEA. International Atomic Energy Agency

ICE. Immigrations and Customs Enforcement

IDF. Israel Defense Force; the name of Israel's armed forces

IED. Improvised explosive device; usually made from artillery shells, mines, or other high explosives—often set up along heavily traveled roads and often detonated by remote control

IFF. Identification friend or foe; a device used to discriminate between friendly and enemy units, individuals, weapons, and aircraft. In aircraft, an IFF device will display altitude, speed, and direction on an air traffic controller's computer display.

IM. Instant messaging; wireless instant messaging differs from e-mail primarily in that its primary focus is immediate end-user delivery and does not use typical computer architecture and hardware.

In Sha' Allah. Arabic, from the Quran, meaning "God willing"

IPSA. An oil pipeline between southern Iraq and northern Saudi Arabia

IR. Infrared

JCS. Joint Chiefs of Staff

JDAM. Joint Direct Attack Munition

JSOC. Joint Special Operations Command

Klick. Military slang for kilometer

LGB. Laser-guided bomb

LHD. U.S. Navy and Marine Corps designation for an amphibious assault ship, helicopter, dock

LMG. Light machine gun

LZ. Landing zone

Maddrassa. Schools for religious instruction in Islamic teaching

MAMs. Military age males

Materiel. Military term for all items necessary to equip, operate, maintain, and support military units

MEU. Marine Expeditionary Unit

MI6. United Kingdom's secret foreign intelligence service; similar to U.S. Central Intelligence Agency

MOPP. Mission-oriented protective posture; designation for the protective suit, mask, and other equipment worn to shield troops from toxic nuclear, biological, and chemical weapons— also called "NBC suit"

MPS. Maritime pre-positioning ships

MSG. Marine security guard

Mullah. A teacher or learned man (Islam)

NBC suit. Nuclear, biological, and chemical protective gear; see also MOPP

NCO. Noncommissioned officer

NCOIC. Noncommissioned officer in charge

NEO. Noncombatant Evacuation Operation

NEST. Nuclear Emergency Search Team

NIC. National Intelligence Council

NMCC. National Military Command Center

NOC. Network Operations Center

NOTAM. Notice to Mariners

NRO. National Reconnaissance Office, located near Dulles, Virginia; handles the operations of U.S. military and intelligence imagery satellites

NSA. National Security Agency

NVD. Night vision device; an optical device for sighting targets in darkness through a scope mounted on a rifle or other weapon

NVG. Night vision goggles; worn by military personnel to enhance vision at night

OIF. Operation Iraqi Freedom

OP. Observation post

OPEC. Organization for Petroleum Exporting Countries

PAL. Permissive action links; devices that prevent the arming, release, detonation, or launch of a nuclear weapon by unauthorized personnel—often supplemented by sophisticated coded switch systems

PAX. Military abbreviation for "passengers"

PDB. President's Daily Briefing

PFT. Marine Corps physical fitness test

PM. Prime Minister

PMMW. Passive millimeter wave; equipment that permits an operator to view through solid objects, producing an image similar to an X-ray

POL. Petroleum, oil, and lubricants

POTUS. President of the United States

PSD. Personal Security Detail

QRF. Quick Reaction Force (U.S. Marines)

RAD. Radiation absorbed dose, which units measure the amount of energy from any type of ionizing radiation deposited in any medium (also see REM)

RAF. Royal Air Force

RCC. Revolutionary Command Council (government of Iran)

RCT. Regimental Combat Team

RDD. Radiological dispersal device; a "dirty bomb" using radioactive materials

RDV. Rendezvous

REM. Roentgen equivalent man/mammal; a unit that measures the effects of ionizing radiation on humans and other animals. One hundred REMs equal one sievert (also see sievert)

ROE. Rules of Engagement

RPG. Rocket-propelled grenade

RTO. Radio transmitter operator; the acronym is used in military jargon for the radio operator.

SAR. Search and rescue

SAS. Special Air Service; elite unit of the British Royal Army and Air Force used for special operations

SAVAMA. Iran's former National Intelligence Security Organisation *(Sazamaneh Ettela at va Amniateh Mihan)* and still the nickname for its current apparatus (see VEVAK)

SBS. Special Boat Service; an elite British Special Forces unit

SecDef. U.S. Secretary of Defense

Sievert. The international standard unit of dose or dose equivalent; one sievert (Sv) is equal to one hundred REMs.

SIGINT. Signals intelligence

SIS. Special Intelligence Service, a British agency.

SOCOM. Special Operations Command

SOF. Special Operation Forces

SOP. Standard Operating Procedure

SPR. Strategic Petroleum Reserve

SSCI. Senate Select Committee on Intelligence

SubLant. Naval submarine force; U.S. Atlantic fleet

SVR. Federal Security Service (Russian Federation, successor to KGB)

SWO. Senior watch officer

TSA. Transportation Security Administration

UAE. United Arab Emirates

UAV. Unmanned aerial vehicle

USCG. U.S. Coast Guard

VBIED. Vehicle-borne improvised explosive device

VEVAK. Iranian Ministry of Intelligence and Security *(Vezarat-e Ettelaat va Amniat-e Keshvar* VEVAK/MOIS). The intelligence service used by the Shah of Iran (SAVAK) has been defunct since 1979, when it was absorbed by SAVAMA *(Sazamaneh Ettela at va Amniateh Mihan)*, which in turn was absorbed by VEVAK. Many Iranians still refer to Iran's primary intelligence service as SAVAMA.

XO. Executive officer

ZULU. Military term for Greenwich Mean Time, used as a reference for all military activities

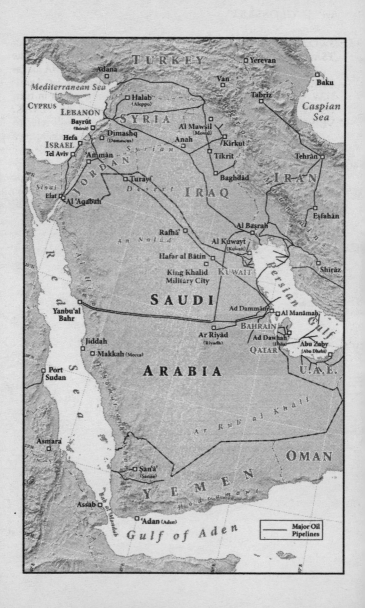

THE
ASSASSINS

PROLOGUE

In the Event of War . . .

Royal Saudi Air Force Early Warning Center
King Khalid Air Base, Saudi Arabia
Sunday, 14 October 2007
1056 Hours Local

When the tiny blip first appeared on his radar screen, Maj. Achmed Musa glanced at it and resumed drinking his coffee. He'd already checked the display next to the screen, confirmed that Iran Air Flight 6 was due to appear at this time, and so he merely shrugged. Musa had seen "IA#6" pop up on the radar console three times a week at this time of day ever since the Saudi government had granted the Iranians over-flight rights for their commercial aircraft heading to and from Egypt.

The Saudi officer glanced at the wide screen at the front of the room. Sure enough, the Japanese computers that drove the American-installed software showed the flight tracks of a dozen aircraft in the air above the kingdom. A few minutes earlier Musa had glanced up to see the flight tracks of two chartered civilian Gulfstream aircraft—both of them on flight plans to pick up VIP passengers—and now he could see the track of IA#6 on a bearing of 285 degrees as the Airbus A300 headed across the Persian Gulf, toward Saudi airspace. Until January this year, Standard Operating Procedures had called for him to contact the Royal Saudi Air Force AWACs aircraft, orbiting at 37,000 feet some 230 miles north. But that part of their SOP had changed—overruling the American military advisors.

Ever since 9/11—as they called it—the Americans had been fanatical about the Persians and were always reminding the Saudi officers about the "jihadist menace."

Maybe they have always been that way, the Saudi major reflected. The Americans had sold the big Boeing 747 AWACs, with their revolving PNQ-41 radar antennas, to the Saudis way back in 1981—when Musa was still in diapers—on the infidels' paranoid premise that the Iranians were a threat to the Saudi kingdom.

"Praise be to Allah," the Saudi major said to himself, "we've gotten a lot smarter since then. Now we know that the real threat isn't our Muslim brothers in Tehran—it's the Zionists and their infidel supporters." And that's why, since the Israelis *were* the real threat, the Saudi AWACs and the Early Warning Center had stopped alerting each other every time an Iranian airplane took off. That's also why the big 747s now took station on Saudi Arabia's northern border. If an airplane got more than a few feet off the ground in Israel, the Saudi AWACs would spot it and respond to the threat.

In the control room of the Saudi Early Warning Center, Major Musa was still contemplating these things when he noticed that Iranian Air Flight 6 was no longer on its normal course.

He stared at the radar image for several seconds before acting on what he saw. Instead of flying straight toward the Jordanian border, IA#6 was now ten degrees south of its prescribed flight path. Musa reached for the hotline phone—another American innovation—that connected him with the Regional Air Traffic Control Center. His hand picked up the telephone handset—but before he could ask what was going on, the blip on his radar screen suddenly disappeared.

Major Musa held the phone next to his chest as he waited for the radar repeater to make another revolution. When it did and he still saw nothing where Flight 6 had once been, he put the phone to his ear to make his inquiry. The line was dead.

ARAMCO Gulf Service Vessel
Safaniya Offshore Oil Field, Persian Gulf
Sunday, 14 October 2007
1057 Hours Local

The 145-foot red and black hydrofoil with the words "ARAMCO Gulf Services" boldly painted on its side was a familiar sight in the northern Persian Gulf. Since the 1980s, ten of the high-speed craft had been routinely delivering crews, parts, mail, and food to the dozens of Saudi and Emirate-owned oil platforms up and down the Persian Gulf.

On the bridge of the vessel, Ibrahim al-Hadid, the youthful pilot, spoke softly in Arabic to the helmsman—a fellow Yemeni. "Keep on this course, and maintain your speed. Ignore their signals to slow down. We do not want to be late making our delivery of this precious cargo to Safaniya." If the two men were nervous, they didn't show it.

Looming just a few hundred yards directly in front of the vessel, a massive, towering structure with sixteen huge steel legs, anchored atop the largest oil field in the Persian Gulf, rose up out of the blue water. The giant rig was much more than an oil platform. Since it was first towed into position in 1975, Safaniya had been transformed into the offshore hub for a spiderweb of seabed pipelines connected to scores of offshore rigs. On the huge platform's main deck, eighty-five feet above the water's surface, forty-six carefully calibrated pumps and hundreds of valves controlled the distribution of heavy crude and natural gas through a network of submerged pipes, sixty miles south to the supertanker terminal at Ras Tanura.

But the biggest—and by far the most critical— pumps, valves, and controls aboard Safaniya didn't move oil or gas. Instead they moved millions of gallons of seawater—through pipes hundreds of feet underwater— injecting it deep into offshore and onshore pockets of heavy crude. The water was needed to force the diminishing supply of crude to the surface.

As widely suspected, but known for certain by only a few dozen petroleum experts and oil geologists, the vast Saudi oil fields were slowly running dry. The myth of "gushers"—spouting black gold high in the air above a drilling rig—had been just that, a myth, for decades.

The most critical function performed by the 343 Filipino, Bangladeshi, Pakistani, Indonesian, Yemeni, and Turkish workers aboard Safaniya was to ensure that the thirty-one enormous seawater pumps on the platform's 01 Level, immediately below main deck, never faltered. If the water stopped flowing, so, too, would the oil— from beneath the seabed as well as the huge Ramallah oil field ashore. Well over half of Saudi production depended on the seawater delivered by Safaniya.

Ibrahim al-Hadid knew all this, for he had worked on the Safaniya platform for nearly five years—three of them after he had been recruited by Ansar al Islam. For the last two of those years the Islamic terror group that considered al-Hadid to be a member of their sleeper cells never contacted him. When he left the rig two weeks ago for his quarterly "shore rotation," al-Hadid had planned on spending the time at home with his family in Yemen. But two days after arriving in Sana, an official from the Iranian Embassy had quietly approached him at his mosque. The Iranian simply said, "It is time.

You have a mission from Allah." Al-Hadid was given a ticket to Kaki, Iran, and when he arrived there, was introduced to the five young men now aboard the hydrofoil with him. Together they had been taken to the naval base at Mal Gonzel.

It was there that the five men were escorted aboard the hydrofoil. The utility ship was tied up beneath a large canvas awning—not as protection from the sun, but to hide the vessel from the prying eyes of American, Indian, French, Russian, and Chinese intelligence satellites.

For a week the five radical Muslims had gone out each night with an Iranian Navy officer who taught them the rudiments of navigation and seamanship. Each day they studied the Quran with a mullah from the nearby maddrassa. For two days prior to departing, al-Hadid and the others helped Iranian sailors load tons of ammonium nitrate in large barrels aboard the boat. Then, the five "volunteer martyrs" watched as a team of Revolutionary Guard explosives "experts" mixed diesel fuel with the white, powdery granules, tied the detonating charges together with primacord, and wired them together with eleven blasting caps—all of which were then connected in serial to an electric switch on the bridge.

Before leaving the five men, the head of the explosives team showed al-Hadid how to hook up the battery to the blasting circuit—a lesson the Iranian concluded with the admonition, "Make this connection last, just before you approach your target."

The trip across the gulf had taken less than two hours and was totally uneventful. Now, as the huge platform loomed before them, al-Hadid connected the red and black leads from the battery to the open switch on the bridge and made a final check of the wires taped to the deck and running aft to the blasting caps. Behind the pilothouse in the galley, his three other colleagues were poised with AK-47s and hand grenades—a precaution against being stopped and boarded. He nodded to them and said, "It is almost time. We will strike a blow for Islam and against the infidels!"

"Allah be praised. It will happen as you say," one of them replied more perfunctorily than enthusiastic.

"We will meet again in paradise! We go in triumph to meet Allah, bringing with us the heads of our enemies." Al-Hadid turned back to the young jihadist at the steering station, put his hand on the helmsman's shoulder, and said, "Do not change course even if their security force begins firing. They have heavy firepower, but we are going fast enough that I think we can get through any attempt to stop us. Just keep speed and course steady. Estimated time—thirty seconds." No one spoke as the ship hurtled toward the huge Safaniya oilrig while al-Hadid completed arming the terminals of the blasting circuit.

"Are you ready?" al-Hadid asked in the direction of the boy.

"Yes," came the reply, almost a croak.

"Good," said al-Hadid. Then, a few seconds later, he reached for the switches on the console and shouted, "Now! Full speed. Allah Akbar!"

Chartered Gulfstream V
Heading 130° at 30,000'
Approaching Abqaiq Processing Center, Saudi Arabia
Sunday, 14 October 2007
1058 Hours Local

Muammar al-Qutb was comfortable at the controls of the chartered Gulfstream V. An experienced, senior Egypt Air commercial pilot, al-Qutb had more than eight thousand hours in various commercial and charter aircraft. His employers knew that he often supplemented his income with charter work—a lucrative sideline in his home country and throughout the region. What they did not know was that the forty-two-year-old father of three was also a member of the Egyptian Islamic Brotherhood—and had been for more than two decades.

On Thursday, 11 October, al-Qutb had departed from the Charter FBO at Cairo's Marsa Alam airport after filing a flight plan for Maan airport, just outside of Amman, Jordan. Upon arrival, he taxied the Gulfstream into a hangar on the south side of the field, opposite the main passenger terminal. Once the hangar door closed, five of his Islamic Brotherhood colleagues immediately began stripping the interior out of the luxurious plane. Once the luxurious leather seats, plush carpeting, lavatory, even the sound-deadening insulation were all removed, the formerly posh passenger cabin resembled the inside of a boxcar. It was then packed floor to ceiling with more than five thousand pounds of Libyan-made plastic explosives.

By the time al-Qutb left for evening prayers at the nearby mosque on Friday afternoon, the luxury aircraft had been turned into a flying bomb. His only admonition to his associates: "Please ensure that the load is properly balanced—and that you do not add any more fuel than necessary." What the pilot al-Qutb knew, but the others did not, was that an identical chartered Gulfstream was being similarly modified in a hangar at the Beirut International Airport.

Al-Qutb spent Saturday at Amman's most famous bordello on Al Bassah Street in the company of a Swedish prostitute. He arose early Sunday morning, and after filing a flight plan from Amman to Al Jubay, Saudi Arabia, he took off at 0855 without incident and, once at his cruising altitude, gently turned the heavily laden Gulfstream southeast. By 0955 al-Qutb was at 27,000 feet, the nose of the sleek jet pointed toward the sprawling Abqaiq processing facility off in the distance. He knew, from detailed briefings he had received almost a week before in Cairo, that two-thirds of Saudi Arabia's crude oil was exported from the gulf via the processing facility—amounting to a staggering ten million barrels a day.

As he soared toward his destination, al-Qutb routinely responded over the radio to the series of instructions from Saudi air traffic controllers who periodically told him to change his IFF transponder code and vectored him over various waypoints—all designed to ensure that he avoided "sensitive" areas in the royal kingdom. On two occasions he heard controllers talking to the other Gulfstream that had left Beirut, en route to "pick up a VIP" at the port city of Yanbu—terminus for the sixty-inch liquid natural gas (LNG) pipeline that snakes parallel to the Petroline Pipeline for 750 miles from Shadqam to the Abqaiq processing facility, and then to Yanbu al Bahr, at Ras Tanura on the Persian Gulf—the "load point" for more than four thousand mammoth tankers annually. The export terminals at Ras Tanura on the Persian Gulf were, al-Qutb had been told, the largest in the world. What he didn't know was that nearly all of the royal kingdom's wealth passes through these critical nodes.

Without them, the only way the Saudis could move any quantity of crude was by way of the old sixty-inch Trans-Arabian Pipeline that ran through Saudi Arabia and Syria to Az Zahrani on the Mediterranean Sea in Lebanon—but it had been shut down since the Lebanese civil war in the 1970s. The only other oil conduit through the kingdom was the old forty-eight-inch IPSA Pipeline that ran from the southern Iraqi border across Saudi Arabia. But it had been taken off-line in August 1990 as part of the UN oil embargo against Iraq, and Bedouin thieves had scavenged whole sections of it.

Muammar al-Qutb knew all of this from the extensive briefings he had received in Cairo a week before he chartered the Gulfstream. He also knew that his fellow pilot—and fellow member of the Muslim Brotherhood—was supposed to depart Beirut that same morning on the other Gulfstream on a similar mission. But al-Qutb knew nothing of Iran Flight 6, the hydrofoil off the coast, or the four Ansar al Islam cells poised to strike at the Kirkuk-Baji and Ramallah-Basra pipelines in Iraq. Nor did he know about the scores of six-man teams of well-armed "Brothers" who had slipped into Saudi Arabia from Yemen, Oman, Kuwait, and Jordan earlier in the week or the others who had surreptitiously crossed the Red Sea into the kingdom from Egypt, Sudan, and Somalia. Riding motorcycles and using handheld GPSs, these highly trained young zealots had traversed the largely uninhabited, trackless desert and assembled undetected at their staging areas near every Saudi city and royal palace.

At 1058 on Sunday, 14 October, Muammar al-Qutb began to nose his Gulfstream down in a long straight trajectory toward the Abqaiq processing facility and the Ghawar oil field. Few of the 471 young men involved in this action knew more than their own role in the largest terror operation in history. Though it was an incredibly complex undertaking, there were no electronic instructions passed by radio, telephone, or the Internet. No calls were made that could be intercepted by the technology of the infidels. Instead, trusted couriers had hand-carried all necessary commands from Tehran to each of the participants.

As the Gulfstream descended, al-Qutb shut off his IFF transponder, pushed the throttles forward, hard against the stops, and muttered to himself, "Allah Akbar." The jet aircraft was now a hurtling guided bomb.

National Reconnaissance Office Operations Center
Chantilly, VA
Sunday, 14 October 2007
0359 Hours Local

Chief Warrant Officer Dan Peters loved his job—flying satellites. The KH-13 that he was "piloting" over the Middle East was traveling at 26,000 miles per hour, at 102 miles above the earth—and he never even had to leave Virginia. From his "cyber-cockpit" in the basement of the NRO Operations Center, less than a mile from the back gate at Dulles International Airport, he could point a satellite's long lens at just about any point on the planet that mattered and "take your picture." At least that's the way he often put it to friends who had the security clearance to know what he did for a living.

Making all this possible, of course, were the arrays of computers behind him. Peters could do this—and often did—taking "snapshots" of various places that were of interest to someone high up the food chain of the federal government or intelligence community. Usually it was some place in Iraq, Iran, Pakistan, or Afghanistan—and had been for over six years—ever since U.S. troops had deployed in the region for Operation Enduring Freedom in 2001.

The middle of the day in Southwest Asia was normally "quiet time" for KH-13 #62B—the newest "Keyhole" imagery satellite "working" the region. From long experience Peters knew that the hours between 1030 and 1430 local time beneath the satellite were never the optimum time for doing the kind of imagery that the "heavies" liked to see in their morning intelligence briefs. They wanted nice, crisp, clear photos of their targets—and for that there had to be shadows. Those shots were best taken when it was early morning or late afternoon beneath the satellite—while the sun was lower in the skies in "his" part of the world.

That's why Peters volunteered for the midnight to 0800 watch. Most nights, unless there was a crisis, by this time in Virginia, the "tasking orders" for imagery from KH-13 #62B—one of more than a dozen such "birds" high above the earth—would already be completed. That meant he could sit down beneath the sign that read MANUAL CONTROL—AUTHORIZED PERSONNEL ONLY, insert his "credit card" identity badge into the slot, take the control yoke with its toggle switches in his hands, and "fly the bird."

Using the GPS display as a navigation aid, Peters flicked a switch on the yoke labeled IR and the image on the monitor in front of him changed from what first looked like an HDTV color TV picture to what now appeared as a color negative image. As he did so, the word *thermal* appeared in the upper right side of the screen.

Peters panned the lens west across Saudi Arabia and zoomed in, "hitting" various installations, pointing the camera at things *he* wanted to look at. As the satellite passed over Ras Tanura, a sudden bright flash flared on the screen, "blinding" the bird and blotting out the image in front of him. Peters recoiled in the ergonomic seat, his first thought, *The lens was hit by a laser!*

It was a logical assumption. All of the NRO watch officers had been briefed on the ground-based, Chinese laser attacks on U.S. intelligence satellites. But in seconds, the powerful computers slowly restored the image on the screen. As the picture came back on-line, Peters blinked and said, in an awe-filled, prayerful gasp, "Oh, my God!"

The deputy watch officer, an Air Force master sergeant, heard Peters' intake of breath. He glanced up at the TV monitor and stood up so quickly that he knocked over his chair. Both Peters and his assistant leaned over to look at another monitor with a normal optical image, confirming what they were watching, live, on the screen. Then Peters shouted an expletive and hit an alarm switch on the console with his left palm. There was no mistaking what they were seeing on the monitor.

Department of Homeland Security Operations Center
Nebraska Avenue, Washington, DC
Sunday, 14 October 2007
0401 Hours Local

The metallic sound of the klaxon over the map display sent a squirt of adrenaline through Matt Roderick's gut. The retired Marine infantry officer pushed the button on his desk, shutting off the annoying sound—just as he had done in more than a dozen national emergency preparedness exercises. He—and all twenty-seven of his watch officers—looked at the map display on the large plasma screen on the front wall. On the map of the Middle East there was a bright red icon, blinking over Saudi Arabia. Then, almost as though they were choreographed, they all moved their eyes at once—from the large map display to the red-bordered message that appeared on every computer screen in the room:

NRO KH-13 #62B REPORTS LEVEL FOUR EXPLOSIVE
FLARE.

Then, just seconds later, another message:

CORRECTION: MULTIPLE EXPLOSIVE FLARES IN NE
SAUDI ARABIA. IMAGERY TO FOLLOW. STAND BY.

Roderick felt his heart begin to race as he focused on the large-screen map and the computer monitors around the room. Within minutes, additional markers showed up on the display, matching the original single red icon on the plasma screen. Roderick called to his

CIA and DIA watch officers monitoring the intelligence situation: "Any word yet?"

By 0420 they had spoken with their respective points of contact and verified Roderick's hunch. "Somebody's bombing the oil fields of Saudi Arabia!" he said into the phone, after getting the Secretary of Homeland Security out of bed an hour earlier than usual.

At 0445 Roderick called the Secretary again and recited what little additional information he had been able to collect: "Between thirty and fifty explosions so far, highly strategic and apparently very accurate. We're getting some more satellite imagery. NRO will need to analyze it to confirm, but right now it looks like someone has taken out just about all of the Saudis' oil production facilities and crippled their pipeline and distribution installations—even the offshore stuff.

"NSA says there are no ELINT emissions from radios or even cell phones, except for Saudi first responders. Nobody has claimed credit yet. Radar confirms that it wasn't done by any of our aircraft or cruise missiles. None of our ships in the Persian Gulf tracked any strike aircraft or missiles from Iran. The Brits are on the line asking what *we* know, so it's logical that *they* probably didn't do it. And I can't see either Israel or the Russians doing something like this. My gut tells me it's a terror attack."

Roderick listened as the DHS Secretary gave him instructions and he wrote the words down on the pad in front of him. The Ops Center was focused on the "event," and as he spoke, one of his watch officers handed him a printout that had just been decrypted.

As Roderick scanned the summary, he could see that it was a detailed confirmation of what he had just shared with his boss. When he finished his "speed read" of the report he said, "I think you might want to wake the President. This looks really bad. All hell has broken loose in Saudi Arabia, and nobody here, the Pentagon,

State, or Langley, has comms with our embassy in Riyadh."

What he didn't know then, but would find out within hours, was that nearly all of the Saudi royal family was already dead or dying.

CHAPTER ONE

Gathering Fury

Situation Room
The White House, Washington, DC
Sunday, 14 October 2007
0846 Hours Local

By the time the armored Cadillac entered the Southwest Gate, West Executive Avenue was already crowded with dark blue government sedans, glistening in the crisp, clear, early autumn air. As the car stopped next to the green awning, Army Staff Sgt. John Houston, jumped from the right front seat of the vehicle, opened the heavy right rear door and stood back. Dan Powers, the grim-faced Secretary of Defense, emerged first, said, "Thank you, John," and entered the West Wing. He was followed by Gen. George Grisham, USMC, Chairman of the Joint Chiefs of Staff.

Immediately inside the door, a cheerless Secret Service agent placed their briefcases on the conveyor of an X-ray machine, and the two men were waved through an airport-type metal detector—despite the machine's muted electronic protest prompted by the ribbons and badges on the Chairman's chest and the four stars on each epaulet.

Powers and Grisham were quickly ushered into the

White House Situation Room by the Senior Watch Officer. They stepped down into the small executive conference enclosure just as the Vice President was taking his seat at the foot of the table.

"Better get a cup of coffee," said the unsmiling Vice President. "It's going to be a long morning." But before Powers and Grisham could comply, the door they had just entered slid open again as the SWO announced, "Ladies and gentlemen, the President."

Powers and Grisham stood when everyone else rose and the President entered the now hushed room. Powers noticed that his hair was still wet—as though he had just toweled it dry. As the President moved past him, Grisham glanced at the digital clock over the plasma screen mounted in the south wall and thought, *It's only 0852 . . . We're going to start eight minutes early. Good thing we were here on time. This guy could have been a Marine he's so punctual. I wonder if he's ever late . . .*

Without preamble, the President removed his suit coat, draped it over the back of his chair, sat down, smoothed his tie, and said, "Thank you all for coming on such short notice. It doesn't look like any of us are going to get to church this morning so let's start with a word of prayer." Turning to the young man on his immediate right, he said, "Jeb, why don't you take this one?"

"Jeb" Stuart, National Security Advisor to the most powerful man on the planet, had been up since the SWO first called him at 0415. He had hastily shaved, showered, dressed, and raced to the White House. For the past four hours he had been furiously trying to assess the magnitude of what had happened in Saudi Arabia. Right up until a few minutes before coming to the Sit Room he was still assembling information and recommendations from State, Defense, the Director of National Intelligence, FBI, DHS, and the Departments of Treasury and Energy.

The National Security Advisor hadn't thought of starting the meeting with prayer, but with all that he'd seen since 0445 that morning, it seemed particularly appropriate. He and the others bowed their heads and Stuart said, "Lord, You are our hope and salvation. Please grant us wisdom. Guide our discussion. Help us to make sound decisions . . ."

As his National Security Advisor awkwardly paused, the President concluded the time of prayer with, "And God, please protect our country and keep our people safe from those who would do us harm and bring us evil . . . amen."

The Chief Executive raised his head and said, "Thank you, Jeb." Then he turned to the Director of National Intelligence and said, "All right, Perry, what do we know?"

Like the others, Perry Straw, the DNI, had been up since shortly after 0400. He had sped to his office at the Reagan Building on Pennsylvania Avenue and immediately ordered every possible collection resource pointed at Saudi Arabia. By 0530 he had directed a worldwide alert to all CIA and NSA bases and stations around the globe, called in all his deputy directors, and ordered preparation of an immediate assessment.

Straw picked up what looked to be a TV remote, pushed a button, and a map of Saudi Arabia came up on the plasma screen. As those in the room shifted in their seats, a series of red dots, more than seventy of them, appeared on the map as the DNI began his briefing. "Based on information about thirty-five minutes old, these are the places where we *know* some kind of violent action took place this morning. We don't have KH-13 imagery in from all of these yet, and there may be more that we don't yet know about. But what we *do* have looks very bad."

As the DNI spoke, a series of satellite "photos"—each with a Chyron-generated label identifying the location and time—appeared on the screen. There were more than thirty images—showing raging fires, burning oil facilities, and blown pipelines pouring oil into huge pools onto the sand.

"We don't know the full extent yet, but it appears that at about 1100 this morning Saudi time, a carefully coordinated attack was launched against the royal kingdom's entire petroleum production and distribution infrastructure," said the DNI. As the horrific scenes flashed on the screen he continued, "As best we can tell, the Abqaiq processing facility at Ghawar and the Yanbu installations have been taken out. The Qatif Junction manifolds, valves, and control center look to be wrecked. The Safaniya Offshore Pumping Station that delivers seawater to most of the Northeast Saudi nodes and controls the undersea distribution network in the northern Persian Gulf is simply gone. The only thing we can see there now is a burning oil slick."

No one said a word until the terrible "slide show" finished. When the screen went blank, the President said simply, "Casualties?"

"Not known yet," Straw replied. "Several thousand at least. Probably multiple nationalities since very few Saudis actually work in their oil industry."

"Americans?" asked the President again.

"Don't know, sir," said Straw. "The CIA's secure fiber-optic and microwave comms with their station in Riyadh went down at the same time the oil infrastructure was hit. We're back up via satellite now, but the station chief is 'flying blind' right now because all official Americans have been told to report to the embassy and he apparently can't get any of his Saudi liaison people to answer the phone."

"Any idea who did this?" asked the President.

"No, sir. We can guess, but that's all," answered the DNI. "The CIA, NSA, and FBI are all listening, but no one has yet made any announcement claiming credit.

Saudi TV and radio are off the air. An Al Jazeera broadcast about an hour ago from Qatar speculated that it was the work of Al Qaeda—but they also only made mention of Ras Tanura being hit. I don't think anyone but the perpetrators really knows how widespread the attack was."

"Is it over?" asked the President. "Have any American installations been hit? How about our diplomatic, commercial, and military facilities in Iraq, Kuwait, Bahrain, and Qatar?"

This time the Secretary of State answered first. "All official Americans in Riyadh have been accounted for. As of 0800 here, no attacks have been reported on any of the 'Western Enclaves' in Saudi Arabia—but we have to assume that American citizens working at the oil sites that were hit are among the casualties.

"We've sent an emergency recall message to all our embassies in the region and told them to dust off their NEO Plans—uh—Non-combatant Evacuation Operations. It's a contingency plan used by every embassy for a safe evacuation of American citizens out of a country or region," the Secretary of State said without missing the cadence in her quick briefing. "Ambassador Kenneth Snelling in Riyadh has been trying to contact the Saudi Foreign Minister without success since noon over there. The only thing I can add to what Perry has already reported is that our embassy security chief told Ambassador Snelling that he had heard explosions in the vicinity of the king's palace and that from the roof of the embassy he can see a pall of smoke over that part of the city."

Turning to the Secretary of Defense, the President simply said, "Dan?"

At seventy, Dan Powers was the oldest one in the room and known as a man who wasted few words. He was also perceived to be closer to the President than anyone in Washington except the Vice President. Everyone knew that in the cabinet he was first among equals—and that he had the President's ear anytime he wanted it.

Unlike the rest of the principals around the table, Dan Powers had no pile of papers in front of him. Seated directly behind him, General Grisham held several folders in case they were needed, but the SecDef waved them off. Powers folded his hands in front of him and began:

"We have dismissed the possibility that this is an overt military act by any of Saudi Arabia's neighbors. We have two carrier battle groups operating in the Northern PG and neither spotted any unusual air activity prior to 1100 Saudi time or since. The USS *Abraham Lincoln* did report that an Iran Air civilian aircraft disappeared off radar at 1058 local and an E-2C off the *Ronald Reagan* lost two other 'bogeys' over northeast Saudi Arabia at about the same time."

Though briefing without the aid of notes or Power-Point slides, the SecDef was speaking quickly. From his vantage point behind the Secretary, Grisham could see several in the room struggling to keep up in taking notes.

Powers continued, talking directly to the President: "As you know, sir, General Grisham here was CinC CENTCOM from 1998 to 2003, and he still has many close friends in the region. In the last four hours he has spoken with every military chief in the theater, and I have spoken directly with all of our senior military commanders out there. Other than two large detonations in Iraq, one on the Kirkuk-Baji pipeline and the other that shut down the Ramallah-Basra Gas-Oil Separation Plant, there have been no attacks anywhere near our troops, ships, aircraft, or installations. We've ordered a Marine Expeditionary Unit that was returning from Iraq to Camp Lejeune to divert to Qatar to beef up security for the Umm Sa'id POL storage facility."

"How much fuel do we have there?" interjected the Commander in Chief.

"We have nearly fifty million gallons of fuel stored at Umm Sa'id—about 750,000 barrels of JP-8 and 150,000 barrels of JP-5. It's the principal POL storage point for CENTCOM," explained the SecDef.

"Any indication of an attempted attack there?" asked the President, directing the question to Grisham.

"No, sir. We're putting the MEU in there as a precaution. We'll also keep their amphibious shipping there in case we need them for rescue and recovery operations—like we did with the Tsunami Aid in December '04—but we have no threat warning indicators. It's a very secure facility."

Several in the room visibly started to sigh in relief—a respite abruptly stifled by the remainder of Powers's assessment. The SecDef continued, "Even though Saudi Arabia seems to be the locus of the attacks, we have concluded that *we* are the principal target."

The President's brow furrowed and everyone else leaned forward as he asked, "Dan . . . General Grisham . . . why do you assume that?"

"Because," Powers replied, "based on what we now know—and we should expect the word from Saudi Arabia to get worse not better—this morning's attack is aimed at the heart of our economy. We have concluded that this morning's attack destroyed at least 50 and perhaps as much as 80 percent of Saudi Arabia's oil production capability and wrecked nearly all export capacity. It's possible that they will not be able to resume significant oil exports for three to five years."

The Defense Secretary's pronouncement stunned the room. In the silence, Jeb Stuart, the National Security Advisor, suddenly realized why Powers had urged him to invite Sam Browning, the Secretary of Energy, to the meeting. Stuart turned to Browning and in a voice that was suddenly hoarse said, "Sam, could that be right?"

The Energy Secretary, attending his first National Security Council crisis meeting, nodded and replied, "If the attacks this morning hit all the nodes described by the DNI, it's entirely possible that Saudi production could be off-line even longer. Unfortunately there's very little in their extraction and distribution system that is common in the rest of the world. Most of the valves, fittings, manifolds, control instrumentation, even piping in the Saudi system is unique.

"Their system is their own, and most of the parts aren't interchangeable or standard. Replacing the pipelines, repairing the 'plumbing' and especially rebuilding the GOSP infrastructure is likely to take *years*."

"I want to get back to the intelligence and what options we need to consider, but first—what's your best guess as to what this is going to do to the price of oil, Sam?" the President asked his Energy Secretary.

Browning thumbed through the stack of paper in front of him and replied, "Hard to tell how high it's going to go. I don't want to step on the toes of Commerce or Treasury, but an hour ago oil futures on the international commodities markets were already at sixty-five U.S. dollars per barrel and headed higher. My guess is that it could break a hundred dollars, maybe even one-fifty by this time tomorrow when our exchanges open."

"Frank," said the President, turning to his Treasury Secretary, "what's going to happen when the markets open tomorrow?"

Frank Kilgannon had made Wall Street his life. He knew "the street" as well as anyone, and everyone in the room respected his opinion on matters of finance—personal and national. He got right to the point: "This could be even worse than 9/11. The market is going to go into a tailspin. And it's not just the NYSE, NASDAQ, AMEX, and the Commodity Exchanges. I think we'll see every exchange in the world take a big hit. We probably ought to call for our exchanges not to open tomorrow—perhaps take a bank holiday, like after 9/11—just to keep the bottom from falling out. Of course we can't keep 'em closed forever. How bad it gets and how long it stays bad is going to depend a lot on what we say and do. I recommend a three-day 'holiday' to let the panic subside."

When the Treasury Secretary finished his blunt assessment, the President said, "Do it, Frank. Get the appropriate Emergency Executive Order out of the Presidential Emergency Action Documents that Jeb keeps locked up down here somewhere and bring it by the Oval Office this afternoon." He then turned back to his Energy Secretary and asked, "Is there anything we can do short-term to replace the Saudi production? Winter is coming on and people need to heat their homes and businesses."

Once again Sam Browning delved into his stack of paper, grasped a sheet, and held it in front of his corpulent stomach as he began to speak. "We currently have about 900 million barrels in the SPR . . . the Strategic Petroleum Reserve. We're currently using about twelve to fifteen million barrels a day just for American autos and trucks. At current consumption rates our reserves would only last sixty days. We're maxed out in Texas, Oklahoma, the Gulf, and the North Slope—although at higher prices per barrel, producers will be able to squeeze more out of low yield wells—maybe 5 percent of what we got from the Saudis. Too bad Congress killed ANWR. If it was on-line it could replace about 20 percent of what we just lost."

Browning fumbled through a few more pages and then added, "At the higher price, Mexico will be able to crank up some low-production wells and get us another 5 percent . . . the Brits, Dutch, and Norway—another 5 percent from the North Sea; the Russian Caspian and Siberian fields maybe another 5 percent or so."

The Energy Secretary then drew an even bleaker picture. "With their political instability, Venezuela is a wild card—I doubt that they'll help us. Neither will the Iranians. The Chinese are still working on getting their own strategic reserves up to a billion barrels, so it's unlikely they will want to sell any. Japan and India are going to want everything they can get from the Indonesian and the South China Sea fields. The Europeans are going to grab every bucket of Libyan sweet crude they can get. About the only hope we have is that some in OPEC will want to cash in on the higher per-barrel price. If they really crank up production, they *might* be able to replace 20 to 25 percent of what we've just lost. But that's pure speculation."

While his Energy Secretary was talking, the President, a former oil man himself, was jotting down the figures on a notepad in front of him. He looked up and said, "What you're telling us is that for the foreseeable future the best we can hope for is 40 to 45 percent of the oil we were getting from Saudi Arabia. And on top of the shortfall, every drop we use is now going to cost up to three times more than the highest price we've ever paid."

Browning nodded somberly and said quietly, "Yes, sir."

The President grimaced, looked back to his Defense Secretary, and said, "What about Iraq, Dan?"

"Iraqi oil, sir?"

"Yeah, how are the Iraqis doing on our little project?" asked the President. Then realizing that most of the rest of the room didn't know what he was talking about, the Chief Executive added, "A while back I asked Dan to see what it would take to get the Iraqis up on the step for full production."

Powers had been silent for several minutes while the Treasury and Energy secretaries had been making their gloomy forecasts. Now, still without the aid of notes, he spoke quietly to the rest of the room. "What you're about to hear has been discussed only with the President, Vice President, the National Security Advisor, and General Grisham here. Until now it has been known to only a very small circle, and given what's happened today, we need to keep it that way."

The SecDef cleared his throat and continued, "Shortly after the Iraqi elections in January '05, I asked the Defense Intelligence Agency to give us a scientific assessment of Iraqi reserves." As he said these words he could see Perry Straw silently bristle. Collecting this kind of information was clearly within the mandate of the DNI, and everyone in the room knew it.

Powers decided to nip the bureaucratic "turf war" in the bud before it escalated outside the room. Looking directly at the DNI for the first time, he said, "Perry, I had DIA do this because the President told me to. But it was my decision not to bring your folks in because your National Intelligence Council—which ordinarily would have gotten the report—leaks like a sieve—as you are well aware."

Straw began to argue. "That's still no reason—"

"Enough!" said the President. "What's the bottom line, Dan?"

The President's mild rebuke brought Powers back to the issue. He continued, "Our guys discovered that there hadn't been a realistic assessment of Iraqi oil reserves in more than thirty years. We used some of our new overhead stuff—both satellite and 'air breather'—and integrated that data with geologic, seismic, and tectonic information collected over the last eighteen months. The study concludes that *Iraq* probably has two or three times more recoverable crude than Saudi Arabia possesses today."

"If that's true," said Sam Browning, the Energy Secretary, "it's the first good news I've heard all morning. Who did this assessment, if I may ask?"

"Doctors Edmond Sarrini and Josef Hussman," Powers replied.

Even Perry Straw was impressed. Both Sarrini and Hussman had impeccable credentials, but he had to ask, "You talk about leaks—how'd you keep them from talking about their work? They're both well known in the very small but loquacious universe of oil exploration experts."

"Unfortunately, they cannot talk. They're both dead," Powers replied bluntly. "They were killed by a roadside bomb in Iraq four days ago. The media haven't picked up on the story yet. They delivered their final report the night before and were on the way to the airport when they were hit. Our people in Baghdad believe that someone—perhaps from one of their own survey teams—fingered them."

"Well, you managed to keep the lid on this one," interjected the DNI, still smarting from the earlier exchange. "I haven't seen a word of this come through channels. Did we or the Iraqis catch anyone involved?" asked Straw.

"The Iraqi National Police arrested four people that they believe were involved. Unfortunately, the suspects are also dead."

"Who were they? How did they die?" Straw inquired even though he knew that the President was impatient to move on.

"They were Iranians—and they poisoned themselves . . . with Ricin," answered Powers tersely.

Before the President could interrupt again, Jeb Stuart spoke up. "Again, it is important that none of this be discussed outside this room. Mr. Secretary, could you please summarize what the Sarrini/Hussman assessment says about how long it could take to get these Iraqi reserves into full production?"

"Shortest time, twelve months for seven to ten million barrels," the SecDef replied. "Longer term, two to four years to bring Iraqi production up to twenty-five to thirty million barrels—roughly double what Saudi production was yesterday. But equally important, both Sarrini and Hussman maintained that Saudi production was about to drop off precipitously. Sarrini reported that the amount of seawater the Saudis were using to maintain positive pressure to push the crude to the surface had gone up dramatically in the last few years."

Powers nodded to the Energy Secretary and said, "Sam, this is something that you understand better than I do, but Sarrini claimed that over the past four years the water being pumped into the wells increased from 18 percent to more than 30 percent. And in April of this year the ratio got *as high as 52 percent.*"

"That can only mean that their recoverable reserves were being depleted at an alarming rate," Browning said, almost to himself.

For the first time the Vice President spoke up. "What connection does any of this have to what happened this morning in Saudi Arabia?"

"We're not sure, Mr. Vice President," Powers replied deferentially. "It's still too early and we clearly don't know enough, but the one country in the region that stands to gain the most from a collapse of Saudi production is Iran."

"Why?" asked the Energy Secretary who had been listening intently.

"Because, Sam, knocking out Saudi production sends world oil prices skyrocketing—hurting us the most. It leaves Iran as the biggest producer in the Gulf and able to call the shots in OPEC as the Saudis have done since the '70s. If Saudi Arabia goes broke, their monarchy is ripe for overthrow—leaving the country open to takeover by radical Wahhabi clerics. They may be Sunni and not Shia like the Iranians, but it means another theocracy on the western side of the Persian Gulf. If that happens, in six months there won't be an 'infidel'—

meaning 'Westerner'—remaining in the Gulf or anywhere near it."

Browning and the others were listening intently, so Powers continued. "Once the Western oil expertise is gone, the moderate emirs and princes running the oil-producing emirates won't last a year. At that point radical 'Islamicists' are sitting on more than half the world's known reserves of oil. By then we'll be paying a hundred and ten dollars or more for a barrel of oil. Gasoline in the U.S. will be seven-fifty to eight bucks a gallon, our trade deficit will be out of sight, foreign aid to Egypt, Jordan, Afghanistan, or Turkey will be out of the question—and they'll be the next to go. Within eighteen months to two years it's possible that every Islamic state but one in the Middle East and Southwest Asia will be a radical theocracy. The Europeans, with fewer resources than we have to fall back on, will want to cut some kind of deal so we won't be able to count on them for any military support. We will have lost all of our bases in the region—with the exception of Iraq—which by then will be impossible to get to. You see where this is headed?"

The room was silent, taking in Powers's terrifying scenario, when the President leaned forward, his elbows on the table, and said, "So how does the killing of those two scientists—and the hit on the Iraqi oil facilities this morning—fit in all this, Dan?"

The SecDef turned back to the President and said, "The fact that Sarrini and Hussman, two of the world's preeminent oil experts, were killed by an Iranian hit team—and the fact that the only places attacked this morning outside Saudi Arabia were *Iraqi* oil facilities—indicates to us that the ayatollahs in Tehran are behind it. Finally, the Iranians are the big losers if Iraq really does have the kind of exploitable reserves Sarrini and Hussman believed they have. We think it's likely that their murders and the events of this morning are in some way connected, but right now we just don't know."

"Is there any indication that the Iranians knew the Saudis were running dry or that the Iraqis have these enormous reserves?" asked the President.

"We think it's unlikely that they knew that much about the Saudi problem," the SecDef replied. "The Saudis were playing that one so close to the vest, we didn't know about it until Sarrini and Hussman turned in their report. On the other hand it's possible—perhaps even likely—that the Iranians have long believed Iraq had significantly greater reserves than have previously been exploited."

"Are we seeing any mobilization in Iran?" asked the Vice President.

"This morning, after the explosions in Saudi Arabia, all Iranian Air Defense units were put on alert," Powers answered. "They've also publicly announced that Iran Air Flight 6 is missing and overdue in Cairo. Other than that, so far there's no discernable military activity. Iranian naval units are still in port. Their air force was still on the ground when we left to come over here this morning."

"But if the Iranians are behind this, wouldn't they be mobilizing? They know what we did in Afghanistan in 2001. Isn't it possible that this could have been done by bin Laden or some other terrorist group?" asked the President.

"It's too big an operation for bin Laden," said the SecDef. "If the reports we're getting now are right, there were more than seventy Saudi installations hit. We estimate it took anywhere from four hundred to a thousand trained terrorists. Al Qaeda hasn't had a place to train, prepare, and mount an operation this large and complex since we shut down Al Qaeda and the Taliban in Afghanistan. Bin Laden wanted the downfall of the Saudi government, but we just don't think he could pull off something as big as this."

"DNI would agree on that point," interjected Straw, trying to play catch-up.

"Is this the extent of the attacks, or should we expect something here at home?" asked the President, turning for the first time to Sarah Dornin, his Secretary for the Department of Homeland Security.

"We've activated T-PLAN 3, Mr. President," she responded. "At 0800 this morning we increased the National Terror Alert Level from yellow to red. All of our border-entry points with Mexico and Canada are closed until you give the word to open them again."

Then, consulting her notes, the DHS Secretary continued, "The Coast Guard has notified all non-U.S. flag vessels already in U.S. ports to cease unloading and stand off in designated at-sea anchorages until further notice. No foreign-flag ships en route will be allowed into U.S. waters or ports until their manifests are checked and they are searched. With the cooperation of both the Mexican and Canadian governments, all international flights en route to U.S. airspace are being diverted to preplanned airfields in their countries. U.S. citizens aboard these ships and planes will be bused to U.S. entry points where we will provide them with vouchers to fly on U.S. domestic carriers to their destinations and—"

"What about 'other nationals' who were scheduled to depart on foreign carriers?" interrupted the President.

"T-PLAN 3 calls for us to provide vouchers for them to return to their home countries aboard U.S.-flag aircraft as soon as we can," the DHS secretary responded. She then continued, "We've cancelled all leave for Coast Guard, Border Patrol, TSA, Secret Service, ATF, and ICE personnel and placed all Civil Reserve Air Fleet aircraft on standby for mobilization."

"Thank you, Sarah. Please make sure that we summarize this for my remarks this afternoon," said the

President. Turning to his National Security Advisor, he said, "Jeb, what time is my address to the nation?"

"We've alerted the networks that you will be making a statement at 4:00 p.m. (EST) from the Oval Office. We'll be doing a WHCA pool feed so there'll be no press in there with you," Stuart responded.

After consulting his notes he continued, "I've also told the Press Office to put out the word that the only Q & A today will be conducted upstairs, after your statement, and that it will be a 'backgrounder' by a 'senior administration official.' "

"Who's going to do the 'backgrounder'?" asked the President.

"Secretary Powers, sir."

Turning to his SecDef, the President said, "We need to reassure people, Dan. I think the American people can handle bad news—and we need to be straight with them about the very damaging effects the Saudi attacks are going to have on our economy. But until we have more information, I don't think we ought to lay out the 'worst-case' scenario you described. Let's not assume the collapse of moderate governance in Saudi Arabia and the rest of the region. We just don't know enough right now—at least for me to go on the air this afternoon and point the finger at the ayatollahs and mullahs in Tehran."

Leaning back in his chair, the President looked around the room and asked, "Does anyone disagree? Does anyone here have any indication that the Iranians are planning anything else?"

When no one said anything, the Commander in Chief turned to his DNI and asked, "Perry, are the boys at NSA picking up any 'chatter' coming from Tehran or Qum?"

"No, sir," responded Straw, glad to be consulted. "As of an hour ago we had no intercepts that would indicate Tehran had anything to do with the Saudi or Iraqi attacks. Their state-run media had announced only that they had a commercial aircraft missing."

The President turned back to his SecDef and said, "Dan, do you have any more proof?"

Powers paused for a moment before speaking, then said very quietly, "No, sir. But I still think there's more coming. I believe that we're going to hear a lot more from the Iranians before this is over."

"But, Dan, what more can the Iranians do to us?" asked the President. "Surely they know if we confirm that they are behind this, that we'll respond with overwhelming force. There's no way they can win a war with us. They have no surprises of military consequence. Last week, the President's Daily Brief had an assessment of Iranian nuclear capabilities. According to the PDB, the blueprints, and materials that Iran received from that Pakistani nuclear scientist—"

"Dr. Abdul Qadeer Khan," interjected Perry Straw.

"Right," said the President with a nod toward the DNI, and then finished the thought, "according to the PDB, the Khan network was broken up before the Iranians could enrich enough uranium for a bomb and that they are unlikely to be able to build one for the next twelve to eighteen months at the earliest. Are you now saying that the PDB was wrong? Were any nuclear weapons used in the attack this morning in Saudi Arabia?"

"No, on both counts, Mr. President," Powers replied. "We think the CIA assessment is right about Iran's inability to make nuclear weapons on their own just yet. And we haven't detected any radiation from any of the Saudi detonations."

"Then if the Iranians don't have nuclear weapons yet, why would they launch something like this now—why wouldn't they wait until they do?" asked the President.

Once again, Powers paused before speaking. "They had to do it now, Mr. President. General Grisham and I believe that the Iranian government is on the ropes," he said. "In a way, we're a victim of our own success in Afghanistan and Iraq. After the Afghan elections in October '04 and the Iraqi elections in 2005, student unrest in Iran grew dramatically. Following the referendum on the new Iraqi constitution in October that year, it got worse. When the new Iraqi parliamentary government was elected with an overwhelming turnout in December of '05, the ayatollahs in Tehran had to cope with youth protests all over the country demanding free elections for Iran. They now have a democratic Iraq to their west and a democratic Afghanistan to the east. It's very threatening to their hold on power. The clerics running Tehran believe that they can hang on if they drive the 'infidels' out of the region, establish theocracies in the neighborhood, and take control of Middle East oil. And they know that their time is running out."

Jeb Stuart shook his head and interjected, "But getting back to the President's question: How can the Iranians hope to do any of that if they don't have any nuclear weapons ready for delivery yet?"

Instead of answering the National Security Advisor, Powers looked the Commander in Chief in the eye and said, "Mr. President, I don't think they have been able to build any nuclear weapons of their own yet. But that doesn't mean the Iranians haven't been able to *acquire* nuclear weapons from *somewhere else.*"

"Where?" the President shot back, clearly upset by his SecDef's assessment.

Powers leaned back in his chair and replied, "We don't know. But I suspect we're about to find out."

Department of Homeland Security Operations Center
Nebraska Avenue, Washington, DC
Sunday, 14 October 2007
1000 Hours Local

Brig. Gen. Peter Newman, USMC, was used to coming to work early. But the call from his deputy Matt Roderick at 0425 this morning had propelled him out of bed and into the shower an hour earlier than even he was used to rising—especially on a Sunday in a stateside duty station.

Newman had raced to the Operations Center from his townhouse on Foxhall Road. Most days he ran up the hill—showering and changing from his jogging suit into his civvies when he arrived at the DHS facility on Nebraska Avenue. On the rare occasions when he drove, the commute usually took about eighteen minutes. This morning he made it in less than ten.

Now, five hours after arriving in his office beside the DHS Operations Center, he was fully frustrated. An act of war—or at the very least, a major international terror event—had occurred in Saudi Arabia, and he was relegated to the sidelines.

His assignment as the Director of Operations for the Department of Homeland Security sounded important—coordinating the crisis operations of the far-flung but disparate activities of what he had taken to calling "the DHS alphabet soup." But in his four months on the job he had quickly learned that the USCG (the Coast Guard), TSA (the Transportation Security Administration), ATF (Alcohol, Tobacco and Firearms), ICE (Immigrations and Customs Enforcement), FEMA (the Federal Emergency Management Agency), and the host of other organizations under his purview—from the Border Patrol to the Secret Service and to the state and local agencies represented in his Operations Center—already knew what to do and how to do it. The DHS Opera-

tions Staff functioned so well without his direct involvement that he complained to his wife, Rachel, that
he felt like "the fifth wheel on a tricycle—lots of revo-
lutions in small circles—but going nowhere."

Newman had taken this assignment on the advice of
Gen. George Grisham when his mentor had been named
as the first Marine Chairman of the Joint Chiefs of Staff
in June. Grisham had said, "Pete, if you are going to
pick up your next star—and you deserve it—you need a
'joint tour' here in Washington. Besides, if I'm going to
be the JCS Chairman, I want somebody over at DHS
watching my back."

But since June, Newman hadn't been watching any
backs except those of the more than capable watch officers in the DHS Operations Center. There was little for
the Marine Brigadier General to lead or even manage.
His deputy, Matt Roderick, capably handled almost all
day-to-day problems. This assignment was a definite
letdown for Newman. The one good thing that it gave
him, however, was what he called his "family time."

For the first time in his military career—which began
when he graduated from the Naval Academy in 1978—
Newman now had reasonable hours. And for a change,
neither he nor his family was in any kind of danger—
other than the bustling traffic that seemed to race up
and down Foxhall Road.

✪

Thanks to General Grisham—and a powerful member
of the House Armed Services Committee—Newman's
career had been effectively rehabilitated from what he
and Rachel privately called the "1998 debacle in the
desert." From March of that year until February 2001,
he had served at MacDill AFB on Grisham's Operations
and Planning staff at CENTCOM. That month, when
the new president picked Grisham as the next Marine
Commandant, Newman went to Washington with him
as staff secretary.

Though the hours were long, Newman was working at the side of the man to whom he owed his life, his marriage, and his faith. Grisham had also made a personal mission out of seeing to it that Newman's controversial past did not hinder his future. While the general never acknowledged it, Newman was convinced that his promotion from lieutenant colonel to colonel in July 2000 was the direct result of Grisham's intervention.

And he also suspected that it was General Grisham who had orchestrated the invitation to the Oval Office on 24 March 2001, where, with his wife and two children watching, the new President awarded Col. Peter J. Newman, USMC, a second Navy Cross and a second Purple Heart for the highly sensitive action in Iraq three years before.

It was a deeply emotional moment for the entire Newman family. Even though James was barely six and little Elizabeth Anne was just two, they both seemed to grasp the gravity of the moment as the President's military aide read the classified citation and their mother's eyes welled up with tears. Afterward, when Newman tried to thank Grisham, the general simply said, "Well, I guess that this should remove any doubt about your three and a half years of 'detached duty' being a blot on your military record."

The general's personal involvement in Newman's military career didn't stop there. As Commandant of the Marine Corps, Grisham personally selected the commanders of all his field units. In January 2003, with war looming in Iraq, he picked Newman to command the Third Marine Regiment—which had already deployed to Kuwait. Newman had packed his "fly-away kit" and departed for his new command with less than forty-eight hours' notice. He left Rachel and their two children in their Foxhall Road townhouse to fend for themselves once again, a condition all too familiar to most military families.

Newman's assignment as the commanding officer of Regimental Combat Team 3 wasn't really a matter of favoritism on the part of the Commandant. Making him the CO of RCT-3 took advantage of all the planning Newman had done while on the CENTCOM staff. It also put him in the van of the First Marine Expeditionary Force (I-MEF) attack up the Tigris River from Kuwait to Baghdad, over terrain that he'd come to know in 1995 during the UN's ill-fated assassination attempt against Saddam, and his 1998 involvement in the highly classified joint U.S.-Israeli raid into Iraq.

Newman had commanded RCT-3 through the swift battle to depose Saddam's brutal regime and the subsequent effort to establish an interim government in Baghdad. In January of '04 he had been handpicked by the Commanding General of the 1st Marine Division to become Division Chief of Staff. And in June that year, during his eighteenth month "in theater," Newman was selected for Brigadier General.

Though most of his contemporaries had long since rotated home, Newman accepted the post of Assistant Division Commander of the 1st Marine Division and stayed in Iraq. Aside from a brief two-week leave to fly home in September of '04, he remained with the 1st Mar Div HQ at Ramadi, Iraq—in the heart of the so-called "Sunni triangle" about forty-five miles west of Baghdad.

Finally, following the Iraqi elections in 2005, and after two long years in the field, Newman returned to the U.S. to take up a new assignment in the office of the Deputy Chief of Staff for Air-Ground Operations and Plans at the Marine headquarters.

After a month of leave with Rachel, James, and Elizabeth Anne, Newman had literally jumped into his new job. To almost anyone else, an assignment at HQMC would be a welcome respite for an officer coming from two years of duty overseas in a combat zone. But within days after reporting to his new job, Newman was on the road again.

Between March of '05 and June of '07, Newman had thrown himself into the task of ensuring that Marine units being rotated to Iraq and Afghanistan were fully trained, equipped, and ready. In sixteen months he made a dozen trips to the two war-torn countries, as well as countless other inspection visits to Marine battalions and squadrons in the Carolinas, California, and Japan.

Each time her husband departed for Southwest Asia, Rachel would put on a brave face, kiss him good-bye at the front door, and hold her tears until after the staff car had pulled out of their driveway headed for Andrews Air Force Base. And though Peter called and e-mailed frequently while away from home, there were many nights when young James and "Little Lizzie"—as Newman called his daughter—often heard their mother crying softly in her bedroom.

Newman had been on a trip to Iraq in June of 2007 when the President chose General Grisham to become the first Marine Chairman of the Joint Chiefs of Staff. Peter and Rachel had been invited to a White House reception for the new chairman the day he was confirmed by the Senate. It was the kind of event Rachel usually declined when her husband was away; however, George Grisham and his wife Barbara weren't just part of the Washington military hierarchy—they were *friends*.

Rachel decided to go, and it was there, in the midst of the crush of congressmen, senators, well-wishers, lobbyists, and sycophants in the East Room of the White House that General Grisham had spotted her.

"It's great to see you, Rachel," Grisham said warmly. "I guess one of my last acts as Commandant was to send Peter on another trip to Iraq. I'm sorry he isn't here with you."

"So am I," Rachel replied, tears suddenly welling up in her eyes.

Grisham immediately put his arm around her shoulder and turned her away from the crowd, toward a window facing south toward the Ellipse, asking, "Rachel, is everything all right?"

"Oh, I'm so sorry," she said, grabbing a handkerchief from her purse. "This isn't like me. It's such a wonderful day for you and Barbara, and here I am crying like a teenager," she said, biting her lower lip.

"Tell me what's on your mind, Rachel. You and Pete mean too much to us to have you unhappy. How can I help?" the senior military officer of the U.S. Armed Forces asked her.

Rachel took a deep breath and plunged in. "I know I shouldn't be worried about Peter. As you know better than almost anyone else, he and I have been through an awful lot over the past dozen years. But now, even with a stateside assignment, Peter's never home. He'd be upset if he knew I was telling you this, but I know Peter had some very close calls when he commanded the regiment in Iraq—and that he's had others—like the time just before he rotated home when his helicopter went down outside Ramadi while he was Assistant Division Commander."

The general looked at this emotionally vulnerable woman whom he loved as if she were his own daughter. "Pete knows the ropes. He can take care of himself," he said, trying to be reassuring.

"I know. But I can't help but wonder how many other 'close calls' he's had that he never tells me about."

General Grisham sighed, feeling the depth of her frustration and concern.

Rachel said, "We need more time together—but there isn't any and meanwhile young James and little Elizabeth are growing up without him." She finally stopped talking and noticed that her second-favorite general was staring out the window toward the Washington Monument.

After a moment Grisham spoke, as much to himself

as to her. "Peter is an exceptional officer, but I've asked too much of you both. The Corps always asks a lot of those who have a lot to give. But I also know it hasn't been fair. You have both been asked to give a lot."

Then looking directly into Rachel's eyes, he continued, "I still have a little pull in the Marine Corps. I'm going to see to it that when Pete returns from this trip to Iraq he's reassigned to a job where he'll have no reason not to be home. We have an opening at the Department of Homeland Security, right up the road from your home on Foxhall Road."

"Oh General, I'd love that," said Rachel. "But if Pete finds out that I've caused him to be sent to some dead-end job, he'll be miserable."

"Don't you worry about that," Grisham replied, now smiling once again. "It's not a dead-end job—it's very important—he'll be the senior military officer at DHS. Pete needs a 'joint' assignment like that if he's going to pick up a second star. And you and the children will get to see him more. This will be good for both of you."

The Oval Office
The White House, Washington, DC
Sunday, 14 October 2007
1535 Hours Local

While the White House Communications Agency techs quietly and competently completed the hookups for the lights, cameras, and Teleprompter, for what they called a "national feed," the most powerful man in the world was already seated behind his desk, reviewing the statement he would make to the nation and the world in less than half an hour. It was only four pages long, double-spaced in 15-point type. He had already been through it twice, inserting a word here, deleting a phrase there.

Standing beside him was Miles Johnson, his ch.
speechwriter. Johnson duplicated each alteration in th
text on his laptop computer on the desk by the Chie.
Executive's left arm. As he inserted each change, a wireless encrypted data link automatically updated the version in the Teleprompter. Once "the boss" was satisfied,
it would take less than a minute to produce a "final
smooth" on the printer just outside the Oval Office
door in the Staff Secretary's office. This paper copy
would be in front of the President when the cameras
went "live" just in case there was a glitch in the
Teleprompter.

The President looked up from the text and looked
around the room. Spotting his National Security Advisor near the fireplace talking quietly with Defense Secretary Powers, he said, "Jeb, I'm still concerned about
this wording here." Looking down he read: " 'I have
tried to reach the Crown Prince of Saudi Arabia to ex-
tend my personal concerns and offer our condolences
for the loss of life in the country.' Doesn't that beg the
question as to *why* I haven't been able to reach him?"

"Yes, sir, but I think we have to say something to reassure the royal family."

"Well, what's the problem?" asked the Commander
in Chief, his frustration showing. "Why can't we contact anyone over there? It's been almost twelve hours
since the attack! I thought you said that our comms
were back on-line."

"Sir," the National Security Advisor responded,
"that's true, but WHCA has been trying to get your call
through since before the NSC meeting this morning. It's
the Saudis who are not responding. State says the Saudi
Foreign Ministry won't tell us anything and won't put
anyone above some desk officer on the phone. The
Agency can't find anyone to talk to in Riyadh because
the main telephone exchange is apparently shut down.
Our ambassador reports that the Saudi National Guard

...l has our embassy surrounded and refuses to let any ...r our people out of the compound on the premise that ...t's not safe for 'Westerners' to be on the streets. Prince Bushir, their ambassador, is out of Washington and incommunicado, and their DCM isn't taking calls. I don't know what else we can say except the truth—that you've been unable to reach anyone there."

The President grimaced, looked at his Defense Secretary, and said, "Dan, we're about to interrupt the NFL football schedule on national television and I'm going to have my head handed to me by the 'Armchair Admirals,' 'Barroom Brigadiers,' and the 'Sound-bite Special Forces.' Every talking head in the country is going to have their own spin on why I can't reach the Crown Prince. I'd like to tell my own version. Got any ideas?"

Powers was about to reply when there was an abrupt double knock on the door that leads from the Oval Office to the hallway outside the Roosevelt Room. It was such an extraordinary breach of protocol that no one said anything. Jeb Stuart walked over to the heavy door, opened it, and stared into the ashen face of the duty military aide, an Air Force major. "Yes?" said the National Security Advisor.

"Sir," said the aide, "I have an emergency call from the Chairman of the Joint Chiefs for the Secretary of Defense. It came through on the 'NCA Red Phone.'"

The major was holding in his hand what appeared to be an ordinary cell phone but was actually a highly sophisticated, encrypted satellite-cellular communications device. One of these phones was always in the immediate vicinity of every officer in the National Command Authority "nuclear chain of command." The aides to the President, Vice President, SecDef, and each of the commanders of America's nuclear forces always had one with them. So did the Chairman and Vice Chairman of the JCS, though technically they were not in the direct NCA "chain." The phones, and the system to support them, had been created by the Defense Communications Agency with one purpose: to alert key decision makers that a weapon-of-mass-destruction attack—nuclear, biological, or chemical—had been launched against the United States.

Thinking of that, seventy-year-old Dan Powers practically jumped over the wires and cables that the WHCA TV crew had sprawled over the floor of the Oval Office as though he were still the college athlete he had been fifty years earlier. Taking the phone from his aide's outstretched hand, he said, "Thank you, Charles," and put the phone to his ear. "Powers here," he said.

For twenty seconds, he listened and then said, "Hold on, George, I want the President to hear this directly. I'm in the Oval Office with him right now. Are you in the NMCC? . . . OK . . . good. I'll ask the President to call you there immediately."

The SecDef pressed the button labeled END CALL on the phone, handed it back to his aide, and said, "Mr. President, we have some very disturbing news from the JCS Chairman that may change the tenor of your remarks completely. If I may, sir, I think we need to clear the office so that you, Jeb, and I can hear this directly from General Grisham."

The four WHCA technicians were already moving to the door on the opposite side of the fireplace before the National Security Advisor had to hasten them out of the room. As the door closed, leaving Powers and Stuart alone with the Commander in Chief, he pressed a button on the secure phone labeled NMCC.

Immediately, a slightly garbled voice came over the speaker: "This is General Grisham, sir."

"What do we have, General?" asked the President, glancing at his watch. It was 3:45. In fifteen minutes he was supposed to deliver a reassuring address to the nation.

Grisham's voice came back through the fiber-optic link: "Sir, five minutes ago the NCOIC of the Marine Security Guard Detachment in Riyadh called in on an open line from the Marine House, which is about a block from our embassy. He reports that an hour ago, Sheikh Abdullah al-Aziz, the cousin of the Saudi Interior Minister, rushed into the detachment's billet, badly wounded and covered in blood. Shortly thereafter, twenty-five to thirty well-armed militants attacked the Marine House. The Marines have beaten off two assaults and are holding their own, hoping they don't run out of ammo before dawn."

"Any of our boys casualties?" asked the President.

"One Marine KIA, three wounded," answered Grisham.

"How many Marines are in the house?" asked the President.

"Seven still alive."

"How about this Saudi—is he likely to make it?"

"No, sir, he died," answered Grisham. "But before the Saudi expired, he was very insistent that the Marines get word to you that his entire family has been killed. His words were, 'There is no one left.' "

"That's a terrible shame," said the President, "but at this point, I'm more concerned about my Marines."

"Yes, sir, so am I," interjected the Chairman of the Joint Chiefs. "But please understand, Mr. President, Sheikh al-Aziz wasn't just talking about his wives and children. He was talking about the *royal* family—the House of Saud. The entire royal family of Saudi Arabia seems to have been assassinated."

CHAPTER TWO

Know Your Enemy

Lourdes Signals Intelligence Facility
Bejucal, Cuba
Sunday, 14 October 2007
1610 Hours Local

Dimitri Komulakov was not a happy man. As the "retired" KGB general pored over printouts of satellite imagery, he kept checking his watch. The American president was to have spoken by now, yet he had received nothing from his "communications experts."

Long, one-meter-wide sheets of paper, their edges curled from the humidity, were spread out on a large table in the middle of the room. Each strip, from successive satellite "passes," clearly showed the devastation wrought by the attacks on the Saudi facilities. Komulakov had just bent over the table to examine the image of a destroyed GOSP, black smoke churning from a flaming caldron, when there was a knock on the door.

"Who is it?" the Russian snarled in his native tongue.

"I have brought you some food, sir . . . from *our* commissary," said a familiar voice on the other side of the door.

"Come in, Viktor," replied Komulakov, softening his tone.

The door opened, but as the man entered carrying a tray, the general said, "Thank you, Major, but I am not hungry."

"But, sir, you must eat. You have eaten nothing all day. I saw you in the communications monitoring cell at four this morning. My orders when I was sent here by Moscow Centre were to make sure that you kept your strength," the younger Russian replied earnestly.

Komulakov, attired in a tropical shirt, khaki slacks, and American Dockers shoes, stood in sharp contrast to his subordinate, dressed in the dark, heavy cotton fabric of Cuban camouflage fatigues. The junior officer, tanned and fit, was still standing just inside the open doorway, holding the tray.

Komulakov looked him over and said, "Come in, Major Sakharovsky. Shut the door. This miserable air conditioner, undoubtedly made by some corrupt 'entrepreneur' in Moscow, can't even cool this little office, much less the rest of Cuba."

The major entered, closing the door with his foot, and the general motioned for him to set the tray on his desk at the far end of the room. When he had done so, the major asked, "Is there anything else I can get for you, sir?"

"Not right now, Viktor Sakharovsky, but tell me," the older man asked, "you say your orders from Moscow Centre were to ensure that I kept my strength, eh? What *other* orders did our new 'leaders' give you?"

The younger man, looking hurt, replied, "Only to assist you in this mission as you direct, General."

"And did they tell you what this mission was about?"

"Only that it was very important and of great sensitivity. I was also told to do as you ordered and that you would tell me what I needed to know when I needed to know it," Sakharovsky replied.

"That's true—and your discretion is important," Komulakov said. "As I told you and your men when you arrived last month, there can be no letters, calls, or Internet messages back to your families while we are here. Also, our 'hosts' are to know nothing about what we do. I hope you are enforcing these orders."

"General," said the major, now standing at attention, "my Special Tasks Unit of the SVR 8th Department has twice been commended for its work on behalf of our country—and our activities have never been compromised."

"Yes, yes, Viktor Sakharovsky, I know all about how you helped Señor Chávez hold on in Caracas and about the bomb you planted in Beirut to 'eliminate' Rafiq al Hariri for the Syrians in February of 2005. As a matter of fact, that's why I asked for you," said the general. "But I remind you, Major, that today's 8th Department is not the same as the First Counterintelligence Directorate your grandfather headed, nor is the SVR the same as the KGB that your father, Igor Aleksandrovich, and I worked for in the old days."

Having heard his father and his friends musing many times about the "good old days," the major said nothing. Komulakov shrugged, ended his lecture, and returned to the task at hand. "Why have I not heard the American president's remarks? Wasn't he supposed to make some kind of televised statement a quarter hour ago?"

"Yes, sir," the major responded, "but at 4:00 their television and radio networks announced that the statement had been postponed. Their news organs are saying it is because he was afraid of a backlash for disrupting their football games. In the United States, football on Sunday afternoon is very important and—"

"Please, Viktor," Komulakov interrupted, holding up his hand. "I lived in Washington and New York for many years. I know all about their penchant for football. Now, go to the Communications Monitoring cell and find out why he *really* failed to make his statement. I want to know if they have discovered what has happened to the Saudi 'princelings.' "

After the door closed behind the SVR major, Komulakov went to his desk, chose a sausage, some cheese, and a piece of bread from the selection on the tray, and returned to the map table. As he once more peered at the devastation with a mouthful of food, he thought, *Ahh . . . a taste of home.*

✪

For Dimitri Komulakov "home" was an indistinct term. During his more than two decades' tenure in the KGB and since, he had spent more time outside his native Minsk, Belarus, than in it. He had lived in Russia, East Germany, Yugoslavia, Vienna, Paris, Afghanistan, Syria, and Washington. By 1995 he was enjoying the good life in New York as a senior United Nations official when his career was abruptly terminated because of a U.S. Marine named Peter Newman.

After "retiring" in Sweden with his mistress, he returned to Russia and became wealthy beyond his wildest dreams by illegally selling weapons and military equipment from old Soviet inventories. After a brief dalliance in "new Russian politics"—and defeat by a fellow KGB officer, Vladimir Putin—Komulakov returned full time to the black market arms trade. By 1998 his most expensive products for sale were stolen Soviet Army nuclear artillery rounds, and his best client was Saddam Hussein.

Though never one to reflect long on his failures, Komulakov sometimes wondered if the effort to sell nuclear weapons to Saddam in '98 would have succeeded but for the incompetence and paranoia of the dictator's two sons, Uday and Qusay. In the end, the venture had collapsed in a blaze of gunfire at a secret base on the Syrian border. And once again, Peter Newman had been the primary reason why the Russian barely escaped with his skin, his fortune—and a nuclear weapon. Though the thought of Newman could make the bile boil in Komulakov's gut, the face of the "retired" KGB general's dead business partner, Leonid Dotensk, never came to mind. But that was understandable—it was Komulakov who had killed him.

By 2001, when the Americans launched their invasion of Afghanistan, Komulakov was a very wealthy man. His network of "former KGB officers" and access to stolen Soviet-era military hardware had helped him make more than $500 million, which he had stuffed into Swiss, Panamanian, and Cayman Island bank accounts. And by then he had found a new, affluent client base—the mullahs and ayatollahs in Tehran.

Well before Komulakov appeared on the scene, the Iranians had obtained blueprints of a Chinese nuclear bomb from the Pakistani nuclear scientist, Dr. Abdul Qadeer Khan. It was the same design that Khan and his associates also sold to the Libyans, so they, too, could become an "Islamic nuclear power." But the Pakistani engineer was unable to deliver more than a small amount of enriched uranium—far too little for either country to build a bomb, much less an arsenal.

By 2001, when Komulakov first appeared on the scene in Tehran, the Iranians were already struggling to convert the Khan design into a workable nuclear weapon. The Russian arms merchant immediately established a close relationship with the Iranian military and intelligence hierarchy—and started making deliveries. Their first requests were relatively simple: air defense weapons and black market aircraft parts for Iran's aging, American-built air force. But within a matter of months the Iranians began asking Komulakov about materials and equipment for the nuclear weapons that A.Q. Khan had shown them how to build. The Russian promptly delivered some spent nuclear fuel, centrifuge parts, and sophisticated machine tools for honing heavy, radioactive metal into warheads.

Two months after the first "nuclear delivery," Qorbanali Darri Najafabadi, Komulakov's Iranian intelligence point of contact, asked the black market arms dealer if he could provide "plans for a small nuclear device." Komulakov, always alert to an opportunity, offered to deliver—for $25 million—"a single nuclear artillery round" so they would have a prototype to copy.

The Iranians jumped at the offer—and began talking to each other about it. In the summer of 2001, NSA intercepted several Tehran telephone conversations about the deal, and a subsequent top secret CIA report in August, entitled "Proliferation of Weapons of Mass Destruction," charged that "individuals in the Russian Federation appear to have established contact with elements in the Islamic Republic of Iran for the purpose of selling Soviet-era nuclear weapons and/or fissile materiel to the Iranians." Fortunately for Komulakov, all of this was promptly forgotten by nearly everyone in the U.S. intelligence and military establishment a month later when nearly three thousand Americans perished on September 11.

In the months afterward, Komulakov practically took up residence in Tehran. The Iranians were stunned by the swift American victory next door in Afghanistan and, like the rest of the world, recognized that Iraq was next. The theocrats running Tehran paid the Russian arms trader handsomely to deliver weaponry of every sort—from small arms to air-to-air missiles, radars, even two diesel-powered coastal submarines. Nothing was too hard for Komulakov. And best of all, from his perspective, the Iranians paid top dollar—half up front—half on delivery. All of it was deposited directly into the Russian's overseas bank accounts.

Of course, the Iranians weren't Komulakov's only clients. Syria, Libya, Yemen, Somalia, Hamas, Fatah, Hezbollah, and Islamic Jihad all called upon his services. He even opened an office in Caracas to support Castro's new friend, Hugo Chávez. From 2004 until 2006 he supplied most of the detonators, plastic explosives, and communications gear used by Baath party remnants in Iraq to build what the Americans called "Improvised Explosive Devices" or IEDs. But these contracts were small potatoes compared with the Iranians. Komulakov let his lieutenants handle the other clients. He handled "business" in Tehran himself.

It was through his Iranian "clients" that the Russian had ended up in Cuba. Having established himself as a discreet, reliable provider of arms and materiel, the Iranians came to have confidence in Komulakov for much more than weaponry. His skill at building personal relationships, carefully nurtured during his KGB career, enabled him to keep their trust. This was the case even when Ali Yunesi succeeded Qorbanali Darri Najafabadi as head of Iranian intelligence in February 1999—when Najafabadi resigned after admitting that his agents had been killing dissidents.

Before becoming Minister of Intelligence and Security, Yunesi, a powerful, well-connected Shiite cleric, had headed Iran's military tribunals—the arm of the "judiciary" that investigated, apprehended, tried, and sentenced dissidents, spies, and traitors. It was Yunesi who had convinced the Revolutionary Command Council (RCC)—in effect, the government of Iran—that they needed to avail themselves of "outside expertise" in order to carry out what they were tentatively calling "Operation Dawah."

Within a week of the 31 January 2005 elections in Iraq, students rioted in Tehran, Qum, Tabriz, Mashhad, and Esfahan, demanding similar elections—including women's suffrage—in Iran. The RCC convened in secret on 15 February to consider courses of action. On the second day of the covert session, Yunesi, as spokesman for the RCC "hardliners," rose and delivered a blistering condemnation on "the failure of current tactics for driving infidels and Zionists out of Islamic lands." The next day he was unanimously selected by Iran's most powerful clerics to "immediately develop and implement a strategy for protecting Islamic territory from infidels and to ensure the propagation of Islamic law."

On 18 February 2005, as the RCC recessed to observe Ashura—the Shia holy day—Yunesi was secretly allocated $500 million to carry out what he called Operation Dawah—Arabic for "the call." Two weeks later he "retained" Dimitri Komulakov as his personal advisor in planning the most audacious act of state-sponsored terrorism in history.

○

At their first planning meeting in March of 2005, Yunesi began with a lesson in radical Islamic thought. "Last year," he said in English, "a respected Saudi cleric announced a new fatwa from Allah. Normally we Shia don't pay much attention to these Sunnis, but in this case what he said applied to all Muslims."

Komulakov tried to appear attentive. Though the Iranian money was good, he found these interminable religious lectures to be mind-numbingly tedious.

The cleric continued, "In his fatwa, the imam declared that under Islamic law, it is permissible to use nuclear and other weapons of mass destruction to attack the United States, Great Britain, and other infidel nations—including even their women and children. Because Muslim civilians were killed in the Iraqi war, it is justifiable to kill American civilians."

"I see," Komulakov said, appearing interested but, in fact, he couldn't care less about such intersections between religion and politics.

The Iranian cleric then said bluntly, "Our scientists are having great difficulty in building a workable nuclear device that can be easily transported."

Komulakov shrugged, but then decided that such indifference was not a proper response, based on the look he received from Yunesi. So he improvised a query. "What is it you want me to do? I offered to hire some Russian nuclear weapons scientists, but you did not want them here."

"That is true," replied the cleric. "We do not want your scientists. There is not time. How many more of those weapons like the one you already delivered can you provide?"

The Iranian now had the Russian's full attention. Komulakov pondered the question for a moment, quickly considering the risks of raiding the relatively unsecured stockpile of Soviet-era tactical nuclear devices in the Ukraine. He responded, "It would depend on how many you want and how quickly you want them—and the price, of course."

The Iranian responded without hesitation: "We will need eleven nuclear weapons on hand by September 2007."

"May I ask why that many?"

"No . . . for now, it is enough that you know how many weapons we require, and when we will need them. Please be prepared to give me a price tomorrow."

With that, the first of their many meetings had ended—and Komulakov knew that he was going to be a very wealthy man. He also realized that a lot of American civilians were likely to die, but that part didn't bother him a bit.

❂

On 15 January 2006, with the plan for Operation Dawah nearly finalized, Ali Yunesi arrived at the Russian's luxurious suite on the top floor of the old Hilton Hotel, perched on a hill overlooking Tehran's northeastern suburbs. As always in their meetings, Yunesi got right down to business.

For three hours the mullah and Komulakov reviewed the intricate details of the plan. Before departing, Yunesi asked the Russian to prepare recommendations for how the ambitious plot could be "improved."

When the two convened again the next day, Komulakov was ready. The arms dealer-turned-"advisor" had prepared several charts and had on the table a number of sheets of paper—all composed on his IBM computer.

"Here are your best targets," the Russian said, handing Yunesi a sheet labeled "target list." On it were the key nodes of the Saudi oil industry.

He then handed the Iranian a second sheet and said, "Here are the people you will have to get. They won't all be in Saudi Arabia. For an additional fee, I'll help you find and kill them."

The Iranian listened intently—though he didn't need to. Their entire conversation—like every one that they'd had here—was being picked up on microphones carefully implanted throughout the suite, most of which Komulakov had already discovered.

The Russian was blunt. "You can't run this operation—particularly the second and third phases—from Tehran."

"Why?" asked the Iranian.

"Because the Americans will know that you are behind it and if they can prove it, they will destroy you within hours."

Yunesi furrowed his brow and said, "What about all the radars, communications equipment, fighter parts, and anti-aircraft weapons you have delivered—and we have paid you for?" he added testily.

"Forget about it," answered Komulakov. "I delivered exactly what you wanted. You never asked me, but it's nearly all useless against the Americans."

The mullah, his eyes wide, started to protest. Komulakov raised the palm of his hand, despite knowing it was considered rude, and said, "Please, I'm not finished."

The Iranian intelligence chief closed his mouth and sat back in his chair as the Russian continued. "Within two hours of their decision to attack, cruise missiles launched from their submarines and ships in the Persian Gulf will have flown twenty meters above the earth to explode on targets in Tehran. Your radars will not be able to see them. A few minutes later, more than one hundred aircraft launched from their carriers will have eliminated your air force. Then, scores of the U.S. Air Force aircraft from Iraq will take out what's left of your radars and your command and control facilities. For the next thirty-six hours you will be subjected to nonstop, air-launched cruise missile and JDAM attacks from their twenty-five B-52s out of Diego Garcia and their twenty-one B-2 bombers all the way from the middle of the United States."

When Komulakov finished his soliloquy the Iranian sat with lips pursed and said nothing for almost a minute. He then asked, "From where should this operation be run?"

"Cuba," answered the Russian.

"Why Cuba?"

"Because it's perfect," Komulakov replied with a thin smile. He continued, "If you initiate this as I suggest—without any electronic signals whatsoever, the Americans will be uncertain. They will want to believe you are behind all this, but they won't be able to prove it. All of their attention, all of their intelligence assets will be focused on Iran shortly after the first phase of the attack. They won't be looking in Cuba, it's much too close for them to ever suspect. It's the perfect place from which to coordinate the second and third phases of the attack."

Ali Yunesi was nodding now, clearly seeing the wisdom in what he was hearing. "But where in Cuba?" the mullah asked. "Our embassy in Havana is watched around the clock. We know the American Satans have it under surveillance and probably have spies inside it."

"Correct," said Komulakov. "Not your embassy. I have just the place in Cuba to run this. That's where I should be." What Komulakov didn't say was that if the Americans responded with overwhelming force—perhaps even nuclear weapons, as *this* American president was liable to do—Komulakov didn't want to be anywhere near Tehran.

"What is this place in Cuba?" asked the Iranian.

Komulakov unrolled a satellite photo of Cuba and explained, pointing to a location on the chart: "This place is called Lourdes. It's fifty miles west of Havana. More than forty years ago Castro provided the USSR with access and control over this twenty-nine-square-mile facility. In exchange, my country provided Castro with oil and hundreds of millions of dollars' worth of aid. We used this facility to monitor American communications—everything from satellite to their 'long lines' microwave telephone conversations. The USSR manned this site more than three decades with nearly two thousand technicians, engineers, analysts, and military personnel. During that period as much as 75 percent of all intercepted intelligence that was sent to Moscow originated from Lourdes."

Though he knew some of this already, the Iranian was trying hard not to appear to be impressed. To stop the history lesson he asked, "But didn't your President Putin shut all this down years ago?"

"Today, Lourdes looks mostly abandoned," Komulakov answered, pointing to the aerial photo. "From the air or a satellite all that shows are these scattered buildings and old satellite tracking dishes. But what most people do not know is that the site is still picking up military signals to and from the U.S.

"Putin told the world that he was shutting Lourdes

down after the Americans went into Afghanistan, but that's not what happened," continued the Russian, exhibiting pride even for the man who had destroyed his political ambitions.

"The Russian intelligence services knew that the location of the facility—little more than one hundred miles from Key West—made it too valuable. It is still one of the largest and most sophisticated SIGINT collection facilities in the world—equal to one of the West's ECHELON sites in Australia or the ones they have built next door to you in Iraq and Afghanistan. Today it still serves Russian military intelligence (GRU), the Federal Agency for Government Communications (FAPSI) and in a separate area, the Cuban military and secret police intelligence services."

"But I saw pictures of the place being dismantled," said Yunesi.

"True," the Russian responded. "But the crates of communications equipment loaded onto cargo ships and aircraft bound for Murmansk were merely for show. Only the obsolete technology was sent back to Russia. We cut our personnel by more than half, but improvements in technology had made them obsolete anyway. Putin's grand gesture was bogus. We brought in new equipment and still operate the Lourdes facility pretty much as before but with greater effectiveness."

"But I cannot go to Cuba," protested the Iranian. "I must be here."

"Of course," replied Komulakov smoothly. "You will be in complete control at all times. All orders to those who will be carrying out phases two and three will originate with you—but they will be transmitted from Lourdes. Best of all, there is a totally secure fiber-optic cable that runs between Lourdes and Murmansk—and the Americans know nothing about it. That is how I shall communicate with you—from Lourdes, to the

SVR communications center outside Moscow. There, I will set up a secure satellite link to you, here in Iran."

"If we do as you suggest, what will Castro know about this?" asked Yunesi. "I met him at a 'non-aligned meeting' many years ago. He makes very long speeches and seems benign in his old age. But I would still be worried if he knew."

"Do not be concerned about Mr. Castro, my friend," the Russian replied. "He will know nothing about this."

❂

Now, twenty months after that conversation in Tehran, Komulakov was absolutely convinced that the plan was flawless. It had taken a year and a half to put in place all of the necessary personnel and equipment. Multiple small shipments of gear, much of it purchased in Europe and Japan, had been delivered to Cuba and installed in the old Lourdes bunkers and above-ground buildings.

To ensure that American spies in Cuba—and their satellites overhead—could not detect any changes at Lourdes, Komulakov insisted on two iron-clad rules. First, no exterior structural changes were permitted. Second, overall Russian personnel strength at the site was unchanged. To ensure this, the "retired" general simply arranged with Moscow Centre to substitute one of his own "contractors" each time a Russian government technician rotated home. His only personnel concerns were the four Iranians Ali Yunesi had insisted on sending to Lourdes to ensure that at least one of his countrymen was on watch at all times in the communications center.

By September 2007, the Lourdes-Murmansk-Moscow-Tehran encrypted voice communications link had been tested twice. A week before "Al Dawah" began, all of the primary and secondary Internet Web sites that they would use for relaying messages to operatives in the field were up and running. Komulakov was confident that the changes at Lourdes had gone undetected by the Americans. He was correct in that assessment.

The Russian had also convinced himself that Fidel Castro, the old fool, was blissfully unaware that his island paradise was being used as the command and control center for a global terror operation of unprecedented proportions. Yet, like so many others over the years, Komulakov had underestimated Fidel.

Department of Homeland Security Operations Center
Nebraska Avenue, Washington, DC
Sunday, 14 October 2007
1610 Hours Local

Matt Roderick's early morning call was the first exciting event for Brig. Gen. Peter Newman since he'd been appointed as the DHS Operations Director in June. In the intervening months he had made a number of "survey" trips—with the Border Patrol along the Mexican border, to the Energetic Materials Research and Test Center in Socorro, New Mexico, and to inspect First Responder training at College Station, Texas.

In August, Newman had gone to Charleston, South Carolina, with the Coast Guard to supervise a "No-notice Emergency Preparedness Exercise." Afterward, he'd assessed the local, state, and federal participants to be well prepared to handle an actual biotoxin terror attack.

Since his arrival, Newman had been impressed with the dedication of the DHS scientists and employees, as well as the new technologies they were developing. He judged the coordination, cooperation, and communications issues that had been identified as "problem areas" by the so-called "9/11 Commission" in 2004 to be much improved. After returning from each of these inspections, Newman prepared reports and briefed DHS

Secretary Sarah Dornin, though he was frustrated when his recommendations for further improvement were swallowed up in the bureaucracy.

But in the immediate aftermath of the attack on Saudi Arabia, there was no evidence of any bureaucratic wrangling. By the time he arrived at the DHS facility at 0505, the Operations Center was humming like a well-oiled machine. Within minutes of initial notification from the NRO, every relevant agency of the federal government had been alerted, the National Terror Alert level had been elevated from yellow to red, the borders had been closed, and emergency recall notices had gone out to all DHS agencies.

Before Secretary Dornin departed at 0820 for the NSC Crisis Team meeting at the White House, Newman and Roderick had briefed and armed her with a sheaf of reports. By then, every item on the Operations Center's automated Emergency Checklist had been completed.

After Secretary Dornin returned from the White House at 1030, Newman had helped her draft the DHS input for the President's statement and then spent the early part of the afternoon reviewing reports and responding to requests from the six DHS regional field offices, the Border Patrol, Coast Guard, the FAA, and TSA. He had spent almost three and a half hours in phone calls and e-mails with his counterparts in Canada and Mexico who were dealing with dozens of diverted aircraft and thousands of passengers stranded in Gander, Newfoundland, and Mexico City.

By 1555 every task that appeared on Newman's automated checklist had been completed. He had just poured himself a fresh cup of coffee, intending to sit at his desk and watch the President's televised address to the nation, when he saw the FLASH precedence electronic message from the White House pop up on his computer screen:

UNCLAS
FLASH

141557ZOCT07
FROM: WHITE HOUSE
TO: ALL USG
SUBJ: POTUS STATEMENT RE SAUDI ATTACK POST-
           PONED

THE PRESIDENT'S LIVE TELEVISED ADDRESS FROM THE
OVAL OFFICE SCHEDULED FOR 1600 EST HAS BEEN
POSTPONED. REFER ALL MEDIA INQUIRIES TO WHITE
HOUSE PRESS OFFICE. NO BACKGROUNDERS

AUTHORIZED.
FOR THE PRESIDENT, JEB STUART
BT

UNCLAS

Newman stared at the message for a moment, said
uh-oh to himself, and grabbed the TV remote on his
desk. Pointing it at the TV set mounted on the wall opposite his desk, he dialed up the volume in time to hear
one of the NFL talking heads say, ". . . and now this just
in from the White House: the President had asked for a
ten-minute 'time out' in all of this afternoon's games to
address the nation regarding the attack in Saudi Arabia.
But we've just been informed that his statement has
been postponed indefinitely. Stay tuned to this FOX station for more news as it happens. Now, back to the
game . . ."

Hitting "Mute" again on the remote silenced the announcer. Through the large glass window that separated
his office from the DHS Ops Center, Newman could see
phone lines begin to light up on the watch officers'
desks. He shook his head at the thought of what the
next few hours were going to be like but was glad he
wasn't the White House Press Secretary.

At that moment, the intercom on his desk buzzed, and the voice of DHS Secretary Sarah Dornin came through the speaker. "Peter, would you come over to my office in ten minutes, and let's see if we can figure out where we go from here?"

"Be right there," the Marine responded, grabbing a small green notebook. But before heading off down the hall he remembered that he had promised Rachel that he would call if he were to be late.

Standing at his desk, he picked up the receiver of the "outside" phone on his desk and dialed his home number. On the third ring a voice answered with a polite, "Hello . . . this is the Newman residence, James speaking."

"Hi, Jimmy . . . it's Dad." Newman was proud of the boy's manners. It hardly seemed possible that it had been nearly twelve years since he was born. "How was church today, buddy?" he asked his son.

"We didn't go. Mom said we had to stay home because of the red alert. What's a red alert, Dad?"

Newman paused. He didn't want to frighten the boy but didn't want to deceive him either. He finally replied, "It's a security measure we take because some bad guys blew up some oil wells in Saudi Arabia last night."

"Oh yeah," the boy responded. "I saw that on the TV news this morning. Does this mean you're going to have to go away again, Dad?" Though not yet twelve, his son had already learned that when bad things happened in the world, his dad had to leave home and take care of the problems.

His son's question hit Newman with two conflicting emotions: a pang of guilt that he had spent so much of his son's life away from home and the fleeting twinge of desire for action he felt in his gut at the thought of "going somewhere." But he answered, "No, Jimmy. I don't think I'll be going anywhere this time."

"Good," said the boy, "because I'm supposed to have a basketball game tomorrow if they have school. The

TV said all the schools in the city are probably going to be closed tomorrow. But I'm hoping we have school cuz our sixth grade team is playing against 'Schuyler'—and most of them are seventh and eighth graders—but I think we can beat 'em. Do you think you can come and watch the game, if we have school tomorrow, Dad?"

"Well, things are pretty busy here at work, champ. I won't know until later tonight. I'll have a better idea of what my workload looks like by then, and we should know pretty soon if the schools are going to be open tomorrow." Then Newman asked the boy, "Is your mom there, Jim?"

"She's with Lizzie. Just a minute, Dad—I'll get her."

A moment later Rachel was on the line. Normally she'd begin by telling him about some new achievement of their eight-year-old daughter Elizabeth or son James. But this time she got right to the point. "Honey, why did the presidential statement get cancelled?" Rachel asked, posing the question that most of America was probably asking by now.

The FLASH precedence notification that Newman had just seen hadn't revealed the answer to his wife's query.

"I really don't know," Peter replied. "All I know for sure is that around noon the White House asked the networks and the NFL for ten minutes starting at 4:00 p.m. so the President could address the nation from the Oval Office. About three minutes ago they sent out an advisory that it was postponed. No reason given, though I guess this means it's going to be a long night. The Secretary just called and asked me to come over to her office."

"When *is* the President going to speak?"

"I don't know."

"What does this mean?" she posed, almost as though she was thinking out loud.

"I don't know that either," Peter replied. "But even if

I did, I doubt that I would be able to tell you on this line, honey."

"OK, I understand that, but tell me, you're not going anywhere, are you, Peter?" Rachel asked hesitantly.

Once again Newman felt a pang of disappointment, but tried not to let it show. "No . . . I don't think so. If anything comes up, the Pentagon has teams already in the region," he told her.

But her husband's tone told Rachel more than his words. She knew he wanted to be where things were happening—and that he was very good at the terrible business of war. She loved and respected his courage, but she craved his presence, feared for his safety, and prayed daily for his protection.

Rachel's response was tempered by all of this. She spoke softly and with deep understanding. "Peter, I know you'd like to be out there. But I want you to know that our children and I need you more than they do. And my loyalties are different from yours. I love you more than the Marine Corps."

It wasn't a rebuke, but Peter heard her words in a way he'd never heard them before.

MI6 Headquarters
Vauxhall Cross, London
Sunday, 14 October 2007
2030 Hours Local

MI6 agent Joseph Blackman had been at his desk for almost twelve hours. Within minutes of the attack in Saudi Arabia, the Prime Minister had alerted the Chief of the British Secret Intelligence Service to call up all of his personnel and then attend to an immediate analysis of the Saudi oil-field attacks. MI6 had departments related to activities in the Middle East, and each department head was given the responsibility to cull through their most active case files for answers to the questions the PM was likely to raise.

Six of Blackman's colleagues were working with intelligence reports from Syria, Iran, Iraq, Afghanistan, Saudi Arabia, and Egypt. Other departments, including Jordan, Yemen, Libya, and Sudan, were also hard at work looking for any links to what had happened in Saudi Arabia that morning.

Three of the top MI6 agents were assigned to examine the SIS "Name Files"—highly sensitive material on individuals who were "of interest" to British intelligence. Because of its extraordinary sensitivity—much of it relating to senior officials, even heads of state in other countries—this information was never entered into the MI6 computer database. Instead, only a single paper copy was kept—filed alphabetically and secured in four drawer combination-locked safes under round-the-clock monitoring.

At 0915 that morning, a records clerk had delivered to Blackman five boxes containing the A through K "Name Files." After signing a receipt for the documents, the MI6 agent began a systematic review of the folders—each with a neat label bearing the name of the subject. It was just after 1930 that Blackman pulled out the thick file labeled "Komulakov, Dimitri."

The MI6 officer smiled as he thumbed rapidly through the mass of paper. Blackman was pleased to see that his 1998 report on the former KGB general, turned arms broker, was included. He also noted that after his brush with Komulakov, others in Her Majesty's Secret Intelligence Service had documented the activities of the notorious Russian. Reports on the "retired" KGB officer were fairly regular up through 2001 when he had been spotted coming and going from Tehran. There was also a lengthy assessment for that year from the Americans that concluded Komulakov was supplying Iran with materiel and equipment for the manufacture of nuclear weapons. A 2003 entry indicated that the Russian had become Iran's "number-one supplier of conventional munitions."

Blackman had nearly completed his review of the file and was about to place it in the large stack of "No Current Interest" folders he had already perused when he came to the four final entries in Komulakov's record. Though the reports were all very brief, he picked up the phone, called the Chief of SIS, and asked for an appointment.

"Have a seat, Joe," he said to Blackman. The chief, or "C" as he was known to the MI6 staff, motioned toward the small conference table on the back wall of the office.

Blackman wasted no time. "Sir, there may be something of interest here with our old friend Komulakov."

"Now, Joe," the chief retorted, "you're not getting your blood up . . . making this personal, are you?"

"No, sir," Blackman replied, "these entries are all well after my run-in with him in Iraq back in '98."

"Go ahead, then," the British spy chief said. "What are the dates and who filed the reports?"

Blackman continued, "If I may sir, we have to go back a little further."

When C nodded, the MI6 agent pressed on. "In August 2001 the Americans concluded that Komulakov was providing the Iranians with Soviet-era nuclear weapons and/or fissile materiel. In the spring of 2002—after the Americans were in Afghanistan—our Kiev Station reported that Komulakov was providing the Iranians with massive quantities of conventional munitions."

Again C nodded. "Go on."

"In April of 2003 our station in Damascus filed an unconfirmed report from an Israeli source that Komulakov had engineered the last-minute movement of Saddam's biological and chemical weapons out of Iraq, through Syria and into the Bekka Valley of Lebanon.

Later that same year an American source—an Iraqi named Eli Yusef Habib who's apparently a personal contact of Bill Goode at Langley—reported again Komulakov's involvement in the delivery of a Soviet nuclear artillery round. This Habib fellow claimed that the Iranians were trying to reverse engineer the weapon."

C, listening intently, said, "That could be circular reporting, but continue."

"Well, after that there's very little on Komulakov except for these three brief entries. The first one is an unsubstantiated report from one of our sources—an Iranian defector. He claims that he was a driver for the Iranian Intelligence Service, and previously was the personal chauffeur for Qorbanali Darri Najafabadi and then for Ali Yunesi. According to this source, during 2005 and early 2006, Yunesi met frequently with Komulakov at the Hilton Hotel in Tehran."

"There's a *Hilton* in Tehran?" asked C incredulously.

"Not anymore, sir," Blackman hastened to clarify. "It *was* the Hilton Hotel, but now it's just a place where the Iranians put their 'foreign guests.' The place is actually run by their intelligences service."

"I see," said C, somewhat nonplussed. "When did we interview this driver and where is he now?"

"In April of 2006 during one of those appalling sandstorms they have out there, our boy apparently loaded up his entire family in Ali Yunesi's car and drove it across the border into Iraq." Blackman consulted the file and continued, "When he got to Basrah on 16 April he drove up to the front door of the British garrison and asked for asylum. Our man Snipes interviewed him there."

"And where is our 'car thief' now?" asked C, genuinely amused by the audacity of the Iranian defector.

"He's running an Indian restaurant here in London," answered Blackman.

"Well, Joe," said the chief, "you may bring him in

and sweat him a bit, but I don't see what this tells us about this morning's attacks in Saudi."

Blackman hastened on. "The next entry is a report from Venezuela. Over the last twelve months our 'gate watcher' at the Caracas airport has filed seven separate reports of Komulakov and several other Russians transiting through Caracas en route to and from Cuba."

"*Cuba!*" said C. It was more of an exclamation than a question.

"Yes, sir," said Blackman, pleased that he was able to surprise his boss twice. "And on his last trip in he was apparently accompanied by four males who appeared to be of Middle Eastern origin. As of the 5th of last month, he was still there—unless he slipped out through a transit point other than Caracas."

"What the devil is he doing in Cuba with four Middle Easterners?"

"Don't know, sir," replied the MI6 agent, "and not too sure how we find out, but there is one final entry that may be relevant."

"Go ahead."

"Two weeks ago Madrid Station reported on a 'walk-in' who claims he is a defector from the Cuban DGI. This individual insisted to our man Potts that he was with Castro last month and the old Stalinist was ranting about the Russians 'playing games' at their old Signals Intelligence site at Lourdes."

"Now, Joseph," the chief interrupted, "I know that Cuba isn't exactly the part of the world where you've spent most of your time and I don't mean to be pedantic, but nearly all of these so-called DGI defectors are doubles. They're well trained at what they do—they can even pass a polygraph. Remember how badly they snookered our friends at Langley? What was it, back seven or eight years ago, when seventy-five or so of their 'Cuban defectors' turned out to be double agents? They even held a press conference to show how the Americans had been duped!"

"Yes, sir," continued Blackman, "but there were two bits of information in this defector's debrief from Madrid that caught my attention. When Potts was chatting him up, the Cuban claimed that he was present when Castro was howling at his brother Raul about why the Lourdes site once again had a Russian general at it—and he even named the general."

"Komulakov?"

"Yes," said Blackman.

"Hmmm," was C's response.

"And there was one more thing," Blackman added. "The Madrid defector said that Castro was on a bit of a tear because the Russians had not informed him that there were four Iranians living at Lourdes."

C sat bolt upright in his chair. "Iranians? At Lourdes? Why?"

"Don't know, sir," Blackman replied.

C, staring off into the distance, said, "Where is this Cuban defector now?"

"In a safe house in Madrid. Potts is waiting for instructions."

Rising, C looked at his young protégé and said, "Send Potts a cable and tell him to get to Gibraltar with this Cuban right away. I want Potts to come with him. Ring up the RAF and tell 'em I've authorized a special air mission. When they get here, put the Cuban on 'the box' and let's see what the polygraph wizards tell us about how truthful this Cuban is. By the way, what do you think, any sign of the Russian's fingerprints or MO on what transpired this morning in Saudi?"

Blackman was standing now as well. He stopped shoveling papers into the Komulakov folder, looked directly at the British Intelligence chief, and answered thoughtfully, "None that I can find. . . ." Then he added, "But then, that's the way he would have done it."

C connected the dots: "If those earlier reports about Komulakov and his involvement with the Iranian nuclear weapons are true, and these more recent entries about Cuba check out, our American friends may have more trouble closer to home than they think."

CHAPTER THREE

Pennsylvania Avenue

Situation Room
The White House, Washington, DC
Monday, 15 October 2007
0815 Hours Local

Perry, are you saying that we have no idea whether a single member of the Saudi royal family survived and is still alive?" the President asked his Director of National Intelligence, interrupting his brief.

"That's correct, sir," the DNI replied, looking extremely uncomfortable as he consulted his notes. "There appears to be widespread anarchy and looting in Riyadh, Jiddah, and Medina. A group calling itself the 'Islamic Brotherhood' has apparently taken over several broadcast facilities and made the claim that the House of Saud has abdicated the throne."

When the DNI finished it seemed as though all the air had been sucked out of the Sit Room. Jeb Stuart, the National Security Advisor, seated to the right of the President, looked around the table. Everyone was seated in exactly the same chairs they had occupied less than twenty-four hours earlier. The men had changed their shirts and ties, and the two women were wearing different business suits. Only Gen. George Grisham, the

Chairman of the Joint Chiefs of Staff, appeared the same—wearing a khaki shirt and tie with the Marines' forest green blouse. But even he looked as grim, frustrated, and fatigued as the rest of them.

"Well, who's in charge in Saudi Arabia? Do we know if this was a coup?"

Once again Straw had to admit, "We just don't know, Mr. President."

The President leaned forward in his chair, elbows on the table. "It seems to me that it'd be almost impossible that every member of the royal family was in Saudi Arabia yesterday morning when all that hell broke loose. There had to be a good number of them out of the country. Have we checked in Monaco? Have we asked the Italians, the French? How about the Swiss?"

"Yes, sir, the CIA has queried every base and station since yesterday afternoon when we got the word on the assassinations in Riyadh," Straw responded. "We have some solid but quite a few unconfirmed reports of killings outside of Saudi Arabia. And thus far we're unable to confirm the location of any surviving member of the royal family."

"That's an awful lot of people. I can't begin to imagine the logistics of carrying out an assassination plot of such magnitude. Do any of our embassies have anything?" the President asked, turning to Helen Luce, his Secretary of State.

"I went personally to the Saudi Embassy here in Washington last night and, after a fifteen-minute wait, was finally admitted," she began. "Their Deputy Chief of Mission told me that they've had no communications with the ambassador since he left for Riyadh toward the end of last week. The DCM also told me that Prince Bushir was supposed to have headed back here on Sunday morning, but it's pretty clear that they don't know where he is either—or even if he's dead or alive. And everyone at their embassy here is in a major state of panic."

"How about our embassy over there?"

Referring to a sheet of paper in front of her, she tried to bail out the DNI as she responded: "As Perry said, Riyadh is still locked down. The Marine Security Guards who were in the standoff yesterday at the Marine House managed to break through to the embassy last night with one killed and all seven others wounded. All of our people and their dependents are accounted for and are inside the compound. Communications are still out all over the country—they're getting word back to us via portable satellite feed."

Consulting her notes again, Luce continued, "Our Counsel General in Monaco reports that one of the royal yachts is in the harbor there. Embassy Rabat believes that two aircraft belonging to the Saudi royal family are in Morocco and that one of the royal yachts is in Casablanca. A royal Saudi aircraft is at Lucerne, Switzerland, and there is another in Kuwait City. Our Counsel General in Palma, Majorca, indicates that a yacht belonging to a Saudi royal was in port yesterday. Athens is checking on two other yachts that have been in and around the Greek islands, and we have an unconfirmed report that another is or was at Port Louis, Mauritius. Supposedly two other yachts have been operating between Cabo San Lucas and Puerto Vallarta in Mexico. And we have a report that a Saudi yacht is in port in Colon, Panama—"

"Good grief," interrupted the Chief Executive. "How many royal yachts are there?"

"At least twenty that we know of," the DNI responded, glad to have an answer to at least one of the President's questions.

"Are any of the princes or royal family members with any of these boats or aircraft?"

Straw instantly regretted his zeal. Shaking his head, he quietly answered, "We don't know, Mr. President."

"Look," began a clearly exasperated president. "I've

got to address the nation in less than two hours. The statement we issued last night saying that we're looking for the perpetrators, announcing a three-day bank and financial markets holiday, as well as our plan to release oil from the SPR won't hold 'em off until noon. The Congressional leadership is also demanding action. The *New York Times,* the *Washington Post,* and the TV networks are after my scalp for 'hiding in the Oval Office.' It sounds like Jimmy Carter hiding in the Rose Garden during the Iran Hostage Crisis."

Every eye in the room was focused on the Chief Executive. He continued: "It took us less than twelve hours after the 9/11 attack to confirm that it was bin Laden and get a pretty good fix on where he was. Five days later we had our first Special Ops teams in Afghanistan. Twenty-four days later we had Marine boots on the ground in Khandahar. We need to do at least as well this time. That means we have to find out who did this and get moving. We also need to be clear about the situation in Saudi Arabia, and I need to be able to reassure the American people that we're doing all we can to restore our energy supplies."

The DNI swallowed hard and nodded. Dan Powers, lips pressed into a thin line, looked from the President to the DNI. When Straw said nothing, the SecDef cleared his throat and said, "Mr. President?"

"Yes, Dan," responded the clearly agitated Commander in Chief.

"In accord with your guidance last night, we've prepared a tentative Op Plan to move U.S. troops into northeastern Saudi Arabia and secure about 75 percent of their oil infrastructure."

As usual, the SecDef was speaking without the aid of notes or briefing cards. He continued. "We don't think that U.S. forces entering the country will encounter substantial resistance. But even if we don't have any significant armed opposition, that's not going to get the oil flowing again anytime soon. As the DNI indicated, it appears from the 'overhead' imagery that somewhere between 75 and 90 percent of Saudi production has been destroyed. And according to Sam, that's not the only problem in their oil patch."

Sam Browning, the Energy Secretary, picked up without losing a beat. "I went over to the Pentagon with some of my folks last night and looked carefully at those satellite shots. Whoever did this knew precisely what they were doing. In addition to the physical damage to the infrastructure elsewhere, it looks like they also took out the stabilizing towers at Abqaiq, Al Jubayl, Ad Damman, and Al Qatif. They're all gone. That means no 'de-sulfurization' for whatever oil we might be able to recover—but it also means that there's undoubtedly a serious downwind drift hazard."

"Drift hazard? From what?" the Secretary of State asked.

"From a hydrogen sulfide gas plume. In fact, by now, it may well have already killed *thousands*. But even after it dissipates, anywhere that it combines with moisture it forms sulfur dioxide—it's like pouring sulfuric acid on metal. Everything out there that's corroded will probably need to be replaced."

At this point, the SecDef picked up again. "What this means, Mr. President, is that if we put troops in, they're going to have to go with full MOPP—gas masks, chemical suits—just like the opening days of Operation Iraqi Freedom. And if we take in any civilian oil techs with us, they'll have to live and work in the same equipment."

"For how long?" interrupted the President.

"It depends on atmospheric conditions," his Energy Secretary interjected. "It could be anywhere from several weeks to several months. It argues strongly for us to use some of your emergency powers to fund a couple of pilot 'coal-gasification' plants. My people tell me that we have the technology that can convert low-sulfur coal into gas at break-even costs when oil is more than eighty or ninety dollars a barrel—which is what they're predicting it's going to be for a good while."

"Where would we do this?" the Chief Executive asked.

"In West Virginia and southern Virginia," Browning replied. "Virginia Tech, down in Blacksburg, has been working on this for years. When I talked to them last night, they were confident we could even be producing home heating oil, diesel, and gasoline in some quantity inside of eight to ten months."

As the Energy Secretary was talking, General Grisham slipped a note to Dan Powers, who read it and looked back at the general for confirmation. Grisham nodded affirmatively. Powers slipped the note into his side pocket and finished listening to the plan offered by Sam Browning regarding the feasibility of converting American coal to other fuels.

"Well, this problem isn't going to go away anytime soon. So do it, Sam," said the President. "Get the wording for the Emergency Executive Order from Jeb—and make sure we include this in my ten o'clock statement.

"What do you recommend I say about our military options, Dan?" the Commander in Chief asked, looking at his watch.

"We'll continue planning," the SecDef responded. "We've already alerted the 82nd Airborne and the 2nd Marine Division. We can get them there fastest. We've ordered the MPS—Maritime Prepositioning Ships—vessels to get under way from Diego Garcia and steam north."

"How's all this going to be coordinated over there?" the President asked.

Powers gestured to the man sitting behind him in the Marine uniform and said, "General Grisham is leaving for CENTCOM Forward HQ at Doha, Qatar, this afternoon. When he gets there tomorrow morning we'll look at what forces we can pull out of Iraq. He has some initial ideas, which he'll finalize when he gets to CENTCOM."

General Grisham offered the ideas he'd presented to Dan Powers earlier. "We can probably use the armor elements of the Army's 3rd Infantry Division, and 1st Cav," he said. "There may be some political issues in play if the Kuwaitis won't give us transit rights from Iraq to Saudi Arabia. But rather than complicate the situation we can move across the Iraqi desert and cross into northern Saudi Arabia there."

"I'm not sure I should be that detailed in my talk at ten this morning," the President suggested.

Powers shook his head. "That's just so *you* know that we're working on something. I agree that you *not* get into those specifics. You might just say something like, 'We're positioning our military forces for contingency operations as necessary.' That's probably too nebulous for the press, but it should hold 'em for a few hours while we try to get a handle on just what's happening in Saudi Arabia."

"OK, Dan," the President said. "Anyone have anything else to add?"

"Yes, sir," said the SecDef. "There is one good piece of news—but I'll let George tell you since he discovered it."

"General Grisham," said the President, "you have some good news? We need some. What is it?"

The Marine, seated behind the Defense Secretary, leaned forward and said, "Mr. President, since coming in here this morning I've been informed that we have found at least one surviving member of the Saudi royal family—and he's here in the U.S."

There was an almost audible sigh of relief around the table. The President, brightening for the first time since the meeting began, said, "Who is it, George, and how did you find out?"

The Chairman of the Joint Chiefs held up what looked like an everyday PDA and said, "It came across this, my D-DACT—something new that our troops are using. It's used to transmit data—totally secure—on the battlefield. It has built-in GPS—and we have 'em down to the squad level in the Army and Marines. As Secretary Powers and I were coming over here, I remembered that the Saudi ambassador, Prince Bushir, had a son who attended the Naval Academy. I asked the CNO to check and see if he was still enrolled. He is. He's a Second Class Midshipman—a junior—and he's in an engineering class right now."

"That's great news!" said the President, smiling for the first time. "Is he in line of succession to the crown? Seems like I read in one of Perry's briefing books that there are five or six thousand 'princes' in the royal family."

"Well, sir," explained Grisham, "technically there is no established line of succession. It's not really determined by primogeniture from one king to his son. All that's required is that the person on the throne be a blood relative of the original King Saud. Prince Bushir is his great-grandson, so *his* son at the Naval Academy is certainly eligible."

"Good. Now what do we do with him? He may be the new king of Saudi Arabia."

"I've sent a message to the superintendent's office and ordered the Marine security detachment to guard him until we can get a helicopter there to pick him up and bring him to the Pentagon so we can better protect him while we figure out what's happened to his family," Grisham replied.

"You did all that with that little thing?" asked the President.

"Yes, sir."

"Well done, General," said the President, rising. And then, as the others stood, he added, "I think we need to make sure that we keep this last bit of news to ourselves. If there really has been an effort at a coup we may have found a legitimate heir to the crown. We don't need to let the perpetrators know he's alive."

As he exited the door, with his National Security Advisor following close behind, the President turned to him and said quietly, "Jeb, ask Secretary Powers and General Grisham to join me in the Oval Office in five minutes, please." With that, the Chief Executive turned and headed up the stairs, taking them two at a time.

The Oval Office
The White House, Washington, DC
Monday, 15 October 2007
0910 Hours Local

As the Secretary of Defense and the Chairman of the Joint Chiefs joined the President in the Oval Office, the slightly curved door opposite the fireplace opened, and Bruce Allen, the White House Chief of Staff, entered carrying a file. All four remained standing in front of the famous "Queen Victoria desk."

"Dan, just a quick heads-up, because in fifty minutes I have to get ready to swim with the sharks in the press room and I need a few minutes to prepare," said the Commander in Chief. "Since you're going to follow me for the 'backgrounder' Q and A, you need to be aware that Senator Waggoner is brewing up a kettle of trouble up on Capitol Hill."

"What's the old phony up to now?" the SecDef muttered.

The President glanced at his watch and continued. "He's called twice since last night—he's threatening to introduce his Assassination Bill again—the same one that he wanted right after 9/11."

"Well, the situation is no different today than it was then," replied Powers, alert to the President's schedule.

"As I explained to the closed session of the Armed Services Committee back in 2001, Executive Order 12333 and the others prohibiting U.S. government agents or officers from engaging in assassination give us the moral high ground in dealing with a world full of thugs. If Congress vacates those orders and Waggoner's 'Assassination Bill' becomes law, we lose whatever moral high ground we still have. Some radical Islamic cleric will immediately issue a fatwa calling on every Muslim to kill you—and any other U.S. government official or employee they can find. It was a terrible idea then, and it still is."

"Well, now he says he's got the solution for that problem," said the Chief of Staff.

"Which problem, the moral issue or the fact that we all become targets once you sign an 'Assassination Bill' into law?" Powers asked.

"Well, as you might imagine, matters of right and wrong aren't very high on Senator Waggoner's list of priorities," Allen replied. "He's been after the President's hide ever since the Intelligence Reform and Terrorism Prevention Act passed in 2004 in spite of him. Now Waggoner says that the reason we couldn't prevent the Saudi attack on Sunday is because we still don't have decent human intelligence and we're not 'proactive' in preventing these attacks."

"Well, that's not new," answered the SecDef. "But usually the carping comes from the other party. This isn't the time to reopen the debate on whether we need a Director of National Intelligence or not. I don't need to tell anyone in this room that I didn't like the idea—but that's not the issue here—no matter what Waggoner thinks."

"I agree, Dan," interjected the President. "And you've been a good soldier on that whole DNI thing. But Senator Waggoner told Bruce just before our meeting this morning that he has the votes to override my veto for a bill authorizing assassination, and he wants the Congress called into secret session for a vote on the bill."

There was a moment of stunned silence as Powers stared, first at the President and then at the Chief of Staff. He then said, as much to himself as anyone: "The *whole* Congress in secret session? Has that ever been done before?"

"Not since 1781—when it was the Continental Congress," Allen responded. "But back then it was because they were afraid that if the British learned about where they were meeting they'd be attacked. But Waggoner's right about being able to do it—Article I, Section 5 of our Constitution clearly envisions the ability to convene joint sessions in secret."

"But it would leak immediately," Powers protested. "There are 535 of 'em up there, and it doesn't matter how many votes Waggoner has for this crazy idea of his; there will be dozens of people in the House and Senate who'll be opposed. Those who vote 'no' will let it leak that they tried to prevent the measure. It won't be a secret for ten minutes after that vote! Why is Waggoner doing this? Does he really think this is going to improve his prospects for president next year?"

"I don't know what his plans are for 2008," said the President, once again checking his watch. "But I wanted you to be aware, since you're doing the 'backgrounder' Q and A after I issue our statement—just in case he's planted a question with the press corps."

"Yes, sir, I understand," the SecDef responded. "If it does come up, what do you want me to say?"

The President and his Chief of Staff looked at each other silently for a moment, and then Bruce Allen said, "If it comes up, just say that 'the President reaffirmed E.O. 12333 at the beginning of his administration and all options remain open for bringing terrorists to justice.' "

Office of Sen. James W. Waggoner
Dirksen Senate Office Building
Washington, DC
Monday, 15 October 2007
1020 Hours Local

The President closed his televised message to the nation with his usual ". . . and may God continue to bless the United States of America." Senator James Waggoner, Chairman of the Senate Select Committee on Intelligence, watching it on television in his office, grabbed his remote, pointed it at the TV set, hit the red button, and the screen immediately went dark. He then pushed the "intercom" button on his phone and snarled, "Ralph, come in here!"

Seconds later, Ralph Monroe, chief of staff to one of the most powerful men in the U.S. Senate, was standing in front of Waggoner's enormous desk.

"Sit down, Ralph," said the senator, leaning back in his leather chair, his shoeless feet resting on the top of the desk. "What did you think of what our beloved President had to say?"

Monroe knew from the tone of Waggoner's voice that it was in his best interests to criticize the President. "Nothing but platitudes," the younger man said, seating himself in a wooden armchair opposite the desk. "They clearly don't know who pulled this off and therefore don't know what to do about it."

"Exactly," replied the man who liked to be referred to as his state's "senior senator." "But did you also notice all the business of 'calling on the civilized world to join us in reviewing options for securing the Saudi oil fields'—that means they have no idea whether the royal family is still in power. It's also likely that they have no idea when or if we'll ever get another drop of oil out of Saudi Arabia. That's why they released oil from the SPR and all this long-winded business of converting coal to kerosene."

"And diesel and gasoline," Monroe added, but bit his tongue for giving the President more credit for the idea than he should have.

Waggoner had done his ruminating from his desk chair but suddenly swung his feet to the floor, leaned over his desk, and asked, "What's the tally on who would support my 'active measures' proposal?"

Ralph Monroe had spent his political life on Capitol Hill. He "had the book" on every member of Congress—both parties, both houses. Monroe had been on Waggoner's staff since the senator had arrived on the hill with his movie-star wife more than two decades ago. He knew that they were little more than a year away from a national election, and that Waggoner had to make a choice in the next few weeks as to whether he would run for reelection to the Senate or make a run for the White House. Either way, Ralph Monroe planned to be there when Waggoner was sworn in.

With this in mind, he replied, "Everybody is scared that this attack is the start of a jihad. You have enough votes to override a veto in the Senate—and by this time tomorrow, we'll have enough in the House to do the same. Of course the White House is going to come down hard against it."

The senator was silent for more than a minute, musing about the possibilities and what taking on the White House might mean for his future. Waggoner was from the President's party, but his politics were more closely aligned with the opposition. *If I can get votes from our party and show that I can also get votes from the other side of the aisle—while taking on a "lame duck" White House, that might make me a very attractive candidate for president,* he thought.

Waggoner finally responded, "Y'know, Ralph, I

kinda like the idea of bucking this White House. The people who think of themselves as 'Independents' are tired of all this ultraconservative and Christian-right preaching they've been getting for the last seven years."

Monroe leaned back; he'd heard this speech before—and he enjoyed it when his boss got "fired up" at what he called the "holy rollers running the show at 1600 Pennsylvania Avenue."

"The American people want somebody who is willing to take action—and that's just what my bill will do, Ralph. We're going to start bringing people together behind a course of action that doesn't threaten American civil liberties. It only threatens those who would try to take away Americans' most basic right—the right to *life!* Ralph, write that down."

Monroe was already taking notes, realizing that Waggoner was crafting more than just another of his harangues against the so-called "Patriot Act"—this time he was outlining the basics of a campaign platform.

"It's time that America stopped being the punching bag for all these crazy radicals." Waggoner was getting wound up. He continued, "We've tried giving 'em liberty in Afghanistan and Iraq—and in return they killed our boys. We tried making nice to 'em in OPEC, and they messed with us by jacking up the price of oil. We pandered to the Israelis and even offered the Palestinians their own country—and all we get is grief and more dead Americans. You getting all this, Ralph?"

Monroe nodded and kept scribbling as Waggoner continued, "Now, because the White House bent over backward to these mullahs and imams and ayatollahs, we're gonna be paying ten bucks for a gallon of gas. Well, the American people deserve better than what we've gotten in return for all this high-sounding moral crap. We need to take the fight right to the door of every terrorist. Anybody out there who has committed an act of terrorism—or is even *planning* on committing one—

needs to go to bed at night not knowing if he'll get up in the morning. He needs to know we're out there hunting for him, and when we find him, we're going to kill him before he can kill another American."

The senator paused and before he could go on, Monroe stood up and said, "I can work with this. What do you want me to do with it?"

"Clean that up and turn it into a press release," said the senator. "But before you leave, do we have any friends inside the administration on this bill?"

Monroe flipped open his notebook again and scanned down a page. "State and Defense will fight it because they'll do what the President tells 'em to. We might be able to count on help from DHS—Secretary Dornin is pretty frustrated that she isn't getting all the funding she wanted for the border problem. And I know we can count on a quiet 'assist' from the DNI—Perry Straw. He hates Powers and feels impotent. CIA should help, but the Deputy Director for Operations is a very strange guy, and he has people at the White House and the Pentagon who pay attention to him."

"I met him last time I was out there at Langley," Waggoner interrupted. "Old guy—kind of a creepy fella—what's his name?"

"Goode, William Goode," Monroe answered. "They treat him like some kind of legend out there."

"How old is he?" the Chairman of the Senate Select Committee on Intelligence asked.

"I'll get his bio out of the file, but he's got to be in his seventies."

"He's too old for the job," the senator retorted. Monroe started to smile—Waggoner was in his seventies as well—but he checked the urge. Waggoner said, "Tell 'em it's time to get rid of Goode and get some young blood in that job—preferably somebody off my SSCI staff—somebody that we can control."

"Yes, sir," Monroe replied.

"By the way, Ralph . . . have you read this report that the CIA sent to the committee last Friday?" Waggoner asked, changing the subject yet again. He picked up a thick dossier with a red-bordered cover sheet emblazoned with the words TOP SECRET at the top and bottom, along with the warning "For U.S. Eyes Only."

"Not yet," Monroe answered.

"Well, you need to before you put on the full-court press for this bill," Waggoner responded. "It's an analytical response to the questions the committee put to the CIA Director when he appeared before the SSCI last month. It lays out who our targets ought to be—and what we should be doing about it. Here, read the Executive Summary," the senator said, handing the sheaf of paper to his aide.

Ralph Monroe did as he was told. Taking the document, he sat back down in the chair, flipped open the cover, and began to read:

TOP SECRET

NO FORN/WNTEL/EYES ONLY FOR SSCI MEMBERS
DOCUMENT NO: 1007C135.3
COPY # 2 OF 4 COPIES
EXECUTIVE SUMMARY
SUBJECT: NEAR TERM THREATS IN THE PERSIAN GULF
REGION

The effectiveness of USG policy in the "Global War on Terror" has created new, near-term vulnerabilities in the Persian Gulf and South West Asia. The successes of "Operation Enduring Freedom" in Afghanistan in 2001–02 and "Operation Iraqi Freedom" in 2003–2006 have exacerbated the desire of radical Islamic militants with access to weapons of mass destruction to bring about an immediate change in the direction of the region.

The installation of democratically elected governments in

Kabul and Baghdad and the universal acceptance of the Palestinian-Israeli "Treaty of Mutual Recognition and Assurance" are all taken as "signs" by the most radical Islamic leaders that they must act quickly to "preserve Islamic law" in what they regard to be "Islamic Lands."

Available U.S. and allied military forces may be inadequate to prevent the collapse of friendly regimes that have been targeted for "Islamification." Given U.S. and European dependence on Persian Gulf oil, such an outcome would represent a profound strategic reversal that could take decades to alter.

Radical Islamic leaders in the region are increasingly concerned that indigenous terror groups are NOT achieving sufficient momentum through insurgent actions such as those taking place in Afghanistan, Iraq, Israel, or even in the West (including the 2004 attacks on Madrid). Though Western media generally portray these terrorist organizations as achieving significant and strategic results through suicide bombings, IEDs, and other such localized attacks, radical Islamic leaders know better. These events, though causing casualties to USG civilian and military personnel, are not of sufficient magnitude to cause a withdrawal of U.S. or Western presence from what radical adherents refer to as "Islamic Lands" and are unlikely to alter USG near-term or long-range objectives. The attendant media exposure given to these events creates a perception of success and makes recruiting additional "martyrs" easier for peripheral and affiliated groups such as Al Qaeda, Islamic Jihad, Ansar al Islam, Hezbollah, the Islamic Brotherhood, etc. But recent intercepts of telephonic and electronic traffic among the most radical Islamic clerics in Iran, Saudi Arabia, Syria, Egypt, Yemen, and Pakistan indicate an awareness that such tactics are never going to alter USG policies, force a withdrawal from Afghanistan or Iraq, or bring about an end to what they call the "Zionist occupation," i.e., Israel.

In recent months it has become increasingly evident to radical Islamic leaders that localized terror movements are "helpful," but what is most necessary is a coordinated effort to ignite anti-Western Islamic militants on both sides of the Shia-Sunni sectarian divide. To that end, Wahhabi Sunnis in Saudi Arabia and the Shia clerical leadership in Iran may be nearing an informal accord with the goal of driving Western commercial, military, and diplomatic personnel out of moderate Gulf states and establishing radical theocratic governments on both sides of the Persian Gulf.

Should any government or extra-governmental entity in the Middle East or Southwest Asia succeed in uniting the two principal Islamic sects for this common goal, it is possible that Western influence and institutions could be replaced in a matter of months by Islamic theocratic bodies that would govern every aspect of day-to-day life in the region: civil authority, business, judicial matters, the media, and foreign policy. We should expect that such an outcome would create a regime or regimes innately hostile to the U.S. and our allies in the region. Under such circumstances it is unlikely that any pro-American governments in the region (e.g., the UAE, Bahrain, Afghanistan, Iraq) would long survive the transition.

Recent technical intercepts indicate that a highly structured effort to create a "cataclysmic event" may be in the late stages of planning in Tehran. It is possible that the event could be on the scale of the 9/11/01 attack on the U.S., although a specific target is undetermined. Intensive collection efforts have been undertaken with U.S. diplomatic, military, intelligence, and commercial activities in the region. To date, all reports from the field, based on queries to "moderate leaders" in the region, have dismissed the possible action as "unfeasible."

Two reporting agencies take exception to this finding:

1. The British SIS report in Addendum A indicates that Russian nuclear scientists have been tracked entering and leaving Tehran consistently for the past three years. The SIS report also surmises that Russian President Vladimir Putin has "closed a deal" with the Iranian leadership—that in ex-

change for Tehran's help in Chechnya, the Russians are providing the nuclear technology and materiel sought by the Iranian regime.

2. The CIA CT Branch, as indicated in Addendum B, notes that all of those who have been intercepted and/or observed discussing the aforementioned "cataclysmic event" are clerics or government officials who are beyond the reach of U.S. counter-terrorism units under current guidelines. The analyst notes that they all appear to be aware that they are "protected" from any USG action by Executive Order 12333.

When he finished reading the last line of the Executive Summary, Ralph Monroe whistled through his teeth and looked up at his boss. Senator Waggoner stood there grinning and said, "Well, what do you think?"

"Good grief, this is exactly what we need to get your bill passed."

"Exactly."

"But how do we get this around to the naysayers?" Monroe asked. "It's restricted dissemination."

"Well now, son, you're just going to have to make some copies of this thing and get it around to the people who need to see it," Waggoner replied, in his best, southern, "good ol' boy" twang. "You know how to run a copy machine, don't you?"

"Yes, sir," Monroe responded, unsure of himself for the first time. He thought, *People could go to jail for making copies of classified documents.*

"Well good," said the senator, still smiling. "Send one of the 'gofers' or interns out to buy some cheap copy paper and plain white envelopes at a busy office supply store somewhere in Virginia—the older the better. Have 'em pay for it with cash. Burn the receipt. Tonight, use the copier down in the mailroom—not ours. Make thirty copies of just the summary. Cover up the document and copy number—and make sure you don't touch any of the paper copies with your bare hands. Bring the originals and those copies back here. I'll tell you what mail boxes to stuff 'em into."

Monroe stood, marveling at the "senior senator's" guile. But as he started for the door, his boss called to him yet again.

"Ralph—wait. I almost forgot. Make thirty-one copies—and on your way home tonight, stop at a mail-box in Virginia and send the extra one to that nice boy, Alan Michaels, down at the *Washington Post.*"

Home of Eli Yusef Habib
Anah, Iraq
Sunday, 14 October 2007
2230 Hours Local

"Welcome home, Samir," Eli Yusef Habib said, rising to greet his son as the younger man entered the comfortable living room.

"Thank you, Father," Samir answered, embracing the patriarch of the family. Even in his stocking feet, the forty-six-year-old son towered over his father, as they held each other with sincere affection.

"Where is Mother?" the young man finally asked.

"She is next door at your house, talking to your wife," the old man replied. "The women have been anxious for you since you called yesterday to tell us that you were on the way home. With all of the news of what's happened in the neighboring kingdom, they were worried when you did not arrive before dark."

"But you were not worried, eh?" Samir asked with a smile.

"Ahh, no," Eli Yusef replied, "I do not worry, my son. I pray."

Samir laughed, but he knew *that* was true. His father

was one of the most devout men he had ever met. The old man prayed and meditated several times a day—not in the words of the Quran—but using a different text—the Holy Bible.

"Go now, to your wife and children," the old man commanded. "Bathe the dust of the desert from your body and then return with Hamilah." Then he added with a smile, "Your mother has prepared a feast for the return of our 'prodigal' son."

"All right, Father," Samir said. He walked down the carpeted marble floor and out the front door. As he slipped his shoes back on he looked northeast across the broad Euphrates. *It seems as though there are more lights on every night,* he thought, seeing the reflections in the barely moving water.

Walking the twenty meters to the large house next door, Samir waved to one of the many guards that were posted both outside and within the walls of the large gated compound. As he approached his front door he could hear the sound of music. His mother Zahira and wife Hamilah were singing hymns to the accompaniment of the Sony sound system that he had brought back from Beirut on one of his many trips to the "Pearl of the Levant" for the family import-export business.

A half hour later, bathed and wearing a clean linen shirt and trousers, Samir, Hamilah, and his mother and father were seated around the parents' dining room table. Before they ate, Eli Yusef prayed—first in thanksgiving for his son's safe return, then "for all the blessings bestowed on this faithful family," for the food set before them, and last, "for all those in peril in Saudi Arabia and particularly for 'the believers' who may be in jeopardy from evildoers."

As they passed the trays of garlic-covered lamb, seared vegetables, spinach pie, and fresh-baked flat bread, the old man said, "Tell us, Samir, about your journey. You left Beirut with four truckloads of appliances and other goods almost a month ago. How do things look in Tehran? Were you able to meet any 'believers' among the Persians?"

Samir smiled at the way his father had worded the last question. *That's the old British spy in him,* he thought. And indeed Samir was correct. To Eli Yusef, the World War II, teen-aged spy for the British, the Iranians would always be known as "Persians."

The younger man leaned back in his chair, took a long drink of tea from his cup, and said, "Ahh, first . . . Mother, thank you for a delightful meal. It is good to be home. Now—where to begin? Well first, let me tell you about Iraq. Baghdad is much more peaceful than it was on last year's trip. The road through Ramadi and Fallujah to Baghdad is now free of bandits. Other than a few flat tires, we had no trouble whatsoever anywhere in Iraq." Samir told them about other things that he'd seen in Iraq that were also encouraging the spread of democracy in the ancient land. "But I am getting tired now," he said, putting his teacup back on the saucer.

The two women got up and began clearing the table, leaving the men to their conversation. "How about crossing the borders?" asked the old man.

"I want to talk to you about Beirut and Syria in the morning, Father," Samir said. "I believe we have some great opportunities there if the rail line opens as planned. But tonight, let me tell you about Iran because I am wondering if we should close our offices there."

The old man frowned at the thought. He had been building their little trading business for more than five decades—through four Arab-Israeli wars, the Lebanese Civil War, the Soviet invasion of Afghanistan, the Iran-Iraq war, the first Gulf War, the American-led invasion of Afghanistan to throw out the Taliban, and finally, Operation Iraqi Freedom and the removal of Saddam Hussein. Through it all he had persisted—never closing an office or trade route once opened. In reply to his son's suggestion, he asked, "If we shut down in Iran, how would we supply our customers in Afghanistan?"

"I don't know, Father," Samir answered, "but I just spent a week in Iran. We were able to make all our deliveries, but it is the first time I have actually felt what you described to me about that place—that 'real evil' resides there."

The old man nodded because he understood. There had been many times in his life when he had felt the presence of what he called "real evil." He said simply, "Tell me about what you saw and heard."

"Well, first of all, I could not locate any of our friends from the 'Fellowship of Believers,' " said Samir, reaching in his pocket and holding up a tiny metal fish. "In Ahvaz I went to the address of your old friend, Petra—the family you stayed with on your last trip three years ago. Petra and his whole family are gone. None of his neighbors could—or *would*—tell me anything about where they had gone."

"I hope that nothing has happened to them," said Eli Yusef. "What else did you find in Iran?"

"The *Pasdaran*—the Iranian Revolutionary Guard Corps—are everywhere. So are the ayatollah's secret police. Every time I turned a corner—you know, using the techniques that Peter Newman taught me when we were helping the Americans find the Baathists and the foreign terrorists here four years ago—I could tell that I was being followed. And on Iranian state radio every day there are reports of people being hung, beheaded, and having their tongues cut out for not abiding by the Quran—or for violating some new Islamic regulation. One afternoon in Tehran while I was waiting for one of our trucks to be repaired I was even questioned about why I was in Tehran by two *Russians*."

"Russians?" the old man asked.

"Yes," Samir said. "There are hundreds of them in Tehran. My truck broke down near that place you once reported on—the Centre for the Development of Advanced Defense Technology—and I went to a coffee shop to wait for a mechanic. The two Russians spent about an hour questioning me, asking why I was there, what I was doing and the like."

"But such things have happened in the past—the Russians come and go. And some authority is always checking your documents or asking questions."

"No," Samir said. "It is different this time. You can feel the evil everywhere. On Friday I was passing by a mosque during afternoon prayer. Over the speakers on the minaret the mullah who was preaching kept calling on the people to prepare for what he called 'the last jihad'—for 'the final conflict.' On the street even the Iranian people looked afraid."

"Hm-m, yes, I see," Eli Yusef said.

"I also heard many Iranian Muslims talking about the number eleven. Do you know anything about that?"

"The number eleven? Yes . . . I have heard something about that too," the old man replied. "I heard it from one of our Fellowship of Believers, who passed through here several weeks ago on his way to Kuwait from Syria. He said that in the Bekka Valley—among the Hezbollah who offered themselves to be martyred—there were young men who asked if they could choose to die on the eleventh."

"It sounded to me from what I heard in Tehran that it has some significance to their jihads. But I do not know what it means," Samir told the old man.

Eli Yusef was silent for a few moments, but his son could see that he was deep in thought, and did not interrupt. Finally the father spoke. "I have noticed that some of the terrorist attacks on the West took place on the eleventh day of the month—September eleventh in America, and the train attacks in Madrid on the eleventh of March. Perhaps the number eleven has something to do with their attacks and jihads."

"I wonder, though," said Samir. "The attack this morning in Saudi Arabia—today is the fourteenth. That does not seem to fit with our theory."

"Perhaps . . . and then again perhaps not," said the old man, clearly now deep in thought. "Please, Samir, bring me my Holy Bible and a copy of the Quran off the bookshelf in my library, and I will study the matter and pray for discernment. Now, you must go to your wife and get some rest. We will talk in the morning and see if the Lord has something to show me besides your smiling face."

CHAPTER FOUR

Ultimatum

Filaya Petroleum Building
14 Al-Aqsa Street
Riyadh, Saudi Arabia
Monday, 15 October 2007
1718 Hours Local

Nikolai Dubzhuko was watching the BBC International news satellite feed on the top floor of the dummy corporation's offices when the German-made secure telephone on his desk buzzed. The gray-haired, former KGB colonel picked up the receiver, listened for the *ping* as the system engaged—and after a momentary hiss of static as his encryption unit synchronized with the caller's, heard the slightly garbled voice of his superior say, "Nikolai, how are you?"

It was the first time that the two men had spoken since the operation began. All other communications had been encrypted electronic data exchanged via the Persian Gulf undersea cable—to Iran and then on the secure Tehran-Moscow-Murmansk-Lourdes circuit. Dubzhuko replied, "I am well, General Komulakov, as I trust you are. I hope for your sake that things are not as exciting for you, wherever you are, as they are here."

Standing at a communications console in Lourdes, Cuba, Dimitri Komulakov smiled at his subordinate's clumsy attempt at figuring out where his "employer" was. "Nikolai, all the years we worked together you never mastered your insatiable curiosity. You're like the 'Elephant's Child' in Kipling."

Now it was Dubzhuko's turn to smile, and he replied, "Ah, yes, my dear General—and I should much prefer to be young again and with you back on the banks of 'the great gray, greasy Limpopo River' rather than here right now."

Komulakov was suddenly all business. "Enough reminiscing about our youth, Nikolai. You are being paid much more these days. How are things there?"

"Well, General," Dubzhuko replied formally, catching the change in tenor, "things have gone according to our plan—but we may have succeeded beyond our client's expectations. I have received positive reports from all but one of our teams. All but two of the Saudi individuals were successfully located and eliminated. It will all be in my next report in less than three hours."

"Yes, your reports have been good," Komulakov said, "but what did you mean by 'exciting' and 'better than our client expected'? Is everything all right?"

"Well," the KGB colonel continued, "all of our 'Muslim allies' performed well, but I had forgotten how bloodthirsty they can be. I well remember how the Afghanis and Chechnyans were toward us—but I expected them to be somewhat more considerate toward their own kind. The women and children . . ."

Komulakov waited for Dubzhuko to finish, but when he heard nothing for a moment he interjected, "You aren't going soft on me are you, Nikolai? How can you talk this way—you were my best executioner. I used to give you the toughest missions. I sent you to kill that Roman priest in Warsaw back in '86 with your bare hands because we knew the Poles would mess it up. What do you care about these people—they're just Arabs!"

"Yes, General. I understand—you're right—it is just Arabs killing Arabs," the KGB colonel replied. "But now it's out of control. The police have abandoned their stations, and the Saudi National Guard has stripped off their uniforms and deserted faster than Saddam's army fled from the Americans in 2003. Mobs have taken over the streets and sacked every palace, government building, and most businesses—not just here in Riyadh, but in every other Saudi city as well. The locals finished what we started and managed to kill some of the members of the royal family before our teams even got there."

"Are you sure that all the 'princelings' are dead?" asked the general.

"We're quite certain that there are none left alive here in Saudi Arabia," Dubzhuko responded, as though he were talking about exterminating insects. "I trust you have seen the follow-up report from Yemen that there were three, not two, who were in the car explosion. In my next report I'll summarize all this, but as of now, two more members of the royal family were caught and killed in Geneva just an hour ago. Another three were killed in Thailand, and Prince Al-Habib Rasul and his family members were ambushed outside their hotel in Paris. I'm still waiting to hear from our teams that followed other 'princelings' to Marseilles, Rio, South Africa, Hong Kong, and Belgium. We didn't hear from our teams in London or Montreal, but if you've watched the satellite news channels, you no doubt saw the reports of the successful operations there. Apparently the police in London killed three of our men. The BBC announced that two members of the 'Russian mafia' accompanied by a Middle Eastern male killed five of the Saudi royal family. That would be Dusko's team."

"What about Australia?" Komulakov asked.

"That's Voytetsky," Dubzhuko responded. "He reported from Sydney that his targets got some kind of warning and all three Saudis fled by chartered airplane. He thinks they may be in New Zealand. If they are, he'll get them. But the explosion aboard the yacht was an accident. It's floating firewood now."

"Well, we need to make sure when all this is over, we have eleven of their boats and aircraft," Komulakov said. "Our client made it very evident that he wants eleven royal Saudi aircraft as well as eleven yachts."

"What's so special about eleven?"

"He hasn't told me, but you must see to it. That's one of the reasons they are paying so much for this operation," Komulakov said, smiling broadly across the miles. "Do you have confidence in the backup teams that are in place for those who escaped the first assassination attempt?"

"Yes, General. As you will see in my next report, I have already implemented the backup South Africa. I may even hear something before nightfall here."

"Are you secure there?" Komulakov asked, concerned that he could lose his operations center in the Saudi capital.

"Yes," Dubzhuko answered. "I've pulled most of our people back here, inside the Filaya compound. This is the most secure building in Riyadh. We have plenty of food, water, arms and ammunition, and three good generators if the power goes out. We can hold off just about anything unless the 'crazies' get their hands on some of the National Guard tanks or some of the Royal Air Force F-16s or Mirages."

"In your last report you said the Royal Saudi Air Force had fled," the general snapped. "Is that correct?"

"That is correct," Dubzhuko replied stiffly. "The King's personal 747, with the Crown Prince and his family aboard was shot down on takeoff as you ordered. All of the Royal Saudi Air Force aircraft that could fly are now in Kuwait, Bahrain, Qatar, UAE, and Jordan. The rest were destroyed on the ground. The King's yacht was burned at Jiddah before our team could get to it, but we now have possession of five of the 'princelings' yachts and six of their aircraft, including two Gulfstreams, a Hawker, a 737, a 767, and an Airbus 319. Rest assured, by the time we are finished our client will have his eleven yachts and eleven aircraft."

"Good, Nikolai," said Komulakov, softening slightly. "Where are those boats and personal aircraft now?"

"The aircraft that we took here in Saudi Arabia have been moved to our facilities in Damascus, Mogadishu, and Sana. The boats are all at sea. I'll put it all in my next report."

"You have done well, Nikolai Dubzhuko," said Komulakov, now considerably warmer. "Do your people still have control of all four big radio and TV stations?"

"We had to give up one. That was where Captain Kryuchkov and his whole team of Egyptians were killed—when several thousand rioters burned down the TV station around them. The other three radio and television stations are still in our hands."

"Good," said Komulakov, ignoring the fact that one of his Russian team leaders had been killed. "Do you have the 'ultimatum' tape ready for broadcast at 1800 there in Riyadh?"

"Yes," said Dubzhuko, checking his Rolex watch. "There is a copy of the tape at each station and they will broadcast it as planned in twenty-eight minutes."

"Very well," said Komulakov. "And I assume that the next event on the schedule is ready as well—because we know that the Americans will not comply."

"Yes, General, the next event is ready for midnight. Major Zarubin assures me that he is ready to make the hour before midnight into noon if that is what you want."

The Oval Office
The White House, Washington, DC
Monday, 15 October 2007
1116 Hours Local

Jeb Stuart hadn't "buzzed" the President's intercom once in three years. But seconds after the FLASH precedence message from the American Embassy in Riyadh popped up on his computer screen, he simultaneously hit the Print icon on his computer and the intercom button on his phone labeled "Oval Office."

"Yes, Jeb," said the President, "I'm just wrapping up the meeting on wage and price controls. Can this wait?"

"No, sir," the National Security Advisor replied— surprising not just the secretaries of Treasury, Labor, and Commerce, but himself.

"OK, then, come on in," the President replied.

It took less than a minute for Jeb Stuart to click the tool bar on his computer labeled DISSEMINATE TO CRISIS GROUP 1, grab the two copies of the message off his printer, and traverse the back corridor from his office in the northwest corner of the West Wing to the Oval Office. He nodded to the unsmiling Secret Service agent posted outside the door, knocked twice and entered, as the President was ushering his three cabinet officers out the door on the opposite side of the room.

"I'm sorry to interrupt, sir," Stuart said as the President returned to his desk. "But this is very important." Handing the Commander in Chief one of the sheets of paper he had printed from his computer, he continued,

"It's an ultimatum from the people who now appear to be running Saudi Arabia."

The President slipped on his reading glasses and read:

SECRET
FLASH

151912ZOCT07
FROM: AMEMB RIYADH
TO: WHITE HOUSE; SEC STATE; SECDEF; DNI
SUBJ: ULTIMATUM DELIVERED ON SAUDI RADIO/TV

AT 1800 HOURS LOCAL, AN ANNOUNCER DESCRIBING HIMSELF AS "THE SPOKESMAN FOR THE ISLAMIC BROTHERHOOD" MADE THE FOLLOWING STATEMENT IN ARABIC AND ENGLISH ON SAUDI RADIO AND TELEVISION:

1. IN THE NAME OF ALLAH THE MAGNIFICENT, THE ISLAMIC BROTHERHOOD HEREBY DECLARES THAT THE COUNTRY PREVIOUSLY KNOWN AS THE KINGDOM OF SAUDI ARABIA WILL FROM THIS DAY FORWARD BE KNOWN AS "THE LAND OF THE HOLY PROPHET."

2. BECAUSE THIS IS THE BIRTHPLACE OF MOHAMMAD, THE TERRITORY ON WHICH THE GREAT TEACHER WALKED, PRAYED, AND TAUGHT, IT SHALL NO LONGER BE SULLIED AND DESECRATED BY THE PRESENCE OF INFIDELS.

3. ALL THOSE WHO DO NOT PROFESS THE ONE TRUE FAITH OF ISLAM, ALL SPIES AND THOSE WHO REPRESENT OTHER NATIONS, ALL THOSE WHO HAVE COME TO THE LAND OF THE HOLY PROPHET TO TAKE FROM ALLAH'S PEOPLE WHAT HE PUT HERE FOR THEM TO ENJOY, MUST DEPART IMMEDIATELY SO THAT THE LAND CAN BE PURIFIED.

4. BECAUSE ALLAH IS MERCIFUL, ALL FOREIGNERS AND INFIDELS WILL BE ALLOTTED THE TIME OF TWO SUNRISES TO DEPART THE LAND OF THE HOLY PROPHET.

5. THOSE INFIDELS THAT REMAIN HERE AFTER THE TIME ALLOTTED SHALL BE SLAUGHTERED LIKE UNCLEAN ANIMALS BY THE WARRIORS OF THE ISLAMIC BROTHERHOOD.

6. THOSE WHO PURPORT TO LEAD OTHER NATIONS MUST CLOSE THEIR EMBASSIES AND WITHDRAW THEIR PEOPLE IN THE TIME ALLOTTED.

7. ALL THOSE WHO WISH TO REMOVE THEIR CIVILIAN INFIDELS FROM THE LAND OF THE HOLY PROPHET MUST DO SO IN THE TIME ALLOTTED.

8. ONLY CIVILIAN COMMERCIAL AIRCRAFT AND VESSELS WILL BE ALLOWED INTO THE LAND OF THE HOLY PROPHET FOR THIS PURPOSE OF EVACUATION.

9. ALL ISLAMIC PRISONERS OF CONSCIENCE BEING HELD BY THE SATANIC AMERICAN IMPERIALISTS AT THEIR NOTORIOUS CONCENTRATION CAMP IN CUBA MUST BE SET FREE WITHIN THE TIME ALLOTTED.

10. THE GODLESS, IMPERIALIST REGIME IN WASHINGTON MUST ACKNOWLEDGE THIS MESSAGE FROM THE ISLAMIC BROTHERHOOD WITHIN FIVE HOURS.

11. FAILURE TO COMPLY WITH THIS MESSAGE IN THE TIME ALLOTTED BY THE ISLAMIC BROTHERHOOD WILL RESULT IN A PURIFYING FIRE BEING UNLEASHED ON EVERY INFIDEL MAN, WOMAN, AND CHILD IN THE GREAT SATAN'S CAVE.

BT

SECRET

It took the President less than a minute to read the terse warning through twice. When he had finished, he looked up at his National Security Advisor and said calmly, "Jeb, convene the Crisis Team by secure videoconference in five minutes. Have those who can't make it to a video-link dial in by secure voice. I'll meet you in the Sit Room in four minutes."

The National Security Advisor practically ran out of the Oval Office, hurried down the south passageway to

the stairs and raced down the steps, taking them two at
a time. When he arrived in the Situation Room he was
winded but managed to tell the SWO, "Notify the Crisis Team that the President wants a secure video conference in four minutes! I'll activate the monitors and
cameras in the conference room."

Even before responding, "Yes, sir," the Senior Watch
Officer had tapped the touch screen on his desk, selected a menu, touched a red-bordered box labeled
"Emergency," and typed in "3 min. 30 sec." on his computer keyboard. Meanwhile, Stuart entered the conference room and opened the wooden panels on the north,
west, and south walls, exposing three built-in, flat-panel
video screens and miniature cameras. Emblazoned on
the solid blue-colored screens in white letters were the
words SECURE VIDEO-CONFERENCE CONVENES
IN: and below that, a digital countdown was progress-
ing 3:12, 3:11, 3:10, 3:09 . . .

As soon as he was sure that all the equipment was
functioning properly, Stuart placed a wireless microphone, a standard television remote, and a note pad and
pencil on the table in front of the President's seat, pulled
open a small drawer built into the table at the President's position, lifted out a red telephone receiver, and
put it to his ear. An instant later the voice of the WHCA
secure voice operator said simply, "Yes, sir."

"This is Jeb Stuart; please connect me with the Crisis Team Operations Centers." In seconds the National
Security Advisor heard the operator calling roll and
other voices responding: "State"—"here" . . .
"NMCC"—"here" . . . "DNI"—"here" . . . "Justice"—
"here" . . . "DHS"—"here" . . . "Treasury"—"here" . . .
"Energy"—"here."

In less than thirty seconds all the Ops centers were
linked into the conference and the National Security
Advisor said, "This is Jeb Stuart. Please ensure that

when your principal joins the conference, he or she has a copy of American Embassy Riyadh flash precedence cable, date-time group fifteen-nineteen twelve zulu."

●

After a chorus of near-simultaneous "Roger that," NSA Stuart hung up the phone, picked up the remote, and pointed it at the north wall monitor. The countdown clock disappeared and was replaced by FOX News anchor David Asman who was in midsentence, ". . . according to Al Jazeera, the ultimatum was issued over Saudi state radio and television by a group calling itself the Islamic Brotherhood . . ."

At that moment the President entered the conference room. Stuart hit Mute, looked up, and said cheerlessly, "It looks like the networks already have it."

"Well," said the President, taking his seat, "let's make sure we tape what they have to say in case they know more about it than we do."

Stuart sat next to the President in his customary seat. As he pulled his chair up to the table, Secretary of State Helen Luce appeared on the monitor to the President's left. Within seconds, Dan Powers, the Secretary of Defense; then DNI Perry Straw, DHS Secretary Sarah Dornin, Energy Secretary Sam Browning, and Attorney General Paul Skinner were all suddenly visible on the flat screen arrays.

The President began without preamble. "Hopefully you've all seen the cable from our ambassador in Riyadh. Apparently the media is also reporting on this ultimatum. Perry, do we know anything more about this group?"

The DNI shook his head and said, "No, Mr. President. The CIA has no record of it." Then someone passed a note to him off screen and he added, "Nor has NSA ever picked up anything on a group going by this name prior to this."

"Sarah, have you had time to check with the FBI, Secret Service, Coast Guard, Customs? Any of your agencies have anything on these people?"

The Secretary of Homeland Security responded immediately. "Nothing so far, Mr. President, but I'm still waiting to hear back from Customs and the Coast Guard. It takes a while to go through every database. As you know, we're still struggling to integrate them all."

"Dan, what do you think?" asked the President.

"Nothing here in our database. It's totally new to us, too," said the SecDef.

"Anyone got *anything* on this Islamic Brotherhood?" asked the President.

When no one answered he said, "OK, let's move on. It seems to me that the threats in paragraphs one thru eight are pretty clear—they are going to kill any Westerners left in Saudi Arabia sixty hours or so from now. Paragraph nine is a warning to release the terrorists at Guantanamo. Dan, how many do we have left there?"

"Five hundred and thirty-seven," answered the SecDef.

"All right, that gets us to ten and eleven. Anybody got any idea what they mean?"

When no one else spoke, the DNI said, "It seems to me that in paragraph ten they want a USG spokesman to simply acknowledge the Islamic Brotherhood's message. But it's eleven that has us worried. That seems to be a threat that this 'purifying fire' will be used against American civilians if any of the prior ten paragraphs are not done as they want."

"What's the purifying fire part mean?" asked the President.

Again there was a pause until the Secretary of Defense said, "I believe it's their euphemism for a nuclear weapon."

"But Dan," the Commander in Chief responded, "where does a never-before-heard-of terrorist group get a nuclear weapon?"

"I don't know, Mr. President, but I am increasingly convinced that all of these Saudi events are somehow tied to the ayatollahs in Tehran."

"Do we have anything more than intuition to substantiate your suspicion?"

"No, sir, just my gut," answered the SecDef, staring directly at the camera mounted in front of him in the NMCC. "But as I said at our first meeting on this matter, the only ones in the region with the ability to pull something like this off—and the ones with the most to gain from all that's happened—are the people running the Iranian theocracy. Aside from the Pakistanis, the Iranians are the only other Islamic power with the potential for having nukes."

"Perry, what do our intelligence services say?" asked the President.

"Well, sir, we haven't had a chance to do a full voice analysis of the broadcast yet. One of the NSA analysts who listened to the broadcast when it first aired says it sounds like Ayatollah Ali Yunesi, the head of the Iranian Intelligence Service, but we won't know for certain for several more hours—if at all. Those tapes are generally second generation, and not the best quality. As to who might be behind this, the DNI analysts agree with Defense on Iranian motivation and capabilities—except for the nuclear issue. We continue to believe that the Iranians are at least a year away from being able to build their own nuclear weapons."

"That may well be," interjected the SecDef, "but that doesn't rule out the Iranians having obtained nukes from someone else."

"Who?" asked the President. "The Pakistanis?"

"Not likely," answered the DNI.

"Let's move on for a moment," interjected the President. "We're going to have to respond to this quickly. My inclination is to have the State Department issue a statement saying that we don't negotiate with terrorists and downplay what this means. Anyone else have a better suggestion?"

Helen Luce, the Secretary of State, spoke for the first time. "We agree that State should issue a statement along those lines, but also believe that we need to announce that anyone who harms U.S. civilian nationals in Saudi Arabia will be held accountable and that we do not recognize anyone other than the royal family as the legitimate government of Saudi Arabia."

"What about the reports that the entire royal family has been assassinated?" asked Perry Straw.

"Well," Luce replied, "we know we have at least one surviving member of the Al Saud line—safe in our protection—unless that has changed since we last talked."

"That's correct," interjected the President. "It's not for public consumption, but Secretary Dornin has him in a safe place. Right, Sarah?"

"Yes, Mr. President, he is alive and well in a very safe place," replied the DHS Secretary—without divulging that Prince Arshad had been moved from the Naval Academy to the Mount Weather Emergency Relocation Facility in Virginia's Blue Ridge Mountains. Nor did she reveal that she had dispatched Marine Brig. Gen. Peter Newman, the DHS Operations Director, to "ensure the prince's safety and comfort."

"Then all the more reason why we need to add the 'recognition' statement to whatever comment we make on this," the SecState replied.

"Very well," said the President. "Does anyone think we need to say anything about the detainees in Guantanamo?"

"No, sir," replied the SecDef. "The more we say, the more we'll have to defend if anything changes. But I do think we'd better take a quiet look at our options in Saudi, just in case this is not some kind of a bluff. Gen. George Grisham is en route to CENTCOM Forward.

He'll arrive there about midnight our time. Between now and then I suggest we get a good estimate on how many AmCits we have out there and start looking at how quickly we can get enough chartered civil aircraft to evacuate them if it becomes necessary. Unfortunately, once we start contacting civilian airlines, it's sure to leak."

"You're right, Dan," the President responded. "Start pulling the numbers together to see how many charter flights we would need, but hold off on contacting the airlines. Sarah, check with the FAA to see how many U.S. flagged aircraft got grounded outside the U.S. yesterday when we closed our airspace. Helen, draft up a statement along the lines we just discussed and circulate it around to principals only. I'd like to have this out by noon at the latest. There'll be no 'backgrounders' from anyone. Let the statement stand on its own. Now, let's go back to the hanging question—who's behind this and do they really have nukes?"

Helen Luce answered first. "State agrees it's likely the Iranians, but we also doubt they have any nuclear weapons."

The DNI spoke up next: "The DNI concurs that the Iranians *may* be behind this, but we don't believe that the Iranians—or whoever issued this statement—has access to nuclear weapons."

When nobody else spoke up, the President said, "Dan?"

The Defense Secretary's expression had not changed once during the twelve-minute teleconference, and it did not now. "Though we cannot prove it, we believe that the group calling itself the 'Islamic Brotherhood' is actually either the Iranian Intelligence Service, or the Iranian Revolutionary Guard Corps—maybe both. We also believe that they already possess nuclear weapons—and fully intend to use them to force us to comply with the demands in this statement."

"But once again, Dan, where would they get the weapons?" asked the President, preparing to end the conference.

The Defense Secretary pursed his lips, then asked rhetorically, "How about the Russians?"

Mount Weather Emergency Relocation Facility
Bluemont, VA
Monday, 15 October 2007
1450 Hours Local

Prince Arshad Ali Akbar-Salah was taking it all fairly well, Newman thought. The Marine Brigadier General had been dispatched to meet the young Saudi prince when he arrived at the Pentagon LZ aboard the VH-60 that had picked him up at the Naval Academy.

Before reboarding the helicopter for the thirty-minute flight to Mount Weather, the twenty-one-year-old midshipman had exchanged his uniform for jeans, a dark blue flannel shirt, and a nondescript Navy windbreaker. Aside from the regulation academy haircut, the Saudi prince now looked much like any other college junior.

Newman, the prince, and his Naval Academy roommate, Ken Carlton, were sitting in what *appeared* to be a comfortable, well-appointed apartment—except that they were nearly a thousand feet beneath the crest of Mount Weather. The sign outside the "apartment" door read: "VIP Suite 3."

The three men had already enjoyed a late lunch prepared by stewards in the galley a level above them. The two midshipmen, seated on a comfortable couch, and Newman in a leather easy chair, were now in the "living room" of the suite watching the afternoon news. As the television went from the latest on the situation in Saudi Arabia to a commercial, Carlton asked Newman, "Have you ever been here before, sir?"

"Only once," the Marine brigadier responded. "I came here on an inspection shortly after joining the Department of Homeland Security."

"I had no idea anything like this existed," the midshipman continued. "How many places like this are there?"

Newman paused a moment and answered, "Enough so that we can relocate all of the functions of the federal government in an extreme emergency. But we probably can't say much more than that."

At this the Saudi smiled and interjected, "I'll bet you don't have too many foreigners as guests."

The Marine, smiling as well, responded, "That's certainly true. But the cover for this place got fairly well 'blown' after 9/11. This was the 'Undisclosed Location' for the Vice President. It's actually been around since the Eisenhower administration built it to withstand a Soviet nuclear attack."

At this, the smile left the prince's face and he suddenly became serious. "Other than what we have seen on the news, is there any other word on my mother, father, or my sisters?"

Since being dispatched to pick up the prince, Newman had been provided with regular updates, transmitted by the DHS Ops Center to the ERF Communications suite a hundred feet below them in the heart of the underground warren of concrete tunnels. In the hours since they had arrived at the mountain bastion, the two midshipmen had seen couriers delivering messages in sealed envelopes to their escort. And all three of them had watched rebroadcasts of the State Department's spokesman rejecting the "ultimatum" issued by the "Islamic Brotherhood."

Newman chose his words carefully, calling the prince by the name that his classmates used. "There has been no official confirmation, Arshad. Our embassy in Riyadh is surrounded by angry mobs, there are quite a few wounded inside, and we have very little verifiable information. As we heard just a few minutes ago on TV, your country's entire diplomatic mission in Washington, and those in London, Paris, and Berlin, have asked for asylum. Our government has promised to notify me immediately whenever we learn anything about your parents, siblings, or the rest of your relatives in Saudi Arabia."

"But it doesn't look good, does it?" said the prince.

Again, the Marine paused before answering. "No, it doesn't. I'm not going to lie to you, Arshad. As of an hour ago, our government has been unable to confirm that any members of the royal Saud family are still alive—except you. That's why we're here."

The young man leaned back in his chair and said nothing. Carlton reached over and pressed the prince's arm as Newman watched in silence.

The briefing paper on the young Saudi prince described him as an "enigma" to his family and countrymen. While the licentious lifestyle of most Saudi males was legendary, the ambassador's oldest son was clearly cut from a different bolt of cloth. He was widely respected at the Naval Academy for his diligence, academic performance, and athletic abilities. Though his father was one of the wealthiest men on the planet, Arshad lived the same austere existence as any other midshipman. The only exception from the usual rules that he had ever requested was that he be allowed to keep Ken Carlton as his roommate after "Plebe Year." His request had been quietly granted.

Because the prince had asked that his Bancroft Hall roommate be allowed to accompany him when he was hastily evacuated from Annapolis, Ken Carlton's background had also been included in the documents Newman had inside his locked briefcase. In those briefing papers, the Chicago native was described as a "natural athlete and leader" and "academically proficient"—as reflected by his 3.7 grade point average—only one tenth of a point lower than the prince's. Newman had also read that Carlton was the leading halfback on Navy's varsity football team, the vice president of his class, and the leader of an Officer's Christian Fellowship Bible study.

After a long silence, Carlton asked, "Can I call home and tell my folks where we are, sir? I usually e-mail them every day and they'll be worried about both of us. Arshad has been a guest in my parents' home many times."

"You can call home on that phone right there," Newman replied, pointing to a telephone on the table beside the couch. "But please don't tell them where you are, simply that you are in a safe place."

"How do I make the call?" Carlton asked. "There is no number pad for dialing."

"Just pick up the phone and tell the operator the number," Newman replied.

Carlton was reaching for the phone when FOX News' Shepard Smith interrupted a report on oil reaching $154 a barrel and announced, "Ladies and gentlemen, this is a FOX News Alert. My producer is informing me that there has been a large explosion in southeastern Saudi Arabia. We're going live to our chief Pentagon correspondent, Brett Baier—Brett, what do we have?"

Newman grabbed the remote off the table in front of the couch and increased the volume as the image on the screen changed to the Pentagon pressroom.

"Shep, we have just been informed by the Office of the Secretary of Defense that a large explosion has been observed in southeastern Saudi Arabia. I'm going to read this exactly as we just received it from the Pentagon Public Affairs Office moments ago." Baier held up a piece of paper and read, "At 2300 Saudi Arabia time—1500 Washington Time—that's three p.m.—a

National Reconnaissance Office satellite observed what appears to be a *nuclear detonation* in southeastern Saudi Arabia at 21 degrees north latitude, 54 degrees east longitude. The epicenter of the explosion is approximately seven hundred miles southeast of Riyadh, in the vicinity of the Saudi Arabia-Oman border. Based on the size of the flare, it is estimated that the yield of the device was between one hundred and four hundred kilotons. A radioactive plume is evident, indicating that the detonation occurred at or near ground level. Prevailing winds in the lower atmosphere indicate a probable high risk of near-term radioactive fallout east of the detonation to include Muscat, Oman, south to Duqm, Oman. Upper level winds indicate a mid-term radiation hazard to vessels and aircraft transiting the Arabian Sea, east to the Indian subcontinent including Bombay, Sholapur, and Akola, India. The Secretary of Defense confirms that the 'Washington-Moscow Hotline' was activated within three minutes of the suspected nuclear event . . ."

The three men listened to the simple recitation in stunned silence as a map appeared on the screen showing the area of the world that had just been described. While they watched, the prince muttered, "That's Rub al Khali."

Newman turned to him and asked, "What's that, Arshad?"

The prince looked at the Marine and replied, "If they are right about where the explosion occurred, that's called 'Rub al Khali'—it means the 'Empty Quarter' in Arabic. Nobody but a few Bedouins live there."

As Newman was about to ask more questions, there was a knock on the door. He walked to the portal and opened it to see one of the civilian communications technicians standing next to the armed U.S. Army sentry who had been posted outside the VIP suite since he and the two midshipmen had arrived.

The civilian, clad in a blue jump suit, said, "General Newman, you're wanted in the communications center."

"Very well," he replied. Then turning to the two men who were now standing he said, "Ken, better make that phone call sooner rather than later. I've got a feeling that the U.S. long-distance system is about to get very busy. The phone call will be monitored, so be careful not to reveal where you are. Please wait here for me. I'll be right back."

As Newman turned to leave he looked at his watch. It was 1520.

Dirksen Senate Office Building
Washington, DC
Monday, 15 October 2007
1905 Hours Local

Senator James Waggoner was pacing back and forth in front of his desk, TV remote in hand. His skillfully trimmed and tinted mane of white hair was carefully combed and sprayed, and he was still wearing makeup from his fourth TV interview of the day. Two more cable news crews and a print reporter were waiting in his outer office.

Waggoner had just switched the channel to C-SPAN's live coverage of the UN Security Council's emergency session on the crisis in Saudi Arabia when Ralph Monroe knocked on the door and entered. Before the "senior senator's" chief of staff could speak, Waggoner asked, "Are we ready for the next interview?"

"Yes, sir," Monroe answered, "but before I bring them in here, the White House is returning your call."

"Which call? I've been calling down there every half hour since that bomb went off four hours ago. Which line, Ralph?"

"Line 5, sir," the aide replied.

The Chairman of the Senate Select Committee on Intelligence returned to his desk and reached for the phone. Every line was lit up and blinking. He punched the button labeled 5, picked up the receiver, and said, "Senator Waggoner."

At the other end of the line an operator's voice said, "This is White House Signal, please stand by for the National Security Advisor."

A look of disgust appeared on the senator's face as he heard a click on the circuit and then, "Good evening, Mr. Chairman, this is Jeb Stuart. I'm sorry it's taken me so long to get back to you, but it's been very busy this afternoon as I'm sure you understand."

"Understand? Well no, I don't understand! I've been calling for hours, boy," Waggoner began. "You people don't seem to know what you're doing down there and I'm just trying to help you out! This thing has been going on now for two days and all you can do is hold meetings, issue statements, and call on the UN for help. We've had a friendly government toppled, our supply of oil cut off, and now a nuke has killed God knows how many people and all you people can do is call another meeting—"

"Now, Senator—" the National Security Advisor tried to interrupt the barrage.

"Don't 'now senator' me, son," Waggoner continued. "I didn't call for *you*, I called for *the President*. Now get your tail over there to the Oval Office or the gym or wherever the President is napping right now and you tell him that the Chairman of the Senate Select Committee on Intelligence is hopping mad and wants to talk to him—not to you, not the head of Legislative Affairs, not the Chief of Staff, not the Vice President—I want to talk to *him*, pronto. You got it?"

The National Security Advisor did not answer. He was seething. Though he held his temper in check, he finally spoke but his voice had a steel edge. "Rest assured, Senator, I shall apprise the President of your call. Could you tell me the subject matter? It may help expedite his response."

Waggoner instantly shifted to his more familiar "good ol' boy" persona. "Sure, son. You tell the President that in accord with Article I, Section 5 of our beloved Constitution, I want the Congress to meet immediately in secret session to pass my 'Terrorist Threat Mitigation Bill.' And you can tell him that I have the votes necessary to override his veto—in both houses of Congress."

"I shall pass it on to the President, Mr. Chairman," Stuart responded coolly. Then, in a none too subtle reference to the senator's penchant for disappearing for hours on end with his "lady friends" or drinking buddies, he added: "Will you be reachable this evening?"

"I'll be right here, son, doing my part to save the Republic. I have a few more press interviews to do about us not knowing who's running this 'Islamic Brotherhood' outfit."

"Yes, Senator, I saw your last interview on NBC. If you'll permit me, I can tell you that the President is none too happy about the Chairman of the Senate Select Committee on Intelligence telling our adversaries things they don't need to know."

"Well now, young fella, if the President is unhappy with me, please have him call and tell me so," Waggoner said with a syrupy drawl. "Now y'all just run along and talk to your boss. I don't like to keep the Fourth Estate waiting."

Waggoner hung up the phone, looked at his chief of staff, smiled broadly, and said, "I think we got their attention. We do have the votes, don't we, Ralph?"

"After the nuke exploded, there's no doubt about it," Monroe answered. "There's not a member of Congress who hasn't had their phone ringing off the hook with constituents calling, demanding action."

"You have the bill in final form?" Waggoner asked.

"Yes, sir, it's all ready to go," Monroe responded.

"Good. Call the mailroom and have a courier hand-carry a copy to the White House. Stamp the envelope 'Eyes Only for the President' from me. That should be all it takes to make our Chief Executive want to pick up the phone," the senator instructed. He then added, "While we're waiting for the White House to call back, send out to the Capitol Grille for a bite to eat."

"Yes, sir," the aide said. "Do you want me to bring in the next camera crew now?"

"No. Let 'em wait 'til I eat."

The Oval Office
The White House, Washington, DC
Monday, 15 October 2007
2030 Hours Local

By sunset, the President had spent more of the day in the Situation Room than in the Oval Office. The detonation of the nuclear device in southeastern Saudi Arabia had driven the price of oil over $225 a barrel and precipitated panic in several European cities. The London Stock Exchange closed early following the worst trading losses in its 205-year history. It was much the same in Paris, Geneva, Bonn, and Tokyo. When a report of the explosion was announced over the public address system at a soccer game in São Paulo, Brazil, several hundred fans were trampled in the ensuing melee.

Secretary of State Helen Luce missed the Crisis Team meeting that convened in the Sit Room at 1930. She had been dispatched to New York City to urge the United Nations Security Council to act on a joint US/UK resolution calling for an "International Stability Force" to take control of Saudi Arabia. The President and the others in the Situation Room had watched the live feed from the United Nations as Secretary Luce made her brief but impassioned plea to the international body:

"I call upon all nations to join the United States of America and the United Kingdom in condemning these actions, and to give no aid or comfort to those who are responsible. Already, on the heels of the initial terrorist aggression, other appalling actions have been triggered by these same unlawful elements. These also threaten the lives and property of a peaceful people and have placed others, thousands of miles away at grave risk of sickness and death from nuclear radiation. Anarchy exists all across Saudi Arabia, while various outside terror elements seek to take advantage of the instability and chaos within the country. We must act now to keep this terrible tragedy from gathering momentum. We must protect the lives and property of those who are not able to protect themselves. And we must act swiftly and decisively."

She had completed her presentation just minutes before the President walked back into the Oval Office, accompanied by his National Security Advisor and Defense Secretary.

As the President entered the room, the red phone on his desk rang once. He walked over to it, picked up the receiver and heard, "Mr. President, this is WHCA Secure Voice Operator. I have the Secretary of State on the line from her portable secure unit in New York."

"Go ahead and put her through, and tell her I'm with the Secretary of Defense and the National Security Advisor on a speaker," the President said, activating the device beside the phone. After the usual clicking, *pings*, and whooshing noise, the three men heard the garbled but unmistakable voice of Helen Luce say, "Sorry to bother you, Mr. President, but the Security Council has recessed to go into executive session and it doesn't look good. We made our strongest case, but both the French and Russian ambassadors told me privately that they have been instructed by their governments to veto the resolution."

The weary President shook his head and visibly slumped in his chair, then said, "I'll call Putin and Chirac right now to see if we can move them. I'll also call London and ask Tony to do the same thing. You try to get hold of the Russian and French Foreign Ministers—though getting anyone over there in the middle of the night is going to be a problem."

"You're probably the only one who can move them now, Mr. President," the Secretary of State responded. "Do you want me to stay here until the vote or head back to Washington?"

"Well, you did a fine job and gave it your best shot, Helen," said the President, noticing that both his National Security Advisor and Defense Secretary were now talking quietly into their secure cell phones. "I think you can be of more help here with things changing so rapidly."

"I'll be back at Andrews in an hour and call White House Signal as soon as I arrive at Foggy Bottom."

"Thank you, Helen. I appreciate your effort," said the President as he hung up the phone.

As soon as he did so, Jeb Stuart interjected, "While you were on the phone with Secretary Luce, I told 'Signal' to connect you with Presidents Putin and Chirac as fast as possible. Dan contacted the NMCC and told them to send another message on the 'Moscow Hotline' that you're calling President Putin regarding today's 'nuclear event' in Saudi Arabia."

The President nodded, said "Thank you," and picked up the envelope that was sitting in the middle of his desk marked "Eyes Only for the President from the Chairman, SSCI." He looked at it, noticed that it had been stamped, SECURITY SCREENED USSS PASSED, and asked, "What's this?"

"More bad news, Mr. President," Stuart answered.

"It's a copy of Senator Waggoner's bill. He wants a vote on it in a secret joint session of Congress. This is what he's been calling about all afternoon."

"I'm surprised he's had time to make any calls or send anything to anyone with all the interviews he's been doing on television," the exhausted Commander in Chief responded, unfolding the three sheets of paper.

After quickly scanning the document, the President shook his head and handed it to the Defense Secretary, saying, "How can we ever agree to this, Dan?"

While Powers read the bill, the President asked, "Jeb, have you talked to Carl about this?"

Carl Rose, widely regarded—and feared—as the most astute political operative in Washington, had engineered the Presidents two elections. Rose and the National Security Advisor were close friends—yet often had fiery debates about the wisdom of various policies and courses of action. Stuart responded, "Yes, sir. Carl is heading back here tonight on the 'Red Eye' from California. I don't want to misrepresent his views, but he believes you ought to sign this because Waggoner has the votes to override and when it leaks out, you don't want to be seen as opposed to something that most people believe is necessary. But you know I disagree."

The Defense Secretary finished reading the bill and said, "This is essentially the same 'Assassination Bill' that Waggoner wanted after 9/11. We stopped it then but now he's got the votes to roll us. Apparently the Majority Leader and the Speaker don't feel that they have the backing to stop this secret session from happening tomorrow or keep it from coming to a vote. I agree with Jeb that this is bad all the way around for all the reasons we've already discussed. But last I checked, gasoline was already at four dollars a gallon and headed higher by the minute. Politically, everyone is going to tell you to get aboard this train before it runs you over. Morally, it's just not right. If you're going to call Waggoner back, ask him what happens when his 'Commission' and this 'Special Unit' target the wrong person or accidentally kill a bunch of innocent people. Accidents *do* happen. I wonder if he remembers what we went through in 2002 when some Canadians were killed during close air support training in Afghanistan or in 2005 when that Italian journalist and her rescuers got shot up in Baghdad in the middle of the night."

"Let's get this over with," the President said emphatically. He picked up the phone and an operator instantly said, "Signal."

"Get Senator James Waggoner for me, would you, please," said the President and put the receiver back on the phone.

Twenty seconds later the phone rang once. The President picked it up and said, "Yes . . . fine, please put him on." After a momentary pause he said, "Good evening, Mr. Chairman. I'm here with Secretary Powers and Jeb Stuart. You don't mind if I put you on the speakerphone, do you?"

There was another momentary pause and then the President forced a slight chuckle and said, "No, Senator, Lyndon Johnson and Richard Nixon were the last two to tape record their phone calls from the Oval Office. . . . OK then."

The President pushed a button on the phone, placed the handset back in the cradle, and said, "Go ahead, James."

For the next ten minutes Dan Powers and Jeb Stuart listened as the two politicians discussed their divergent positions on the Assassination Bill. The President made all the arguments about the moral issues and what might happen to those carrying out the bill, if—as inevitably happens—"mistakes are made." The SSCI Chairman ignored it all.

The National Security Advisor was amazed at how different Waggoner's demeanor had become, from the coarse way the senator had spoken to him earlier in the evening. But behind his new amiability was a stubborn resolve. And in the end it was obvious that Waggoner was going ahead with his plan for a secret joint session of the Congress on Tuesday—and that, shortly there-after, the bill was going to land on the President's desk.

As he prepared to end the conversation, the President said, "Well, Senator, you go ahead and do what you feel is necessary, but I cannot support assassination. We will of course say nothing about your secret session, but I'm going to have to think long and hard about signing this bill into law if it gets to my desk."

"Well now, Mr. President," Waggoner said with in-flection as thick as molasses, "you don't want to be known as someone who tried to stand in the way of protecting the American people from terrorists, do you—particularly since I have the votes up here to over-ride your veto?"

The President leaned forward, put his arms on the desk, and put his face directly over the speaker before responding. "You know, that's the second ultimatum I've received today. I don't like ultimatums. Good night, Senator."

CHAPTER FIVE

"The Congress, in Secret Session Convened, Does Hereby . . ."

MI6 Headquarters
Vauxhall Cross, London
Tuesday, 16 October 2007
0900 Hours Local

Seated in the ancient leather chair in C's anteroom, Blackman suddenly realized he was exhausted. With the exception of a brief nap at his desk and a quick trip back to his flat for a shower and a change of clothes, he'd been at MI6 headquarters nonstop since the Saudi crisis blew up on Sunday morning. As he stood to stretch his back, the door opened and C said, "Come in, Joseph. Found something, have you?"

"Yes, sir," responded the MI6 field officer, closing the door behind him and taking the proffered seat beside C's battleship of a desk. "We've gotten a bit more out of the two defectors that we pulled in. We've been sweating 'em for about twelve hours, and both seem to be very cooperative."

"Good, because the PM has already had a pound of my flesh over the nuclear detonation in southeastern Saudi—railing on about how poor our intelligence is," said the head of the British Secret Intelligence Service, looking at Blackman over his glasses, "He's on a bit of a rip with all of us, I'm afraid."

"How's that, sir?" asked Blackman, trying to appear sympathetic.

"Well, Scotland Yard has identified one of the bodies of the three who were killed in the shootout with Prince Atif's bodyguards in Eaton on Sunday night," C said. "Two of them are clearly of Middle Eastern origin. The Yard thinks they're Egyptian. But it turns out the third was indeed a Russian, as the news on the 'telly' claimed."

"How is that our fault?" asked Blackman.

C continued. "The forensics people say his name is Iosif Dusko. And it turns out—Dusko was already in our files as a suspect in killing our military attaché in Thailand back in '99. Apparently we never notified the Home Office or Scotland Yard, so when he came into Heathrow last week nobody knew to 'pull him aside' as it were."

Blackman, having nothing to add, simply nodded.

"So what have our two defectors told you, Joseph?" asked C, changing the subject. "Did either of these two characters know anything about the Iranians having a nuclear device?"

"No, sir, not exactly," the MI6 officer replied, "but given that one is an Iranian and the other is a Cuban—and neither apparently ever met the other—there seems to be some considerable overlap in what they are telling us."

"Why are they cooperating?" asked C.

"Very simple. Neither one of them wants to be sent back to his respective little dictatorships."

"And you suggested that possibility?"

"Something along those lines, yes sir," responded Blackman with a straight face. "It seems to have worked. Both of them are chirping like pigeons in Hyde Park."

"Yes, I'm sure," responded C. "And what's the gist of what they have to say?"

"The Iranian—the one who used to drive for Ali Yunesi—says that as far back as 2005, his boss was putting together 'a big operation' that Yunesi referred to as 'Operation Dawah'—which means 'The Call' in English," Blackman added.

"Yes, thank you, Joseph, I speak the language," the director said dryly. "Anything else?"

"Potts brought the Cuban DGI defector in from Gibraltar last night. The Cuban apparently neglected to tell Potts in Madrid that Castro believes the Russians brought the Iranians to Lourdes to help engineer some kind of prison break from the American detention center at Guantanamo," continued Blackman.

"That's an interesting angle," said C staring off in the distance. "But when you called me for this meeting you said that you had another idea on what Komulakov was up to. Is that it?"

"No . . . at least not all of it. Our Iranian 'restaurateur' now tells us that shortly before he stole his boss's car and drove to Iraq with his family, he took Ali Yunesi and his deputy to a meeting with Komulakov and another Russian, a chap named . . ."—at this point Blackman consulted his notes—"a Russian named Dubzhuko. Apparently on the way back from this meeting, our Iranian overheard Yunesi and his deputy trying to figure out which four of their agents they could trust enough to send to Cuba with Komulakov."

"That gives us two independent sources that put Iranians in Cuba with Komulakov," said C, connecting the dots. "But where is this chap Dubzhuko now, Joseph?"

Blackman smiled for the first time in the meeting. "Right at this minute I don't know for certain," answered Blackman, "but when his name popped up during the interrogation of the Iranian, I ran it through our database. It turns out that Mr.—or I should say

Colonel—Dubzhuko and General Komulakov served together in the KGB, going all the way back to the 'bad old days' in the Congo—"

"Yes, yes, Joseph," C interrupted impatiently. "One assumes that they have a long and nefarious association, but what does this Dubzhuko character have to do with the current state of affairs in Saudi Arabia and a nuclear detonation going off?"

Glancing down at his notes, Blackman skipped ahead and continued, "Ten months ago, our airport 'gate watchers' in Riyadh began reporting on regular arrivals and departures of Nikolai Dubzhuko. After his eighth trip in five months, a liaison inquiry was made by Riyadh Station with the Saudi Interior Ministry. The routine report that was filed at the time indicated that Dubzhuko was registered as an engineer with a Russian-Saudi joint venture named 'Filaya Petroleum.' "

"Blast it, Joseph," said C, feigning anger. "Where is he *now*?"

Blackman couldn't resist dragging it out a little further. Smiling, he said, "Eight days ago Dubzhuko returned to Riyadh—accompanied by 124 other 'Russian petroleum engineers and geologists,' ostensibly for a meeting with their Saudi partners."

"Let me guess," said C, now leaning over his desk toward his subordinate. "This Dubzhuko chap isn't on the list of 'infidels' scheduled to be evacuated before the deadline set by this unknown group calling itself the Islamic Brotherhood."

"Correct," replied Blackman. "But it's even better than that. After I couldn't find Dubzhuko's name on any of the evacuation lists, I called Patterson at GCHQ and asked him to tell me what he could about the Filaya Petroleum facility in Riyadh. It's a very large complex on Al-Aqsa Street. It turns out that Filaya Petroleum is one of the few businesses in the whole country that hasn't been sacked—and it has enough radio-electronics emanating from it to replace the BBC."

C was now staring wide-eyed at his subordinate. "What language?" he asked quietly.

"Mostly Russian, some Arabic, a lot of it encrypted— what we would call 'long and short range tactical comms,' if this were a military operation," Blackman replied.

"Anything to Cuba or any in Farsi?"

"Not that GCHQ can hear, but they've only had a few hours to work on it."

C leaned back in his chair and thought for a moment then said, "This is very good work, Joseph. Ring up the RAF and tell them I want you on the fastest plane they can find to Washington. See if GCHQ can spare Patterson to go with you. I'm going to call Langley and attempt to get their attention on this. Then I'll run over to Number Ten and talk to the PM. I think he needs to talk to the President. Unfortunately, our friends in 'the colonies' seem to be completely distracted by the latest maneuver by their Congress."

"Sir?" said Blackman, now standing.

C stood as well and said, "I guess you haven't seen the latest out of Washington Station. At some point later today their Congress is going to meet in secret session."

"Good Lord," Blackman exclaimed, "are they going to declare war on Iran?"

"No," C replied. "Apparently they have decided to go into the assassination business."

The Oval Office
The White House, Washington, DC
Tuesday, 16 October 2007
1035 Hours Local

"How does this happen in this town, Jeb?" the President asked his National Security Advisor. He was hold-

ing the front section of the *Washington Post* and pointing to the article, upper right, above the fold with the
headline: "Top Secret CIA Report Says Islamic Terrorists Do Not Fear U.S."

"I don't know, sir," Stuart replied. "The CIA says
there were only four copies of that report. I compared
the article to our copy, and this guy Alan Michaels has
direct quotes from it. He has to have an actual copy
rather than some statement somebody leaked."

"Well, get the Attorney General on the phone for
me," the clearly agitated Chief Executive muttered. "It
may not be against the law for a newspaper to print
classified information—but it sure is illegal for someone
in the government to be handing out copies of Top Secret documents. Let's see if we can—"

A knock on the door stopped the President midsentence. Bruce Allen, the White House Chief of Staff,
stuck his head in and said, "The Vice President is on the
way back here, sir. It passed."

The President shook his head and said, "Come on in,
Bruce." As the Chief of Staff entered the Oval Office,
the President glanced at his watch and said, "That
didn't take long. How long were they in session?"

Allen looked at the note he'd attached to the bill in
his hand and said, "According to the Vice President, the
Congress convened in secret at 0630 and they started
voting at ten o'clock."

"After just three and a half hours of debate?" The
President shook his head then said, "How long before
the bill gets here?"

"The Vice President is bringing it with him," the
Chief of Staff answered. "That's highly unusual, but—"

"—but these are unusual times . . . yes," the President finished for him. "Bruce . . . Dan Powers and
Sarah Dornin are headed over here for the 11:00 a.m.
in the Sit Room. Call and ask them to meet me up
here first. And Jeb, ask Carl to come in so that

they're all here when the Vice President arrives with the bill."

Five minutes later they all arrived almost simultaneously. When the Vice President entered the Oval Office—followed by Sarah Dornin, the Secretary of Homeland Security—Carl Rose, the Counselor to the President and Jeb Stuart, National Security Advisor were having a hushed but heated argument by the fireplace. Dan Powers, the Defense Secretary and Bruce Allen, the Chief of Staff, were watching the news on a television set that had been placed on a table against the east wall of the office, near the doors leading to the Rose Garden. As he entered, the Vice President asked, "Where's the boss?"

"He's in his study. I'll tell him you're here, sir," said the Chief of Staff.

"Wait," said the Vice President. "Take this to him," he said, holding out a large envelope. "It's the bill."

Allen exited through the doorway on the west wall of the Oval Office, and the Vice President said, "Pennsylvania Avenue is practically deserted. What's been happening since I've been up on the Hill?"

"Nothing good, sir," answered Jeb Stuart. "Sam Browning announced even-odd-day gasoline rationing about an hour ago from the Department of Energy, so the press is beating us up pretty well over that. The retail price of gasoline hit five bucks a gallon this morning—so maybe that accounts for a lot of people staying home from work. And of course the banks and markets are still closed, so that may explain some of the lack of traffic."

"Well, it's probably going to get lighter still," said the Vice President. "As I was leaving the Hill the Speaker told me that since the nuke went off in Saudi Arabia a lot of the members have been agitating for a Congressional recess until after Thanksgiving. He says they want to 'set an example for energy conservation,' but a lot of the members in both parties are scared. They think Washington is next. I told the Speaker that talk like that could create panic and if they really want to set an example, they should knock it off—talking about a recess when the country needs to see strength, unity, and resolve. But I'm afraid that they're so gutless they may actually go home to their districts."

In his private study the President, leaning over his stand-up reading desk, finished reading the bill, handed it to his Chief of Staff, and said, "Bruce, make copies for everyone in the Oval Office and bring them back to me, please."

Allen left the room to use the copier, as the President looked around the room where so many important decisions had been made—all the way back to Harry Truman. On the walls were neatly framed and matted photographs of soldiers, sailors, airmen, and Marines—all of them in combat attire, taken in Afghanistan and Iraq. Beneath each picture, some handwritten, others typed, one obviously penned on a cardboard field ration sleeve, were the prayers that these young Americans had included with the photographs that they had sent to their Commander in Chief.

When the Chief of Staff returned from his chore he found the President on his knees, his head bowed and his arms resting on the leather armchair next to the stand-up reading desk. Allen backed silently away and said nothing. After a moment the President rose, turned, put on his suit jacket, and said, "Well, Bruce, let's go face the music."

Together, the two men walked back into the Oval Office.

Lourdes Signals Intelligence Facility
Bejucal, Cuba
Tuesday, 16 October 2007
1100 Hours Local

"Excuse me, sir," said Major Sakharovsky, standing at attention outside Komulakov's open door. "There are two Cuban officers at the entrance to our compound demanding a meeting with the senior Russian officer."

"Come in, Viktor," said the general. "As always, you are wasting what little air conditioning we have. Did you tell them that they are not allowed to enter this facility? As you know I have been up almost all night for a week. Can't you just take down whatever their problem is and tell them that we'll deal with it later?"

"Yes, General," replied the aide, clearly upset. "I told them that, but they say that they have been sent by 'Comrade Castro' and they will speak only with you."

Komulakov thought for a moment. The American satellites would surely pick up Cuban government officials "chattering" over their telephones about "problems with the Russians at Lourdes." He didn't want this distraction with so much going on but nodded and said, "Very well, Viktor. Tell them I will receive them at the gatehouse. Don't let the Cubans inside any except that building. I'll be right over—and tell all our people to stay out of sight."

Komulakov arrived minutes later in civilian attire. With Major Sakharovsky serving as translator, the Cuban officers were introduced as Colonel Ramirez and Major Cruz. They wasted no time getting to the point of their visit.

"Chairman Castro dispatched us to inquire why you have Iranians here at this facility, without the permission of the Cuban government," Colonel Ramirez said bluntly.

Though he didn't show it, Komulakov was astounded by the question. *How in the world did they find out about the Iranians,* he thought.

At first he considered lying outright about the presence of the four Iranian communicators. They had, after all, arrived via Caracas with perfectly forged Russian passports. But recalling his well-practiced KGB tradecraft he decided to lie only about those things he was sure they could not verify.

"Well, Comrade Colonel, there must have been some terrible oversight on our part," Komulakov said with an ingratiating smile. "We do have several people here who were born in Iran, but they are immigrants to Russia and they work for our International Communications Monitoring Service. They provide translations of various broadcasts. With all that's happening out there in that part of the world, we believe it is very important to monitor Iranian communications. I'm sure you agree?"

The Cuban colonel was not impressed. "How many are there?" he asked.

Komulakov appeared to ponder the answer, then replied, "Four, I believe. One for each watch section."

The two Cuban officers looked at each other, and then the major said firmly, "We want to see their documents."

Now it was time for Komulakov to stand on principle. "Out of the question. Our two governments have a formal agreement that governs the operation of this facility. That agreement clearly states that we are to provide to you only the number of technicians here, no names. *We* are abiding by our part of the agreement. We have paid our lease fee a year in advance. It is to be renewed in January. Am I to inform my government in Moscow that your government is no longer going to live up to its end of the bargain? Please return to Havana and inquire if this is the message you wish to send to my government."

This was clearly not what the Cubans had anticipated. Colonel Ramirez wavered and said, "This is beyond my responsibility, General. We were instructed only to ask about the presence of Iranian nationals. I believe you have answered our questions."

Komulakov, though still deeply concerned, was suddenly affable again. "May I ask, Colonel, what gave rise to this inquiry?"

Ramirez, anxious to avoid being the cause of a diplomatic flap between Moscow and Havana, also wanted to be seen as a "fellow intelligence officer." He responded, "We have many sources, Comrade General, but one of our air force pilots flying over Lourdes last week noticed two men kneeling on prayer rugs, facing east, on top of one of your buildings. This confirmed some intelligence that we got from our people in Caracas."

For the second time in minutes Komulakov was stunned, but rising to his feet he said, "Well, thank you for pointing that out. We certainly don't want the American satellites seeing that now, do we?"

"No, not at all," replied the colonel, realizing that their audience was over.

As they reached the door, Komulakov said, "I trust this has cleared up any misunderstanding. Please transmit my good wishes to Comrade Castro. I look forward to coming to Havana soon to pay my respects to Comrade Raul. Of course, I don't need to caution you about the need not to discuss any of this over the telephone or radio. The Imperialist eavesdroppers are very good, as you know." They parted smiling.

But when Major Sakharovsky returned from escorting the Cubans outside the perimeter, Komulakov exploded, "What is going on here? Don't the Iranian fools know that the Americans have this place under constant surveillance? If you ever see them outside on their idiotic prayer rugs again, shoot them!"

Komulakov was still fuming when he returned to his

quarters and turned on his Chinese-manufactured, Japanese computer. As the screen lit up he saw an urgent message—an encrypted e-mail communiqué from Nikolai Dubzhuko in Riyadh:

SEVERAL OF OUR PERSONNEL IN CHARGE OF ELIMINATING THE SAUDI ROYALTY AND SEIZING THE YACHTS AND AIRCRAFT ARE DEMANDING MORE MONEY. THEY CLAIM THAT THEY WERE NOT TOLD ABOUT THE NUCLEAR DEVICE BEING USED AND THAT AS A CONSEQUENCE, THEIR RISKS HAVE INCREASED SUBSTANTIALLY. THEY ARE ASKING FOR AN ADDITIONAL 200 THOUSAND DOLLARS U.S. CURRENCY EACH. I MUST HAVE YOUR ANSWER QUICKLY AS THEY ARE THREATENING TO LEAVE TOMORROW MORNING SAUDI TIME IF YOU DO NOT AGREE TO THE NEW TERMS.

Komulakov did not appreciate extortion—although it never bothered *him* to engage in such tactics. Nevertheless he decided that, for the most part, the work had already been done and quite successfully.

Sitting at his computer, the general typed a hasty reply:

HOW MANY ARE THREATENING TO QUIT?

Komulakov then resumed other duties while he awaited a reply to his e-mail. Not long after his query his computer chirped, announcing an incoming encrypted message. The Russian spun his chair around to face the computer and clicked the mouse to open Dubzhuko's message:

THERE ARE SEVEN WHO THREATENED TO LEAVE IF YOU DO NOT AGREE TO THEIR TERMS. THERE MAY BE MORE IF THEY BEGIN TO TALK AMONG THEMSELVES. WHAT SHALL I TELL THEM?

Komulakov quickly typed a response:

TELL THEM NOTHING.

Dubzhuko asked next:

THEN WHAT SHALL I DO?

Komulakov's terse reply sent a chill through his deputy:

KILL THEM. AND KILL ANYONE ELSE WHO FAILS TO DO HIS DUTY.

Situation Room
The White House, Washington, DC
Tuesday, 16 October 2007
1130 Hours Local

It was the first meeting any of them could remember that the President had started late. He had arrived from the Oval Office at 1105, just seconds after the Vice President, Sarah Dornin, Dan Powers, and Bruce Allen. As they took their places, Jeb Stuart arrived and took his seat, placing a stack of paper upside down on the table.

The President wasted no time. "I'm sorry to have kept you waiting. Perry, give us the latest."

The DNI's recitation, accompanied by the usual satellite imagery, was more of the same that they had been getting since Sunday. There was as yet no further intelligence on the group calling itself the Islamic Brotherhood. But there were many more reports from around the world where Saudi royalty were apparently being systematically hunted down and killed. There was also information about radiation sickness in Oman, the

UAE, and coastal India. More than 50,000 "foreigners" were begging to be evacuated from Saudi Arabia, but as Straw pointed out, "That's likely just the tip of the iceberg. We estimate that there are still almost 200,000 'non-Arabs' still in Saudi Arabia. Though many who were working outside Riyadh were able to escape, those in the capital and others without their own vehicles remain trapped."

Sarah Dornin, the Secretary of Homeland Security, reported next. "Last night agents from ICE and the FBI arrested four Venezuelan males in McAllen, Texas—across the Rio Grande from Reyrosa, Mexico. They all had forged passports, and each was carrying $30,000 in counterfeit hundred-dollar bills. They apparently were part of a group being smuggled in by Salvadoran *Mara Salvatrucha* gang members. The smugglers and the suspected terrorists have been interrogated, but they don't have much to say. The FBI Special Agent in Charge doesn't believe that they are connected to the current situation in Saudi Arabia but has asked the U.S. Attorney to hold them until we learn more. The governors of Texas, New Mexico, Arizona, and California are all petitioning to call up the National Guard to protect our border with Mexico. Other than that, the only thing that is new is the rash of gasoline and home heating oil thefts that began yesterday. Again, we believe that this is simply criminal activity reacting to the current shortages, rationing, and high prices."

Secretary of State Helen Luce had about the only good news. "The Swiss," she said, "believe that they have established contact with someone in Saudi Arabia who purports to speak for this Islamic Brotherhood group, and they think there will be an extension of the deadline on evacuating foreigners. Operating through the offices of the International Red Cross and the Red Crescent, the Swiss have agreed to evacuate our nationals—if we can get them out of the embassy. Many of the

Americans who were living outside the capital seem to have had escape plans and have apparently succeeded in making their way overland to Oman, Yemen, Qatar, Iraq, or Jordan."

Dan Powers waited until the rest were through, and kept his report very brief: "General Grisham is in Qatar at CENTCOM forward. We have released the MPS shipping which departed Diego Garcia en route to the Gulf to CINC CENTCOM. It will be available in three days—if we have a secure port for offload. The Marine Expeditionary Unit that was ashore in Qatar has been back-loaded aboard their amphibious assault shipping and is available now. If we put them ashore in Saudi Arabia to seize a port, we'll time it to parachute in a brigade of the 82nd Airborne right afterward to get a nearby airfield. The 1st Cav and the 3rd ID are mounted up in Iraq and ready to move across the border into Saudi Arabia whenever you give the word. We're flying more chemical protective gear and equipment, and that should all be there by tomorrow. Finally, I have given Jeb a draft Decision Directive on forward deploying another Special Operations unit that SOCOM will have available for immediate use."

"Will we be able to get them out of the States to wherever they are going to be pre-positioned without it making the front pages?" asked the President.

"Yes, sir. It will probably be a Marine unit out of Camp Lejeune," answered Powers.

The President nodded, then looked around the room and said, "Thank you, everyone. Now, there is a new matter on which I want your advice. A little over an hour ago, the Congress met in secret session and passed a bill that they believe will help us deal with the present crisis. Jeb, hand the copies out to everyone, please."

As the National Security Advisor handed out the stapled copies of the bill, the President said, "The Vice President attended the joint session, and he'll give you a report on what he observed."

The Vice President cleared his throat and said simply, "Though they met in joint session, each house voted separately. It passed the House by 425 to 6 with 4 abstentions. The Senate passed it 92 to 3 with 3 abstentions and 2 absent. After the nuclear detonation yesterday and this morning's piece in the *Washington Post,* there was almost no debate."

When the Vice President finished, the President said, "Now, if you will each take a few minutes to read the bill, I'll tell you what I have decided to do."

The room was silent except for the rustle of paper as the President's most trusted advisors read what the Congress had passed just hours before:

110th CONGRESS
2nd Session
J.R. 1

To nullify the effect of certain provisions of various executive orders and compel the Commander in Chief to take certain measures in the National Interest.

IN THE HOUSE AND SENATE, JOINTLY CONVENED
October 16, 2007

Senator WAGGONER of West Virginia and Mr. WILSON of Connecticut jointly introduced the following bill, which was referred to a Special Joint Session of the Congress, convened in secret session.

A BILL

To nullify the effect of certain provisions of various executive orders and compel the Commander in Chief to take certain measures in the National Interest.

Be it enacted by the Senate and House of Representatives of the United States of America in Congress assembled,

SECTION 1. SHORT TITLE.

This Act may be cited as the "Terrorist Threat Mitigation Act of 2007."

SECTION 2. FINDINGS.

Congress finds that:

(1) Presidents have issued executive orders, which severely limit the use of the military and intelligence services when dealing with potentially serious threats against the United States of America;

(2) these executive orders limit the swift, sure, and precise action needed by the United States to protect our national security;

(3) present strategy allows U.S. military forces to bomb large targets hoping to eliminate a terrorist leader, but prevents our country from designing a limited action which would specifically accomplish that purpose;

(4) on several occasions the military has been ordered to use a military strike hoping, in most cases unsuccessfully, to remove a terrorist leader who has committed or who is planning crimes against the United States;

(5) as the threat from terrorism grows, America must continue to employ more effective means of combating the menace posed by those who would murder American citizens simply to make a political point; and

(6) action by the United States Government to remove such persons is a remedy which should be used sparingly and considered only after all other reasonable options have failed or are not available; however, this is an option our country must maintain for cases in which international threats to United States national security cannot be eliminated by other means.

SECTION 3. NULLIFICATION OF EFFECT OF CERTAIN PROVISIONS OF VARIOUS EXECUTIVE ORDERS.

The following provisions of the enumerated executive orders shall have no further force or effect:

(1) Section 5(g) of Executive Order 11905; to wit: No employee of the United States Government shall engage in, or conspire to engage in, political assassination.

(2) Section 2-305 of Executive Order 12036; to wit: No person employed by or acting on behalf of the United States Government shall engage in, or conspire to engage in, assassination.

(3) Section 2.11 of Executive Order 12333; to wit: No person employed by or acting on behalf of the United States Government shall engage in, or conspire to engage in, assassination.

SECTION 4. IMPLEMENTATION OF TERRORIST THREAT MITIGATION MEASURES.

(1) The President shall immediately cause to be formed a Threat Mitigation Commission comprised of five American citizens.

(2) The Threat Mitigation Commission shall be chaired by a sitting or former Justice of the Supreme Court and consist of a former Secretary of State, a former Attorney General of the United States, a former Director of Central Intelligence, and a former Chairman of the Joint Chiefs of Staff.

(3) The Threat Mitigation Commission shall convene as necessary to identify and compile a list of foreign persons who pose sufficient risk to the National Security Interests of the United States to warrant the sentence of death.

(4) The list of persons sentenced to death by the Commission on Threat Mitigation shall be submitted to the President for appropriate and timely action by the Executive Branch. Said list of individuals so sentenced shall be maintained at not more than one hundred persons.

(5) The President shall immediately cause to be created within the Executive Branch a Special Unit of sufficient size, background, and experience to carry out the sentences imposed by the Commission.

(6) Members of said Special Unit shall report to the Pres-

ident through the Commission on Threat Mitigation and shall be afforded all necessary diplomatic and other protections to preclude prosecution for executing their duties under this Act.

SECTION 5. AUTHORIZATION AND APPROPRIATION.

(1) The sum of Five Hundred Million dollars is hereby authorized and appropriated to the Executive Branch in the Classified Annex to the Budget for the Central Intelligence Agency for FY 2008.

(2) In the event that additional sums are required to carry out the purposes of this Act before the end of FY 2008, the President shall report such requirement to the House Permanent Select Committee on Intelligence and the Senate Select Committee on Intelligence as necessary.

SECTION 6. CLASSIFIED INFORMATION.

(1) The President shall designate all information pertaining to the provisions of this Act the highest level of National Security classification.

(2) The names and duties of those serving on the aforementioned Threat Mitigation Commission and the Special Unit shall remain classified Top Secret.

(3) The President shall provide a quarterly report to the Senate Select Committee on Intelligence and the House Permanent Select Committee on Intelligence regarding the activities of the aforementioned Threat Mitigation Commission and the Special Unit. Said reports to be designated the highest level of National Security classification.

❂

When everyone in the room was again looking at him, the President said, "Notwithstanding deep reservations and very serious concerns about this bill, I have decided to sign it."

Hearing this, Helen Luce slumped back in her seat and audibly sighed. No one else in the room moved. The President continued, "I believe that this is *not* a wise course of action to pursue. However, after praying about it and listening to wise counsel, I've decided that this may be the only option we have open to us at this point. If any of you feel that such action is inconsistent with your moral or ethical beliefs and think that you must choose to resign, now, or privately later, I'll understand."

There was a long moment of silence. When Helen Luce finally spoke, her voice was barely above a whisper. "Mr. President, if you sign this bill, we will forever lose any moral authority we have as a nation."

"Helen, I know. That may well turn out to be true. But if I veto it or don't sign it—it'll still become law. And in the ensuing fight over the bill we could cease to be a nation. As all of you have seen in the news, Washington is not the only city where Americans did not come to work today. The fear of a nuclear device going off in any one of our major metropolitan areas may not be reasonable, but it's still very real."

"May I ask who urged you to sign this, Mr. President?" the Secretary of State persisted. "We don't have to stoop to the level of these savages in order to prevail against them. I recall when this came up after 9/11, Dan, you were opposed," she said, looking directly at the Defense Secretary. "So were you, Mr. Vice President," she said, gazing at the man who had been in the House chamber for the secret vote. "And so were you, Jeb. You were all against assassinations. Who now thinks this is a good idea?" When she finished she had tears in her eyes.

Again there was a moment of silence and then the Vice President spoke very quietly. "Helen . . . none of us thinks it's a good idea. But as the President said, it's a necessary one. When I was coming back down from the Hill this morning, I jotted down all the reasons why I was going to recommend that the President veto this bill."

The VP removed a folded sheet of paper from inside

his coat pocket. It was covered with his handwriting. "But then I looked up and saw the empty streets and it suddenly occurred to me, who of us wouldn't have assassinated Adolf Hitler—*before* he could murder millions of people. If Josef Stalin had been dispatched in the 1920s, *tens* of millions would have been spared. How do you measure 'moral high ground' in a situation like *that*? Would assassinating either of them have been anymore immoral than letting them do what they did? That's what changed my mind."

There was a brief silence as the people in the room grappled with the possible consequences of implementing the bill. The Secretary of State took a deep breath, looked at the President, and brought the matter back into focus. "What else do you want from us, Mr. President?"

"I'd like your suggestions as to who might serve on this Commission that the Congress has called for. I'll get with Dan separately to determine how we're to form this Special Unit. I'd appreciate you sending me your suggestions by mid-afternoon. I'll make the calls myself so that the names won't leak out quite as quickly as other things do in this town."

Everyone nodded—even Helen Luce. The President then took a pen out of his pocket and signed his name to the bottom of the bill.

2nd Force Reconnaissance Company, FMF
Camp Lejeune, NC
Tuesday, 16 October 2007
1230 Hours Local

Sgt. Maj. Amos Skillings reached into an open cardboard case labeled "Meals Ready to Eat," grabbed a brown plastic pouch without looking at its contents, and deftly sliced it open with his Kabar knife. The well-muscled sergeant major had just led his Recon Marines on a three-mile race through the swampy terrain on the banks of the New River. As he sat down with a bottle of water and prepared to eat from the combat rations pack, his black skin was glistening with sweat.

"Hey, Sergeant Major," a Marine corporal called to him. "You didn't even read what was on the label. Don't you want to pick out something good?"

"You mean the Corps would give us something that *wasn't* good?"

The forty-nine Marines and four Navy medical corpsmen taking a meal break from their Special Ops training laughed and continued their good-natured chatter while they ate. It was always a bit of a risk, kidding their legendary sergeant major. They held him in awe, but not just because he was a highly decorated warrior, now at the top of the enlisted ranks. The troops also knew that Skillings was the best shot in 2nd Recon Battalion, that he always "maxed" the monthly physical fitness test, had made more parachute jumps than anyone around, and could still beat every one of them on the rugged Recon obstacle course. And yet, by way of contrast, many of them also knew him as the leader of the "Thursday Night Bible Study" in the Recon Battalion recreation room.

All of the Marines had seen Skillings in his service dress uniform with his five rows of ribbons—topped by the gold "parachute wings" worn by SEALs, Recon Marines, and few others. Though Skillings himself never talked about his personal heroism, the younger NCOs would often tell tales of Sergeant Skillings's daring in 1990 when the Iraqis invaded tiny Kuwait and how he had received his first Silver Star and Purple Heart. And even the newest Marines in the battalion knew how in 2003, then-First Sergeant Skillings, though badly wounded, had saved Col. Peter Newman, his Regimental Commander, during Operation Iraqi Freedom—resulting in a second Silver Star and Purple Heart. But almost no one knew the *real* story behind the Bronze Star with Combat "V" that the Sergeant Major wore on his blouse. When one of his young Marines would ask about it, Skillings would simply reply, "It was for a little gunfight near the Iraqi border." He never bothered to explain that the "little gunfight" was actually a bloodbath on the Syrian side of the Iraqi border in March of 1998, or that he was then a Gunnery Sergeant on a covert mission with then-Lt. Col. Peter J. Newman.

As one of the most decorated Marines in the Corps, many assumed that Skillings was a "natural" for eventual selection as Sergeant Major of the Marine Corps—the top enlisted spot in the small, elite force. He not only had more "combat time" than many Marines would ever have, but had also proven himself to be more than capable of serving in high-level staff assignments. He had somehow made time to earn a Bachelor of Arts degree in Management from the University of Maryland Extension School and had twice worked for Gen. George Grisham—one of the most revered officers in the Corps.

Skillings had never married. At thirty-nine, nearly twice the age of the Marines around him, the sergeant major had come to the simple acceptance that he was never going to find "the right woman." Behind his back, some jealous detractors called him "the black monk" or said that he was "married to the Corps." But even his most cynical critics had to admit that Sgt. Maj. Amos Skillings was the one man they would want beside them in a gunfight. And everyone who had ever served with him knew that he would also take a bullet for them, without thinking twice.

The Marines and Corpsmen of 1st Platoon, 2nd Force Reconnaissance Company that Skillings was training with were all "Special Ops Warriors"—designated as

"Marine Detachment Two" for the U.S. Special Operations Command. SOCOM Det-2 was in the midst of preparing for a seven-month deployment to Afghanistan in January 2008. There, they would "work" the mountainous border region with Pakistan where the remnant of Osama bin Laden's Al Qaeda terrorist network was still making mischief.

Despite Sunday's attack on Saudi Arabia, they had gone to "the field" as scheduled early Monday morning for what was supposed to be a five-day training exercise. This was all part of a three-month pre-deployment training cycle that would take them from the coastal lowlands of Camp Lejeune to the high desert at Twenty-nine Palms, California, and eventually to the icy cold mountains of Fort Drum, New York.

At 0300 on Monday morning the Marines and their faithful Corpsmen had dutifully reported to the parachute loft at the Marine Corps Air Station New River. There, they strapped on their chutes and before dawn had dropped into a gridiron-sized DZ at the east end of Camp Lejeune.

At 1525 on Monday afternoon, Capt. Andy Christopher, the Det-2 Commander, and Sergeant Major Skillings had both received the same "Flash" message on their D-DACTs:

FLASH
SECRET

151525ZOCT07
FM: C.O. 2nd FORCE RECON, FMF
TO: DET 2 C.O.; 2nd FORCE RECON ECHO NINE
SUBJ: NUKE WARN
   1. NCA INFORMS TAC NUKE DETONATED IN SE SAUDI ARABIA.
   2. NO KNOWN U.S. CASUALTIES.
   3. ORIGIN OF NUKE UNK.
   4. ALL U.S. FORCES OCONUS REPORT DEFCON ONE.

5. ALL U.S. FORCES CONUS REPORT DEFCON TWO.
6. DET 2 BE PREP TO RET ONSLOW BEACH ON 4 HRS.
NOTICE.
BT

After receiving the message, Captain Christopher, his XO, the three team-leader lieutenants, and Sergeant Major Skillings had huddled briefly. They then pulled the rest of troops together, briefed them on what little they knew, and continued to carry out the training schedule. For the next twenty hours they had continued to scramble through the thick brush—trying to avoid detection by one of the 2nd Marine Division's Infantry Battalions, while calling in simulated fire missions on their "opponents."

Now, as Skillings and the rest of the Marines were finishing their hastily eaten rations, his little D-DACT vibrated in the cargo pocket of his digital camouflage trousers—a silent alert that he had received a message.

He pulled out the small, rugged green device that served as a combination computer, GPS, and data communications system, marveling at the technology. At a mere thirty-one ounces, the Dismounted Data Automated Communications Terminal system allowed a combat leader to send and receive encrypted messages in total silence—literally around the globe. With a D-DACT—or the vehicle mounted M-DACT—a small unit leader in combat could receive images from satellites or UAVs, call in air or artillery strikes, and instantly mark his position for casualty evacuation or reinforcements.

Skillings looked at the screen and saw that he had received another message from Recon Battalion HQ:

FLASH
SECRET

161745ZOCT07
FM: C.O. 2nd FORCE RECON, FMF
TO: DET 2 C.O.; 2nd FORCE RECON ECHO NINE
SUBJ: EMERGENCY RECALL

1. EFFECTIVE 1800 LOCAL, SOCOM AIR ALERT TETHER FOR DET TWO REDUCED TO ONE HOUR.

2. DET TWO RET IMMEDIATELY TO ONSLOW BEACH VIA MOTOR-T ASSETS EN ROUTE YOUR LOC.

3. ON ARRIVAL ONSLOW BEACH, RETAIN MOTOR-T ASSETS TO XPORT DET TWO PAX & UNIT FLY-AWAY MOUNT OUT TO HANGAR FOUR, MCAS NEW RIVER NLT 1700 LOCAL.

4. USAF TO PROVIDE TWO C-I7 A/C AT MCAS NEW RIVER FOR ONWARD DEPLOYMENT OF DET TWO PAX & EQUIP.

5. FLY-AWAY MOUNTOUT LIMIT: 56 PAX W/ T/E WEAPS & AMMO, FOUR HUMVEE MK-16 AND 5,300 CUFT EQUIP/SPARES, DESERT PREP.

6. REPORT MSN CAPABLE THIS HQ ON ARRIVAL MCAS NEW RIVER.

7. CHOP TO SOCOM ON ORDER.

8. ADCON REMAINS 2nd FORCE RECON CO., FMF.

9. COMM SOP XT21A & EMCON EFF IMMEDIATELY.

BT

After reading the message through quickly, Sergeant Major Skillings pushed the red button labeled ACK on his D-DACT—sending a microburst transmission via satellite back to the Recon Battalion to acknowledge that he had received the message. He then pushed the button labeled SAVE, and the message on the screen disappeared from the screen into the tiny computer's digital memory.

He shoved the D-DACT back into his cargo pocket as Capt. Andy Christopher walked up and said, "Well,

Sergeant Major, looks like training just got cancelled for the real thing."

"Yes, sir," Skillings replied, "but they've all seen action before. They're ready. I wonder where SOCOM is sending you. The message didn't say."

"No, it didn't," the captain replied. "Did you notice something else? The message specified fifty-six passengers—but there's only forty-nine Marines and four Corpsmen in this Det. Who are the extra three who will be going along for the ride?"

"Don't know, sir," Skillings replied with a smile. "But if you're going to get into a gunfight, sure wish I was going to be one of 'em."

Captain Christopher—a veteran of a tour of duty in Iraq and another in Afghanistan—looked at Skillings and said, "So do I, Sergeant Major, so do I."

From the hardball tarmac road a quarter mile through the woods came the sound of trucks slowing and braking to a halt. The captain turned to Skillings and said, "That must be our ride back to Onslow Beach. Better get 'em up and moving, Sergeant Major."

"Aye aye, sir!" Skillings said. Then turning to the Marines resting in the thicket, he bellowed, "Listen up, ladies! Contrary to Marine Corps policy, training has been cancelled in lieu of a war. SOCOM wants your sorry butts on Air Alert at New River by 1800 tonight. We're headed back to the barracks at Onslow Beach. When we get there you will grab your fly-away kits, put the tops on your mount-out boxes, draw ammo, load it all on the trucks, clean your weapons, shower, put on a clean set of 'desert digitals,' and be ready for inspection with all personal combat gear, desert side out, on the Company street at 1645, ready to roll. Any questions?"

"Yes, Sergeant Major," said a young corporal. "Where are we going?"

"Well now, son, if they had wanted you to know that they would have told me and I would have told you,"

Skillings said with a laconic grin. "But no matter where you go, remember that there is no greater friend and no worse enemy than a U.S. Marine. When you get to wherever you are going, just tell the first guy you meet to choose one or the other. Now, if there are no other questions, mount up! Get your gear and get your rear. Put 'em both in those 'six-bys' out on the road. Let's go!"

The Oval Office
The White House, Washington, DC
Tuesday, 16 October 2007
2130 Hours Local

By nine-fifteen that evening they had their Commission on Threat Mitigation required by the "Top Secret" bill that the President had signed into law at noon. The essential elements of the bill had of course leaked to the press by 3:00 p.m. Media speculation began immediately as to who would serve on what they called the "Assassination Commission."

Defense Secretary Dan Powers, the Vice President, National Security Advisor Jeb Stuart, Secretary of State Helen Luce, and the President had been calling potential Commission members since 1:00 p.m. They automatically eliminated anyone who called in to volunteer their services—and it had taken the personal intervention of the President in each case to convince the five who finally agreed to serve.

Chief Justice Anthony Scironi had reluctantly accepted the post of Chairman. At sixty-eight he was one of the youngest on the panel. The rest, as required by the law, were all former high-level officials of previous administrations: James Cook, now seventy, had been Secretary of State; Russell Bates, once the Director of Central Intelligence, was seventy-four; and seventy-six-year-old Gen. Conrad Vassar, once Chairman of the

Joint Chiefs of Staff, was the oldest. The youngest member of the new Commission was former FBI director Gerald Donahue. They all agreed to serve a one-year term on the Commission for Threat Mitigation—with the proviso that their names not be revealed during their lifetimes or that of their children.

The National Security Advisor arranged for Gulfstream jets from the 89th Special Air Squadron at Andrews—the same Air Force unit that flies and maintains *Air Force One*—to bring the four from around the country to meet privately with the President on Wednesday. In an effort to lighten the heavy atmosphere, the Vice President suggested that the meeting be held at an "undisclosed location" in hopes that the identities of the candidates could be protected. They agreed on Camp David.

As the two cabinet secretaries and the National Security Advisor were preparing to depart for home, the Vice President said, "I know it's been a long and tumultuous day, but we haven't given any thought to who is going to head up this 'Special Unit' called for in the legislation."

"Yes, sir, I have," said Dan Powers. "I believe it has to be a military man. Someone who is experienced, disciplined, has proven himself to be level-headed in combat, and knows how to follow orders."

"Why not someone from the CIA, the clandestine service?" asked Jeb Stuart.

"Because anyone who *really* knows how to be a covert operative—from the days when the Agency *had* a clandestine service—would be as old as our Commission members or older," Powers retorted. "We haven't had any *real* spies out there since the '60s or '70s—and most of them were 'holdovers' from World War II or Korea."

The SecDef had been complaining about the poor quality of human intelligence collection at the CIA for years and as far as he was concerned, the Intelligence Reform and Terrorism Prevention Act, signed by the President on 17 December 2004, and the creation of the DNI had made things worse instead of better. "The only *real* spy left at Langley is old Bill Goode—and he's the Deputy Director of Operations. He might make a good 'advisor' to this 'Special Unit,' but he's too old to run it."

The weary President had heard much of this before, and despite his respect for his Defense Secretary, he tried to short-circuit the diatribe: "Do you have some candidates, Dan?"

"Well, sir, I talked to George Grisham after you signed the bill. He says there is only one man he knows of who can handle this assignment, but he wants to talk to him first—before you or the Commission see him."

"Why?" asked the Vice President. "If he's a serving officer, it shouldn't be a problem."

"Yes, that's true, Mr. Vice President, but I agree with something else General Grisham said to me about this assignment," Powers responded. "As you probably know, George didn't think this bill should become law either—but he's a good Marine and he's loyal. He said that the man we want for this job has to have nerves of steel, a heart full of compassion, and want no recognition."

"Those are qualities I admire," the President said. "Do you know who this man is, Dan?"

"Yes, sir, but without insulting anyone here, I think his name should be known only to a very small number of people—perhaps you, the Vice President, and the Committee Chairman."

"And of course you and General Grisham," said Jeb Stuart, showing his fatigue and seeing where this was heading.

At this the Secretary of State interjected, "I think Dan is right, Jeb. Whoever carries out the mission of this 'Special Unit' is going to be in grave jeopardy. The smaller the number of people who know who he is, the safer he and his family—if he has one—will be. Let's go."

Stuart, realizing he had been petulant, shrugged his shoulders and said, "You're right. I don't need to know who it is. My apologies, Mr. Secretary . . . Mr. President, good night. I'll be here at seven in the morning."

"Thank you, Helen . . . Jeb," the President said as they gathered up their notes. "I appreciate your good advice and hard work on another difficult day."

After the door closed behind Luce and Stuart, the President said to Powers, "Who is it? Do I know him?"

"You met him, Mr. President—right here in this office, shortly after the start of your first term—on 24 March 2001. He was a new Marine colonel then, and you awarded him the Navy Cross—his second—for a very sensitive mission in Iraq during your predecessor's term. Today he's a Brigadier General, assigned to a slot at DHS, as Sarah Dornin's Director of Operations."

The President leaned back in his desk chair, looked up at the ceiling, and said, "I recall the event. If I remember correctly, it was a classified citation. What's his name?"

The SecDef handed the President a file he'd been carrying all evening and said, "This is his Officer's Qualification Record—his whole military history and background. His name is Peter John Newman."

CHAPTER SIX

Prey without Ceasing

Filaya Petroleum Building
14 Al-Aqsa Street
Riyadh, Saudi Arabia
Wednesday, 17 October 2007
0430 Hours Local

Former KGB colonel Nikolai Dubzhuko groaned as the discordant warble of the secure telephone dragged him out of the depths of sleep. He had gotten so used to his employer calling in the middle of the night that he'd taken to sleeping on a cot near the communication equipment in the conference room on the top floor of the Filaya Petroleum Building.

Dubzhuko had also concluded by now that his boss had to be running this whole operation from somewhere well west of Riyadh. *There is no way that Comrade General Komulakov is losing this much sleep. He can't possibly be in Tehran or Moscow. The reprobate's probably on some Caribbean island,* he thought as he stumbled in the darkness toward the incessant noise.

"This is Dubzhuko," he said, trying to sound wide-awake.

Komulakov didn't bother to identify himself, but he didn't have to. Dubzhuko knew his voice, and besides—

who else would be calling him on this phone? "What is your latest count on the mission objectives?" Komulakov asked without preamble.

"Which mission objectives?" Dubzhuko asked aloud, while thinking: *Why do you always ask me such open-ended questions and keep me on the defensive?* But then he clarified the question by further asking Komulakov, "Do you mean how many of the royal family have been located and dealt with? Or are you referring to how many of our rebellious mercenaries I have had to shoot?"

The inquiry was met by silence at the other end of the connection. "Did you hear my question?" Dubzhuko asked.

"Yes. But you weren't paying attention to my question. I wouldn't be calling you to ask about the trouble-makers there—I already told you to deal with them, so I presume you did. I want to know about the primary mission."

"That number has not changed since my last report six hours ago," Dubzhuko said dully.

"Then there are still four 'princelings' and five female royal family members that are unaccounted for or under the protection of other nations."

"That is correct," Dubzhuko replied. "The two in New Zealand with their wives, the one in Italy with his wife and two daughters, and the prince studying at the 'main adversary's' Naval School."

Komulakov did not react to Dubzhuko's use of the old KGB term for the United States. Instead he said, "Good. I will activate two backup teams to take care of the ones in Italy and Australia and send you instructions later today about what to do about them after I talk to our 'client' in Tehran. I am not sure what to do about the 'princeling' in the United States. He's the son of the Saudi Ambassador to Washington. Are you sure that his parents have been eliminated?"

"Yes," replied Dubzhuko. "They tried to flee in their aircraft, but one of our 'Muslim allies' machine-gunned them as they were ·boarding. Unfortunately the plane burned as well. The fool had tracer bullets in his weapon when he fired."

"Too bad," said Komulakov solemnly. "We could have used the aircraft." The former KGB general continued. "Our client wants us to make some minor alterations in our plan. The American television networks are saying that Washington has troops all ready to move into Saudi Arabia. Wait, let me read this to you."

There was a pause while Komulakov consulted his notes. Dubzhuko, now fully awake, said nothing—but wondered if what he was about to hear was going to alter his contingency arrangements for escaping Riyadh if their plans went awry. Nikolai Dubzhuko was being paid 2.5 million euros for this job—half of which was already in his account in the Caymans. But none of it would be his if he didn't survive the experience.

Finally Komulakov continued, "Here is the transcript from CNN just an hour ago: 'American and British military units are poised to act preemptively and invade Saudi Arabia. According to highly placed sources in London and Washington, U.S. assassination squads will accompany conventional military units when they enter the country which the new government in Riyadh is calling "The Land of the Holy Prophet." According to our sources, neither Washington nor London is going to wait for the UN to vote again on sending in a peacekeeping force. Apparently the "hawks" and influential oil interests in both capitals have convinced government decision makers that the anarchy in Saudi Arabia will only get worse by waiting on the UN, and they need to try and contain it now . . .' and the rest is irrelevant," Komulakov said.

"Then they know of our plans?" said Dubzhuko.

"No. That's just their media talking. They hate

America as much as you or I do. But there is very likely some truth in this report. There have been other stories about some new American assassination organization. Perhaps it is just propaganda, but I doubt it. As for preparations for a military invasion, I believe that part of it. That's all the cowboys in Washington know how to do."

"Then what are we to do here?" asked an increasingly dubious Dubzhuko. "Do we just wait here for them to arrive and find out that there is no such thing as an 'Islamic Brotherhood'?"

"No, you fool," responded Komulakov, harshly. "Listen! I have talked to our friends in Tehran, and they are going to go to the UN this morning and demand that any intervention in Saudi Arabia only be undertaken by an Islamic coalition. They are going to urge that Kuwait, UAE, Bahrain, Jordan, Oman, Egypt, Syria, and Yemen join them in such a venture," Komulakov said.

Dubzhuko was incredulous. "And the UN will agree?"

Komulakov was becoming increasingly exasperated but also knew that Dubzhuko had to remain in place for several more weeks. Otherwise the Iranian plan would collapse—and he would not receive his full compensation.

The Russian general took a deep breath and continued patiently, "Nikolai Dubzhuko, I know you are tired. But please, comrade, listen carefully—the Iranians are simply trying to delay any American or British military intervention by going to the UN. That also means you're going to have to help from there as well. We need time to finish exterminating any of the other princelings so that our friends in Tehran get the time they need to create their new theocracy to rule from Riyadh."

"Yes, General, but—"

Komulakov kept talking, ignoring the interruption,

"As you know, the Iranian clerics are already working with several of the imams in Medina, Mecca, and Jeddah. But I need you to create more disorder to exacerbate problems for any use of American military force. That will give the Iranians the time they need."

"What do you want me to do?"

"How much of that nuclear material that you removed from Iraq in 2003 did you bring with you?" Komulakov asked.

"Just six barrels. It's all we had room for on the truck from Syria. It's about five hundred kilos, but almost all of it is very low level."

"That doesn't matter," the general replied. "Send some of the men you have there in the compound out to get a large panel truck. Then, have them go out to one of the abandoned Saudi National Guard ammunition dumps and fill it up with ordnance—explosives, artillery rounds, bombs—whatever you can find. Intersperse among the ordnance the barrels of nuclear material. Wire the truck with a remote detonator that you can control from where you are. Do you understand me?"

Dubzhuko felt a knot forming in his stomach. While he knew that the "dirty bomb" would create limited damage, it would also leave a radiological hazard zone that could spread out to one or two miles in diameter from the site of the detonation, depending on wind direction and velocity.

"Where do you want it to go off?" he asked.

"For the most strategic effect, I think you park the truck as close as you can get it to the Diplomatic Quarter. That's well away and downwind from your location, and it will prompt an international backlash against any American intervention."

SOCOM DET 2
Marine Corps Air Station, New River, NC
Wednesday, 17 October 2007
0030 Hours Local

For the Marines and Navy Medical Corpsmen of 1st Platoon, 2nd Force Reconnaissance Company, it had been another case of "hurry up and wait." On Tuesday afternoon they had dutifully raced back to the Recon Battalion HQ at Onslow Point, packed their pre-staged "Fly Away" combat gear aboard trucks, and then convoyed to the Marine Corps Air Station, just across the New River from Camp Lejeune.

To any curious reporter, the ten seven-ton trucks and four Humvees rolling through Jacksonville, North Carolina, looked like any other military motorcade ferrying Marines back to Camp Geiger, beside the Air Station, from the "Mainside" area of Camp Lejeune. But a trained observer would have noted that the four desert-camouflaged "up armored" Humvees towing trailers all had rolls of concertina wire lashed to their hoods, were equipped with M-DACTs, and lacked the normal stateside "Tac Marks" on their doors and bumpers. And if they had followed the little convoy, they would have seen that it passed the main gate at Camp Geiger and rolled instead into the Marine Air Station.

By the time the sun was low on the horizon at 1830, the Marines had off-loaded all their equipment and the entire platoon was sequestered inside hangar 2 at the east end of the north-south runway. Though the ten trucks had long since departed, the four Humvees and trailers were lined up inside the hangar, ready to drive aboard the two USAF C-17s they had been told to expect.

At 1930, shortly after the last tinge of orange disappeared from the western sky, another Humvee pulled up in front of the hangar. The Marine corporal posted on security near the hangar, just outside the pool of light from the sodium vapor lamps overhead, was prepared to challenge the two men who exited the vehicle when he recognized Lt. Col. Dan Hart and Sgt. Maj. Amos Skillings. Before the two men could enter the personnel portal built into the large sliding door, the corporal sprang to open the hatch. As he did so, he sounded off, "Attention on deck!"

As Hart and Skillings stepped through the entry, there was the sound of troops scrambling to their feet as they rose to stand silently beside their flak jackets, helmets, rucksacks, and weapons. "Stand at ease," barked the Sergeant Major.

Captain Christopher stepped over his grounded gear, walked up to his commander, and said simply, "Sir!" It was both a salutation and a question.

"Gather the Marines around your Humvee, Andy," the lieutenant colonel said, as Skillings unrolled a large chart and several aerial photographs and started taping them to the sides of the armored vehicles. As the captain assembled his troops, the agile lieutenant colonel bounded up the front bumper to stand on the hood of the Humvee so everyone in the unit could see and hear him.

"All right, listen up. I have an update on the situation and your mission. Effective immediately, you are redesignated as Marine Detachment Two, Special Operations Command. Your mission orders from this point on will come from SOCOM until such time as you are 'chopped' back to 2nd Force Recon. SOCOM has dispatched two Air Force C-17s here to transport you to Doha, Qatar, to carry out contingency operations in the CENTCOM Area of Operations. On the aircraft when they arrive will be two officers from the Nuclear Emergency Search Team out of Los Alamos, New Mexico. These NEST scientists are accompanying you with some specialized equipment to see if we can determine whether there are additional nuclear weapons in Saudi

Arabia. Based on the radiation from the one that was cracked off Monday, the experts believe it was an old Soviet 'tac nuke' artillery round detonated at ground level. They have also concluded that the weapon wasn't fired from an artillery piece or delivered by an aircraft or rocket. The satellite imagery that Sergeant Major Skillings has with him shows truck tracks about a mile from 'ground zero' that are from the vehicle that they think probably delivered the nuke. Any questions so far?"

"Yes, sir," replied Sergeant Holland, one of the team leaders. "How did they set it off?"

"Good question," responded Hart. "And the answer is we don't know. It could have been by timer or a remote control device—either radio or wire. There are truck tracks headed to the site from the paved highway to the west and tracks headed back to the highway, so we're assuming that whoever did it intended to survive the experience and probably did. It's also likely that if this really was an old Soviet nuke, the people who did it were Russian—not local 'jihadis'—since it's unlikely that the Russians were going to give up their PAL codes."

Several of the Marines nodded their heads in agreement with this assessment. Hart continued, "A half hour ago I was told by the SOCOM planners that they intend to use one of your squads to assist in the evacuation of the American citizens currently barricaded inside the American embassy in Riyadh, one squad to see what can be learned from a covert visit to the 'ground zero' site—that's what the NEST scientists are for—and one squad with Captain Christopher's command group are the QRF."

At this, some of the Marines started to jostle one another over which team would get which mission. Skillings, seeing the reaction, growled, "Knock it off!" and there was again silence.

Lieutenant Colonel Hart ignored the interruption and resumed his briefing. "The team going to the nuclear detonation area will be transported to and from by CH-53 from the 21st MEU deployed offshore in the Persian Gulf. Sergeant Major Skillings will accompany the team that goes to the site to look after the two scientists.

"The team going to the embassy will HALO or HAHO into the compound to get things organized for evacuation aboard the MEU's V-22 Osprey detachment. The MEU has also been ordered to provide QRF backup and whatever additional support you may need. Your radio frequencies, encryption instructions, and protocols are contained in the Comm Plan that Captain Christopher will have. Everybody going into southwest Saudi Arabia will wear full MOPP and carry chemical and radiological sensors because of the potential for contamination. We want you all coming home safe. Any other questions?"

While the Marines gathered around the maps, charts, and satellite images that Sergeant Major Skillings had taped to the Humvees and trailers, Lieutenant Colonel Hart jumped down off the slanted hood and took Captain Christopher aside, away from the hubbub, and said, "Andy, I know Amy is about to give birth any day now. Lieutenant Weiner can handle this if you want to stay back until the baby is born."

"No, sir," Christopher replied. "Bob Weiner is a great XO, but these are my Marines. Amy can handle it. Her mom is coming down from Virginia, and our next-door neighbors are going to look after little Joshua."

"Weren't you in Iraq when Josh was born?"

"Yes, sir. But I don't want these guys to do this mission without me. We've all worked too hard for too long getting ready for this kind of thing, and Lieutenant Weiner has only been with us for a month. Besides," the captain said with a smile, "if I stay back, who's going to look after Sergeant Major Skillings?"

"OK," Hart said, putting his hand on the younger officer's shoulder, "just don't get hurt over there. I don't want to have to tell Amy that something happened to you."

❂

Lieutenant Colonel Hart spent another half hour talking with individual Marines and their Navy Corpsmen. After he departed, most of them lay down on the concrete floor and dozed, their heads resting on rolled-up poncho liners, rucksacks, and flak jackets. While the troops rested, Captain Christopher gathered his squad and team leaders off in a corner of the hangar, and they reviewed the Operations Order, load plan, and communications annex. Finally, two USAF C-17s landed, taxied up to the front of the hangar, and dropped their ramps, exposing their cavernous interiors. By the time the screech of their engines had died away and the big hangar door was slowly opening, the Marines were on their feet and gathering their gear.

Without being told to do so, they formed up in two columns beside the Humvees while Captain Christopher and Lieutenant Weiner checked their names off on the manifests. On a signal from the Air Force crew chiefs, the two columns of Marines, looking like two long, sand-colored centipedes, shuffled up the ramps, then all the way forward in their respective aircraft. In addition to his own weapon, each man wore or carried more than a hundred pounds of gear.

As soon as the troops were belted into the four rows of red, webbed seats, the four Humvees and trailers rolled aboard—two sets on each C-17. As soon as the vehicles were positioned inside the fuselage, Air Force crewmen strapped them down. Finally, after everything else was loaded, two large diesel-powered forklifts, each carrying an enormous pallet of ammunition and ordnance, approached the aircraft. That's when it happened.

While the troops and vehicles were being loaded,

Sergeant Major Skillings had been talking to the two NEST scientists beside the ramp of the C-17 parked to the right of the hangar door. The men from Los Alamos, dressed in Air Force flight suits, had shown him their ID badges and introduced themselves as doctors Reynolds and Chaisson. They were clearly excited about the prospects of putting their highly specialized education, training, and unique equipment to work.

Skillings was listening carefully. While genuinely interested in how they did their job, the sergeant major was also sizing the men up, trying to estimate how they would handle themselves on the mission deep into Saudi Arabia's empty—and now radioactive—southeastern desert.

Dr. Reynolds, having just described one of their radiation detection devices, suddenly said, "Wait, I'll show you one . . ." and he turned to board the ramp—directly into the path of the oncoming forklift.

The equipment operator, his view blocked by the large metal pallet and the heavy load of ammunition lashed atop it, couldn't see the green-clad scientist who was about to be crushed from behind by three tons of ordnance. But Skillings, facing the hangar, saw it all and reacted instantly.

Yelling "Duck!" at the top of his lungs, Skillings lunged through the air, hitting Reynolds in the right rib cage just as the scientist was raising his right foot to step up onto the ramp. The impact of Skillings's 212 pounds hurtling into Reynolds threw him across the entire width of the ramp, well away from the oncoming pallet and left the two men sprawled on the tarmac.

The scientist's body was completely clear of the calamity—but Skillings's left foot was not. The forklift operator, wearing ear protection against the roar of the diesel engine, hadn't heard the sergeant major's shouted warning and couldn't see the two figures flying from right to left beneath the pallet. By the time the loadmaster standing inside the C-17 reacted and raised his hands to signal the driver to stop, Skillings's left foot was beneath the forklift's left front tire.

The driver immediately backed up, but the damage was done. Though his foot had only been pinned for a few seconds, Skillings had felt the crunch of bone being crushed against the tarmac. "Doc" Doan, one of the detachment's Navy corpsmen, was there in an instant. He didn't even have to remove the desert-tan boot to see that blood was already soaking through the nylon canvas upper.

The corpsman gently probed with his fingers, and though Skillings never uttered a sound through his clenched teeth, neither one of them needed an X-ray to tell that something was broken. Doan shook his head and said, "Don't move it. We need to stabilize this, Sergeant Major. I'm going to get an inflatable splint."

The corpsman ran up the ramp and returned in seconds with his canvas Unit One First Aid Kit. He withdrew what looked like a rolled up, double-sided plastic bag. Doan deftly slid the bag up over Skillings's leg, hit a small compressed air cartridge, and the bag inflated around the sergeant major's injured extremity.

By now the apologetic forklift operator and several of the Air Force crewmen were standing around the injured sergeant major and the corpsman kneeling beside him. Skillings looked around and growled, "What's wrong with you people? Haven't you ever seen a black Pillsbury 'doughboy' before? Get back to work!"

At that point Capt. Andy Christopher arrived from the other aircraft and said, "Lying down on the job again, eh, Sergeant Major?" But his voice showed his concern and compassion as he asked, "What's it look like, Doc?"

"Broken ankle, sir," replied Doan in a matter-of-fact manner.

"Can he go with us?"

"No, sir," answered the corpsman. "He needs to see a medical officer, get an X-ray. Depends on how bad his foot is; it might need surgery."

"Button it up, Doc, and help me up," said Skillings through clenched teeth. "I'll be OK in a couple of days."

The corpsman stood, looked at the captain, and shook his head.

Christopher thought for a moment, then said, "No, Sergeant Major, you need to sit this one out. I'm going to get the Air Station duty officer to send an ambulance and run you over to Hospital Point. If the docs say you're good to go, you can catch a hop to Doha. We'll probably still be sitting there waiting for something to happen."

Twenty minutes later Skillings was riding prone on a gurney in the back of an Air Station ambulance headed toward the Camp Lejeune Naval Hospital when the roar of the two C-17s lifting off reverberated through the vehicle. The youthful hospital corpsman seated beside him checking his vital signs said, "Hey, Sergeant Major, your pulse and blood pressure just spiked. Don't get so worried. This isn't combat. That's just the noise of a couple of planes taking off."

Skillings looked at the young man, leaned back on the pillow, and said, "Yeah. Thanks, Doc. I wonder where they're going."

Operations Directorate, 7th Floor, CIA Headquarters
Langley, VA
Wednesday, 17 October 2007
1300 Hours Local

"I'm telling you, Bill, there is something going on at that Filaya Oil Facility in Riyadh." Joseph Blackman, the British MI6 officer sitting across the desk from his friend William Goode, spoke earnestly to the CIA's Deputy Director for Operations. He continued, "Patterson here says that the GCHQ listening post at our embassy in Riyadh and our El Auja base in Jordan are both picking up Russian, Arabic, and Farsi—all coming out of the Filaya site."

Goode, in his shirt sleeves, with hands clasped and his arms resting on his elbows, leaned forward across his desk, looked from Blackman to Roy Patterson, the young GCHQ "Emissions Technician" who had accompanied Blackman "across the pond." Their hastily arranged RAF flight from London had landed at Andrews Air Force Base at 1200, and a CIA car had whisked them directly to the Agency's Langley, Virginia, headquarters.

Patterson, suddenly realizing he was expected to speak, stammered: "Yes, quite, Mr. Goode. Just as Mr. Blackman said, we've been picking up quite a montage of language coming from the Filaya site. It appears to us that it is some kind of command and control node for what's been happening in Saudi Arabia—and perhaps elsewhere around the world involving members of the Saudi royal family."

"Have you been able to translate any of what's being said?" asked Goode.

"Some. I brought a number of transcripts," Patterson replied, reaching into his briefcase and withdrawing a sheaf of paper. Handing Goode the top sheet, the GCHQ expert said, "This is the last one to come in before we left London. It's a cell phone conversation 'in the clear' between two males speaking Russian. Both El Auja and our embassy site intercepted it early this morning. It's only a partial, but it appears that the person initiating the call is in the Filaya building and the person taking the call is a subordinate somewhere in

King Khalid Military City, the big Saudi Army and Air Force base northwest of the capital."

Goode nodded and read the intercept:

MOST SECRET
SIGINT
INTERCEPT POST: GCHQ/AD BRICKMAN
DATE: 17 OCT
TIME: 0545-0547 LOCAL
LANG: RUSSIAN
CIPHER: CLEAR
MODE: VOICE CELL BAND GSM SA 825-894 MHZ

TARGET/SOURCE:
   A. ID UNK, MALE, VIC FILAYA COMPLEX, RIYADH
   B. ID UNK, MALE, VIC KING KHALID MILITARY CITY
   A. YOU AND (UNINTELLIGIBLE) MUST COME HERE IM-
MEDIATELY.
   B. WHY ARE YOU CALLING ME ON THIS PHONE? WE
ARE BUSY HERE WITH THE AIRCRAFT.
   A. THERE HAS BEEN ANOTHER CHANGE OF (SEVERAL
WORDS UNINTELLIGIBLE). I NEED YOU HERE WITH THE
BARRELS OF SPECIAL MATERIAL. IT (SEVERAL WORDS
UNINTELLIGIBLE) READY FOR USE BY THE DAY AFTER
TOMORROW.
   B. YOU KNOW NIKOLAI THAT THE MEN ARE NOT
GOING TO LIKE THIS. AFTER THE LAST ONE (UNINTELLI-
GIBLE) HAD A MUTINY.
   A. GREGOR DO NOT (UNINTELLIGIBLE) ME. THIS IS
NOT A REQUEST IT IS AN ORDER.
   B. WHEN DO YOU WANT ME THERE?
   A. YOU KNOW BETTER THAN I HOW (UNINTELLIGIBLE)
PUT THIS TOGETHER. WE HAVE TO HAVE IT IN PLACE BY
FRIDAY MORNING.
   B. YOU UNDERSTAND THAT THIS WILL NOT DO ANY
SERIOUS DAMAGE OTHER THAN (UNINTELLIGIBLE).

A. THAT IS NOT THE ISSUE (SEVERAL WORDS UNIN-
TELLIGIBLE) WE HAVE BEEN TOLD WHAT TO DO AND
WHEN IT HAS TO BE DONE.

B. I WILL (UNINTELLIGIBLE) TONIGHT.

A. AS LONG AS YOU HAVE ENOUGH TIME TO (UNIN-
TELLIGIBLE).

TRANSMISSION TERMINATED 0547:23

When Goode finished reading the transcript he looked up and said, "Are the others much like this one?"

"There are only a few cell phone calls like this," Patterson answered. "Most of what we're getting is short-range radio with commercial encryption. There are multiple bands and frequency ranges in use, and it is in various Arab dialects, some Farsi and, of course, Russian, like this one."

"What do you make of it, Joseph? Could this be Russian diplomatic or commercial people communicating with the locals, perhaps trying to arrange safe passage out of the country?" Goode asked, turning to Blackman.

"We don't know—but here's what I think," Blackman said emphatically. "Person 'A' at the Filaya Complex is the man in charge of some activity in Riyadh—but he has a superior somewhere—because even though 'A' initiates the call, he's clearly relaying someone else's orders to 'B' at King Khalid Military City. 'B' is a subordinate, likely some kind of technical expert that 'A' needs back in Riyadh to repair or build something, using 'barrels of special material.' Person B is not happy about what he's being told to do, but he's going to comply."

"And we have no idea who these people are or what it is they are planning to do?" asked Goode.

"Officially? No," replied Blackman, "but Patterson and I think we know who 'A' and 'B' are—though we can't confirm it with our voice recognition software."

"Who are they?" asked Goode, looking now at the GCHQ expert.

"We believe 'A' is Col. Nikolai Dubzhuko, the Russian who Mr. Blackman says arrived in Riyadh eight days before all hell broke loose in Saudi Arabia. And we think 'B' is Lt. Col. Gregor Pokrovsky, who was the *SVR Deputy Rezident* in Damascus in 2003."

Goode squinted at the two men and said, as though to himself, "Why do I know that name, Pokrovsky?"

"He's a man your DIA believed to have taken part in removing Saddam's WMD stocks and equipment, shipping them into Syria just before we launched Operation Iraqi Freedom," answered Blackman.

Goode nodded his head, leaned back in his chair, and stared at the two men for a long moment, then said, "And, Joseph, if I understood your call last night, you think that Dubzhuko is working for Gen. Dimitri Komulakov, whom you believe to be in Cuba."

"Yes, William," said Blackman. "And now that I've had some rest coming here on that delightful RAF transport, I now believe that Komulakov is somehow orchestrating this whole Saudi Arabian fiasco from Cuba—including the murders of royal family members elsewhere around the world—and I believe he's doing it all at the behest of Tehran."

"That's a stretch," said Goode with a half smile. "Did you find *any* comms among Dubzhuko in Riyadh? Or from Komulakov in Cuba—and from anyone in Tehran?"

"No," said Blackman, "but you're a lot closer to Cuba than we are, old friend."

"True," said Goode. "But I'm not sure I'm going to get a lot of help from NSA to start poking around Mr. Castro's little island. Things have changed a good bit over here since we 'reorganized.' I now have to put a request in for that kind of coverage through our DNI, and Mr. Straw seems to be fairly well preoccupied with Southwest Asia right now."

Patterson simply shrugged and said, "Quite."

Goode picked up the transcript again and asked, "Any thoughts on what your Col. Nikolai Dubzhuko wants Lt. Col. Gregor Pokrovsky to do with these 'barrels of special material' by Friday?"

Blackman took a moment to answer and then responded: "Since you asked, William, I believe that the 'barrels' contain either chemical, biological, or radiological material that has been brought into Saudi Arabia from Syria by Pokrovsky. I think that our Russian 'friends' intend to use it to create more havoc on behalf of the ayatollahs in Tehran."

"Can we prove any of this, Joseph?"

Blackman slumped back into his chair, looked Goode in the eye, and said, "No. I'm afraid not. But if the worst happens—as I think it's about to—everyone is going to wish we had some proof."

Office of the Chairman, Joint Chiefs of Staff
The Pentagon, Arlington, VA
Wednesday, 17 October 2007
1500 Hours Local

"Quite a view you have from here, Mr. Chairman," said Brig. Gen. Peter Newman with a smile. He was standing by the triple-pane, Mylar-coated window, looking northwest at the lengthening shadows from the top floor of the Pentagon. To his left he could see Arlington Cemetery—rows of white markers surrounded by green, overlaid by a blaze of orange, yellow, and red leaves—on his right, the muddy Potomac, and in the distance, Memorial Bridge and the Lincoln Memorial.

"I appreciate you coming over here on such short notice, Pete," Gen. George Grisham said, taking off his medal-laden blouse and hanging it on a hanger in the wardrobe on the wall opposite his desk. The general

walked over to the window and stood beside his protégé. After a moment he said quietly, "You're right—it
is quite a view. You know, this is the third office for the
Chairman of the Joint Chiefs since 9/11. And some time
next year it'll probably get moved again. Apparently
your experts at Homeland Security think the SecDef and
the Chairman are too vulnerable."

Newman looked at his mentor and noted there was
a little more gray in his temples than he remembered.
Grisham's wide, deep-set blue eyes were still bright but
tired. "You didn't fly all the way back from Qatar to
call me over here to look at the scenery, General," the
younger officer said.

"No, I didn't, Pete. I asked you over here for a reason—
but before we get to that, how is Prince Arshad taking
all this?"

"He's doing all right, sir," Newman replied. "He's
more concerned about his parents than anything else.
We still don't have any word on whether they are alive
or dead. Matt Roderick is with him now—Matt
switched off with me this morning so I could come in
and get some work done. At some point in the near future we're going to have to make a decision as to what
we're going to do with the prince. We can't hide him
and his Naval Academy roommate at Mount Weather
forever."

Grisham nodded and motioned toward the brown
leather couch to the right front of his desk. "I'll talk to
Secretary Powers about it this afternoon—but I think it
may be premature to send him back to Annapolis until
the mess in Saudi Arabia shakes out a little more."

As Grisham sat in a nearby leather armchair, Newman took a seat on the end of the couch. The Chairman
continued, "I trust you were able to follow this business
about the so-called 'Threat Mitigation Bill' while you
were out there in the Blue Ridge Mountains?"

"Yes, sir," Newman answered. "We saw it on the

news—and of course it was in all the papers. This town leaks like a sieve. When I got back to my office this morning, Secretary Dornin let me read the bill—I mean the law. I couldn't help but wonder—why would the President sign such a thing?"

Grisham shook his head and said, "Apparently the Congress was going to override his veto. Secretary Powers sent me a lengthy backchannel cable while I was in Doha about all the palace intrigue behind it. And unfortunately, it's now the law of the land, and we're bound to uphold it."

"Secretary Dornin told me that the Commission—the one the media calls the 'Assassination Committee'—is meeting with the President this afternoon at Camp David to discuss its implementation. Is that correct?"

"That's right," Grisham replied, nodding.

"Who would want such a job?" Newman asked rhetorically, as though to himself. "That's about the only thing that wasn't in the papers."

The Chairman rose, went to his desk, and returned with a red folder. Opening it, he handed Newman a sheet of paper. Newman read:

TOP SECRET
PRESIDENTIAL COMMISSION ON THREAT MITIGATION

CHAIRMAN: Chief Justice of the Supreme Court Anthony Scironi
FORMER SECRETARY OF STATE: James Cook
FORMER DIRECTOR OF CENTRAL INTELLIGENCE: Russell Bates
FORMER CHAIRMAN, JOINT CHIEFS OF STAFF: Gen. Conrad Vassar
FORMER FBI DIRECTOR: Gerald Donahue

The members of this Presidential Commission on Threat Mitigation shall serve a one-year term. The names of these

members shall not be revealed during their lifetimes or that of their children.
BY ORDER OF THE PRESIDENT OF THE UNITED STATES. SET UNDER MY HAND ON THE 16TH DAY OF OCTOBER, IN THE YEAR OF OUR LORD 2007.

"Well," said Newman handing the sheet of paper back to Grisham, "that answers 'who' would serve. Perhaps 'why' is the more appropriate question?"

George Grisham paused before answering. "I asked Secretary Powers almost the same question. He told me that none of these men wanted the job. They only took it because the President begged them to—and because they're patriots."

"*Are* they?" Newman said in a somewhat cynical manner, so much so that he surprised himself. He belatedly added, "Sir."

"I hope so, is all I can tell you, Peter," said Grisham gravely. "I pray that these are wise men who'll do what's right in the most terrible of circumstances for our country. I have no doubt about the Chief Justice. I know him well; I've hunted with him, spent time with him, and admire him. I feel the same way about General Vassar. I've known him for too many years to think of him as anything but a fine soldier. I also have high regard for Secretary Cook. I don't know him as well as the Chief Justice or General Vassar, but everything I've seen leads me to believe he is a man of integrity. I don't know about Bates or Donahue except by reputation. Both are highly respected. And now all this Commission needs is an equally fine American to head up the Special Unit that's called for in the legislation."

Newman suddenly realized why he was here. He felt a rush of adrenaline in his gut, and he sat bolt upright on the edge of the couch. For a moment, Grisham thought he might actually flee.

"That's why you called for me, isn't it, General?" Newman said hoarsely.

Grisham looked at the younger man, pressed his lips into a thin line, nodded his head, and finally said, very quietly, "Yes."

For what seemed a full minute, neither man said anything. Then, Newman sighed and asked, "Do I have a choice?"

"Of course," Grisham answered. "But if you turn me down, I don't know anyone else I can turn to. Yours was the only name given to the President."

Newman leaned forward, put his elbows on his knees, and rested his chin on his fists. For a long while he stared off into the distance, and after a moment he said quietly, "I thought I was done with all that . . ."

"So did I, Peter," replied Grisham. "I've thought and prayed about this the whole way back from Doha. It's certainly not what I wanted for you, but the President and Secretary Powers each asked me to give them the name of the best officer I had for this assignment. If there was anyone else who could handle this, I wouldn't have chosen you."

"Who would I . . . I mean, who does the head of this Special Unit report to, sir?" Newman asked—giving away that he had accepted his lot.

"Nominally, the Chairman of the Commission," Grisham replied. "But you—" Grisham checked himself, not wanting to presume too much. He continued, "—but the head of the Special Unit will be able to call on me—and the Secretary for whatever support that's needed . . . and to help resolve any problems."

Newman's mind was now fully engaged with the challenge. "Where do the troops come from for the Special Unit?"

"SOCOM. You get your choice."

"Can I take one of the Marine SOCOM Dets?"

"If that's what you want."

"How many personnel?"

"Tell me what you need. If it's within reason, you'll have 'em. Same goes for airlift, maritime support, mobility assets," said Grisham emphatically. "The President has told Secretary Powers to 'make sure that the Special Unit gets what it needs.' And according to the SecDef, he meant it."

"How about staff support?"

"We'll detail a Comm detachment from Defense Communications Agency, and a few good admin types from my front office," answered Grisham.

"Can I have Sgt. Maj. Amos Skillings from 2nd Force Recon to keep things squared away?"

"Sure."

"Intel support?"

"The Commission will get targeting intel from the DNI. Operational intelligence will be available from DIA. We may be able to task CIA directly. I'll have to check on that," said Grisham, making a note and slipping it into the red folder.

"I'd like to be able to talk directly to Bill Goode out in Langley, at the least, sir."

"I'll tell the Secretary and we'll find a way to make it happen."

"Where is this outfit going to be headquartered?"

"In one of the Presidential Commission townhouses over on Lafayette Square, across from the White House."

"How about the troops?"

"Don't know yet. That will be your call," Grisham responded, pleased at the way Newman was thinking. "Andrews, maybe—so you have immediate access to airlift. On the other hand, Quantico might fill the bill so that your troops can train."

"How long is this assignment for all the military personnel?"

"A maximum of one year—same as for the Commission members. And this is important," Grisham added, pulling a copy of the legislation out of the red folder and pointing to the phrase in Section 4.(6), "everyone involved is fully protected under the law."

Newman read the passage and then looked at Grisham. "General, I owe you my life—and more. I trust you like few others. You more than anyone else know what Rachel and I went through back in the '90s. If you tell me that this is something that has to be done, I'll do it. I know it's not my place to set conditions, but there are just two more issues."

"Go ahead, Pete."

"Can you assure me that this is only for a year—and that when it's over, I can come back to the Corps?"

"You have my word. What else?"

"Who else is going to know about this assignment— not just about me, but the rest of my troops? Everyone involved needs to have the same kind of anonymity as the members of the Commission."

"We'll have ISA build identities and a legend for everyone in the unit. Of course some people will have to know the truth: The President and the Vice President will. The Secretary and I will know. So will Chief Justice Scironi." Then, looking Newman straight in the eye, Grisham added, "And there is one other person who needs to know everything, Pete."

"Who?"

"Rachel."

Habib Trading Company
Anah, Iraq
Wednesday, 17 October 2007
2330 Hours Local

"What brings you here so late this evening, Father?" said Samir, rising to greet the old man as he entered his son's comfortable second-story office. The "headquarters" of the Habib Trading Company were within the same walled compound that enclosed the homes of Eli Yusef and his son Samir. Years before, the building had been a combination warehouse and maintenance building for the tiny fleet of trucks used by the enterprise. But as their consumer products business grew, they had converted the building into the "home office" for the company. Now, the warehouse and truck facilities occupied a full city block in Anah—and Habib Trading Company was the town's largest employer.

"I saw the light on from my bedroom," replied Eli Yusef, "and wondered what could be so troubling in our business that it would keep my son from his wife's bed," said the old man as he took a seat in a comfortable chair. "Paul found it necessary to admonish the husbands of Ephesus and Colossae to love their wives. Am I now to do the same for the husbands of Anah?" he asked with a good-natured smile.

The son took the chair beside his father's and while pouring the old man a glass of chilled water responded with good humor, "Ahh . . . my father, Hamilah knows well that I love her as Solomon loved his Shulamite wife. I only came here to the office because I wanted to respond to an e-mail that I received from Zufar al Nadar, in Dezful."

The old man, suddenly serious, asked, "Are things getting worse in Iran?"

Samir returned to his desk, picked up a sheet of paper off his printer, returned to his seat next to his father, and said: "Zufar reports that this morning, the 'Religious Police' raided our offices on As Sharaf Street. The police said they were searching for 'infidel literature.' While the police were tearing our offices apart looking for Bibles among the cartons of toasters and microwave ovens, Asher arrived from Tehran."

"Asher, from the Fellowship?" interrupted Eli Yusef.

"Yes," Samir replied. "And when they searched Asher they found his 'Sign of the Faith' in his pocket and dragged him away."

Hearing this, Eli Yusef instinctively put his fingers to the tiny metal fish that Samir had never seen his father without. The little stainless steel icthus was worn thin and smooth from decades of being rubbed between the old man's fingers as he prayed, meditated, and read from his Holy Bible.

The old man looked up from the ancient symbol of early Christianity and said to his son, "For more than twenty centuries this has been the sign of 'true believers.' In Rome, those whom Paul called to conversion were crucified for having this sign of faith in their homes. In my lifetime I have even seen those who lived beneath this symbol persecuted and killed. As you know, until recently it was that way here in our country. It has often been so in this part of the world—but the persecution has ebbed and flowed. Now it is getting very bad again. This is a time for us to be very careful. Does Zufar know what has happened to Asher?"

Samir nodded. "According to his e-mail, Zufar went to the police station to inquire and they told him he was to 'forget about the infidel from Tehran.' Zufar also says that he has heard many rumors of other Christians being picked up—not just members of the Fellowship."

"What else?" asked the old man, now clearly concerned.

"According to Zufar's brother Najahm, the one who has the fishing business, the 'Islamic Brotherhood' is planning to poison the air and soil of the Saudi capital because the city has been polluted by infidels. According to Zufar, many people are already fleeing Riyadh—not just Westerners—but Muslims as well."

"This may be the kind of rumor-mongering that many of the Islamic radicals engage in," said the old man, trying to separate fact from fiction. "Remember a few years ago how some of the imams said that the Americans were coming to Iraq to rape our wives and sisters and kill our children to eat their organs—and many of the people believed it!"

"Yes, I recall it well, Father, but that wasn't true. What if *this is?*"

Eli Yusef, rubbing the tiny fish between his thumb and forefinger, thought for a moment and then said, "I was going to talk to you about my concerns in the morning, but perhaps things are more urgent than I understood. My son, do you recall the discussion we had on last Sabbath, after dinner on the night you returned from Iran?"

"Yes, Father."

"Well over the last three days, I have studied the ancient texts and thought and prayed much about it. I have concluded that there is very likely something to this matter of the number 'eleven' and this 'jihad' that we talked about. I wrote it all down and was going to think and pray about it some more. But based on what you are saying, I may have waited too long."

"Too long for what, Father?" asked Samir—knowing from long experience not to ignore what some called his father's "premonitions"—but what Eli called "the gift of discernment." Samir had no doubt that whatever his father's gift was called, it explained how this Christian family had not just survived wars, Saddam, and Islamic terror—but prospered. He leaned attentively toward the old man to listen.

"You had asked how it was that the number eleven could be relevant to the jihad that began in Saudi Arabia on the fourteenth of October," Eli began. "Well, if you write the date as 14 October 2007 in the Christian calendar, that's 14/10/07. Subtract ten from fourteen. That equals four. Now add that four to the remaining integers, zero and seven and the sum is . . ."

"Eleven!" Samir practically shouted. "And you say,

Father, that in the Quran you have found this number to be relevant to this jihad?"

Eli nodded and said, "Yes. I have it all written down over in my house. And because of what you have told me here this evening, I now believe that we must somehow get this information to our American friends before it is too late."

"Tomorrow, I shall drive to Baghdad to see if I can find someone at their embassy who will accept what you have discovered," said Samir. "It will seem strange to some. Perhaps I should ask them to pass it to William Goode?"

"Yes," replied the old man. "He is a believer. He will understand."

"I shall do as you suggest, Father. But why did you say that it may be too late?"

The old man sighed deeply and said, "The day after tomorrow is the nineteenth of October. It is the nineteenth day of the tenth month. Add the integers—one plus nine plus one plus zero . . ."

This time Samir's voice was almost a whisper as he said, "Eleven."

CHAPTER SEVEN

Dirty Bomb

Newman Residence
Foxhall Road
Thursday, 18 October 2007
0605 Hours Local

Hey there, man of my life, what time did you get home last night?" Rachel said lightly to her husband as he entered the kitchen wearing his running shoes and a jogging suit. She stopped unloading the dishwasher and added, "I didn't even hear you come in, but when I got up—there you were."

Newman walked over to her, put his arms around her, and pressed his face into the hollow of her neck, inhaled deeply and said, "You smell good."

Her medium length hair was tied back in a ponytail, and she tossed it back and forth as she giggled and wriggled free of his arms, saying, "Hold on, Romeo! The children will be down here in a few minutes and you don't want them asking what Mommy and Daddy are doing in the kitchen! Now, you go on and run up the hill to work and come home early tonight and pick up where we left off here," she said playfully.

Newman smiled, backed up against the island in the center of the kitchen, and, suddenly serious, said, "I'm not going to work, today—at least not going to work at DHS. I have a new assignment."

Rachel reacted to his change in tone by reaching for her glass of orange juice and saying, "OK, Pete, let's sit down and talk before Jimmy and Elizabeth come charging in here. School is cancelled again—and it's raining. This is not shaping up to be a great day. Where are you going this time?"

As they sat next to each other at the round kitchen table, Newman told her about his meeting with General Grisham the previous afternoon, how he had returned to DHS and reported to Secretary Dornin and then spent the better part of the night "snapping-in" his "temporary replacement"—FBI Special Agent Martin Hinton—as the "Acting DHS Operations Director."

When Peter finished, Rachel was silent for a moment. Then, she nodded her head as though making up her mind about something and said, "I guess this is never going to end, is it?"

"What's never going to end?" he asked—but knowing the answer.

"These kinds of assignments for you are never going to end," she began quietly. "They couldn't just leave you behind a desk at the Department of Homeland Security. This is what it's always going to be like with us, Peter. A crisis comes along and they call for you. Will this be as dangerous as some of the other assignments you've been sent on?" Rachel asked him plainly.

"I don't think so. My job will be to coordinate everything. I don't think that they expect me to go on missions with the Special Unit," he told her, trying his best to reassure her.

"Where will you be going to work?"

"The Commission is headquartered in a townhouse on Jackson Place, next to Lafayette Park, across Pennsylvania Avenue from the White House. I'll have an office there."

"Can you turn this down?"

He hesitated before answering, then said, "Yes. And if you tell me that it's too much for you, I will."

Rachel looked him straight in the eyes and said calmly, without rancor, "Don't put that on me, Peter. I've been through it all with you. It's not a matter of it being too much for me. I know I married the man that everyone else thinks can save the world. And I don't want you to put our children at risk again. But that's not the point here. The question isn't for me—it's for *you*. When is it going to be too much for *you*—saving the world while your children grow up not knowing who their father is?"

Peter reached out and put his hand over hers and was about to respond when their son Jimmy pushed open the swinging door and entered the kitchen, wearing his pajamas. Seeing his parents sitting at the table, he said, "Hi Mom, hi Dad—what's for breakfast?"

Rachel rose and said to her husband, "Why don't you go out for your run? We can finish this later." Turning to Jimmy, she said, "How about a nice big bowl of oatmeal and honey with some cinnamon toast?"

Newman tousled the boy's hair and said, "I'll be back in half an hour. See you when I get back." As he exited the kitchen door, his wife and son were negotiating how much oatmeal had to be eaten to qualify for cinnamon toast.

Before taking off on his run, Newman warmed up on the sidewalk in front of their townhouse, stretching out his hamstrings and calves in the cool, damp early morning air. Then, having loosened up, he jogged out the gate in front of their little community, turned left and headed up Foxhall Road as the first fingers of a gray, drizzling dawn reached through the darkness, dulling the reflected light from the streetlamps.

As he picked up the pace going uphill, Newman was still distracted by Rachel's question just before their son had entered the kitchen. But as he ran further he began to pay more attention to his surroundings—first the wet leaves on the walk and the cracked concrete. Then he noticed that the thoroughfare, normally clogged with the cars of early commuters, was all but devoid of traffic. A Metro bus rolled by—but it was also practically empty. He started looking at the houses that lined the street. Nearly all of them were dark—only a few showed signs that people were inside, preparing for another work day in Washington.

He turned left on Reservoir Road and stretched out his stride, heading west on what would normally be a busy commuter artery. It, too, was empty of the usual heavy incoming traffic. His disposition was as overcast as the sky by the time he got to the intersection of Whitehaven Parkway and MacArthur Boulevard and saw the signs on the two gas stations: "Regular $5.95." Instead of continuing further west, he crossed over to Whitehaven and turned east, jogging back toward Foxhall and his house. A half mile from home the rain that until then had been a mist, turned into a downpour. He arrived at his front door soaking wet, groped the key out of the zipper pocket on his sweat suit, and let himself in.

Twenty minutes later he was back in the kitchen, showered, shaved, dressed in a civilian coat and tie and carrying his forest green Marine "Alpha" uniform in a garment bag. It was just 7:30, and the room smelled like cinnamon.

Jimmy was alone at the table, playing with a pocket video game from which various sounds emerged as the boy rapidly moved his fingers over the toggle switches beneath the tiny screen.

"Where is your mom?"

"Aww, she's down in the basement with Lizzie the Lizard doing laundry or something." Then, seeing the garment bag in his father's hand, he asked, "Are you leaving again, Dad?"

"Nope, just going to work," Peter replied. "The bag has my uniform in it. Why?"

The boy gave his father a funny look and said, "We have a game tomorrow, Dad, remember?"

Newman didn't but was saved by Rachel's return from the basement with their daughter and a laundry basket full of clean clothing. As the eight-year-old ran to her father and wrapped her arms around his legs, Rachel said, "That's right, *if* they have school, tomorrow is the day for their big game. The coach said James will be on the starting team. He wants you to be there, to cheer for him."

"Well, I don't think there is going to be school tomorrow, Jim, and I'm not sure that I'll be home in time—but if I miss it, I'll catch the next one," Newman said, trying to be helpful.

"Yeah, right," the boy said glumly. "I should've known." With that, he left the room.

"I said we'll do it next time," Newman called after him. Bending to pick up his daughter, he looked at Rachel for help in knowing what to say.

"He doesn't know what you do, Peter. He has no idea. To him, it seems like you're just avoiding him—shutting him out of your life—and that you aren't really interested in his life."

"But . . ."

Rachel touched her finger to his lips, stopping the words. "Just remember, they both miss you when you're away—more than you think."

Rachel had read his mind again. There were times when he thought of how much he was missing by not being with his children during these important years that they were growing up. He frequently resolved to make more time for them but all too often felt pangs of guilt when he realized that he had not done so.

" 'Bye, Daddy," Lizzie said, squirming out of his arms and running out of the kitchen to find her big brother. When she got to the kitchen door she paused and said, "If you're going someplace, be sure to send me a postcard."

Newman grinned and said, "OK" as the child disappeared. Ever since the children were toddlers he had made it a practice to stop in airport gift shops and buy postcards to send to them, each with their own special messages. Over the years they had saved them, many from unusual and exotic places around the world. On short trips the postcards often arrived several days after he'd already returned home. But that didn't matter. The postcards were treasured and on rainy days, or when their father was away, the children would sometimes take the cards out of the shoeboxes in which they were stored, to look at them as a reminder of the man who had sent them.

Alone again with her husband, Rachel said, "Come on, sit down here and have a cup of coffee before you run off to your new job."

As she poured them each a cup of coffee, Rachel said lightly, "This is the first time you have been for a jog through the neighborhood since you left Monday for your 'cave' in the Blue Ridge Mountains. Did you notice anything different?"

"Yeah, there's practically nobody home."

"Right, General Newman—you get an 'A' for observation," Rachel said, smiling. But she suddenly became serious. "Look, Peter, I've been following the news nonstop since this stuff in Saudi Arabia started. Almost all of our neighbors except the Schmidts and the Wilsons down at the end of the cul de sac have gone on early winter vacations. The Armentrouts, across the street—he works for the French Embassy—the couple with the two children the same age as ours—are leaving today to go back to France because they're scared."

Peter's reply was an effort to recapture Rachel's good humor: "Yeah, what do you expect; they're French."

Rachel didn't laugh. "This isn't a joke, Peter. I've been thinking that the children and I should leave town for awhile."

Newman looked at her quizzically. "Leave Washington? Why? Where would you go?" he asked.

"We could go down to Boot Key," Rachel said emphatically.

Peter realized from the way his wife had spoken that this was not a spur-of-the-moment idea. The beach house on Boot Key had been built by Rachel's father in the 1950s as a respite from winters in Charlottesville. Peter, Rachel, and their children had visited there many times over the years. When her father died in the spring of 2002 and her mother, later that same year, Rachel inherited the beach house. Since then, it had become the Newman family "getaway." Rachel and the children had spent most of 2003 and 2004 there while Peter was deployed for Operation Iraqi Freedom.

"Is this because of what's happening . . ." he started to ask her.

"Honey, this town is all but shut down already. Congressmen and Senators are going off on vague 'fact-finding' trips, or returning to their districts. You wouldn't believe the level of anxiety."

"Yes . . . I would," Newman muttered.

"Well, think about it, Pete. When I called the school this morning, a recording said they had to stay closed today because too many teachers called in sick. The shelves in the grocery stores are almost bare. You can't get a flight out of here without waiting for days, maybe weeks. Services are shutting down for lack of help . . . and if we have to do without heat in our house, with winter coming, I don't know how we can live here."

Newman considered what she was saying in light of what *he* knew—things that hadn't yet been reported on the news. From a selfish point of view, he'd rather have her and the children close. But he said, "The only problem with going to Florida will be getting there. I really don't feel good about you and the kids driving there in the Suburban all alone and not knowing how you're going to get gas for that thing. But I *do* think you're right. Why don't you start getting ready, and I'll see what I can figure out. It'll take you a few days to get everything packed, so we'll have some time to talk it over."

After a final kiss, Newman picked up his bag and headed for the front door. Rachel followed him to the doorway and watched as he got into the blue sedan that the White House motor pool had dispatched to pick him up. Then, as she'd done so many times before, she gave a final wave.

She watched as the car pulled away, closed the door, and leaned up against it. With her eyes closed she whispered, "He's Yours, Lord. Please protect him and bring him safely back to us."

American Embassy
Baghdad, Iraq
Thursday, 18 October 2007
1430 Hours Local

"But I have an important message that I must get to an American official," said Samir Habib in English to the impassive Sikh security guard at the gate labeled "Visitors" in Arabic and English.

The contract-sentinel, standing behind thick panes of blast-resistant glass, inside the thick-walled, air-conditioned guardhouse, replied through a speaker, "As I told you, Mr. Habib, you must have an appointment. Otherwise I cannot permit you to enter."

Though he tried not to let it show, Samir's frustration was nearly overwhelming. He had departed Anah early in the morning, endured 145 miles of potholes, bumper-to-bumper traffic at four security checkpoints, and air filled with vehicle exhaust, oil refinery fumes and wind-blown dust—just to *get* to Baghdad. Once he arrived in the city center, he had to park his pickup almost a mile from the four-square-mile, heavily fortified "Green Zone." But even without a vehicle, getting inside the high walls, barbed wire, and sand-filled barriers that enclosed the American Embassy and most of the Iraqi government proved to be an onerous, time-consuming ordeal.

Samir had been frisked and pat-down searched three times, passed through two metal detectors, and forced to transit a 250-yard-long maze of razor wire and concrete jersey walls where he was observed by Iraqi men in blue uniforms carrying submachine guns and wearing helmets and body armor. They had directed him to the proper gate at the next high wall—the one surrounding the American Embassy.

But now this guard was insisting that in order to enter, Samir had to have an appointment with someone inside—and a line was beginning to form behind him at the sentry post. Once again the guard's voice came through the speaker: "Do you have the name of the official you wish to see? Perhaps I can call them from here to have you admitted."

Eli Yusef had told his son to get a message to William Goode at the CIA in America. But Samir had no idea who the Agency's Station Chief in Baghdad was now—and he knew better than to shout out "CIA"—even inside the Green Zone. In desperation, he spoke the name of the only American he could think of, though he knew this person was no longer in Iraq: "Please tell someone inside that I know Marine Col. Peter Newman."

As the Sikh security guard stepped away from the window to consult a list of names on a clipboard, a broad-shouldered American in running shoes, shorts, and a sweat-soaked T-shirt stepped up from the line behind Samir and said suspiciously, "Excuse me, sir. What's your name—and what did you just say?"

"My name is Samir Habib, and I said I know Col. Peter Newman."

"It's General Newman now. How do you know him?" said the man with the close-cropped hair.

Samir noticed that on the man's wet T-shirt was a symbol he recognized: an eagle perched atop a globe and an old-fashioned anchor. He said, "I have helped him on various projects over the years. We're friends and fellow believers."

Until Samir uttered those last two words the perspiring Marine had been unimpressed. He responded, "Fellow believers, eh? What does your friend General Newman carry with him at all times, besides his dog tags?"

Samir reached into his pocket and said, "One of these." In his open palm was a tiny metal fish.

The American grinned slightly, reached down inside his shirt, and withdrew the chain that was around his neck. Hanging from the chain was a dog tag—and an identical, tiny metal fish. The Marine said, "That's good enough for me." Holding out his hand, he said, "I'm Gunnery Sgt. David Pennington. I'm the NCOIC of the Marine Security Guard Detachment inside this embassy compound. Let me get you cleared in here."

Pennington reached into a small zippered pocket in his shorts, withdrew two laminated cards, and pressed them up against the window and said to the microphone mounted beside the window, "I'll sign in Mr. Habib and escort him into the embassy."

Once they were through the gate, Samir asked, "Did you serve with Peter Newman?"

Pennington said, "I was with him in RCT 3 during phase one of Operation Iraqi Freedom. By the time he was promoted to Brigadier General and named as the Assistant Division Commander, I was back out here for a second tour. He led a Bible study and he gave me my 'Sign of the Faith' that I keep with my dog tags. You said you had helped General Newman with 'various projects'—what did you mean, Mr. Habib?"

"Please, call me Samir. My father and I first came to know him in 1995. It was my father who rescued Peter Newman when his airplane was shot down over Iraq. Later in 1998, my father and I helped him on his mission here and in Syria. And of course, we tried to be of help in 2003 and thereafter, when he was here in our country."

Though Pennington knew nothing of the 1995 and 1998 events that Samir was referring to, he was well aware that Brigadier General Newman had served on "detached duty" for a considerable period of time back in the '90s. Like many others who had seen that phrase in Newman's official biography, he assumed it was with the CIA. By now the two had arrived at the entrance of the main embassy building. He said, "So who is it you wanted to see inside, Samir?"

"It would be best if I could meet with the CIA Station Chief. I have some information that must get to Mr. William Goode at the CIA in Washington."

Pennington nodded, motioned to the Marine sergeant standing behind the thick, Mylar-coated, laminated ballistic-glass and lexan window at the security post, and said into the speaker, "Sergeant Nelson, have the Corporal of the Guard escort Mr. Habib to one of the special visitor's waiting lounges. I have to run upstairs to see if there is anyone who can speak with him. Please make him comfortable until I return or someone else comes down to escort him upstairs."

The Marine corporal replied "Aye aye," and picked up a phone inside the booth.

Pennington turned to Samir and said, "I'm going upstairs to see who's about. I'll need to borrow your Iraqi National Identity Card for a few minutes. One of my

Marines will make you comfortable. Either I or some-one else will come for you soon." Samir handed the gunnery sergeant his ID card, and Pennington in turn inserted his own laminated card into the mag-card reader beside the door, stepped up to the retinal scanner, and was "buzzed" through the large steel-reinforced wooden door.

Less than a minute later, another Marine opened the same door and said, "Mr. Habib, please come with me." He escorted Samir through yet another metal de-tector, then to a small but comfortably air-conditioned waiting room, handed him a plastic bottle of cold water, and said, "Sir, if you will wait here, someone will be here to escort you upstairs."

Samir had been waiting less than ten minutes when the door opened and two Americans entered. The taller of the two extended his hand and said, "Good after-noon, Mr. Habib. My name is Bill Ainsworth, and this is Larry Conway. Gunnery Sergeant Pennington says you have some information for us."

Conway handed Samir his Iraqi ID card, shook hands, and said, "How can we help you?"

"Can I speak to the Station Chief?" Samir asked Ainsworth, who seemed to be in charge. "I have some information that needs to get to William Goode at Lan-gley as soon as possible."

When Penninston had walked into his second-floor office and told him about Samir, Conway had groaned at the prospect of interviewing yet another "walk-in." Yet within two minutes of scanning the Iraqi ID card into his computer using a device much like that at a su-permarket checkout counter, his screen had turned red and a notice in large white block letters appeared:

RELIABLE HIGH VALUE PROTECTED ASSET
ADVISE CIA D/O ASAP

Conway immediately summoned Ainsworth from another interminable meeting and the two men read what little information that was accessible on the Station Chief's computer, noted that Samir lived in Anah and that his father, Eli Yusef, also of Anah, was in a similarly protected status. They then proceeded directly to the waiting room, thankful that the Marines had placed Samir in one of the four private rooms off the main lobby instead of having him wait in the much larger public waiting area full of Iraqis and others waiting for appointments with other embassy officials.

"Uh . . . follow us, Mr. Habib. We'll go to a conference room where we can talk." Ainsworth led the way through yet another metal detector, waited for an electrically operated security door to open, and then led up a flight of stairs to a long corridor of offices.

Samir followed Ainsworth to a locked conference room. The Agency officer used a swipe-card ID to get into the room, turned on the lights, and invited Samir to sit.

"Mr. Habib, I'm the CIA Station Chief here in Baghdad. Sorry for any delays you might have had getting in here. If you ever need to see me again, please call Mr. Conway and we can have someone meet you somewhere. It's a lot easier than coming here. Before you leave, Mr. Conway will give you a number where you can contact him any time, day or night. Now . . . what is it you have for us?"

"I believe this information should go directly to Mr. Goode in Langley," Samir began.

Ainsworth noted to himself, *This Iraqi knows where Bill Goode works—maybe he is somebody with something useful.* "Do you mind if I tape our conversation?" he asked.

"It is all right," Samir said.

Ainsworth took out a small digital recording device

and pushed "record." He was of the old school of technology—and used the expression "tape our conversation" although there was no cassette or tape involved. Sound was processed directly onto a tiny, removable digital storage unit. Such inconsistencies slipped by him as he spoke again, this time to create an introduction for the recording. "This is William Ainsworth, at 1455 hours on Thursday, October eighteenth, 2007. The interview subject is Mr. Samir Habib, an Iraqi citizen who resides in Anah. Go ahead, Mr. Habib . . . state your name for the record and begin."

"Uh . . . I am Samir Habib, an Arab Christian, and I wish to inform Mr. William Goode of urgent information that I have." Samir cleared his throat and began his narrative. "My father—Eli Yusef Habib—and I believe that there is going to be a serious attack by the jihadists on Friday, October nineteenth—and many more in November."

Ainsworth sat up straight. "You mean *tomorrow* and *this* November?"

"Yes," Samir replied quietly, in contrast to Ainsworth's agitation. "We believe that they are going to use nuclear weapons—like the one used in Saudi Arabia on Monday night—to prove to the world that they have more of this capability."

Ainsworth knew there was a lot of "chatter" being picked up that hinted at some unspecified acts of terrorism. "Who wants to demonstrate that they have more nukes?" he asked.

Samir placed both hands on the table in front of him and leaned forward to speak. He laid out his narrative as his father had instructed him, and wanted to get it right. "In 2004 there was a fatwa issued by an important cleric—a radical Muslim. He said to all people that the Quran sanctioned the right of Muslims to kill American, British, and Israeli civilians—along with other Westerners they call infidels."

"In 2004? Now, Mr. Habib . . . Samir, these terrorists have been killing people for a lot longer than that," Ainsworth said.

"The fatwa went further than the jihadists have ever gone before. This cleric said that the Islamic holy book authorized and approved the 'use of all available weapons' to kill infidels."

Ainsworth tilted his head and asked, "By that this cleric meant—?"

"Nuclear, biological, and chemical weapons," Samir answered. "The fatwa said that even weapons of mass destruction are 'approved by Allah'—according to the Quran."

The CIA Station Chief recalled something about such a fatwa, but at the time the Agency consensus was that it was simply more posturing by radical clerics to bolster sagging support. "Who are these terrorists who are going to use these weapons of mass destruction, and how do you know?"

"It is the Iranians—not terrorists. I can't explain it entirely. But my father, who has carefully studied all this, knows."

"Your father knows? How does your father know?"

"Through a study of their religious books and their writings and the preoccupation of the radical Islamic leaders with the number eleven. And by the study of our own Holy Bible," Samir said.

Ainsworth thought, *Oh boy—another religious nut. How did this guy get on the "protected asset" list?* But he just said, "Go on."

Samir nodded and said, "My father has discerned that the jihadists are distorting the Quran to achieve their own plans and purposes. They have said that Allah gives them permission to kill infidels through means of mass destruction. And now they have nuclear weapons."

"Do you have any proof?"

"My father has the inner assurance that the fatwa goes against the nature and character of the true God— and God will never condone anything that is contrary to His nature and character."

Yeah, whatever that means, thought Ainsworth. "But Mr. Habib, before we can do anything, we have to have proof. We need proof that they really do have nukes, and proof that they plan to use them."

"But one proves the other," Samir said.

"Huh?"

"If there is proof that they have nuclear weapons, it proves that they intend to use them. They have said it many times over the past several years—particularly and specifically in the fatwa of 2004. For more than a decade they have been seeking an Islamic nuclear weapons capability. They do not believe that the Pakistanis are a reliable Islamic nuclear power since they cooperate with the Americans, who are infidels—so the Iranians have acquired their own. They have already used one—in Saudi Arabia. Tomorrow they will use another and in November, the eleventh month of the Christian calendar, they will use more of them."

Ainsworth was stunned. Some inside the Agency had speculated that what they were calling "the Saudi nuke" had been detonated by Iran, but there was no evidence whatsoever connecting Tehran to the nuclear device. Nonetheless, Monday's nuclear explosion proved that *someone* had been willing to expend a nuke, and Langley had instructed all CIA bases and stations to report any information they could gather on the event. "All right," said Ainsworth, "suppose you're right. Suppose the Iranians have some more nuclear weapons. Why do you say they're going to use them tomorrow—and again in November?"

"It is as I said before. All the jihadists, and that includes the mullahs and ayatollahs in Tehran, are preoccupied with the number eleven. For them it means power and leadership. Jihadists destroyed the two towers in New York on the eleventh. They bombed the trains in Madrid on the eleventh. The jihadist attack on Saudi Arabia occurred at eleven hundred hours on the fourteenth of October. That date can be written as 14/10/07. Subtract ten from fourteen. That equals four. Now add the four to the remaining integers, zero and seven and the sum is . . ."

"Eleven," replied Ainsworth—unconvinced.

"Yes," said the Iraqi. "That is why my father is certain that they are going to use another weapon of mass destruction tomorrow."

"Tomorrow? Why tomorrow—it's the nineteenth of October. And the nuclear weapon that detonated in Saudi Arabia went off on the fifteenth of October. What do *those* dates have to do with the number eleven?" asked Ainsworth, his voice heavy with skepticism.

Samir patiently reconstructed what his father had told him last night. He said, "Write the date 15 October 2007 as 15/10/2007. Then, add one and five. That equals six. Add the ten. That equals sixteen. Add the two—that makes eighteen. Now subtract the seven and that equals eleven."

"It's just a coincidence," said Ainsworth. "What about tomorrow—the nineteenth?"

"Ah yes," replied Samir tolerantly. "Tomorrow is the nineteenth day of the tenth month. Add the numbers, one plus nine plus one plus zero . . . and that too equals eleven. My father explained all this to me last night."

"Tell me again why your father thinks all this is going to happen," Ainsworth said, sensing Samir's respect for his father's opinion.

"My father told me that many of their imams attach great significance to certain numbers—in this case the number eleven. He is still studying the Holy Bible, and he is praying to God, to reveal to him answers about where and when. But because the time is short, I thought I should tell you right away what we do know, and if he discerns more, we will tell you."

As Samir sat back in his chair, ending his "report," Ainsworth leaned in and turned off the recorder. He said nothing for a long while, wondering, *What are people at Headquarters going to think if I include all this weird stuff about the number eleven, the information about God, the Bible, the Quran, and praying in a report? I know that if such an account came to me, I'd dismiss it outright—especially if it came from a "walk-in." Still, this man claims to be a friend of Bill Goode, and the Marine gunnery sergeant had said that this Iraqi knew some general back in Washington. Maybe I'll just kick it upstairs to Goode.*

"Tell you what, Mr. Habib," Ainsworth said, deciding on a way to handle the matter with minimum jeopardy to his career. "I'm going to send along this recording to Mr. Goode right away. Ordinarily I'd write up a report, but I think it's best if I just send him what you've told me. It will be faster that way, and he'll know what to do with the information. And thank you for coming in, Mr. Habib. Mr. Conway will show you out. Please thank your father for his effort on this. Mr. Conway will give you a number you can call if you or your father have information for us in the future."

Camp Snoopy
Doha International Airport, Qatar
Friday, 19 October 2007
0200 Hours Local

The two Air Force C-17s carrying SOCOM Det 2 had required a single aerial refueling from a pair of KC-10s out of the Azores during the thirteen-hour flight to Doha. When the aircraft landed at exactly 0100 Thursday—the men had deplaned, enjoying the opportunity to stretch their legs and get the circulation going again.

Marine Colonel "Buck" Beyer, from the CENTCOM Forward HQ staff had been there to meet Captain Christopher and his men with three buses and two seven-ton trucks, escorted by three of the latest up-armored Humvees. Beyer supervised the offload of the unit equipment and ordnance from the aircraft, stowing it all aboard the vehicles, and then led the little convoy from the airbase, three miles to CENTCOM's whimsically dubbed Forward Headquarters, Camp Snoopy.

Named after the Charles Schultz canine, the base didn't live up to its amusing namesake because all humor ended at the main gate. The high, well-lighted perimeter berm topped with coils of razor wire was interrupted every one hundred yards or so by elevated guard towers—manned by two U.S. soldiers each. Protruding from the towers were the snouts of 240 Golf and .50 cal. machine guns. Outside the perimeter, seven two-man teams patrolled with guard dogs. At the entry portal there was a lengthy delay while U.S. Army MPs in full "battle rattle" inspected every vehicle before it was permitted to enter—using mirrors to peer underneath and insisting that the drivers open the hoods of their vehicles so the spaces could be checked for bombs.

U.S. Seabees had constructed Camp Snoopy on the eve of Operation Iraqi Freedom. The Navy Combat Engineers had begun by moving more than 10,000 cubic meters of soil and sand to build the perimeter berm. Then they chiseled their way through granite-hard bedrock to erect high-security, bomb-proof headquarters buildings and finally, row after row of modular billets. Using some 50,000 pounds of steel rebar and beams, and nearly 700 cubic meters of concrete, they constructed three-dozen "Scud bunkers," with a blast wall almost a hundred meters long, plus a mile of road, and another mile of trenches inside the camp. Army Reserve and National Guard engineers working with civilian contractors built mess halls and recreation facilities, and installed dozens of generators, fuel storage tanks, enormous water purification units, sewage treatment plants, and thousands of air conditioners to keep the heat from setting off the fire sprinklers inside the buildings. Even the water for the swimming pools was cooled to prevent troops from being scalded during training or recreation.

Captain Christopher had been through Camp Snoopy on deployments to Iraq several years earlier, and he noticed that not much had changed since. The most obvious difference was the higher security profile—which provided a certain level of comfort. Once they were inside, Colonel Beyer told him, "Your unit is billeted over at the Spec Ops Compound. You have your own storage area, motor-park, and mess hall. Do you and your officers want to stay over at the CENTCOM BOQ?"

"No, sir," the captain replied. "We'll stay with our men. According to my orders we only have twenty-four hours or so before we have to move. I want to get 'em fed, bedded down for awhile, and have plenty of time to brief before this mission goes down."

"OK by me," Beyer said. "I'll be back here in eighteen hours with the final op order from SOCOM."

✪

At 0100, Friday morning, exactly twenty-four hours after SOCOM Det 2 had arrived at Doha, Capt. Andy Christopher had his three teams back at the air base and mission ready. Inside a large hangar lit with blue lights to preserve their night vision, the members of each team conducted a final gear check. The threat of chemical "poisoning" from the petroleum fires raging throughout the country mandated that everyone wear full NBC protective suits and carry their gas masks. And because of the nuclear detonation, every Marine was also issued a radiation dosimeter and told to hang it on the outside of their armor vests. Outside on the tarmac, three different types of aircraft awaited the troops who would ride them to their designated targets.

Two USMC MV-22, tilt-rotor Ospreys from VMM-263 were waiting to fly Lieutenant Weiner, a portion of the HQ element, and the sixteen men of Team 3 to the USS *Makin Island,* LHD-8. From the Expeditionary Assault Ship, twelve miles off the Saudi coast, they would serve as the Detachment QRF.

Parked beside the haze-gray Ospreys were two CH-53E Sea Stallions—also from the Marine Composite Helicopter Squadron aboard the *Makin Island.* The big Sikorski birds had been selected to carry Team 2 and the two NEST scientists directly from Doha to the Rub al Khali nuclear detonation site in southeastern Saudi Arabia. The sixteen Marines and the two civilians were already perspiring heavily in their full MOPP nuclear, biological, and chemical protective suits. So were the CH-53 pilots, crew chiefs, and the door and ramp gunners.

Further out on the apron, a USAF MC-130, rigged for a rapid parachute drop, waited with its ramp open for the team that would jump into the besieged embassy. Since this was likely to be the most dangerous of the three missions, Captain Christopher, his radio operator, two additional Navy medical corpsmen, an air-control communicator, and a satellite technician were accompanying the sixteen Marines of Team 1 into the heart of Riyadh. The MC-130, with its terrain-following radar, would fly at fifty feet all the way to Riyadh, pop up and drop the twenty-one paratroopers—hopefully inside the wall surrounding the three-acre embassy compound.

The CH-53s with Team 2 and the scientists aboard took off at 0118, heading for the southeastern desert of Saudi Arabia. They were followed minutes later by the two MV-22s—the strange-looking aircraft lifting straight up and rapidly transitioning into forward flight—headed for the USS *Makin Island* with Lieutenant Weiner and the QRF. As soon as the first two teams had departed, Captain Christopher and Team 1 left the hangar for the MC-130. Their heavy gear—primary and reserve parachutes, equipment packs, and NBC protective kit—gave them the appearance of pregnant turtles as they waddled up the ramp.

Once aboard, they "counted off"—one through twenty-one—and Christopher shouted, "As soon as we get the word that the QRF is aboard the *Makin,* we'll fire up the engines and take off. Once we're airborne, everyone puts on his gas mask. As we approach the DZ the crew chief will signal us to stand up and move to the ramp. As soon as the light turns green—exit fast!"

The Marines, facing each other in the eerie blue night-lights, responded with loud, "Oohh-Rahh!"

The captain, standing all the way forward, leaned toward the two rows of Marines facing each other in red nylon web seats and continued, "The aircraft will be nose high and climbing directly over the compound—but we still have to get everyone out in four seconds—or the last guys out may not be able to steer inside the embassy wall. And since I'm the last one out—I don't want to land outside the compound and have Mrs. Christopher get the videotape of some 'jihadi' removing her husband's head from his body. Got it?"

"Aye aye, sir!" the men called out in unison.

"As soon as we're on the ground, everybody move immediately to your assignments—first thing is chain saws to remove the trees we saw in the satellite photos. We need to have the 'landscaping' done before dawn." Turning to the Navy First Class Petty Officer seated beside him, he continued, "Doc—get your corpsmen treating any embassy people who are wounded and start prioritizing the evacuees. The security element will coordinate with the senior MSG Marine to reinforce the embassy perimeter. Communicators—stay with me to get our comms up so that we can tell *Makin* when the LZ is clear enough to send in the Ospreys for the evacuation. And remember, we're supposed to go 'live' with SOCOM and Washington as soon as we get on the ground. Last chance—any questions?"

One of the Marines spoke up in the darkness: "Yes, sir. When do we move back into position to go out?"

"On my signal," Christopher replied. "Radio is primary. A green star cluster is backup. We'll keep any MSG personnel who aren't wounded with us—and we'll go out last."

At 0145 the Air Force crew chief shouted, "The pilot has gotten the word from the USS *Makin Island* that the QRF is in place. Please fasten your seat belts. Thank you for riding Spec Ops Air. We hope you enjoy your one-way flight." The ground power unit beneath the right wing fired up and hydraulic pumps whined as the clamshell ramp on the MC-130 closed. Then, one by one, the Marines heard the four engines begin to turn and the aircraft taxied to the runway. As the big bird lumbered into the air, Captain Christopher checked his watch. It was exactly 0200.

CHAPTER EIGHT

The Sky Is Falling

Situation Room
The White House, Washington, DC
Friday, 19 October 2007
0900 Hours Local

For the first time since the "Saudi Crisis" began, William Goode, the CIA Deputy Director of Operations, had been invited to sit in on one of the now twice-daily National Security Team meetings in the White House Situation Room. But his presence was not without its own controversy.

When he received the audio file of Samir's report from Ainsworth in Baghdad, Goode had dutifully called his boss, the CIA director—who punted the matter to Perry Straw. The DNI dismissed the report out of hand and called Goode, telling him to "stop wasting time with religious nut cases and get back to work finding out who *really* popped the Rub al Khali nuke and whether this 'Islamic Brotherhood' outfit has anymore of them."

After hanging up the secure phone, Goode leaned back in his chair and stared out his seventh-floor window deep in thought—all the while, fingering the tiny fish he wore on a military ID chain around his neck.

After a few moments watching the dawn bring color to the trees surrounding the CIA Headquarters, he made up his mind, picked up the secure phone, and dialed the number of the most senior American official he knew—a man who also carried the "sign of the faith."

Goode heard the phone ring twice, then a whooshing noise and a *ping* as the encryption systems synchronized—followed by a slightly garbled, but familiar voice that said simply, "Grisham."

"Good morning, General. Bill Goode at Langley," the CIA Deputy Director said.

"Good to hear from you, Bill. What's up?"

"I have received an urgent message from one of our 'Fellowship of Believers' in Iraq—Samir Habib. I believe it may have immediate bearing on your operation to evacuate our embassy in Riyadh," Goode began. "I have been unable to get anyone out here or the DNI to pay attention to it. It's an encrypted audio file. If you don't mind, I'd like to e-mail it to you."

The JCS Chairman, well aware of the help that Samir and his father had provided over the years, agreed—and a half hour later called Goode back: "I've talked to the SecDef about the report you sent. He's called the White House Chief of Staff, Bruce Allen, and we all think you should be at the 0900 meeting in the Sit Room."

"If you wish," Goode replied, "but you should be aware that the DNI isn't going to like it."

"Tough," said Grisham. "You're coming at the request of Secretary Powers, Bill. If Straw gets his knickers in a knot, he can take it up with the SecDef. Can you put Samir's report on a disc and come here first? We'll all go to the meeting together."

●

Powers, Grisham, and Goode arrived early—but after the DNI—who seethed when he saw the CIA Ops Chief walk into the Sit Room. Straw, glaring at Goode, started around the table, but the President's arrival preempted any confrontation.

The meeting followed the usual format—Straw presented the latest intelligence, what little there was. Secretary of State Luce was next, and she described the latest diplomatic initiatives; and then Powers outlined the ongoing operation to evacuate the embassy in Riyadh.

After describing how Captain Christopher's detachment had successfully parachuted into the embassy compound and how all American personnel were to be extricated by MV-22 after dark in Riyadh, the SecDef added, "Mr. President, General Grisham and I believe you also need to hear some other information from William Goode, the Deputy Director of Operations at the CIA. He was our last Station Chief in Tehran and knows more about the Iranians than anyone in Washington. I've taken the liberty of inviting him here this morning because, in the process of supporting our military operations in Saudi Arabia, he's come across some disturbing information."

All eyes and faces around the conference table turned in Goode's direction. Without preamble, he stood behind Secretary Powers and spoke in a soft but compelling voice: "Mr. President, based on credible evidence I have concluded that the situation in Saudi Arabia is being fomented by the Iranians with the help of the Russians; that Iran is in possession of a number of nuclear weapons, and that they plan to use them."

There was a collective gasp around the table, and Perry Straw started to sputter. The President simply waved his hand to cut him off and said, "How many nuclear weapons?"

"The bad news is that they very likely have no less than eleven. The even worse news is, we don't yet know where they are."

Once again the DNI started to interrupt. This time

the President scowled at him over his reading glasses. "What's the Russian connection?"

Goode continued: "There's a Russian named Dimitri Komulakov—a former KGB general. He's presently an arms merchant—though we're not sure he's really a freelance operator. He was active in Iraq in the 1990s and again in 2003—just before we launched Operation Iraqi Freedom. He has very good contacts in Syria, and the British have verified that he was seen frequently in Tehran over the course of the last several years. He dropped out of sight just before this crisis."

"Elaborate some, Bill," said Dan Powers. "Tell the President what the Brits told you about this guy."

Goode nodded and then said, "MI6 has sources that claim Komulakov got involved with the Iranians beginning in 2000 or 2001—about the time that the IAEA began to poke into Tehran's nuclear weapons program. They say that in early 2003, just before the start of Operation Iraqi Freedom, Komulakov was hurriedly pulled out of Tehran by Moscow and sent to Baghdad to take charge of packing up and shipping Saddam Hussein's nuclear, biological, and chemical weapons stores and equipment out of Iraq."

"To where?" the President asked.

"The MI6 source says that it was trucked to Syria and Iran."

"Do they—British intelligence—and more importantly, do *you* believe that this Russian is involved in this Saudi situation and the nuclear weapons you mentioned?" asked the President.

"Yes, sir, I do," replied Goode. "But we don't know how—nor do we know where he is at the present. But it's my belief that Komulakov may well be the person who supplied nuclear weapons to the Iranians. The initial findings from the two Nuclear Emergency Search Team scientists who went to the site of the Ar Rub al Khali detonation are consistent with the device having been a Soviet-era 152 mm nuclear artillery round. We're fairly certain that Komulakov had access to a number of them as early as 1994 or '95. It now appears that he has provided at least eleven of them to the Iranians."

The President leaned forward, his arms flat on the table, peered at Goode, and said emphatically, "For more than five years the Iranians have been assuring the UN—as well as the British, the French, and the Germans—that they have no intention of acquiring nuclear weapons. If you're correct, Mr. Goode, we've had an intelligence failure even more colossal than 9/11 or the Iraqi WMDs."

It suddenly seemed that everyone at the table was collectively holding their breath. After a moment of stunned silence the President continued, "If the Iranians are behind what's happening in Saudi Arabia, what do they—and this Russian—want?"

Goode glanced at the DNI, who was leaning back in his chair, his arms folded across his chest. Straw nodded his head—a gesture imperceptible to all but Goode, who responded, "Mr. President, in very broad terms, the 'shadow-ayatollahs' who really run Iran want to be the leaders—not just of Iran—but of a revolutionary, global Islam—a caliphate. They see the West as decadent, dissipated, corrupt, and moribund. For the past year, pronouncements by their leading clerics have emphasized that Europe is now 25 percent Muslim, and they are having a growing influence. They also keep preaching that the all-volunteer U.S. military has been exhausted by operations in Iraq and Afghanistan and that the U.S. and Europe are incapable of stopping an 'Inevitable Islamic Revolution'—particularly if the leaders of that revolution are armed with nuclear weapons."

The President held up his hand and said, "What do you mean by the term 'shadow-ayatollahs' that you used a moment ago?"

"These are the real leaders in Tehran, Mr. President,"

Goode answered. "It's not the 'elected' government that we see in the news or the clerics who meet with foreign leaders. That's a facade. The *real* power resides in the *Tasmimgiran*—the Supreme Islamic Council—held by eight or ten ayatollahs who form the camarilla around their 'Supreme Guide'—a mid-level mullah named Ali Hussein-Khamenehi. He is the ultimate decision maker and he has absolute authority."

"What about all the commitments that the Iranians made to the Europeans in the nuclear talks back in 2004 and 2005?" the President asked. "I thought we confirmed that they had stopped their uranium enrichment."

"By then they likely already had enough enriched uranium—or had closed the deal on acquiring old Soviet-era weapons from Komulakov—or both."

"Then why did they keep the talks going?" asked Secretary Luce, interjecting herself into the discussion for the first time.

"We don't know for certain," Goode admitted. "But it's likely their plans for what we have seen this week weren't yet finalized and so the Iranians used the talks as a diplomatic smokescreen—like the Japanese did on the eve of World War II. And, in the aftermath of Iraq, they continued the talks to serve the purpose of driving more wedges between the United States and our European allies. At this point, it seems to have worked—no European government is prepared to join us in military action to restore order in Saudi Arabia, much less action against Tehran."

At this, Helen Luce nodded her head and slumped back in her chair. What she'd just heard confirmed her most feared suspicions, and she was disheartened.

The President, still uncertain that he understood the full implications, asked, "Bill, several times you have said that the Iranians have eleven or more nuclear weapons. Why eleven?"

For the first time Goode hesitated. He couldn't tell the Commander in Chief that it was information relayed from a praying mystic—although of all the men and women in the room, it was the President who might best understand how a man of deep faith in God could know such things. Still, there were many others in the room who would *not* understand. He simply replied, "Mr. President, the number eleven is from an unconfirmed report from a normally reliable source. We have not yet been able to verify his report—but that source also reported that another nuclear detonation is imminent, and I believe we need to take it seriously."

Nearly everyone around the table looked stunned except the President, who asked, "How imminent?"

"Today," replied Goode, catching in the corner of his eye Straw's grimace.

"Does this source say where?" asked the Commander in Chief.

"No, sir!" Perry Straw interrupted forcefully. "Mr. President, this *source* that Mr. Goode is relying on is a religious nut case who walked into our embassy in Baghdad yesterday with a wild-eyed story about radical Iranians committing all manner of heinous deeds based on some crazy numerology of the number eleven. Secretary Powers and General Grisham apparently think that this is something worth worrying about. My staff is inclined to think that this is bogus at best and disinformation at worst. It certainly isn't worth wasting your time speculating what it might or might not mean."

When the DNI had finished his tirade, the President said simply, "Thank you, Perry. Anyone else?"

Secretary of Homeland Security Sarah Dornin had been silent throughout the meeting. Now she interjected, "If it's possible that a nuclear weapon is about to be detonated here in the United States, we need to put our response teams on alert. And Mr. President, if

Washington is even *possibly* a target, you need to move to one of the emergency relocation sites."

As others began to speak, the President held up his hand and said, "Stop. Sarah, you have the floor. Go ahead and alert your regional response teams. But hold off on any announcement or warning to state and local authorities. We don't know that this report about a nuclear attack is accurate—and we don't *know* the target—is that correct, Bill?"

"Yes, sir, that's correct."

"Well then," continued the Commander in Chief, "I'm staying right here. The Vice President will depart immediately for an emergency relocation site with a Continuity of Government Team. Which one are you going to put him in, Sarah?"

"We've been using Mount Weather too much," the Homeland Security Secretary replied. Turning to the Vice President, she said, "If it's OK with you, sir, we'll fly you and your wife down to the one at Fort A. P. Hill, south of Fredericksburg."

"Fine with me," said the Vice President with a smile. "As the 'government inspector for undisclosed locations' it doesn't matter where the boss sends me, just so long as the microwave works and the popcorn is fresh."

The meeting adjourned, and as the President left the room, Straw said something about ". . . the sky is falling." Goode looked at his watch. It was 1000. If no nuclear weapon detonated in the next fourteen hours, the word would quickly spread around Washington's official circles that Bill Goode was "Chicken Little." As they walked out to their car on West Executive Avenue, the CIA Deputy Director for Operations sighed deeply and said to George Grisham, "Let's pray that I *am* the boy who cried wolf."

Continuity of Government Emergency Relocation Site
Fort A. P. Hill, VA
Friday, 19 October 2007
1455 Hours Local

Seven hundred feet beneath the red clay of Fort A. P. Hill, the Vice President of the United States was perched on a high stool inside the "Coordination Module," calmly watching as some of his 350-member military and civilian staff smoothly went about the business of setting up an alternative seat of government—in the event that the unthinkable happened and Washington ceased to exist.

Two levels below on the "VIP Gallery," his wife was resting comfortably in their concrete and steel encased "suite." They had arrived by helicopter shortly after noon and been whisked through the huge blast doors and into an elevator. As the car rapidly descended, his wife had reminded him to clear his ears—a lesson learned from previous trips to facilities such as this.

Now that technicians had established voice, data, and video links with every government agency in Washington, all U.S. military commands and FEMA Emergency Resource Centers in each of the fifty states, the Vice President was ready for an update on the situation. Having once served as the Secretary of Defense, he was much more familiar than most in government with U.S. military capabilities. Turning to a young Air Force officer, he said, "Major, can you connect us with the NMCC and NRO so that we can see what's happening in Saudi Arabia? The embassy evacuation should be getting under way shortly."

"Right away, sir," the major replied as he sat down at a computer console. In a matter of a few dozen keystrokes a satellite image appeared on the screen and the major said, "This is live imagery from the KH-13 approaching Riyadh from the west right now. Because it's night over there, we're using a 'thermal scope' so it looks like a photo 'negative.' The NMCC duty officer will be on speaker 1, right in front of you. The NRO watch officer will be coming up on speaker 2. We'll have the State Department Operations Center on speaker 3 in just a moment. Just so you know, sir, the mikes on all these circuits are 'open' in both directions—so everyone can hear what's being said at both ends. Anyone else you want on?"

"How about CIA Operations?"

"Yes, sir," said the major, as he typed more commands into the computer. "CIA Ops will be coming up on speaker 4."

A moment later a voice came over speaker 1: "NMCC, Brigadier General Stenner, Marines. Can I help you, sir?"

"What's the latest THREAT-WARN?"

"Nothing new on any WMD. The situation here in Washington is unchanged since you departed, sir."

"Good. Any news from Riyadh, General?" asked the Vice President.

"Sir, it's taken a lot longer than expected to clear the LZ for the Ospreys. About two hours ago someone lobbed a couple of mortar rounds into the compound and wounded two Marines from the extraction force, but things have gotten quiet out on the street. Up until an hour ago there had been sporadic small arms and RPG fire from out in front of the embassy, but that's all stopped. It seems to be very quiet right now. The Ospreys have lifted off from the USS *Makin Island* and are loitering out over the desert east of the capital. SOCOM advises that they plan to start the extract in the next thirty minutes or so."

"Good," said the Vice President. "I don't want to get in the way of any of this so I'll just monitor from here. I'm looking at the current KH-13 thermal pass over Saudi Arabia. When the bird gets closer to Riyadh, can we get a close-up of Embassy Row?" he asked. "Or do they have to reprogram the bird for that?"

As if on cue, a female voice came over speaker 2 saying, "How's this, sir?" as the image zoomed in.

The major sitting beside the Vice President moved the mouse in his right hand, and the image that had been on the computer in front of them suddenly appeared on the large plasma screen in front of the room. After staring at the image for a moment, the Vice President asked, "That building in the center of the screen—with what looks like a truck parked in front of it—is that our embassy?"

The female voice on speaker 2 replied, "I think that's the French Embassy, sir. Ours is coming up."

The next image proved her right. As the satellite's high-resolution lens tracked across the scene, the room suddenly became silent as the camera caught the stars and stripes fluttering in the breeze. In the courtyard behind the embassy, several dozen figures could be seen in the final stages of clearing the last of some forty large trees and uprooting bushes and shrubs. They had even leveled the fountain in the center of the proposed landing zone.

The Vice President squinted at the image and said, "What do those men have in their hands that are glowing? Are they weapons?"

"No, sir," said the female voice over speaker 2. "Those are chain saws. They appear to be glowing on the thermal image because they are hot. If you look on the roof you can see others with weapons—and they aren't as 'white' because they haven't been firing."

"Well, that may be a good sign," said the Vice President hopefully. "Maybe all the terrorists have decided to get a night's sleep and we can get our people out of there. Do we have State on the line yet?"

"Yes, sir, Walter Beasley here at State Department Operations," said a voice from speaker 3. "We're watching the same KH-13 pass you are. And I've got the ambassador on the line via the Sat-Com terminal that the Marines brought with them when they parachuted in this morning."

"What does he say about how soon they can get out of there?" asked the VP.

Beasley replied, "They just reported that the LZ is ready and litter bearers are already moving the casualties out of the embassy. The Marines want to take the wounded out first."

Then from speaker 1: "SOCOM reports that the first two MV-22s are inbound to the embassy escorted by two AV-8 harriers. We also have four F-18s 'upstairs' and an AC-130 orbiting south of the city if it's needed. All of 'em are in contact with the team leader on the ground, a Captain Christopher."

Everyone in the room was now watching the large screen at the front of the room. As the KH-13 satellite soared 101 miles over Riyadh, Beasley's voice could be heard over speaker 3 as he talked to someone on a radio from the State Departments Operations Center: ". . . Roger, I understand, the 113 'pax' are all U.S. nationals. Were you able to contact any of the other embassies?" There was a pause and then: "Understood, negative contact." And then, a few seconds later, Beasleys voice again: "Roger, birds inbound."

The Vice President and everyone in the room stared at the screen as two white shapes materialized over the embassy—the MV-22s. On the ground, man-shapes holding infrared strobe lights could be seen signaling their landing points. The huge aircraft rotated their wings and altered from forward to vertical flight and first one, then the other, settled down into the embassy courtyard.

For nearly thirty seconds the speakers were silent as the dust plume kicked up by the twin rotors of each aircraft obscured the image on the screen. As the cloud slowly dissipated, the satellite image showed litter bearers running out of the ramps of the two aircraft back toward the wall to pick up more of the wounded. In less than a minute they had loaded more patients aboard the aircraft. Then, there was another huge plume of dust as the two Ospreys lifted off, one after the other.

Once clear of the wall around the embassy compound, the two aircraft rotated clockwise until they were pointed east and within seconds transformed to horizontal flight and disappeared off the top of the screen. As they did so, a voice came over speaker 1: "Ospreys One and Two away with fifty-seven 'pax' aboard. Ospreys three and four inbound."

There was a collective cheer from the spellbound audience in the Coordination Module. The Vice President, smiling at the spontaneous outburst, glanced at the clock over the plasma screen labeled "Saudi Arabia" and jotted down the time: 2309.

As the second section of MV-22s approached the embassy compound, the voices of several people could be heard over the speakers. It was clear from the clipped speech and the tone of the people talking that the jubilation deep beneath Fort A. P. Hill wasn't being felt at the command centers in Washington.

On speaker 1: ". . . NRO, SOCOM wants you to pan up the street to the west. The Marines on the roof of our embassy say that the truck parked in front of the French Embassy just started up and they are concerned that it may be a suicide VBIED."

As the voice on speaker 2 said: "Roger, panning," the image on the screen widened to show a large truck moving down the street toward the U.S. compound.

Then from speaker 3: ". . . The Evac Team at the embassy has told the second Osprey section to stand off. They're out of AT-4s and Javelins and are calling in an F-18 to take out the truck."

Once again there was silence in the Coordination

Module. On the roof of the American embassy, prone and kneeling figures were blazing away at the truck. On the screen their firing looked like sparklers on the Fourth of July.

Suddenly, the screen went completely white—and then to black. There was a mumbled "Oh my . . ." from someone in the room. After a moment's silence the Vice President said, "What happened?"

The female voice on speaker 2 replied immediately: "Something exploded. The aperture on the KH-13 lens was wide open and it fried our thermal resolution. We should have an image back in about a minute."

"Was it a bomb from the F-18?" asked the Vice President to no one in particular.

"Negative, sir," said the voice on speaker 1. "The F-18 was just lining up to make a cold pass when the flash occurred. Now SOCOM is telling us that they have lost comms with their Evac Team."

Speaker 3 was next: "We've lost the Sat-Com with the ambassador. Will advise when comms are reestablished."

Three minutes later the black screen changed first to "snow" and then a hazy image as the female voice on speaker 2 said, "All subscribers please take note. At 2311 hours local over Riyadh, Saudi Arabia, an explosive 'flare' damaged the thermal reticle on KH-13 six one alpha. NRO has taken the bird under manual control and we're 'flying' it from here. We have enough fuel to hold it geosynchronous over the target area for three hours and eleven minutes. After that we will have to await standard ninety minute passes by six two bravo. We are also reprogramming another bird for thermal imaging, but it will not be available for tasking over the target area until after dawn. An advisory message to this effect is being sent to all subscribers. Please alert your principals to this change in coverage."

From speakers 1, 3, and 4, came a muted, "Roger."

For several seconds the image on the screen got darker, then lighter as NRO technicians made adjustments to the damaged satellite equipment. Though the picture wasn't as clear as it had been before the "flash," the resolution was sufficient to see that the whole front wall of the embassy was down and that flames were raging from a cauldron where the truck had been. A roiling column of smoke billowed to the east and off the top of the screen. The building across the street had been flattened.

As the Vice President started to reach for the telephone to call the White House, the voice of the State Department watch officer came through speaker 3: "All centers be advised, we have reestablished voice Sat-Coms with the embassy. Wait."

A few seconds passed and then Beasley's voice again: "We're trying to patch this through to the conference line. If this works, please avoid talking on your open mike to prevent override. I have the DCM on the other end."

And then, from speaker 3, the Vice President could hear the *whoosh* and *ping* of an encrypted radio transmission as Beasley talked to Riyadh: ". . . Roger, I understand, the ambassador is dead and you have at least ten more casualties. Say again your last about the radiation alarm."

The satellite transmission from Riyadh was garbled but understandable, and it came through speaker 3 with a slight delay: ". . . alarm has been going off since the explosion in front of the embassy. We thought it was just because the blast had damaged the system, but the Marines are saying that their dosimeters are showing that they have been exposed to radiation."

Beasley, clearly unprepared for this news, replied, "Roger, wait out." Then, speaking over the secure conference link, he said, "Who has an expert on radiation available who can talk to Maynard Redding, our Deputy Chief of Mission in Riyadh?"

Speaker 4, which had been silent until now, suddenly came alive with a voice that the Vice President recognized. It was Goode, the man who had briefed at the morning meeting in the Sit Room: "This is CIA Operations. We have Dr. Elizabeth St. Claire here in our Ops Center. She is a nuclear physicist and weapons expert. If you send us the frequency set and encryption coordinates, we'll come up on your net."

Beasley did as asked, and a few seconds later a female voice came over both speakers 3 and 4: "Mr. Redding, this is Dr. St. Claire. Can you tell me what the reading is on any of the dosimeters around you?"

There was a pause and then the DCM responded, "There is a dead Marine here who was with the ambassador. His dosimeter shows that he's been exposed to two *sieverts*. What does that mean?" Even with the garble caused by the encryption and the satellite delay, his anxiety was evident to everyone listening.

"The dosimeter shows how much of an 'effective dose' the wearer has been exposed to," St. Claire responded. "One sievert is roughly one hundred rads. A *lethal* 'effective dose' is about ten sieverts—and death occurs within hours to a few days after radiation exposure. Where was this Marine when he was killed?"

"He was with the ambassador in his office, not far from the front of the building."

"Then the explosion wasn't a nuclear detonation," the physicist said emphatically.

"How do you *know?*" said the voice in Riyadh. "It was an enormous explosion. It blew down the whole front of the building—and leveled the Dutch Embassy across the street. There was even a mushroom cloud."

St. Claire's answer was delivered with calm assurance: "Even a small tactical nuclear weapon going off at that distance would have subjected everyone in your embassy compound to a minimum of twenty to thirty sieverts. It's possible that what we have here is an incomplete detonation of an old nuclear device—but it's much more likely that this was a conventional explosive into which was packed some low-grade radiological material—a so-called 'dirty bomb.' I'm looking at a satellite shot of where you are. Is anyone there still outside breathing in smoke from that fire?"

"Yes," replied Redding. "There are probably forty or more people still out in the courtyard."

"Is that building at the back of the courtyard big enough to hold the survivors?" St. Claire asked.

"Yes."

"Have them get inside that building," the scientist ordered. "If they have gas masks, tell them to put them on. Soot particles from the smoke will likely be radioactive, and they should try not to inhale any. If they have dust from the explosion on their clothing, tell them to take off their clothes and wipe down their bodies with bottled water—get the dust off their skin—and then put on clothing that hasn't been exposed to the smoke and dust."

"What else can we do?" Redding begged.

"Well, this isn't my call," said St. Claire. "But we need to get those who are still alive out before they are exposed to any more radiation."

At that, Brigadier General Stenner's voice came over speaker 1: "We're in touch with SOCOM. They're sending the MV-22s back in. They have no comms with the Extract Team. Mr. Redding, are you taking any fire right now?"

"Negative."

"Good," replied the NMCC Duty Officer. "Can you ask Captain Christopher to come up on the Air Net?"

"He was on the roof," answered Redding. "He's dead."

Without pausing to reflect on the sadness of those words, Stenner continued: "Get all the survivors to that building at the rear of the courtyard and stand by for the Ospreys. Tell everyone to keep their heads down. SOCOM is sending the AC-130 to cover the extract. Do you have a count?"

"Hold one."

After a lengthy pause, the DCM's voice came back over speaker 4: "We have thirty-seven ambulatory, ten wounded on litters, five dead—including the ambassador and Captain Christopher—a total of fifty-two. We also have four missing. They were probably killed in the blast and are likely buried in the rubble."

"Roger, let me pass that to SOCOM."

The next few minutes seemed like hours to those in the Coordination Module watching the degraded image on the plasma screen. Then, as the two MV-22s appeared on the screen, and started to settle inside the compound in a swirl of dust, the street in front of the embassy erupted in splotches of white light.

"What's that?" asked the Vice President.

"Fire from the AC-130," responded the voice on speaker 1.

As the Vice President watched in awe, a constant stream of fire—looking like water from a garden hose—poured down on the streets and buildings surrounding what was left of the U.S. Embassy compound. Before anyone could ask, Stenner's voice came over speaker 1 again: "The troops call it 'the finger of God.' It's the Gatling gun on the AC-130."

A few minutes later it was over. The two Ospreys lifted without further incident and disappeared off the top of the screen. Within seconds, the voice on speaker 1 announced: "Birds aloft en route to the USS *Makin Island* with fifty-two souls on board." After a pause, the voice continued, "As soon as the MV-22s have cleared the coast line, SecDef has ordered that two F-18s place four, thousand-pound LGBs on the embassy to ensure that there won't be anything left of value to the terrorists."

The Vice President grimaced and, forgetting the open microphone on the speaker array in front of him, said, "Pray that those four MIAs are already dead."

At the NMCC, State Department, NRO, and CIA Operations Centers they all heard his prayer. Nobody answered.

●

An hour later, after watching the air strike on what was left of the embassy, the Vice President had seen enough. He took the elevator down to his quarters and, after giving his wife a hug, sat down at the desk in his "study," picked up the phone and said to the operator who answered, "Get me the CIA Operations Center, please."

The phone rang once and a voice answered: "Operations."

"This is the Vice President. Is Mr. Goode there?"

A moment later a now familiar voice said: "Goode."

The Vice President wasted no time: "Is that Dr. St. Claire of yours still convinced that the explosion was not a nuclear weapon?"

"Yes, sir," replied Goode. "She's been on the secure voice radio with the doctors aboard the *Makin*. They've told her that the largest dosimeter reading from those evacuated from the embassy was five sieverts. She says that's consistent with a 'dirty bomb'—so it's not a 'real' nuclear weapon."

"Is five sieverts enough to kill anyone?"

"According to Dr. St. Claire, it depends on what tissues were irradiated, but almost everyone who is healthy can survive exposures of four to six sieverts, though she says they're liable to suffer 'non-stochastic' radiation damage—meaning long-term complications like cataracts, blood-cell damage, thyroid problems, perhaps cancers."

"I understand," said the Vice President. "It's a good thing you had her there. Is she normally on duty in your Operations Center?"

"No, sir, I had called her in from our S&T Branch because of the nuclear weapon issue I briefed this morning in the Situation Room."

"Yes, I remember," said the Vice President. "This morning you also mentioned an infatuation by the terrorists with the number eleven. Did you notice what time that device went off in front of our embassy?"

"Yes, sir, 2311 local in Riyadh. For civilians, that would be eleven minutes after eleven p.m."

"Correct. And didn't you also brief that your 'source' had said that the Iranians had no less than eleven nuclear weapons?"

"Yes, sir."

"Well, let's assume for a minute that your source is correct," said the Vice President. "We're now fairly certain that the weapon that went off in southeastern Saudi Arabia was an old Soviet nuke, correct?"

"Yes, sir."

"And we're pretty sure that the device that went off tonight in Riyadh was a 'dirty bomb'—made to look like a real nuke?"

"As far as we can tell," Goode replied.

"Well, if your source is correct—that would mean the Iranians have ten real nukes left—not nine—as they may want us to believe."

There was a long pause as Goode mulled over what the Vice President had said. He then replied, "I'm not sure what the ayatollahs in Tehran are up to—or how many nukes they may or may not have. There's no doubt that they often mistakenly believe we know more about them than we do. But if you and my source are correct, they still have ten nukes left—and that makes them very dangerous."

"I agree," said the Vice President. "I also think this is

very important. I'm going to call the President and tell him that I want to get back to Washington. In the next day or two, I want you to come in and brief him and me on this number eleven business—and anything else you have on that Russian fellow."

"Komulakov?"

"Yes. We need to find out where he is and what he's up to." And then after a brief pause the Vice President added, "And by the way, tell your source 'thank you' for the warning about the device today—despite the fact that it almost came too late. Be sure to let us know if he has any more hunches like that."

CHAPTER NINE

Flames and Fury

USS *Makin Island* LHD-8
Central Persian Gulf
Saturday, 20 October 2007
0900 Hours Local

From his elevated, leather chair on the right side of the bridge, Capt. Pat Toomey ordered, "Officer of the Deck—increase turns and bring her up into the wind to receive aircraft."

"Aye aye, sir," replied a khaki-clad Navy lieutenant standing beside him, peering into the fog through binoculars. After glancing at the "Heads-Up Display" on a Plexiglas screen, the lieutenant said to the helmsman, "Come right in a standard turn to course two nine five." Then, turning to the petty officer standing watch on the electronic engine controls he said, "Bring her up to twenty-one knots."

The 884-foot-long amphibious assault ship turned smoothly, cutting a long arc through the water. Northrop Grumman Ship Systems had launched the USS *Makin Island* from Pascagoula, Mississippi, and she was one of the newest ships in the U.S. Navy. Captain Toomey and crew had broken her in and loved each bolt and rivet in her. The LHD had 70,000 total shaft horsepower, and it was at times like this—maneuvering in open waters—that she responded most gracefully to the helm.

The USS *Makin Island* carried a crew of 104 officers and 1,004 enlisted men, but she also transported the bulk of an entire, 1,800-man MEU—a Marine Expeditionary Unit. Jammed onto her flight and hangar decks she carried six AV-8B Harrier attack aircraft, six MV-22, Tilt-Rotor Ospreys, a dozen CH-46 Sea Knights, four CH-53E Sea Stallions, four AH-1W Super Cobras, and three UH-1N Armed Hueys. In her well deck were four enormous sea-skimming LCACs—Landing Craft Air Cushion—high-speed over-the-beach craft capable of forty knots for ship-to-shore amphibious landings. The USS *Makin Island* also carried two sleek, high-speed Kevlar-hulled "penetration craft" for use by the SEAL team that had embarked in Norfolk.

As the wind speed across her flight deck increased, a voice on the 1-MC ship's public address system announced: "Flight Quarters. Stand by to receive aircraft. D-Con Team, stand by in Troop Embark."

Sailors wearing purple and red vests and cranial protectors suddenly appeared on the flight deck, and moments later a Navy H-60 appeared out of the fog and the chopper began a sliding approach to a designated spot on the flight deck already crowded with aircraft.

Captain Toomey rose from his chair and went out to stand on the left wing of the bridge to watch the helicopter land. As the haze-gray bird touched down and the flight deck crew raced to tie it down and refuel it, Toomey saw a single person, garbed in Marine "desert-digitals," exit the aircraft, stride across the flight deck, and enter the island. A moment later the 1-MC speakers throughout the ship announced, "SOCOM DET 2, arriving."

Toomey turned to the Officer of the Day and said, "Tell the XO to have Lieutenant Colonel Hart escorted to CIC. I'll meet him in there. Make sure that the MEU CO is aware."

Moments later, Lt. Col. Dan Hart, USMC, commanding officer of 2nd Force Reconnaissance Company—now designated as Special Operations Command Detachment Two—entered the ship's dimly lit Combat-Intel Center. The ten sailors on watch barely looked up from their scopes and computers as Captain Toomey greeted Hart warmly, took him to the rear of the compartments, and said, "It's good to see you, classmate. You got here fast. I'm truly sorry about your boys in Riyadh, Dan."

Hart and Toomey had graduated from Annapolis in 1990, and both had been starters on the Naval Academy varsity lacrosse and soccer teams. The Marine lieutenant colonel responded, "Thanks, Pat. I was already on my way here when I got the word about the 'dirty bomb' at the embassy. What's the latest?"

"Here's the most recent from 5th Fleet," said Toomey, handing Hart a clipboard with several sheets of paper affixed to it. "Most of it's based on what *we* sent *them*." Hart read the top message:

PRIORITY
SECRET/NOFORN
200521ZOCT07

FM: COM 5TH FLEET
TO: AIG 51.4
SUBJ: NUCLEAR INCIDENT REPORT (NUKE-REP) 10-20-03

1. (S) DECONTAMINATION TEAM ABOARD USS *MAKIN ISLAND,* LHD-8, CONFIRMS THAT DURING NON-COMBATANT EVACUATION OPERATION AT AMEMB RIYADH, SAUDI ARABIA, AN EXPLOSIVE DEVICE CONTAINING RADIOLOGICAL MATERIAL WAS DETONATED VIC AMEMB AT APPROX 2311 HOURS LOCAL, FRIDAY 19 OCTOBER 2007.

2. (S) THE EXPLOSION KILLED FOUR AND WOUNDED

ELEVEN. THE REMAINS OF ONE MSG MARINE AND THREE MARINES FM SOCOM DET TWO WERE NOT RE-COVERED. FORTY-SEVEN OF THE RESCUED AMCITS INDICATE EXPOSURE TO ALPHA, BETA, AND GAMMA RA-DIATION AND TOPICAL/RESPIRATORY CONTAMINATION BY IONIZED RADIOLOGICAL PARTICULAR MATERIAL. ALL EXPOSED AND CONTAMINATED PERSONNEL/REMAINS HAVE BEEN EVACUATED TO USS *MAKIN ISLAND* FOR TRIAGE AND DECONTAMINATION IAW NAVORDDIR 522.4.

3. (S) RADIOLOGICAL DETECTION DEVICES WORN BY SIX AIRCREWMEN AND TWO HOSPITAL CORPSMEN ABOARD TWO MV-22 OSPREY A/C ALSO INDICATED EX-POSURE TO LOW LEVELS OF RADIOACTIVE PARTICU-LATE MATTER. THESE PERSONNEL AND THEIR AIRCRAFT HAVE ALSO BEEN DECONTAMINATED IAW NAVAIRDIR 109.7.

4. (C) ALL PERSONNEL INDICATING EXPOSURE ARE UNDER OBSERVATION BY MEDICAL OFFICERS ABD USS *MAKIN ISLAND.* NO EVIDENCE OF RESIDUAL PATHOL-OGY APPARENT AT THIS TIME.

5. (C) CASREP: IN ADDITION TO CASUALTIES RE-PORTED IN NUKE REP 10-20-02, MEDICAL PERSONNEL ABOARD *MAKIN ISLAND* HAVE CONFIRMED THE RE-MAINS OF AMBASSADOR KENNETH P. SNELLING AND ANDREW J. CHRISTOPHER, CAPT. USMC 196-44-8956. BOTH KIA BY ENEMY.

6. (C) REQUEST CENTCOM DISPATCH MORTUARY AF-FAIRS DET TO RECOVER REMAINS ABOARD USS *MAKIN ISLAND* ON RET. DOHA.

7. (C) REQUEST SECSTATE NOTIFY NOK AMB SNELLING.

8. (C) REQUEST CMC NOTIFY NOK CAPT. CHRISTO-PHER.

BT

Hart finished reading the message, handed the clip-board back to Toomey, and said, "I want to see the wounded guys first, then meet in Troop Ops with Lieutenant Weiner and the rest of the Det."

"That's no problem," Toomey answered. "The wounded and all those who were exposed to any radiation are in the infirmary. If you want, you can meet with your Marines in Flag Plot. It's just below this space and unoccupied since we don't have an admiral or general aboard. It'll give you more privacy than Troop Ops since the MEU staff is using that space."

"That would be great," Hart said. "I also want to see Captain Christopher. Where's his body, Pat?"

"Uh . . . it's in the freezer—along with the remains of the others who were killed in Riyadh. Are you sure you want to do that, Dan?"

"Yeah," said the Marine. "I sent him on this mission. The day I left Lejeune, his wife delivered a baby girl. I stopped by the hospital to congratulate her, and she asked me to bring this picture," Hart said, producing a photograph of a smiling young woman, proudly holding a newborn. "She asked me to bring back his choice of names. Instead, I'm going to bring back the body of her husband."

Both men stood there as tears welled up in Hart's eyes. For a long while neither of them spoke. Finally Toomey reached over and put his arms around his classmate and said, "He's in a far better place, Dan—you and I know that for certain. He knew the risks, but he was willing to sacrifice his life in an effort to save others. Remember, 'Greater love hath no man than he who lays down his life for another . . .' "

The words, spoken by any other person right now, might have sounded glib. But to Hart, struggling to control his emotions, they spoke to his heart. He said, "I *do* know that he's in a better place. But it's still hard to lose one of your own. And it's especially tough when it's one of the really good ones. Andy was one of the best, Pat. I should have kept him back . . ."

The two men stood close together for a moment. Then Hart stood erect, reached into his pocket for a handkerchief, blew his nose, and said, "Ahh . . . I don't have much time. I've got to be on a flight back to the States out of Bahrain tonight."

"What's the rush?" asked Toomey. "You just got here."

"It's not my call," said Hart, his voice tinged with a mixture of sadness and anger. "If I had my way, I'd stay here until we recovered the bodies of those four Marines buried in the rubble of what was once our embassy. But, as they say, orders are orders."

"Who's calling the shots—SOCOM?" asked Toomey.

"No, not this time. These orders are coming from the JCS. Just as Andy Christopher's mission was getting under way, I was given a list of fifty of my best Marines—including Captain Christopher, my Sergeant Major, Lieutenant Weiner, plus sixteen of the boys in this unit—and I was told to send them to Washington, D.C., ASAP."

"What for?" asked Toomey. "I thought you guys were supposed to be a 'national asset' so that other commands couldn't mess around with you."

"That's what I thought, too, Pat. But now Washington wants fifty of my guys for some ultra-classified mission. I think I might know what it is—and I don't like it."

"Can you tell me?" asked Toomey.

"Not supposed to," said Hart. "I don't really know that much myself—*yet*—but I can speculate. Have you heard anything out here about this super-secret 'assassination unit' that Congress wants organized?"

"Only what I've heard on the news over the satellite. There hasn't been anything through channels. Sounds nuts to me."

"It *is* nuts. But I've got a bad feeling that brass at the

five-sided waste-basket in Arlington are planning to put my boys into this 'assassination' thing. If that's what they have in mind, I've got news for 'em."

"Which is what, Dan?"

"If they want my boys," said Hart emphatically, "they're going to have to take *me* with 'em."

Lourdes Signals Intelligence Facility
Bejucal, Cuba
Saturday, 20 October 2007
0420 Hours Local

Dimitri Komulakov received the news of the successful bombing of the American Embassy in Saudi Arabia within minutes after it happened, courtesy of American TV newscasts that were merely repeating an Al Jazeera report that "a nuclear weapon had been detonated by the Americans in Riyadh." He immediately placed a call using the Cuba-Murmansk secure circuit to his "client" in Tehran to report success.

Speaking in Farsi, Komulakov said, "You will be pleased to know that your package was opened at eleven minutes past eleven, as you directed. The gift performed exactly as expected. I hope you are pleased. I will call you again about the next packages."

In response Ali Yunesi exclaimed, "Allah be praised for that good news"—words that stung Komulakov.

If you had wanted Allah to handle this, thought Komulakov, *you should have called him instead of me, you filthy pig. I did it—Allah didn't have anything to do with that explosion!*

Knowing better than to say what he was thinking, the Russian simply grunted. But he was even more surprised by the ayatollah's next statement: "It is important that you start getting the other ten weapons aboard the Saudi aircraft and yachts that you have captured.

You do have a total of eleven boats and planes—is that correct?"

"Yes," replied Komulakov. "But are we going to change the schedule we agreed upon?"

"I will tell you if we are to change the schedule," was Yunesi's curt response. "The problem is not the schedule—the problem is that your 'scientists' have failed to deliver on the *additional* special weapons you promised they would build. Because of that I have had to explain to the Supreme Islamic Council that we do not yet have as many weapons as expected. This has caused me many difficulties with the Council, but I assured them—and Ali Hussein-Khamenehi, our 'Supreme Guide'—that you will deliver them by the deadline as we planned."

Komulakov was suddenly alarmed that the Iranian intelligence chief might be setting the stage for nonpayment of their next installment for his services—a sum of $100 million that was to be deposited in two days. It was also the first time in the history of their relationship that the ayatollah had acknowledged that he was not the final decision maker on Operation Dawah.

Though tempted to remind Yunesi that he had merely promised to *help* the Iranians build their own warheads for their Shabaz ballistic missiles, the Russian said instead, "I will contact the scientists and inquire about their completion dates."

"Yes, that would be wise," was all Yunesi said before ending the call with "Hopefully, *In Sha' Allah*, you will be able to contact me again soon with some good news."

By the time he replaced the receiver on the phone, Komulakov was both furious and fearful. He had no way of contacting his Russian and French scientists in Iran without compromising his communications security. Though they had been working for two years to build a nuclear payload to put on the Iranian Shabaz missile, they had been unable to construct a warhead that was light enough to fit the missile so that the weapon could reach its maximum range. The Iranians had never told him so, but he suspected that for internal reasons they wanted their own nuclear weapon—not someone else's—to be able to reach a very specific target: Tel Aviv.

The obstacle, he knew, was no longer sufficient quantities of fissile material. Selling the Iranians enriched uranium and plutonium from poorly secured Russian stockpiles had solved that problem. But the continuing challenge—as his scientists briefed him before he left Tehran for Cuba—was constructing a workable triggering device for the conventional explosion to properly compress the radioactive material in the warhead so that it would cause a critical chain reaction—and a nuclear detonation.

Komulakov didn't fully grasp all of the intricate physics required to produce a nuclear explosion—but he understood that his scientists had been unable to build timers that would create the absolutely necessary simultaneous, uniform explosion in the sphere of conventional explosive material packed around the radioactive core. Without these timers to perfectly control the conventional detonation within a matter of picoseconds—about 560-billionths of a second—the nuclear weapon would either fizzle or blow up prematurely.

Despite a string of failures, Komulakov had kept promising the Iranians that he would "try" to solve the problem for them, and they had planned accordingly. And he *had* tried—for months—to acquire the timers on the black market before Operation Dawah commenced but had been unable to do so. Two of his "purchasing agents" had spent weeks in Islamabad trying to get them from the A. Q. Khan network, and he'd even sent one of his "colleagues" to Pyongyang—all to no avail.

Now, with the operation under way, he'd have to

find some other way of putting a warhead on the "Islamic Missile." The Russian was painfully aware that it wasn't just a matter of not getting paid. If he failed to deliver by the deadline, he knew that he was a dead man. The ayatollahs had no trouble doing deals with the devil. But even the devil had to deliver. Otherwise he was a liability. And Komulakov knew that the deadline for the devil's delivery was just twenty days away—November 10th.

Office of Senator James Waggoner
Dirksen Senate Office Building,
Capitol Hill, Washington, DC
Saturday, 20 October 2007
1000 Hours Local

"Didn't mean for you to have to come in on a Saturday," said Senator James Waggoner to his chief of staff. Ralph Monroe was standing in the threshold of the senator's office door wearing the uniform for bureaucrats on working weekends in Washington—a blue blazer, a light-blue, button-down cotton shirt, khaki trousers, and topsiders.

"Yes, sir, no problem," said Monroe—not really meaning it at all. Despite the exorbitant price of gasoline, he had intended to drive his latest girlfriend out I-66 to the Skyline Drive. She had wanted to view the slopes of the Blue Ridge Mountains, now in transition from green to riotous hues of red, orange, and yellow. He hoped to seduce her into a night at the Mayhurst Inn, a romantic, century-old bed and breakfast in Orange, Virginia.

Waggoner had called while Monroe and Kathleen were packing a picnic basket. He had left her to finish the task and rushed over to Waggoner's office.

"Come in, Ralph, come in," said the senior senator

looking up from the stack of papers he had removed
from a file box labeled "Confidential" beside his desk.
Waggoner was sporting a carefully pressed pink shirt,
meticulously creased lightweight tan wool trousers,
British-made "field shoes," and a paisley-print cravat.

Catching Monroe staring at his neckwear, Waggoner
said, "Don't get any ideas, Ralph, I'm going to the Gold
Cup Races at Great Meadow this afternoon. Have to
look the part, y'know."

"Yes, sir," replied Monroe—hopeful that this meant
he was not going to have to spend the day poring
through campaign finance documents. "What can I do
to help you get under way?" the aide asked helpfully,
and then added, "You don't want to be late."

"Seems like we have a bit of a problem with our 'We
Want Waggoner' Presidential Exploratory Committee,"
the senator said as he pawed through the pile of papers
on his desk.

"How's that, sir?" asked Monroe.

"I got a call last night from an old friend who told
me that the Federal Election Commission may want to
take a look at the source of some of the contributions to
my '3W Committee.' Seems there is some question
about whether all the funds are legit," Waggoner said.

"Why now?" asked Monroe. "You haven't even announced that you're going to run."

"Apparently an anonymous source called one of the
FEC lawyers yesterday and suggested that some major
donations to the exploratory committee may not be
fully on the up-and-up," said the senator.

"Who?" asked Monroe, now genuinely sharing Waggoner's concern.

"My guess is that this is Carl Rose playing hardball,"
Waggoner replied. "But the 'who' and 'why' doesn't
matter right now. What we have to do is make sure that
this paperwork is in order before the FEC snoops start
poking around. As long as we don't have any problems

with the exploratory committee, we'll have clear sailing until the campaign gets under way in earnest after the New Year."

Monroe shook his head trying to recall how many "problems" there were with the donor list. He walked over to the records box, took out a file marked "Contributors," opened it on the desk, and removed a computer printout. He flipped through several pages, found what he was looking for, and said, "Here are the only two contributions that I know of that they'll have questions about," as he pointed to the spreadsheet.

The senator looked at the two entries, each for five million, dated December 2006. Both were annotated: "Personal Contribution, J. W. Waggoner."

"Why are *those* problems?" the senator asked. "That's how you told me to do it in order to get the exploratory committee rolling. We've already filed reports on these."

"That's true," replied Monroe, remembering the transactions. "The problem isn't with you making two significant contributions to your own Presidential Exploratory Committee—or even your own campaign. The problem is, where you *got* the ten million dollars. If the FEC subpoenas your personal banking records, you're going to have to explain the source of the funds."

"Well, if they ask, it came from the sale of 'Yakona,' my horse farm in Virginia."

Monroe looked at his boss for a long moment. Then, choosing his words very carefully, the aide said, "OK, as long as you can back that up, then we don't have anything to worry about. But . . . if it turns out that they can prove you washed someone else's money through your personal account, *that's* a problem—a big problem."

Waggoner sat heavily in his chair and said nothing for what seemed like minutes. Until now he had been confident that the true source of the ten million he had "contributed" to his presidential aspirations had been effectively hidden. Suddenly he wasn't so sure.

The money had come from Samuel Mubassa, a Nigerian serving at the UN, whose family owned a fleet of oil tankers. Early in 2006, through NSA intercepts made available to the SSCI, Waggoner had discovered that Mubassa's family had made hundreds of millions from the corrupt UN "Oil for Food" program. During a quiet dinner in New York, Waggoner offered to keep Mubassa's name out of Congressional hearings. For "services rendered," the UN diplomat promptly "invested" twelve million in the senator's horse farm. The first six million came by wire transfer from a numbered account in the Cayman Islands—the second six million arrived a week later from a Mubassa affiliate in Caracas. Both deposits were made in the "Yakona Farm Account." When Waggoner sold the farm for sixteen million in October 2006, he made two five-million-dollar contributions to the "We Want Waggoner" Presidential Exploratory Committee. The balance went into his personal bank account.

After a long silence, Waggoner looked up at Monroe and asked, "If the FEC does issue subpoenas, how far would it go?"

"Well," Monroe replied, "they'd surely want to interview anyone with whom you had financial dealings—probably back five or more years. They have the power to call witnesses to testify under oath."

"I see," said Waggoner. Then he abruptly rose from his chair and exclaimed, "Well, thanks for coming in today, Ralph. I've got to be getting out to Great Meadow for the races. You run along now and enjoy your day. We'll talk more about this on Monday."

Monroe said, "Have fun at the Gold Cup," and then he exited the senator's office and headed down the darkened, silent hallway toward the parking garage to his car. As he walked, a strange feeling in his gut startled

Ralph Monroe. It was fear. He had never doubted Waggoner's driving ambition. But now, twice in one week, he had been given reasons to doubt the senator's integrity. First, he had been told to "leak" a classified document to a reporter at the *Washington Post*. Now, it was the matter of campaign finances. As he started his car to head back to his apartment to pick up his date, Monroe vowed to start acquiring some insurance. By the time he reached Front Royal and the entrance to Skyline Drive, he had formulated a plan to protect himself—just in case the senator's sins caught up with him.

Commission Townhouse
5 Jackson Place, Washington, DC
Saturday, 20 October 2007
1530 Hours Local

Peter Newman held up his new White House ID badge as he pulled his car up to the uniformed Secret Service agent at the intersection of 17th Street and Pennsylvania Avenue. The officer, carrying an M-16 rifle and wearing an armored vest, looked glad to see someone. The streets were virtually empty.

The sentry swiped Newman's badge through a portable mag-card scanner, and when the word *Authorized* appeared on the tiny screen he pointed to a parking space just beyond Blair House and said, "Go ahead and park there, sir. There hasn't been anyone in all day."

Newman did as instructed and proceeded up the brick walkway to 5 Jackson Place, carrying his briefcase. To his right, Lafayette Park—once the site for placard-waving protesters—was vacant. As he bounded up the five steps at the front of the townhouse, the door swung open and a voice from the darkened interior said, "Good afternoon, General Newman."

As he strode through the doorway, a young man wearing a blue blazer was standing in front of a large desk, strategically placed in the hallway. Newman said, "You know who I am; who are you?"

"My name is Dick Green, Secret Service."

"Good to meet you, Dick Green. Why are you here?" asked Newman with a smile and holding out his hand.

The younger man shook the offered hand and held out a White House badge similar to Newman's—but his was emblazoned with the letters USSS across the bottom. "I'm one of eighteen Secret Service agents assigned to this protective detail. Until the day before yesterday I was in the Seattle field office. I was told that you would be in this afternoon to get set up, so I thought I'd better be here to introduce myself."

"You're here to protect *me?*" asked Newman, taken aback.

Green chuckled. "No, sir. You can pretty much take care of yourself. My agents and I are here to protect the members of the special committee and this building. We've already swept it for 'bugs,' tested the intrusion alarms, and made sure that nobody outside can eavesdrop."

"I thought this place was already secure," said Newman, placing his briefcase on the desk.

"Theoretically it is," Green replied. "Right outside the front door is Lafayette Square. Across the park, on Madison Place, is the Treasury Department Annex. This townhouse, like all the others here on Jackson Place, backs up on the New Executive Office Building. On both sides of us are offices for other Presidential commissions—but they're all in 'recess.' And of course all of this is part of the White House complex. If you want, I can show you around."

It took less than fifteen minutes for the Secret Service agent to walk Newman through the building. On the ground floor was a comfortable conference room and spaces for several administrative staff. Each of the five members of the Commission on Threat Mitigation had a private office on the second floor. The third floor was Newman's—with three private offices and plenty of space for communicators and an "Ops Center" for his "Special Unit."

"According to what I've been told, there is to be a 'watch section' here twenty-four-seven," Green said at the end of their walk through the building. "I've been given a list of twenty-four military personnel from Defense Communications Agency and WHCA. If there are others who will need access, I'll need to get their names and social security numbers before this place opens for business on Monday morning."

"I'll have that for you by then," Newman replied, appreciative of the agent's no-nonsense businesslike manner. "If I can make a secure phone call, I may even be able to get it for you this afternoon."

"Thought you might need something like that," said Green. "When the WHCA people were here this morning I had 'em activate the secure phone and computer terminal in your office upstairs."

The Marine was bounding up the stairs when his cell phone chirped. Flipping it open, he said, "Newman."

"Pete, can you call me secure?" asked a familiar voice.

Newman replied simply, "Yes, sir. Are you in your office?"

"Yes. And make sure that you're alone."

Seconds later Newman was seated at his new desk and connected with the Chairman of the Joint Chiefs of Staff over the secure telephone.

Grisham began without preamble. "Pete, has anyone informed you that several of the Marines you requested for the 'Special Unit' were killed and wounded at the Riyadh embassy yesterday?"

"No, sir."

Grisham continued, "Here's the picture. Of the fifty you requested by name from 2nd Force Recon, four are dead, five are WIA, and seven have been exposed to radioactive debris and are under medical observation. Ten of those you wanted from 1st Force Recon are committed in Afghanistan and I can't get them home, rested up, and up to you for at least thirty days. Five of the fifteen SEALs you asked for are in the Philippines chasing after Abu Sayef. The same for six of the 'D-Boys' from Bragg. That cuts your total complement to sixty-seven. Is that enough to get you started?"

Newman had anticipated that there would be complications "manning up" the Special Unit but not to this extent. Nonetheless, he replied, "Yes, sir. We'll find a way to make it work."

"Good," said Grisham. "There's another matter that's fairly sensitive. Do you know Lt. Col. Dan Hart, the CO of 2nd Force?"

"Yes, sir. He was a battalion XO in my regiment during OIF One."

"Well," Grisham continued, "I just got off the phone with the Commandant, and Hart is pitching a fit about his Marines being 'requisitioned' without his knowing where they are going. The Commandant is ready to relieve him, but I think the better course would be to assign him to your Special Unit if you're willing to take him."

"That's fine with me, General. Hart's a good man. Most of the troops are coming from his Force Recon Company anyway, so it should work well. Do we have any word yet on when Sergeant Major Skillings will be available?"

"I talked to him this morning," Grisham replied. "He told me that he plans to fly to Washington this weekend and be at work Monday morning."

"Sounds like Amos," Newman said with a chuckle. "Is he able to walk?"

"He mentioned something about the doctor telling him he'll have to wait ten days before he can put his full weight on his foot, so I think he's probably using crutches," replied Grisham, "but you know as well as I do that he'll still be there at your doorstep promptly at 0700 on Monday. I'll bet you'll have to order him to desk duty for a couple weeks, or else he'll suck up the pain and be on his feet no matter what."

"If I know Amos, he won't appreciate the idea of desk duty. As you say, I guess I'll just have to order him to do it. I'm pretty sure I can find something to keep him occupied."

Oval Office, The White House
Washington, DC
Sunday, 21 October 2007
1800 Hours Local

"Thank you again, gentlemen," said the President, rising from his chair by the fireplace as the Vice President arose beside him. "I especially appreciate your coming into town for this meeting on a Sunday. I had intended to do this at Camp David to keep it more private, but this weather precluded any helo flights and it's a long drive." As if on cue, the rain beating against the ballistic panes of the Oval Office windows sounded like pellets being thrown against a wall.

"Not a problem, Mr. President," said Chief Justice Anthony Scironi, now standing before the couch where he had been seated for nearly an hour. He and his five colleagues on the "Commission on Threat Mitigation" had arrived separately via the tunnel from the Department of the Treasury to avoid being seen by the White House press corps. "As you requested, we will convene tomorrow across the street to start our deliberations.

All of us understand the gravity of the situation and will do our best."

"I know you will," said the President. "I trust the Secret Service has taken adequate care of your accommodations—or are you all camped out in the Chief Justice's kitchen?"

Former Secretary of State James Cook chuckled and said, "They have me in a suite at the Willard. I'm just glad I'm not paying for it."

"I'm staying at the Army and Navy Club, Mr. President," answered Gen. Conrad Vassar. "The Secret Service lads think that I should move over to the VIP quarters at Fort Meyer after a few days, but I don't want to get in George Grisham's way," added the former JCS chairman.

"Did your wife come with you?" the President asked Gerald Donahue.

"Yes, sir. We're at the J. W. Marriott—also in a very nice suite," replied the retired FBI director. "Though Mrs. Donahue is glad to be back here, she's a bit disappointed that all her old friends seem to be out of town."

"And where do we hide our former spy chiefs in this town?"

Russell Bates, former CIA director, smiled and replied, "In plain sight, Mr. President. I'm at the Hay-Adams—right across Lafayette Square from the Commission offices. I always stay there when I'm in town. You know, from the top floor of that hotel you can look right into the White House residence."

The President nodded and, as he walked them to the door and their escorts waiting in the Roosevelt Room, said, "I'll be sure to remind the First Lady to keep the drapes drawn."

Once Commission members had departed, the President returned to the warmth of the fireplace. The once crackling blaze was now just glowing embers. He turned to the Vice President and said, "What do you think?"

"With the Chief Justice in charge, they aren't going to do anything rash," the Vice President replied. "You've known Jim Cook for years. And I'd trust old General Vassar with my life. That's three out of five."

"What about Donahue and Bates?"

"I don't know them well, but they're serious men. Do you have concerns about them?" asked the Vice President.

"I'm sorry to say that I don't really know the answer to that. I do know that the Bible says that men's hearts are 'desperately wicked' and 'who can know them?' Even men with the best intentions can sometimes get carried away or stray down the wrong path. I'm just praying that those guys are careful, *really* careful."

Office of Senator James Waggoner
Capitol Hill, Washington, DC
Sunday, 21 October 2007
2100 Hours Local

The operator answered, "Hay-Adams Hotel. How may I help you?" Senator James Waggoner said, "Please connect me to the suite of Mr. Russell Bates."

As the call was being transferred Waggoner pulled out the 3 x 5 card on which he'd jotted a few notes to prompt him in his conversation with the former CIA chieftain.

"Hello . . . ?" a voice on the other end said.

"Good evening, Russell. I trust you're having a good rest for the Sabbath and getting your energy up for your meeting tomorrow. How was your meeting with 'POTUS' this evening?" Waggoner said in his usual vocal version of southern syrup. Bates knew at once who it was.

"Well, Senator, it's been some time since we've talked. Thank you for inquiring about my health. How are you—and how the devil did you know I was here?"

"I'm fine, Russell. And as for knowing where you are—you must have forgotten that I'm the Chairman of the Senate Intelligence Committee. Listen, I need you to come over to my office for a bit. I have some things I'd like to talk to you about," Waggoner said.

Bates had absolutely no intention of going out in the awful weather again—short of some kind of national emergency—and he certainly didn't want to go up to Capitol Hill to meet with the "senior senator." So he offered an alternative: "James, why don't you come here and see me. We can go down to the lobby bar and relax, or have a few drinks right here in this lovely suite they've given to me to use while I'm here for this little 'project.' It's really quite nice."

Waggoner dropped the southern charm and got right to the point. His voice had a sharp edge. "Russell, don't give me that crap. I need for you to come to me. And don't use the car and driver that they've given you. It's better if you take a cab—it's more discreet. I'll expect you in a half hour," Waggoner said, and then hung up abruptly.

✪

Russell Bates arrived at the Dirksen Building fifteen minutes after the call, irked at Waggoner's arrogance, but knowing that the senator still held a good hand if it ever came to a showdown.

The senator was waiting in the lobby of the office building when the taxi pulled up, and he had the security guard buzz Bates inside. The two walked silently to the elevator—and then down the long silent corridor to Waggoner's office.

Once inside the confines of the office, Bates was amazed at the senator's change in demeanor. It was as if Waggoner had found a long lost friend. "Scotch, neat, as I recall," Waggoner said with a smile. He poured the drink and carried it to Bates, who was perched in an overstuffed leather chair, trying to keep his trousers, soaked in the downpour, from losing their crease.

"Russell, I'm sorry I had to be so impertinent with you," Waggoner said, once again wearing his "southern gentleman" persona. "It's just that I have some important things to discuss with you, and I didn't want either of us to be bothered by having to answer questions for the White House or anyone else who's keeping tabs on you—maybe even the CIA."

"I haven't gotten that paranoid, James," Bates said, sipping his drink. "I don't think anyone cares a rat's— uh . . . well, who cares anything about my comings and goings these days."

"Well, once burned, twice careful . . . or whatever that saying is, I always say," Waggoner replied.

"What's so important that you want to sneak me here on a rainy Sunday night?"

"Russell . . . y'all know that we go way back. Remember how thick we were back in '95? I think we were the only Republicans with any sense back when that good ol' southern boy was livin' there at 1600 an' gettin' himself in all that trouble with the ladies. And you remember when his National Security Advisor got in deep . . . uh . . . trouble, he 'bout threw everybody overboard so the ship of state wouldn't sink under his weight—which y'all will recall was ponderous."

Both men laughed at the recollection, but with Bates it was a forced levity. He knew where Waggoner was going with this.

"Jus' think, Russell. Our friendship has weathered all those years." The senator paused for effect. Bates used the hesitation to swallow the last of his drink. Waggoner continued, but this time the drawl became less perceptible and he became more urbane and straight-forward. "Look, Russell . . . I need you to return a favor for me. Think of it as a little 'return' for my keeping you out of various hearings, depositions, and indictments when that Silicon Valley defense contractor's problems* blew up. I'm sure you remember that I was the one who kept you out of that mess and, more specifically, kept you out of jail."

Bates clenched his teeth but said nothing. He knew that the old carpetbagger was right—Waggoner had saved his hide when Congressional committees and Justice Department attorneys were rounding up everyone who was even remotely connected to that scandal.

"Yes, it was surely a scandal of epic proportions," said Waggoner, as if reading Bates's mind. "Actually, I think that it might even have been worse except for the distraction provided by that perky little gal in the blue beret. Remember her? Proof once again, Russell, that sex sells better in the media than any other sin."

Bates had long ago gotten the point. "What do you need from me, James?" he asked.

"I have only one small request," Waggoner said. "I want you to add a name to the list of targets to be as-sassinated—and I want it at the top of the list."

"Who? And why?"

"The name is Samuel Mubassa."

"Mubassa? The UN deputy—*that* Mubassa?" Bates asked, surprised.

"The man's a treacherous terrorist, Russell. I have proof, but to reveal it would compromise national de-fense secrets, and I cannot do that," Waggoner said.

"But you want him killed. Why?"

*From the authors' first novel, *Mission Compromised*, © 2002, Broadman & Holman Publishers.

"Because he's a terrorist, and I've learned that he's using money he made in the 'Oil for Food' scandal to fund Al Qaeda, Iran, and who knows what else."

"But—" Bates started to argue.

Waggoner waved off his objections. "Listen, Bates," he said sharply, "I'm asking you to return a favor—one that I've not forgotten. You owe me; you owe me big time. Now listen to me. You tell that Commission that this guy belongs at the top of the list because he's a dangerous terrorist, using his ill-gotten gains to fund terrorist activities against U.S. citizens. If I have to, I can even provide you with proof that Mubassa is in cahoots with the Iranians and whoever else is behind this Saudi mess."

"What kind of proof?" Bates asked.

"Let's just say we have to be careful here because so much is going on behind the scenes with the State and Defense departments. Some of this stuff we have to keep out of the newspapers. But I can show you documents that prove that Mubassa's daddy had a hand in this Saudi crisis because he wants to expand his Nigerian oil business by taking over the Saudi fields." That statement was an outright lie, but Waggoner had the chutzpa to pull it off. He continued spinning his yarn, with imaginary details of conspiracies and assassinations, so that after ten minutes Bates had almost begun to believe Mubassa really was a "treacherous terrorist" who needed to be assassinated.

"The Commission is going to want evidence that what you're telling me is true. What can you give me?"

"You have my word, Russell. That ought to be good enough. It'd be a sad day in the United States of America if a U.S. senator's word meant nothing. You go in there tomorrow and tell 'em to go after this Mubassa fellow. I'll supply you with what you need to support your case. Do you understand what I am asking of you,

Russell? . . . I am only asking you for a small favor. Like the one I did for you back in '95."

Bates had a bad taste in his mouth but blamed the whiskey. He nodded and reached for his jacket. It was time to leave. He hoped that it was still raining outside. Maybe it would help to clear his head.

CHAPTER TEN

Making a List and Checking It Twice

Counter-terrorism Operations Center, CIA Headquarters
Langley, VA
Monday, 22 October 2007
0545 Hours Local

William Goode glanced at his watch and reached for his cup of black coffee. But it was cold and he grimaced as he swallowed a large gulp. Except for a brief stop home for a shave and shower, and then a trip in the rain to the early Sunday morning service at McClean Bible Church, he had been here in the CT Ops Center or in his nearby office on the seventh floor of the CIA Headquarters building all weekend. He looked out the window as the dawn began to break over the Potomac. The rain had stopped and it promised to be a beautiful, crisp autumn day.

Goode looked down to his computer. The assignment that had kept him—and twenty of his best operations officers and analysts—busy for more than sixty hours was nearly completed.

The "tasking" had come on Friday at 1730—directly from the Vice President. He had called Goode personally, shortly after returning to the White House from his "undisclosed location" at Fort A. P. Hill. The instructions were blunt: "Prepare a list of the one hundred most dangerous terrorists at large in the world today who pose a threat to the United States, regardless of their nationality. Include all available biographical data and everything known or suspected about current location. Have nine copies of this report hand-carried to the White House Situation Room by 0730 on Monday morning."

Goode made a final proofread through the 379 pages of information that he and his team had assembled, and he was fairly confident that their "product" would satisfy their "customer." Though the Vice President didn't say so—and Goode hadn't asked—the old spy was fairly certain that this report, classified TOP SECRET/CODEWORD and innocuously entitled, "100 HVTs," was to be used by the new Commission on Threat Mitigation.

He had been through no less than five drafts of the document in the last ten hours. Over the course of two and a half days, Goode and a handful of his key staff members had debated including this individual and excluding another. There had been some heated exchanges as the experts became advocates for and against certain terrorists. At one point his deputy, Kate Deming, had practically shouted, "Why are we limiting this to just a hundred? We probably have 'the book' on five thousand 'jihadists'—and every one of them is a serious threat to the United States!"

Goode agreed—but patiently reminded them all of their assignment. He had even consulted his old MI6 friend, Joe Blackman—now back in London—regarding some of the names on their list. Now, as he prepared to move the cursor on his computer screen over the "Print" icon, he called Deming in for one last "sanity check."

"Kate, we've all agreed that Dimitri Komulakov belongs on this list. But I want to be sure that we're as certain as possible about the 'Current Location' entry. Why did you put down 'Cuba'? And what are our sources on this?"

Deming said, "I'll be right back," and returned to Goode's office moments later carrying her laptop. Taking a seat in a wooden armchair, she rested the computer on her knees and her fingers flew over the keyboard. After a few dozen keystrokes she said, "Here it is," and looked up at her boss.

"Go ahead," he told her.

"Everything we have on Komulakov's location comes from MI6," Deming said, reading from her computer screen. "We have their 'gate-watcher' report from the Caracas airport that he was last seen boarding a commercial flight to Havana in the company of four men of 'Middle Eastern appearance.' We have an MI6 defector report from Iraq that Komulakov was working with Ali Yunesi, the Director of Iranian intelligence, and we have the DGI defector that MI6 brought in who said that Castro was upset about a Russian KGB general at Lourdes. That's it."

"We have no unilateral confirmation? Nothing from NSA? None of our own sources?" asked Goode.

"No on NSA and nothing from our own stations in Caracas or Havana—but you and I both know our HUMINT collection stinks. We don't have any NOCs down there, and it's hard to collect intelligence on terrorists at embassy cocktail parties. The MI6 stuff is the best we've got."

"So why does Komulakov go to Cuba?" asked Goode. "Is he working with Castro—or was it just a diversion—perhaps a trip to throw us off the trail? And what about the four Middle Eastern males? Were they Iranians?"

Deming looked at her boss and said, "Well, we know that the Iranians have been forging ties to the Valdez regime in Caracas over the past several years. I'd have expected that if they were Iranians they would have gone off with some of the goons working for Valdez, but the MI6 report says they boarded the flight to Havana with Komulakov, and no one has seen or heard from any of 'em since. The only other possible linkage to Cuba is the demand in that missive from the Islamic Brotherhood that the U.S. release all the detainees at Guantanamo."

Goode sat bolt upright in his chair as though he had been shocked by a cattle prod. "Could that be it? Is Komulakov helping the Iranians plan some kind of jailbreak from Guantanamo?"

"Hold on, boss," said Deming. "That's way beyond the scope of this project. Let's get this report into the White House before we chase that rabbit."

"You're right," said Goode. "Print nine copies of the report the way it is. Have one of our couriers run them down to Registry and then deliver them to the White House Situation Room before 0730. After it's gone, tell the crew to head home and get some rest. And Kate, before you go, send a 'tasker' over to DIA. I want the names and backgrounds on every detainee currently held at Guantanamo."

Presidential Commission Townhouse
5 Jackson Place, Washington, DC
Monday, 22 October 2007
0700 Hours Local

With next to no traffic coming into the Capitol, it took Peter Newman less than fifteen minutes to drive his aging Suburban from his townhouse, down Foxhall Road to Canal Drive and then east on the Whitehurst Freeway onto Pennsylvania Avenue. An armed sentry, wearing a blue baseball hat labeled "Uniformed Division, US Secret Service," waved him through the checkpoint at 17th and Penn. As Newman stepped out of his vehicle and walked toward 5 Jackson Place, he could see the back of a tall, muscular African-American man on crutches making his way up the brick sidewalk. The man's left leg appeared to be in some kind of removable cast.

Newman shouted out, "Hey mister! This is a 'No Cripple Zone!' Move along!"

Sgt. Maj. Amos Skillings turned and said with a big smile, "Come a little closer and say that—so I can beat you with my crutch!" And then, feigning penitence he drew himself to attention and said, "Oh, sorry General, didn't recognize you in civilian clothes."

The two men embraced on the sidewalk and then Newman said, admiring Skillings's pin-striped suit and regimental striped tie, "Pretty sharp duds for an old broken-down warrior. I had a bet with General Grisham that you'd be here before 0800 this morning."

"Glad I could help you collect, General."

"Did you have any trouble getting in?"

"No, sir. Flew into Reagan National late last night in the middle of that miserable rainstorm and stayed at my sister's place in Alexandria. Thought that it was going to take me awhile to get here this morning, but there was no traffic at all. Does anyone still come to work in this city?"

"Fewer every day since the Saudi attack," replied Newman grimly. "And it's not getting any better."

By now the two men were in front of the townhouse, and Skillings said, "Nice place you have here, General. How long have you been in these facilities?"

"You mean in minutes or hours?" Newman said, grinning. "I was here for the first time Saturday afternoon and came by yesterday for a few minutes to talk to the guys from DCA and WHCA who are installing computers and communications equipment."

"WA-CA? What's that?" asked Skillings quizzically.

"I know DCA stands for Defense Communications Agency—but what's WA-CA stand for?"

Newman smiled and said, "Welcome to the acronym capital of the universe. It's W-H-C-A, the White House Communications Agency. Come on, I'll show you."

As they went inside, Newman used his photo ID to swipe his code into the electronic door lock system, and it buzzed the two of them in. In the small lobby, Skillings shook hands with the Secret Service agent on duty in the entryway and then took a look at the nearby stairwell, and he asked, "Uh . . . how many floors do you have here?"

"Three," replied Newman.

"And our offices?"

"On the top floor."

Skillings grinned and said, "Great. I should've known." Then using the crutches with something less than the graceful experience of someone who has used the supports before, he headed toward the stairs.

"It's on the top floor," Newman repeated, "but we also have an elevator. Come this way."

Skillings shrugged and said, "Aye aye, sir. They must have put the elevator in for you old folks. I was looking forward to the workout."

"Yeah, right. You can carry me while you're at it," Newman said good-naturedly.

When the elevator doors opened on the top floor, the two stepped into their new "Ops Center." Two WHCA communications technicians in blue coveralls paused from wiring up computers and secure phones and said, "Good morning, sir. We'll be out of here in about half an hour."

Newman introduced Sergeant Major Skillings, and the two men went back to their tasks. There was a steel security door to their right leading to the stairwell and three small glass-windowed offices on their left, facing the "bull pen." Newman pointed to the three office spaces and said, "Yours is the one in the middle. Mine is the one on the left, and the one on the right is for Lieutenant Colonel Hart."

"Lt. Col. Dan Hart, from 2nd Force Recon?" asked Skillings, puzzled.

"Yep," replied Newman. "He'll be here tonight."

"My, my, this is going to be an interesting assignment," said Skillings. "What's in the back?"

"A secure conference room, complete with its own security system. It's been 'Tempest hardened' to prevent eavesdropping. Come on, I'll show you."

As they walked to the rear of the building, Newman added, "It's tight but we can make it work. The only thing I don't like about this setup is that all our communications gear is in what used to be the basement where there was more room, and all we have room for here is our information technology—"

"Computer stuff," Skillings said, nodding.

They arrived at another steel door and Newman punched in a number code, then stood in front of an innocuous smoked-glass plate, mounted at eye level on the wall next to the door. After a second or two the door unlocked with a quiet *thunk*.

Skillings said, "Iris scanner."

"Right," replied Newman as they walked into the sound-deadened space. "Have a seat there on the couch. Let me turn off the alarm system, and I'll be right with you."

"Sir, General Grisham gave me a pretty detailed brief over the secure line before I left Lejeune. He said that we're on a fast track here. When are we expected to be operational?" Skillings asked.

"I don't know the answer to that, Sergeant Major," Newman replied, leaning up against the conference room table. "The Commission that gives us our assignments has its first meeting at 0900 this morning. I was simply told to get this unit up and running as fast as possible."

"Where are the troops going to be billeted?"

"For right now, they're going to be at Quantico—out at Camp Upshur. It's out of the way. There's decent billeting, messing, and plenty of space for training. The first forty-five arrive this afternoon on two C-130s from Lejeune and Fort Bragg. Tonight, we're supposed to get our first SEAL contingent in from Norfolk, and the Delta troopers come in tomorrow from Bragg. We're using the Air Station at Quantico instead of Andrews to keep it out of the news."

"How are the teams set up?" Skillings asked.

"Eventually we're supposed to have a hundred men, fifteen assigned to each of six teams," Newman replied.

"All special ops?"

"Uh-huh . . . You'll know most of the Force Recon guys. I've handpicked all the SEALs, D-Boys, and Rangers. The CIA has also detailed five women to us in case we have to run some 'swallows' against a 'raven,' as the KGB used to say."

Skillings nodded and said, "Let's hope we don't. It's bad enough putting the 'boys' out on these ops. I've never felt right about putting the 'girls' out there with 'em."

Newman shrugged and changed the subject. "How's your ankle?"

"Theoretically three weeks and I can put some weight on it," Skillings replied. "But I heal quickly. I figure I'll be ready for anything in another ten days to two weeks."

"Sure enough, Superman," said Newman with a smile. "Look, we're not going to be doing anything with this outfit for at least two weeks. It will take us that long to sort out where we're going and how we're going to get there—much less what we're going to do when we get to where we're going. I'm going to need you then. I read the orthopedic surgeon's report. He said three weeks before you start therapy. Knowing you, you'll be stir-crazy after ten days. Just to keep you sane, I've got a different sort of assignment for you."

"Whatever you need, General," Skillings replied.

Newman paused and then continued. "The Secret Service is providing security for all the members of the Commission that meets here. They recommended a Personal Security Detail for Rachel and the kids at the house—but she's dead set against a PSD. Instead, she wants to go to the place her folks left her in the Florida Keys. I don't want her driving down there alone. As you've probably heard on the news, people are being held up on the highways just for the gas in their tanks. I just don't feel right about her driving herself and the kids all that way alone. I was wondering—"

"I'd be happy to," Skillings said, finishing Newman's thought. "When would we leave, sir?"

Newman laughed. "Hey, let me at least ask you before you volunteer."

"Yes sir, sorry sir."

"Is that long a drive going to be too painful with that ankle?" said Newman, pointing to the cast.

"Hasn't been so far. I've driven around Lejeune for two days now. I'd be pleased to drive your family and watch over them for you, General."

"Thank you, Amos," said Newman, genuinely relieved. "That's a big burden off my shoulders. Rachel wants to leave in a day or two. The guys at the Pentagon were going to tail her all the way to Florida—and that would have driven Rachel nuts. I figure it should take you no more than five days at a reasonable pace—and by the time you get back, I'll have all your pencils sharpened."

Skillings smiled and said, "What about fuel? That old Suburban of yours has got to be a gas guzzler."

"Well, it's old—but it's also diesel—and we have a DOD-issued fuel ration card. If there's fuel to be had, we're allowed to buy it."

"Ah yes," said Skillings, getting to his feet. "The benefits of military service. You tell Mrs. Newman I'll be ready when she is. Meanwhile, let's get some work done around here, General. What's the next thing that's supposed to be happening?"

Newman looked at his watch. It was 0735. "Well," he said, "in about ten minutes a courier from the White House Situation Room is supposed to deliver the latest intelligence for use by the Commission members when they arrive for their 0900 meeting."

"Intel on what?" asked Skillings as he headed back out the door toward the elevator.

"Apparently," replied Newman as the elevator door opened, "it's the latest HVT listing."

Threat Mitigation Commission
Presidential Commission Townhouse
5 Jackson Place, Washington, DC
Monday, 22 October 2007
1010 Hours Local

The first meeting of the Presidential Commission on Threat Mitigation actually started precisely on time—something unusual in much of official Washington. All of the Commissioners had arrived early, each with their respective Secret Service escort. As they entered, the Chairman—Chief Justice Anthony Scironi—greeted them and then, in turn, introduced them to Brig. Gen. Peter Newman.

Each member of the panel was given a large, red notebook containing a copy of the document that William Goode had prepared over the weekend. The Chairman also admonished them: "This notebook and its contents may not leave this building. Each page is numbered and the document must be returned to Brigadier General Newman or one of his staff anytime you leave the premises. You may not discuss the contents or the material in this notebook with anyone outside this building."

At the start of the formal session, the Chief Justice reiterated the importance of security, then added, "If you will indulge me, gentlemen, I want you to think of yourselves as a jury—and consider the contents of this notebook to be evidence in an indictment—just like a criminal trial. Unless any of you demur, that's how I intend to conduct these meetings."

Scironi paused and looked around the table. He noted that old Gen. Conrad Vassar, the former CJCS was nodding his head as was retired FBI Director, Gerald Donahue. Former Secretary of State James Cook appeared lost in thought. Russell Bates, the retired CIA Director, was paging through the red notebook as though looking for something.

The Chief Justice continued, "With the President's permission, I've added two people to our number as my nonvoting, personal assistants. They will join us this afternoon. Since they're both from this area, their presence here in town should not become an issue for the media. Neal Frey was U.S. Attorney for the District of Columbia before retiring. He has agreed to serve as the 'prosecutor' to clarify any of the information against any of the people charged in this indictment," he said, tapping his copy of the red notebook.

"I've also asked my old friend, Georgetown law professor Richard Chambers, to serve the 'defense attorney' during our deliberations."

At this, Bates emitted a quiet snort. Scironi, peering over his glasses, simply said, "Russell, do you have a problem with that?"

Bates looked right back at the Chief Justice and said,

"I don't know why any of the people in this notebook needs a 'Devil's Advocate.' All of these people deserve to die. That's why we're here."

"If I may, Russell," the Chief Justice responded quietly, and then looking around the room, continued, "all of us—and this includes you, General Newman—are here for a very solemn purpose. We're here to decide whether someone lives or dies. I'm not quite sure what the authors of the bill creating this Commission intended—for debate on the matter was depressingly abbreviated. But I do know what the President told me—and I know my own conscience. We will weigh each individual case presented to us. We will decide each case based on the evidence available—and if we decide that the individual is 'guilty as charged,' General Newman's personnel will carry out the sentence. If any of you do not wish to proceed in this manner, please tell me now so that I may inform the President."

Scironi's soliloquy had the intended effect. Bates nodded his head with the others, and, after a brief pause, the Chief Justice continued, "Gentlemen, inside the red notebook you will find the names of one hundred individuals—and a summary of what our government knows about them. This document was prepared by the CIA, and you will note that the names are listed in alphabetical order. Between now and our next formal session commencing at one thirty this afternoon, I would ask you to peruse this information and come prepared to place them in order of priority, one through one hundred."

Donahue, the former FBI Chief, raised his hand and Scironi nodded and said, "Gerald?"

"What criteria do you want us to use, your honor . . . er, Mr. Chairman? Just thumbing through this notebook since we've been here, I see names that go back to when I was Director—and that's quite awhile."

"I don't want to tell you what criteria to use,"

Scironi responded. "You all have long experience in government. Use your best judgment and assign each name a number. When we reconvene this afternoon I'd like to simply add up the rankings you all assign, and the one with the lowest total will have the highest priority, all the way through to the one with the highest total having the lowest priority. Any questions?"

The only one not nodding his head affirmatively at this point was Russell Bates, who interjected, "What do you suggest we do, Mr. Chairman, if we believe that there are some serious omissions to this list. How do you want us to proceed?"

"I'm not sure that I understand, Russell," answered the Chief Justice. "Do you believe that we need to add some names to this list?"

"Yes, Mr. Chairman, I do," Bates responded emphatically. "Just like Gerry Donahue recalls names from his tenure as the head of the FBI, I have a few of my own from my days at the CIA. I'm asking how we get them on this list."

Scironi sighed and said, "Well, Russell, I was of the opinion that one hundred names was more than enough for us to contend with for the time being, but if you feel strongly about this, or if any of the rest of you wish to add more names to this 'indictment,' I suppose the best way to proceed is for you to give General Newman the names, and he will contact the CIA so that the Agency can provide the same kind of information as we have on these one hundred."

"What if we have sources outside what the CIA knows?" pressed Bates.

The patience of the Chief Justice was wearing thin, but he tried hard not to let his exasperation show. "Well, let's proceed along the following lines. If you will please provide your name or names to General Newman, I'm certain that he will endeavor to amplify your information with whatever our government has, and it will all be added to the notebook. May I inquire whom you wish to add?"

Bates leaned back in his chair and said, "Samuel Mubassa."

Former Secretary of State James Cook reacted as though he had been stuck by a bayonet. Staring at Bates, he said, "The Samuel Mubassa at the UN? If he's a terrorist it's news to me, but if he is, just send the FBI to New York and arrest him."

"First of all, he has diplomatic immunity," replied Bates, almost sneering. "Second, he's not in New York right now—he's in Caracas, Venezuela—very likely cavorting with several others from the Valdez regime who also belong on this list."

Before the meeting could degenerate further, the Chief Justice raised his hand and said, "Very well, gentlemen. Russell, if you would provide your information to General Newman, he'll compile it with whatever the CIA can assemble, and we'll include it in the notebook for our deliberations this afternoon. Are there any other comments or questions before we close this session?"

"Just one, Mr. Chairman," said General Vassar, speaking for the first time. "Perhaps I've been retired too long or I've failed to keep up with the acronym explosion here in Washington, but I'm curious. The title of this document is '100 HVTs.' What does HVT stand for?"

The Chief Justice of the United States looked gravely at the old general and said, "I'm afraid, sir, that acronym is a sad testament to what we're here for. HVT stands for High Value Target. I guess we've just added another one."

No one noticed the smile on Russell Bates's face as he left the room.

Oval Office, The White House
Washington, DC
Monday, 22 October 2007
1130 Hours Local

"Sir, you'd better take a look at this," said Bruce Allen, the President's Chief of Staff, as he entered the Oval Office and walked hurriedly over to the television set across the room. It was already tuned to one of the news channels, but the sound was muted. Allen turned it up.

"—too early to tell. But first, we go to our Middle East correspondent John Corrigan in Baghdad. Tell us about the breaking story over there, John," said the perfectly coiffed and tanned face, sitting at a horseshoe-shaped anchor desk in Atlanta.

"The United States has been given another ultimatum by the Islamic Brotherhood, the same group that exploded a nuclear bomb a week ago today, and on Saturday claimed responsibility for destroying the U.S. Embassy in Riyadh, Saudi Arabia," the correspondent said. Corrigan was standing on a hotel balcony overlooking the city of Baghdad. It was already dark in that part of the world, and the buildings in the background were already lit up. He continued his report. "We've obtained a copy of a videotape that was sent to Al Jazeera studios in the United Arab Emirates this afternoon. The tape claims to be from the Islamic Brotherhood, the organization that issued this newest ultimatum. Here is what they said."

As the control room played the tape, it showed a bearded Arab in dark, clerical robes, reading from a prepared text. His words were in Arabic, but a translator's voiceover gave the message in English: "We send this message to the unholy infidels of America, and to their satanic allies in Great Britain and Israel. You have been warned, and yet you still choose to defy our warnings by trying to ignore us. The holy Islamic Brotherhood has demonstrated its commitment to drive out or destroy all infidels who continue to stay and defile the land where the prophet walked.

"On Monday last we showed you the fire and fury of Allah when we exploded one of our nuclear weapons—a course of action that was taken only after the 'great Satans' did not respond to our ultimatum to leave our lands. Now we give you our final word on this matter.

"Here is the warning to unholy Americans and other infidel nations—if you do not leave all Islamic lands, we will see to it that the next nuclear explosions will take place on *your* lands.

"Each month, beginning with the next month, a nuclear detonation will wreak destruction in one of your cities and kill millions. If you still persist, and do not leave the Islamic lands, another city will be destroyed. And if you continue your defilements, another city—until finally your entire country—will be destroyed. You cannot stop us," the spokesman said, staring directly into the camera lens. "You have been warned. There will be no further warning. If you do not leave Islamic holy lands, then you will die, and your families will die. Your nation will die. In the name of Allah, the Almighty."

The television camera returned to John Corrigan, standing on the balcony overlooking the city of Baghdad, who added, "That tape was given to Al Jazeera this afternoon from a group calling itself the Islamic Brotherhood. That's the third time I've watched the tape today, and it's no less chilling now than when I first saw it."

The picture cut back to the anchor in Atlanta: "John, we noticed that there were a few facts that were different from other information we've been given. Our sources at the White House and CIA have been claiming all along that the only Islamic nation with nuclear weapons is Pakistan, and the White House continues to tell us that Iran doesn't have them—ironically, exactly the opposite of what they told us about Iraq in 2003. And we found out during Operation Iraqi Freedom that Saddam didn't have nuclear weapons. So, John, I guess the question of the day is—just who does have a nuclear arsenal? Who is this voice claiming to speak for all Islamic nations? Do we know anything more about this group calling itself the Islamic Brotherhood? What do the FBI or CIA have to say?"

"Well, concerning the Islamic Brotherhood, out here we're being told that this is a new organization. It has never shown up on the terror watch list before, and apparently nobody in our military or intelligence services knows who they are—or if they *do* know, they aren't telling us," Corrigan said.

"And what about their claim that there's more than the one nuclear weapon—the one they exploded over a remote area of Saudi Arabia last Monday night? What are you hearing from the 'Arab street'? Could this 'Islamic Brotherhood' represent some kind of Muslim coalition? I believe it was Dr. Qadeer Khan, the man who helped Pakistan get the bomb, who had aspirations for an Islamic nuclear arsenal. Do you think that's something that may have happened, John?"

"It's only a guess. Off the record we hear speculation that the Islamic Brotherhood itself is some kind of coalition, but we're also getting a fair share of denials all around. While some in Washington believe that Iran is behind the whole Saudi Arabia crisis, others say no single Arab country—not even Iran—could pull off the creation of nuclear weapons without tipping their hand. Our sources at the U.S. State Department and intelligence agencies say that the administration is pulling out all the stops to contain this crisis and get to the bottom line—the same question you asked of me earlier—'who's behind it all?' Meanwhile, as the crisis continues, the White House seems to be in a state of paralysis. Back to you in Atlanta."

The President's Chief of Staff muted the TV sound once again. "Shall I get Jeb Stuart on the line, sir?" he asked.

The Chief Executive sighed deeply, and then he nodded. "Yeah . . . tell him it looks like another all-nighter in the Sit Room. Tell him to pull the Crisis Team together and meet me there at two o'clock."

CHAPTER ELEVEN

Elevens Everywhere

Guantanamo Naval Base
Guantanamo, Cuba
Tuesday, 23 October 2007
0145 Hours Local

Where did these two 'misfits' come from?" asked
Patrick "P. J." Krull, the CIA's senior interrogator at
"Camp Delta," the U.S. military detention center at
Guantanamo Bay, Cuba. He was looking at a closed-
circuit television monitor in the office of the Camp
Delta executive officer as U.S. Army MPs escorted the
newest "shipment" of detainees into the facility. The
prisoners had just arrived via a USAF C-17, direct from
Jordan.

Lt. Col. Tom Maloney, USMC, the Detention Center's XO peered at the wide-screen TV monitor as a
dozen individuals in orange jumpsuits were paraded
past a row of bright floodlights—and hidden camera
lenses. As Krull and Maloney watched, the disheveled,
bearded men were locked inside 8' x 8' individual
"holding pens" awaiting "in-processing" and medical
evaluation. All were wearing shackles on hands and feet
and around each detainee's neck was a round, white
plastic disc, about ten inches in diameter on which was

emblazoned a number. "Which two?" asked Maloney, now looking closely at the video screen.

"Those last two—numbers 3163 and 7895," Krull said, pointing to the screen.

Maloney manipulated a joystick on the console in front of the TV monitor and the camera zoomed in on two sullen, well-built, fair-skinned, blue-eyed men in their mid-to-late-thirties, now locked inside adjacent isolation cells.

"Hmm . . . they don't look like your typical Taliban, do they?" said Maloney, who then sat down at the nearby computer and entered the registration numbers of the two detainees. Seconds later he said, "No wonder—look at this."

Krull spent some five minutes reading the information that appeared on the screen and asked, "How soon can I send this to the CT Center at Langley?"

"You know the rules, P. J.," said Maloney. "We can't send any of this out until we verify who these guys are and conduct an initial interrogation. Even if we put a priority on these two, it'll be sometime tomorrow."

"OK," Krull replied, "then I need to use your secure phone. You need to find something else to do for five minutes."

Maloney looked at his friend, shrugged his shoulders, and said, "I'm going to go out and get a breath of fresh air. Keep an eye on things here in my office 'til I get back."

As soon as the Marine left, Krull picked up the receiver on Maloney's secure phone and, from memory, punched in a series of numbers on the keypad. After hearing the encryption systems' electronic "hand-shake," a voice on the other end—sounding like it was coming down a long tunnel—answered, "Operations, Stearman. Recording. Go ahead."

"This is Krull at Gitmo. Who is the Senior Staff Duty Officer?"

"Assistant Deputy Director Callahan. He's asleep. Do you want me to put you through to him?"

"Yes."

"Wait one."

Krull heard a click and then the mechanical sound of the extension ringing in the Senior Staff Duty Officer's overnight "Ready Room."

After three "rings" the phone was picked up and Krull heard a voice say, "Callahan."

"This is Krull at Gitmo. It appears that two detainees who just arrived here may have been involved in the Saudi caper."

Krull could tell that the deputy director was still not quite awake, and he could hear him rummaging around for his glasses and turning on the lamp on the bedside table. He was probably also digging out his note pad and a pen. When he asked, "Who are the two men?" Krull knew that Callahan was ready to take notes.

"They are apparently Ukrainians, captured last Thursday, 18 October, off the coast of Lebanon," Krull answered.

Callahan, now fully awake, asked, "Captured? Captured by whom?"

"By the Israeli Navy. These two were in a speedboat, apparently trying to make their way north to Syria when the IDF naval patrol picked them up." Krull, reading from Maloney's computer screen, continued: "According to the info that we have from the Israelis, these two tossed their weapons in the drink when the naval patrol approached, but they kept a bag containing $72,000 in U.S. fifty-dollar bills. The IDF brought them back to the Duvdevan base outside Tel Aviv, suspecting that they might be foreign operatives working for the Syrians or even Chechnyans doing 'bang-bang' for Hezbollah. Both of 'em tested positive for nitrate residue on a standard paraffin test, and their genome blood test came back showing that they were Ukrainians, so the Mossad sweated 'em with psychotropic drugs for the next thirty-six hours straight."

"Did 'our colleagues' ever figure out what these guys were doing in Lebanon?" asked Callahan.

"Oh yeah," replied Krull. "They used a combination of scopalamine, benzadrine, and thiopental sodium—sodium pentothal—and both of 'em sang like canaries. They were apparently sent to Beirut to assassinate several members of the Saudi royal family and seize their royal yacht. Apparently these guys weren't quite as good as they thought they were. They killed the 'royals,' but the yacht caught fire in the gunfight and sank."

"How did they end up in Gitmo?" asked the CIA's increasingly concerned Assistant Operations Director.

"It isn't pretty," said Krull. "Once the Israelis figured out the connection to the Saudi mess, they contacted our military attaché in Tel Aviv, and he apparently unilaterally arranged to have these two characters transported to the U.S. military facility at the King Hussein Military Airfield outside of Amman. Yesterday afternoon SOCOM diverted a regular detainee flight to Amman and put these two clowns aboard. I became aware when they arrived here at Gitmo less than an hour ago."

"Oh great," said Callahan. "So the Jordanians are aware of all this?"

"It doesn't say—"

"Are you *reading* from something?" Callahan interrupted.

"Yes, sir," Krull answered. "All this is in the DTI."

"This is all in the Detainee Transmittal Information?" Callahan sounded physically pained. "Good grief! The Congressional committees are going to skin us alive over this one. What else is written down that we're going to have to answer for?"

"The whole Israeli debrief is attached."

"Oh man!" exclaimed Callahan. "There's going to be

serious repercussions on this one when the press finds out about these guys. Have the ICRC reps down there seen these two people yet?"

"No, and that's why I called," said Krull. "Right now, our hands are clean on these two. Neither Tel Aviv nor Amman stations were even informed about these guys. It's all been handled in military channels. But I want to have these two pulled out of the military side of this place and taken to *our* facility."

"Why?" asked the older spy turned CIA bureaucrat. "What's in it for us besides trouble? Why would we even want to talk to these guys?"

"Because, according to the Mossad interrogation report—which I'm guessing is the result of their psychotropic drugs—these two are apparently part of a much bigger operation," replied Krull. "Separately, they both admitted to being recruited last year by Nikolai Dubzhuko—a retired KGB colonel who is known to have worked for—"

"Wait a minute! Let me think," interrupted Callahan. "Dubzhuko . . . Dubzhuko . . . Ah-h yes—Dimitri Komulakov! Dubzhuko worked for Komulakov years ago—and purportedly still does," the older man recalled, suddenly intrigued. "What else did the Mossad get out of these two Ukrainians?"

Krull read down further in the interrogation debrief and said, "I'm summarizing here . . . The royal yacht they were after was to have been taken to a boatyard in Bilbao, Portugal, where it was to have been given a new name, paint job, and registry number—and then turned over to a 'special crew' that would be arriving on 1 November—are you ready for this—from Iran."

"An Iranian crew?" said Callahan. "What the devil do the Iranians want with a Saudi royal yacht?"

"The interrogation transcript doesn't say," replied Krull. "But I'd like to take these two 'off to the side' for a few days to see if we can find out."

There was a long pause while Callahan contemplated the consequences for the Agency, and himself, of authorizing two Israeli-captured, drug-interrogated Ukrainians, spirited through Jordan—to be held incommunicado at Gitmo. He finally said, "Go ahead and make the arrangements, P. J. I'll draft up a quick message to DOD telling the military what we're doing—but remember, these guys had better be in good shape when the ICRC finds out about 'em. What are their detainee numbers again?"

"3163 and 7895," answered Krull.

"OK, P. J., anything else I should put in this report for Bill Goode when he comes in a few hours from now?"

"Just one more thing. Apparently the boat these two were after is just one of several yachts and airplanes that were to have been seized."

"Does it say how many in all?" asked Callahan.

There was a pause while the field officer scrolled back through the interrogation report. "Yeah, here it is," said Krull. "Eleven."

Threat Mitigation Commission
Presidential Commission Townhouse
5 Jackson Place, Washington, DC
Tuesday, 23 October 2007
1410 Hours Local

"Then it's decided," said Chief Justice Anthony Scironi, sounding resigned. "The seven persons on the list before you are guilty of the crime of terrorism against the United States and are condemned to death. Once again, I ask you to affirm your verdict by so indicating when you are polled by Mr. Frey."

Neal Frey, the former U.S. Attorney for the District of Columbia, looked up from his notes and then around the room. He had spent nearly seven hours over the past two days presenting a bill of particulars against ten individuals whose "indictments" were in the red notebooks before each of the Commissioners. Then, Georgetown law professor Richard Chambers had proffered reasons why these ten should not "suffer the ultimate sanction"—as he had put it.

Chambers had made every argument he could think of to spare the lives of the first ten to be "judged" by the Commission. Several, he pointed out, had families and young children who might well be killed or wounded while the Commission's Special Ops were "carrying out the sentence of this Body." And in three cases, the Commissioners were sufficiently swayed by Chambers's line of reasoning that they decided to "defer a verdict until more information is made available." The trio would remain in the red notebooks— but with a stay of execution.

"General Vassar, your verdict on the remaining seven names on the list?" said Frey, looking at the former Chairman of the Joint Chiefs of Staff.

The old general grimaced and said, "Guilty."

"Mr. Donahue?"

"Guilty."

"Mr. Cook?"

"Guilty."

"Mr. Bates?"

"Guilty."

Finally, Frey turned to the Chief Justice and said, "Mr. Chairman, according to the rules adopted by this Commission, the seven persons on the list before you have been found guilty of the crime of terrorism, for which they are condemned to death."

Scironi nodded gravely and said, "Thank you, Mr. Frey . . . Mr. Donahue. You are both excused until tomorrow morning when we take up consideration of the next ten individuals named in this . . ." and tapping the red notebook in front of him on the conference room table, the Chief Justice concluded, ". . . this indictment."

After Frey and Donahue excused themselves and left the room, the Chief Justice turned to Peter Newman, handed him a single, folded sheet of paper, and said, "General, you have heard the verdict of this Commission. The seven individuals named on that document have been condemned to death. In accordance with the law that created this body, you are hereby ordered to carry out the sentence."

Newman had been summoned to the conference room when the Commissioners returned from a brief recess for lunch. The Chief Justice had called and told him that the first of the verdicts were going to be handed down early in the afternoon and that he should be present for the decision. Now, the Marine rose from his seat by the window, said, "Aye aye, sir," and started for the door.

But before Newman could exit the room, Russell Bates said, "Mr. Chairman, a procedural question."

"Yes, Russell?" said the Chief Justice, looking over his reading glasses at the former CIA Chief.

"Mr. Chairman, don't we need to make clear the sequential order in which these sentences are to be carried out?" asked Bates.

For more than twenty-four hours Scironi had been trying to keep these strong-willed Commissioners in line and focused on the task at hand. On Monday afternoon they had established the priority in which the cases would be determined and had decided, based on input from Frey and Donahue, to take them ten at a time. Throughout the process of presenting the evidence "for" and "against" the accused, Bates had been adamant about only one—Samuel Mubassa.

The information against Mubassa provided by the CIA had been sparse to say the least—and Frey had said so. But when the Commission convened this morning, Bates brought in a sheaf of papers that he said "proved conclusively that Mubassa was one of the most secretive and dangerous financiers of Islamic terrorism in the world today."

When Donahue protested the inclusion of "independently compiled evidence," the Commission split two-against-two on whether the "new information" could be used in the case against Mubassa. In the interest of moving things along, Scironi had broken the tie, and voted with Bates and former FBI Director Donahue to allow the evidence to be considered.

But now, the Chief Justice wasn't so sure he'd made the right decision. In response to Bates's query about the order in which the sentences were to be carried out, Scironi asked a question of his own: "Why does it matter, Russell? Don't you trust General Newman to expeditiously fulfill his responsibilities under the law?"

Bates suddenly realized that he was pushing too hard—and was inviting suspicion upon himself. He looked from Scironi to Newman, now standing by the door, and said sullenly, "I just want to be sure that the most dangerous threats are dealt with first."

"I'm sure that's exactly what General Newman will do," replied the Chief Justice.

Operations Directorate, 7th Floor, CIA HQ
Langley, VA
Tuesday, 23 October 2007
1630 Hours Local

"What have you got for me?" William Goode asked the two women who had just knocked on his open door. Kate Deming, his principal deputy, was standing beside Iris Collins, one of the best analysts in the Operations

Directorate. Collins had done her Ph.D. thesis at MIT in mathematics.

"Well, I'm not sure what we found," Deming replied. "It's really rather strange—even spooky, but if you have a few minutes, I'd like to have Iris explain it to you before we go any further."

Goode set aside the interrogation debrief that he had just received from Guantanamo, arose and motioned them to seats at a round table on the other side of his office. Collins began, "I did a full database search, just as you asked me, going back to the beginning of modern Islamic terrorism in the 1970s. You were right—they really do have what appears to be a fixation on the number eleven. For example: 'New York City' has eleven letters; 'Ramzi Yusouf'—the terrorist behind the 1993 attack on the World Trade Center—"

"I get it," Goode said. "They both have eleven letters. Tell me what else you found."

"Yes, sir . . . there are many more," she said, " 'George W. Bush,' 'Colin Powell,' 'nuclear bomb,' 'Saudi Arabia'—all eleven letters—and I now have compiled a list of three hundred and two dates, names, and places that are linked to radical Islamic terrorism—including 'Afghanistan,' 'the Pentagon,'—*all of them* with eleven letters," she said, breathlessly.

Goode noticed that her eyes were wide from lack of sleep and too much caffeine. He said, "Iris, take a deep breath. This sounds to me like the stuff of pure coincidence—the kind of thing that conspiracy theorists incubate."

"Well, I considered that when I first started my analysis, but that's only a tiny part of my resource material," Iris said. "Most of what I have used comes from CIA and FBI database documents, and includes material taken from interrogation interviews and field reports," she added.

"OK, but I'm guessing that you could do a computer run that would find a string of names and places that had some kind of link to almost any number you used," Goode told her.

"Then what about *these*, sir?" Collins held up another sheaf of paper and began to read from one of the printouts in a quick staccato cadence, "New York was the eleventh state to become part of the U.S. The words 'Trade Center' have eleven letters. The first plane that crashed into the Trade Center was flight number eleven. It was carrying 92 passengers—nine plus two equals eleven. Flight number 77 hit the other tower, which is eleven times seven. It had sixty-five passengers—or six plus five—eleven. The total number of victims in both planes was 254. And September eleventh was the 254th day of the year—two plus five plus four, in both cases, is eleven. And from September eleventh to the end of the year, there are a hundred and *eleven* days."

"Interesting," said Goode, "but I find it hard to believe that the perpetrators of 9/11 were somehow able to orchestrate and coordinate all of those 'elevens' into that event."

"That's not what I'm suggesting, sir," Collins replied. "What this data search and accompanying analysis seems to indicate is that radical Islamic groups intentionally initiate dramatic terror events so that they are coincident with the number eleven—meaning a date or a place or both. Then, in the aftermath, while the world press is reporting on the attack, their sheiks, imams, mullahs, ayatollahs, their Web sites and other propaganda organs connect other coincidental 'elevens' to the event, claiming an even greater correlation. In the minds of their adherents—particularly those who are illiterate or superstitious—such connections tend to give those who plan and conduct the attacks near mystical powers. For example, the Madrid train attack in March 2004. There were eleven bombs planted—though not all detonated. The attack was perpetrated on the eleventh of March—exactly *911 days* since the U.S. attacks happened on 9/11. And 191 civilians were killed that day—one plus nine plus one equals eleven. Great significance was attached to these connections in the radical Islamic media, which went even further by falsely asserting that 111 people were killed at precisely 11:00 a.m. in the morning."

Goode had to admit that these facts were beginning to outweigh his skepticism. He turned to Deming and asked, "Do we have anything on *why* these 'jihadists' are so enamored with the number eleven, Kate? Why *do* they put so much emphasis on the number eleven? Does it have a religious significance? Is it some kind of a code? What's the link?"

Deming, who had served most of her career in the Middle East, replied, "The number eleven is linked in much of the Orient and Middle East to mystery and power, and has been since ancient times—well before Judaism, Christianity, or Islam. It's considered a master number. All forms of ancient studies of numbers—including mysticism, occultism, numerology, and the so-called secret wisdom of Kabala—all give significance to the number eleven, and numbers that can be divided or multiplied by eleven—like twenty-two, thirty-three, and so forth.

"Al Qaeda adherents rely heavily on the significance of the number. Osama bin Laden seems to have based his life on eleven-year cycles," Deming said. "When he was eleven, his father died in a plane crash, and he claims that's when he first became aware of a messianic mission to purify Islamic lands for Mohammed. Eleven years later, when he was twenty-two, the Soviets invaded Afghanistan, and bin Laden says he was 'driven' to expelling them from the country. We know that he never led a column of Mujahadeen against the Soviets as he maintains, but his followers don't seem to care much about the truth. When he was thirty-three, eleven years later, Saddam invaded Kuwait, and bin Laden was enraged when 'infidels' of America and Great Britain 'invaded' Saudi Arabia, then 'occupied' Kuwait, and in the process 'defiled their most holy lands.' And eleven years after that, when he was forty-four, we had 9/11."

Goode was nodding as he listened carefully. "Is bin Laden's the only Islamic terror group with this 'eleven fixation'?" he asked.

"Not at all," Deming replied. "The PLO, Hamas, Islamic Jihad, and Hezbollah all give prominence to September 11, 1922, the date when the British issued the Mandate of Palestine. The literature from all these groups charge that by changing boundaries of Islamic nations to satisfy 'Zionist Infidels' more than 100,000 Muslims were killed outright by the British, and most of the militant Islamic Web sites claim that three million have been made homeless since then. That's another reason that the date and the number eleven have significance."

When Deming paused, Iris Collins picked up, "And exactly fifty years later we were introduced to what we might call 'modern Islamic terror'—during the 1972 Munich Olympic Games."

"That was before you were born, Iris," said Goode with a smile.

"Yes, sir," said Collins without missing a beat. "According to my data, the Olympic games were scheduled to end on September eleventh, and . . ." she paused to check her notes, then added, "there were 121 countries that participated—"

"Which is eleven times eleven," Goode said, beating her to the punch.

Undeterred, Collins concluded, "And there were *eleven* Israeli athletes killed by the terrorists."

Impressed, Goode asked, "Have you worked out any probability factors, Iris?"

She nodded and handed him a single 8 ½ x 11 sheet of paper. It read:

The Significance of the Number Eleven
in Radical Islamic Terror Attacks
IX. Summary Probability of Coincidence

1. This computer-generated probability analysis is based on 845 historical, anecdotal, and database accounts of radical Islamic terror events.

2. All duplications were purged before the final analysis.

3. The analysis also sampled 3,497 non-Islamic terror events since 1972 (M-19, Boeder Mienhoff, Red Army Faction, F-17, FMLN, Red Brigades, Sendoro Luminoso, FARC, etc.) and found only fifteen such events that correlated in any way with the number eleven.

4. In forty-seven of 845 Islamic terror events, no correlation with the number eleven could be established, yielding an error factor of .05563, which has been programmed into the final probability analysis.

5. Nonfactual data, disinformation, mythic and/or disputed examples accounted for 2.635 percent of total content and were discounted for the analysis.

6. The computer ran 200 different probability tests based on the final numerical values of these data, and then the results were averaged for a weighted single probability analysis.

Conclusion: The probability of a future Islamic terror event correlating directly with the number eleven is 94.5 percent. The most likely coincidence is a date in which the number eleven is a base numeral or a master number.

Goode finished reading the summary, looked up at his two assistants, and said, "So the bottom line here is that the next radical Islamic terror attack is most likely to take place on the eleventh or twenty-second of any given month?"

"Or on the twenty-ninth day of any month, for example, where the two integers add up to eleven, or on a date such as 3 Jan 2007—which can be written '03/01/07'—all of which adds up to eleven," said Collins.

"So tomorrow morning," Goode said, "when I'm at that meeting in the White House Situation Room and the President asks when to expect the next attack in this jihad, I should tell him that it is likely to happen next Monday, on the twenty-ninth of this month?"

Collins looked him dead in the eye and said without a moment's hesitation: "No, sir. The twenty-ninth is a possibility. But this probability analysis indicates that the most likely date for the next major attack by Islamic radicals is the eleventh of *next* month—or eleven-eleven."

"And do we dare hazard a guess where it might occur?" asked Goode.

There was a moment of silence, then Deming said, "A place with eleven letters . . ."

Collins finished the thought, ". . . like New York City."

Newman Residence
Foxhall Road, Washington, DC
Wednesday, 24 October 2007
0630 Hours Local

As usual, Peter Newman began the day early. He rose from bed at 0500, put on his PT gear, slipped quietly out of the house, and ran five miles in the cool, clear darkness before returning home. He placed a load of luggage in the old Suburban, then went inside to take a shower and shave. By the time he was dressed, dawn was breaking and Rachel, Sgt. Maj. Amos Skillings, and the children had eaten breakfast and cleared the table.

As she was putting their dirty dishes in the dishwasher, she playfully told her husband, "When you finish eating, General, you can put *your* dishes in and press the little button to turn it on. We're all confident that you can handle this assignment."

To the children's delight, Skillings had spent the night in the family's guestroom. Now he was trying to figure out how to carry his overnight bag out to the Suburban sitting in the driveway, while still balancing on his crutches. Newman called out to him, "Sergeant Major! Leave that baggage alone. That's an order."

Skillings looked up, rolled his eyes, and smiled. He said, "Aye aye, sir," and put the duffel bag down.

"Amos," Newman said to him gently, "please . . . you can't do the things you'd normally do. Rachel and the kids can carry their own bags. I helped her pack so that she could lift each of them. I mean it . . . no lifting. I want that foot of yours to heal, so follow the doc's orders—don't put your weight on it, and don't try to carry anything while you're on crutches."

The big man smiled broadly as young James picked up the sergeant major's duffel bag and half carried, half dragged it outside to the waiting Suburban, and then came back inside for his sister's backpack.

As Newman walked his wife and children out to the Suburban he said, "Honey, are you all set for the road? You've got some cash . . . gas tank's filled?"

"Are you losing it, my graying general?" she asked. "You don't remember filling the gas tank last night and going to the ATM for me?"

They both laughed. "I guess I'm a little preoccupied," he admitted. "Got your cell phone . . . and it's charged?"

"Yes, *Father*," she said, "and I've pinned my name on my mittens."

"All right," he laughed. "I get the point."

Newman turned serious when he looked at Skillings.

"Take good care of them for me, Sergeant Major. I don't know what I'd be doing if it weren't for you."

"General, you've got more than enough on your plate," Skillings replied. "Don't worry about us. We're going to take it easy all the way down I-95 to Miami and then out Route 1 to the Keys. Mrs. Newman and I talked it over at breakfast, and we're going to spell each other at the wheel. Ordinarily I'd drive right through, but she said you wanted to break up the trip."

"Yeah, it's a lot better to sleep in a motel than the back of a car. I'm just concerned that even with a DOD ration card, there may not be fuel available in some places. There isn't likely to be much traffic with gas prices the way they are, but things aren't the way they are supposed to be out there."

"Well, I think we can handle whatever problems come up," said Skillings, raising his sweater so that Newman could see the H&K .45 ACP Mk 23, Mod 0 pistol—the standard offensive handgun used by SOCOM—hanging from a shoulder holster.

Newman nodded and Skillings continued, "I have my D-DACT with me so you can see precisely where we are by our GPS plot—right down to a ten-digit grid coordinate. The main thing, sir, is not to worry. I'm like the insurance company—they're in good hands."

"That I know, Amos."

"Well, you're in good hands too, sir. While you were running this morning, Mrs. Newman prayed before breakfast, and her words were, 'Lord, keep him safe and in Your hands.' "

As Sergeant Major Skillings hoisted himself into the front passenger seat, Peter put Lizzie in her seat, checked James's seat belt, kissed both children, and came to his wife's open window on the driver's side of the big SUV. They kissed briefly and he said, "God-speed, and keep you all safe, honey."

Rachel, perched in the high vehicle, looked at her

husband and said, "You too, Peter. Thank you for arranging to have Amos accompany us. Now do me one last favor . . ."

"What's that?"

"Don't do anything heroic while we're away," she said with a smile.

"I promise, I'll see to it that I'm bored to tears."

Rachel nodded, said, "Good," and the big diesel belched black smoke as it clattered to life.

Newman watched them pull out of the driveway and head toward Foxhall Road. As he turned toward the house to lock up, the cell phone on his belt intruded on his thoughts. He glanced at the tiny screen that said "Unidentified Caller," shrugged, pressed the green button on the touchpad and said, "Newman . . ."

"General, so good of you to take my call so early in the morning. I hope I'm not interrupting something," said a voice coated with southern syrup.

"No problem," said the Marine. "Who is this?"

"Oh, ah am so sah-ry for bein' so rude," drawled the voice. "This is Senator James Waggoner. Do you have a moment?"

Newman had met the Chairman of the Senate Select Committee on Intelligence only once—while accompanying DHS Secretary Sarah Dornin when she testified before the committee. Now he recognized the southern twang.

"Yes, Mr. Chairman, but before you tell me why you called, a quick reminder—this is a nonsecure cell phone."

"That's no problem, son, this here is a social call," replied the senator. "Ah know y'all were given seven exciting opportunities to serve our country yesterday afternoon, and ah just want to make sure y'all have your priorities straight as to which of those seven problems needs to be handled first."

Newman was instantly alarmed. He had no doubt that

Waggoner was referring to the list of seven terrorists who had been condemned to death by the Threat Mitigation Commission on Tuesday afternoon. Not only was this fact supposed to be a closely guarded secret—but so too was his identity as the head of the Special Unit. Somehow, a serious security breach had already occurred.

"Well, Senator," Newman started to reply, "that's just not something I can talk—"

"Now listen here, Brigadier General Newman," Waggoner interrupted—the southern charm suddenly gone, "I don't have time for any nonsense here. Your number-one priority has to be the fourth one on that list. I'm sure you know that I also serve on the Armed Forces Committee that has to consent to every military promotion."

Newman let the reference to military promotions—and undoubtedly a threat for his own future promotion—slide by. He was trying to recall the list of seven men sentenced to death that he had handed to Lt. Col. Dan Hart the previous afternoon. The fourth name on the list stood out in his memory because it seemed so anomalous. Six of the seven were Middle Eastern terrorists. But the fourth person was from Nigeria: Samuel Mubassa.

"Be assured, Senator, there won't be any 'nonsense' as you put it. I will also—"

"Good," interrupted Waggoner again. "Ah just knew y'all would do the right thing, General. Thank you for your time. Good day."

The line went dead and Newman slid the phone back into its holster, concerned about the leaked information of the list and his role with the Commission. As he walked up the steps it occurred to him that he had already broken the promise he had made to his wife just minutes ago.

Situation Room
The White House, Washington, DC
Wednesday, 24 October 2007
0900 Hours Local

The President arrived precisely on time and began the Crisis Team meeting by turning to his Director of National Intelligence and saying, "What's the latest?"

Perry Straw cleared his throat and began, "At our Monday afternoon meeting you directed us to analyze the threat from the Islamic Brotherhood on that tape aired by Al Jazeera. We have identified the individual on the tape as Sheikh Abu Bakr al Fawaz—a radical Wahhabi cleric and so-called scholar. He was last known to be in Mecca—though that was several months ago."

"So the bottom line is that we don't know where he is now?" asked the President.

"No, sir," replied the DNI.

The President grimaced, nodded his head, and said, "Look, what's most important is the claim by this 'Islamic Brotherhood' that they are going to start detonating nuclear weapons here. We've had to close the exchanges and banks again. According to the report I got from Commerce yesterday, 40 percent of our inner-city businesses are shut down. Last night in downtown Detroit, every commercial establishment in a five-block area was looted—then burned. The Justice Department says that 'Blue Flu' is becoming endemic. According to DHS, hospitals are reporting high absenteeism among emergency medical 'first responders.' Is this threat real, is what we've got to know."

Straw looked up from his briefing notes and responded almost formally, "The Office of National Intelligence continues to discount the likelihood that this Islamic Brotherhood group has nuclear weapons."

The President looked around the table and said, "Do we have agreement on that?"

"No, sir, we don't," said the Defense Secretary.

"Dan, what does DOD say?"

Powers, as usual speaking without the aid of notes, replied, "We are increasingly convinced that the Islamic Brotherhood is a front for Iranians intent on establishing a Caliphate in the Middle East."

"And you believe that the Iranians have more nuclear weapons?" asked the President.

"Yes, sir," said Powers. "And as a consequence of our work with the CIA Operations Directorate in support of military operations in Saudi Arabia, we think that we're closer to proving it."

"How?" said a clearly agitated Perry Straw.

Powers ignored the question. Still speaking directly to the President, the SecDef said, "We've been working closely with Bill Goode, the Ops Deputy at Langley. I'd rather he summarized this for you, sir."

The President turned to Goode, who was sitting behind General Grisham, and said, "Bill?"

Goode arose from his chair and said, "Mr. President, I'll make this very brief and I would ask everyone here to please take no notes. First, we have strong evidence that Iranians have acquired Soviet-era nuclear weapons. Second, we have believable interrogation reports that several hundred former or current members of the Russian intelligence service are involved with helping the Iranians. Third, the Iranians are likely—as Secretary Powers just said—to be using this 'Islamic Brotherhood' as a cover for their own activities. Fourth, the Iranians—operating as the Islamic Brotherhood—intend to use nuclear weapons against us, and the weapons are to be delivered to the United States in vessels and aircraft that the Iranians' mercenaries have seized from the Saudi royal family. And fifth, the most likely timing for a major attack is November eleventh."

The room was totally silent as Goode sat down.

After a moment of silence the President turned back

to the SecDef and said, "Dan, is this an assessment that you accept?"

"Yes, sir," Powers responded. "We've now got every available intelligence asset and Special Ops team that we can spare from all of the services looking for these boats and aircraft. We've got the Navy and Coast Guard on alert to check vessels that meet the specs of the Saudi yachts that were stolen. We've got our satellites checking for IFF transponders that fit the frequency ID and tail numbers of the aircraft that are missing. They might repaint the planes, but switching out IFF transponders is a bit more problematic. It'll be like hunting needles in a haystack, but we're on it."

"Anything else?" the President asked.

"Well, sir . . ." Powers said hesitantly.

"Yes, Dan . . . what is it?"

"Sir, I think that with the Iranians planning to use nuclear weapons against the United States, that we must consider initiating a preemptive strike against them. At a minimum, I think we have to take out their nuclear development center northeast of Tehran and their Shabaz missile facilities."

The President did not answer. His face was thoughtful, however, and those in the room could see that he was considering the proposal. After a moment's thought he said, "I don't know, Dan. It might be best if we quietly encouraged the Israelis to do it—like they did when they took out the Iraqi nuclear weapons facility at Osirik in 1981."

"Mr. President, if I may respond . . ." the Secretary of State interjected.

"Go ahead, Helen."

"I do not believe that a preemptive strike on Iran would be wise. If you thought the opposition to our going into Iraq was negative, wait 'til you see the world's reaction to bombing Tehran. I'm not sure that we could do it without getting a retaliatory response from Korea—or even Russia, China—maybe even Pakistan."

The President made his decision, "Dan, give me some other military options that stop short of a direct attack on Iran. And the rest of you, please have your options to me by tomorrow morning. We'll meet again at nine, unless the situation gets out of control."

CHAPTER TWELVE

Needles and Haystacks

Lourdes Signals Intelligence Facility
Bejucal, Cuba
Thursday, 25 October 2007
0720 Hours Local

Please forgive the disturbance, Comrade General," said Mikhail Vushneshko, garbed in the "tropical field uniform" of the Russian Military Intelligence service as Dimitri Komulakov opened the door to his quarters.

Despite his fatigue from being up most of the night, Komulakov smiled at hearing himself addressed by the word *comrade*—a term no longer in use in the "new" Russian military. But he replied, "Please come in, Mikhail, you are, after all, my host here on this island paradise."

"Ah yes, General," replied Vushneshko, "I may be the 'commanding officer' of this Listening Post, but you, sir, are our guest of honor. I would not want Moscow to think I was not providing appropriate hospitality."

"You and your contingent have been most generous— and I shall be sure that our superiors are aware of our appreciation," Komulakov replied, motioning the younger man into the room and closing the door. "I hope that the occasion of your early morning visit is not a problem we have created for you."

"Not at all," said Vushneshko. "We have a few more mouths to feed, and we're using a bit more water for drinking and bathing, but that is not what brings me here. I would not disturb you except that when you arrived here you asked me to notify you if our systems intercepted any American communications traffic that might indicate some awareness of your mission."

"Yes, that's true," said Komulakov. "We're of course picking up their commercial radio and television broadcasts from the equipment we brought with us. But I thought that any of their encrypted military and government communications picked up by your antennas were automatically shipped directly to Centre for decryption and translation."

"That is correct, General. But this was not an encrypted communication—it was a 'nonsecure' cell phone conversation, picked up by our service in Washington," replied Vushneshko, handing Komulakov a single sheet of paper.

"How was this intercepted—at our embassy?" asked the "retired" KGB general, putting on his reading glasses.

"It doesn't say—but that's most likely, since it took twenty-four hours to get here. Normally we wouldn't get something like this unless it pertained to our normal mission here. Someone at Centre must have seen a keyword in it and sent it to me to pass directly to you."

Komulakov looked at the sheet, started reading, and asked, "Who is 'DK Moray'?"

Vushneshko smiled as he said, "That's our codeword for you."

The general resumed reading. Even though the interpreter had failed to capture proper American-English spelling or punctuation, Komulakov instantly realized why the transcript had been forwarded to him:

FROM: MINZ SERVICE CTR
TO: 501.7L
INSTRUCTION: PASS TO DK MORAY IMMEDIATE
ITEM: INTERCEPTED USCELTELCON, POTOMAC BASIN REGION
A = INITIATOR: B = RECIPIENT TRANSCRIPT: B: "NEW MAN"

A: "GENERAL SO GOOD OF YOU TWO TAKE MY CALL SO EARLY IN MOURNING. I HOP I'M NOT INTERPRETING SOMETHING"

B: "NO PROBLEM. WHO THIDS"

A: "OH, AH AM SO SORROW FOUR BIN SO RUDE. THIS IS SENATOR JAMES WAGGONER, DO YOU HAVE A MOMEN?"

B: "YES, MR. CHAIRMAN, BUT BEE FOUR YOU TELL ME Y U CALLED, A CLICK REMINDER—THIS IS ANON SEA CURE CELL PHONE."

A: "THAT'S NO PROBLEM, SUN. THIS HERE IS A SOCIAL-IST CULL. AH NO YAWL WERE GIVEN SEVEN EXACT-ING OPPORTUNITIES TO SERVE YOU ARE COUNTRY YESTERDAY AFTER NOON AND I JUST WANT TO MAKE SHEAR YAWL HAVE YOUR PRIORITIES STRAIGHT AS TWO INCH OF THOSE SEVEN PROBLEMS NEEDS TO BE HANDLED FIRST."

B: "WELL SENATOR THAT'S JUST NOT SOME THING I CAN TALK"

A: "NOW LISTEN HERE, BRIGADIER GENERAL NEW MAN I DON'T HAVE TIME FOR ANY NONSENSE HEAR. YOUR NUMBER-ONE PRIORITY HAS TWO BEE THE FORTH ONE ON THAT LIST. I'M SURE YOU KNOW THAT I ALSO SERVE ON THE ARMED FORCES COMMITTEE THAT HAS TWO CONSENT TO EVERY MILITARY PROMO-TION."

B: "BE ASSURED, SENATOR, THERE WON'T BE ANY 'NONSENSE' AS YOU PUT IT I WILL ALSO"

A: "GOOD AH JUST KNEW Y'ALL WOOD DO THE RIGHT THING, GENERAL THANK YOU FOR YOUR TIME. GOOD DAY."

For several seconds after he finished reading the words on the piece of paper, Komulakov just stared forward, saying nothing. Finally Vushneshko cleared his throat and said, "Will there be anything else, General?"

The older man looked at the communications spook and said, distantly, "From where do I know this name—Waggoner?"

Vushneshko replied, "I believe he is the chairman of the Intelligence Committee of their legislature. I have seen his name many times in the past. He apparently likes to use the telephone. Didn't their press recently say that he was the man who drafted a new secret law authorizing their government to assassinate opponents?"

"Ah yes," said Komulakov recalling now, as a thin smile appeared on his lips. "He is sometimes mentioned as a possible candidate for president of their bourgeois government. Thank you for bringing this to me, Mikhail Vushneshko. Please let me know immediately if you come across anything else we have on either of these names."

"Waggoner and this General New Man?—his sounds like a code name," asserted Vushneshko.

"It's Newman—all one word," replied Komulakov, "and he is a very dangerous person."

Headquarters, National Intelligence Directorate
Madrid, Spain
Thursday, 25 October 2007
1530 Hours Local

Roberto Calderon was a creature of habit, though it was not a quality admired by his superiors in DINA—

the Spanish government's Directorate of National Intelligence. Nonetheless, as he prepared to leave for his midday meal and a short siesta, he did as his usual practice demanded and checked his voice mail before heading off to the *Cabo Tiñoso* restaurant. There was only one message on his machine: "Roberto, it's William from the Fellowship, please give me a call whenever you receive this message. May He bless your work."

That was all. Nonetheless, Calderon smiled to himself. The voice was that of his old friend William Goode. They had first met in 1981, when Goode was the "Political Officer" at the American Embassy in Dakar, Senegal—and Calderon was a junior officer in the Spanish Intelligence Service—sent to Africa to see what the Communists were up to in Guinea Bissau and Mozambique. Goode had introduced the Spaniard to the Fellowship of Believers, and they had met again during a pilgrimage to the Holy Land in 1990. They had sailed together from Israel back to Spain on Goode's sloop, *Pescador*. During the voyage, Calderon had been moved by the older man's simplicity and faith. The two had stayed in touch over the years, but it wasn't until 2004 that Calderon realized that Goode was a senior American intelligence officer.

Within hours of the Madrid train bombings on 11 March that year, Goode had appeared at the DINA Headquarters, leading a delegation of American CIA, FBI, and Justice Department investigators—bringing an offer to help. Calderon was the senior Spanish investigator, and the two worked closely, around the clock, trying to determine who had planted the rush-hour bombs that killed 191 and wounded nearly 2,000 more, just three days before the Spanish national elections.

The conservative government of Prime Minister José Maria Aznar insisted that the bombing was the work of ETA—the terror arm of the Basque separatist movement. But as Goode's forensic team probed more deeply it became apparent that the eleven explosive and shrapnel-laden backpacks—ten of which detonated—had actually been planted as part of a well-coordinated attack by an Al Qaeda cell.

Less than twenty-four hours before the election, Calderon was confronted by the awful reality that what his government had been saying simply was not true. Senior officials in Madrid were telling him to lie about what DINA had discovered. He went to Goode with his dilemma: "If we tell the truth, the conservatives will be swept out of power by the socialists, and they will pull our troops out of Iraq."

"Perhaps," said Goode. "But I have to look myself in the mirror when I shave in the morning. It's much easier to do if the person looking back at you isn't a liar. I suggest that you read Paul's first letter to the struggling church in Corinth—chapter 10, verse 13. It's been my experience that He rewards those who do what's right."

Late that night Calderon made the official announcement—the train bombings had been the work of Al Qaeda. The Socialists were voted into power and his superiors threatened to have him fired. Instead, he was promoted—though much to his chagrin, Spain's 1,300 peacekeepers were indeed pulled out of Iraq.

On 3 April, little more than three weeks after the election, seven Islamic militants blew themselves up as a joint DINA-*Guardia Civil* Special Operations unit moved to arrest them at an apartment in Leganes, a small town just outside Madrid. A video—made by the terrorists as they planned their suicide—was found in the wreckage of the apartment. The video contained an Al Qaeda ultimatum for "the immediate withdrawal of Spanish troops from Muslim lands" issued by a Tunisian, Sirhan bin Abdelmajid Fakhet. Calderon's investigators also found sketches of New York's Grand Central Station and several computer discs in the rubble. As a way of saying "thanks" for encouraging him to do the right thing, Calderon quietly made copies and sent them to Goode.

Though Calderon had not seen Goode for more than three years, the sound of the older man's steady voice on the answering machine brought back warm memories. He checked his watch, calculated that it was a little after 0930 in Washington, picked up his cell phone, and dialed the number his friend William had given him more than a half decade before.

The phone rang twice and Calderon heard a familiar voice say, "Goode. Nonsecure. Cell phone. Go ahead."

"William, it's Roberto, returning your call."

"Ah, *mucho gracias, mi amigo,*" said Goode. Then continuing in English he asked, "Do you remember my friend Jonathan at the American Embassy?"

"Certainly," replied Calderon, remembering the CIA Station Chief from several years before.

"Well, Jonathan has been reassigned," Goode continued. "But I have another friend there in that same capacity named Francis. Would it be possible for you to go by to see him on a rather urgent matter? He will be expecting you."

"Of course," Calderon answered. "I shall go there right away."

A half hour later Roberto Calderon was seated in the office of Francis Fernandez, the CIA Station Chief at the U.S. Embassy in Madrid. Fernandez had received a FLASH precedence, personal message from the CIA Operations Director ordering him to greet Calderon at the front door of the embassy and escort him to a secure telephone—a clear "deviation" from established protocols.

Though the sign on his door said "Cultural Attaché," Fernandez wasted little time on pleasantries. After pouring the DINA officer a cup of strong coffee, he said, "Mr. Calderon, my instructions are to put you on this secure phone with my boss in Washington, Mr. William Goode."

With that, Fernandez punched in a number on the keypad of a strange-looking phone situated atop what appeared to be a safe, positioned behind his desk. After a few seconds he said, "This is Madrid. I have Mr. Roberto Calderon for Mr. Goode." Then a few seconds later he said, "Yes, sir, he's right here . . . Yes, sir, I certainly agree this is very unusual, but these are unusual times. I'll put him right on and I'll be next door in Tom Simmons's office."

Handing the receiver to the DINA officer, Fernandez said, "I'll be right next door, Mr. Calderon—just hang up when you are finished and I'll come right in." With that, the CIA Station Chief left the room.

Calderon spoke into the mouthpiece, "Hello, William, what can I do for you?"

"Thank you for coming on such short notice, Roberto," Goode said through the secure link. "There is a matter of great urgency and sensitivity on which I hope you can be of help."

"Certainly," replied Calderon. "If it is possible for me to do, it will be done, my friend."

Goode got right to the point: "We have reason to believe that the group that overthrew the Saudi government has seized a number of the royal family's aircraft and oceangoing vessels. The Saudi royals called 'em 'yachts,' but most of these ships are more than thirty meters long. The aircraft range in size from Lear jets to 767s and Airbus 320s. We believe that these ships and aircraft are going to be used to bring nuclear weapons into the United States."

Calderon simply said, *"¡Mi Dios!"*

"Es verdad," replied Goode. He then continued, "We think that one or more of these aircraft and vessels may have been brought into Spanish ports or airfields for repainting and reregistration—perhaps in the Belaric

Islands—on Majorca or Minorca, or maybe even to Cartegena, on the mainland. We're looking for help on determining whether that's the case—and if it turns out to be so, keeping those planes from leaving the ground or those ships from leaving port."

"Are the nuclear weapons already aboard?" asked a horrified Calderon.

"The truth is," said Goode, "we don't know. But personally, I doubt it. I think—and this is just my opinion—that the weapons are going to be placed aboard somewhere else—shortly before the ships and aircraft are sent to their targets in the U.S."

"How many ships and aircraft are we talking about?" asked Calderon.

"Well, I'm embarrassed to tell you, we don't know that either. The International Ships' Registry, maintained by Lloyds, lists forty-three vessels owned by members of the Saudi royal family. But we have also learned that in their quest for secrecy, many members of the Saudi royal family didn't register their vessels. Same for aircraft. Many seem to have been 'self insured,' as it were. There may have been as many as forty-five to fifty large, oceangoing ships in all."

"May have been?" asked Calderon.

"Yes," replied Goode. "We know that at least nineteen of them have been destroyed—either in Saudi Arabia or other ports when terrorists tried to seize them."

"How about aircraft?" asked the DINA officer.

"Again, the same problem with the registry records," said Goode. "We're guessing that there may have been as many as sixty-five transcontinental-range aircraft personally owned by Saudi royalty before the shooting started."

"So how can I help you?" asked Calderon. "As you no doubt understand, the current government here in Madrid doesn't want to do anything to offend the Islamicists. They bend over backward to appease them, hoping to avoid anymore incidents like the train bombings. I do not think my government will be of much assistance. But *I* will help in any way that I can."

"Thank you," said Goode. "This afternoon, I will have Mr. Fernandez deliver to you photographs and registry numbers for every Saudi ship and aircraft for which we cannot confirm a location. Please do what you can to see if any of them are in Spanish territory—perhaps being repainted or renumbered. If you find any, please notify me right away, using the phone number you called an hour ago. If for some reason I do not get back to you immediately, please contact Mr. Fernandez. He will give you a number."

"William, I must ask," said Calderon, "if I find some of their ships or planes here in Spain, what will you do?"

Goode paused a moment before answering, then said, "We will take care of it with minimum loss of innocent life."

Oval Office
The White House
Thursday, 25 October 2007
1410 Hours Local

It was the third time in as many days that Secretary of State Helen Luce had served as "simultaneous" translator for the Presidents of the United States and France. Dan Powers, the Defense Secretary, and the Vice President were listening silently on extensions next door in the presidential study.

"No, of course not," said the President, standing behind his desk, a pained expression on his face. "We don't intend to disregard your sovereignty. We'd simply like to have your cooperation in this search."

Luce translated the words into French and then listened for the reply. She held her hand over the mouthpiece before saying, "He's still ranting, Mr. President. He says you're trying to bully France."

The President nodded and when there was a lull in the diatribe, sought again to engage the French leader. "Please just listen to what I'm trying to tell you, Mr. President. The United States has credible intelligence that leads us to believe that there are several aircraft and large oceangoing vessels that are being refitted, renumbered, and repainted in your country in preparation for transporting nuclear weapons to the United States. All I am suggesting is that our two countries work together to stop them," the American President said firmly.

Luce translated again, and listened again as the French leader dug in his heels. "He says, 'You have called wolf once too often. You did not find the weapons in Iraq, so now you think France is hiding them?' "

"No . . . not France. Terrorists—either working out of Iran, or others who may be working with Iran as part of this Islamic Brotherhood," the President said, trying to curb his frustration.

Again Luce translated the reply. "Now he says, 'Take the matter to the UN. And this time, do not blame us. We do not make up crimes and look for someone to charge them with.' "

"What the heck's that supposed to mean?" the exasperated President asked.

Luce shrugged and politely asked the French president to clarify his response. After listening, she put her hand over the mouthpiece again and said, "I think we're at an impasse, sir. He sounds like he's reading from prepared remarks. It's all too rehearsed."

"Ask him once more if we send his government photos and satellite imagery, will he check out these suspicious ships and aircraft in Marseille, Lyon, Nice, Monaco, and Toulon? Remind him that at least twenty-seven members of the Saudi royal family—including eight children—were assassinated on *French* soil. Doesn't that prove that this is a serious matter?"

Luce nodded and asked the French president the question posed by the U.S. Chief Executive. There was a pause. Then she grimaced and said, "*Merci, monsieur Presid*—" but she didn't get a chance to finish. The French president had hung up on them.

When he hung up the phone, Powers and the Vice President rejoined Luce and the President in the Oval Office. As they walked into the room Powers said, "My advice is to have our Station Chief in Paris deliver the photos and registry information to the DGSE right away. My guess is that the French Service will quietly make an effort to check 'em out. The government is paralyzed because more than a quarter of the French population is now Muslim. But their security services know they can't take any chances that there's an impending nuke attack and they didn't look for it."

"Maybe . . ." said the President, "but sometimes you can't reason with an angry, stubborn man. He seems to act as though his lot in life is to keep the United States 'in its place.' I don't think we ought to assume they're going to do it—like my mother used to say, 'If you want something done right, y'all better do it yourself.' "

"What exactly are you suggesting, sir?" asked Helen Luce.

"Well, we've got some Navy SEALs checking out some boats in Spanish waters because Spain won't do it. Let's just add these locations to their list," suggested the President.

"That'd be too much for only two Spec Ops teams, sir," Powers said. "I don't think we can spread ourselves that thin. I'll push SOCOM to see if they can scare up another SEAL team or two to check out possible targets in France. But we'll have to be careful—two of those sites are heavily secured French airports. Checking the ships is one thing. Getting inside those airports covertly will be a real magic act."

"But can we do it?" the President asked.

Powers looked at his boss and said, "If we have to, we will."

Until now the Vice President had been silent, but now he interjected, "I agree with everything you and Dan just said, Mr. President. But what you just went through with that arrogant fool in Paris is symptomatic of our larger problem—we're on defense, we're react-ing—our enemy has the initiative and we're behind the curve playing catch-up. We've got to find a way to get inside our adversary's 'decision-making loop' and throw him off balance—make him respond."

The President, still standing behind his desk, nodded and said, "You're right, of course. That's always been the problem for democracies in general—and the U.S. in particular. How to do that without making a terrible mistake, hitting the wrong target, causing all sorts of collateral damage—those have always been our chal-lenges."

"I understand and accept that, Mr. President," said the SecDef, gravely. "So the question is, how far will you let me go in pushing the Iranians, this Islamic Brotherhood outfit—and maybe even the Russians— into thinking that we're about to act, in hopes that one or all of 'em will tip their hand?"

El Mirage Flight Test Facility
El Mirage Dry Lake, California
Friday, 26 October 2007
1530 Hours Local

"I know what your orders are, Colonel, and I under-stand what FAAD One means—'presidential brickbat' is what we call it out here," said Len Katz, the civilian

Flight Test Supervisor to Lt. Col. Dan Hart. "But just before you got here, I received a *superceding* FAAD One order from the same place you got yours—the Secretary of Defense. He's directing me to immediately make everything here that's flyable, ready for some special mission loads. I got the same order for the big birds that the Air Force has at Nellis, over by Las Vegas. I'm sorry you came all the way out here, but as it stands right now, I can't let you have any of these birds."

"And you're sure that this isn't a case of crossed wires at the Pentagon—that your message and mine might just be pertaining to the same thing?" asked Hart in his most plaintive tone.

"Nope, different Task Assignments," said Katz emphatically. "Your orders say twelve UAVs of mixed type and payload capability for some Pentagon Special Unit and 'Operation Huntsman.' This one," said Katz, waving a sheet of paper stamped "Top Secret" as the two men walked toward one of the hangars in the scorching heat, "this says all UAVs capable of carrying a very specific sensor package—and air-to-air and air-to-ground ordnance—are being requisitioned for Operation Stampede, and it's all for SOCOM."

Hart looked disgusted, but he knew he was up against an impenetrable bureaucratic wall. He settled for, "Can I use your secure phone?"

Katz unlocked the door of a modular office—much like a mobile home—motioned the Marine lieutenant colonel into the air-conditioned space, and pointed to a secure voice instrument beside a desk in the cluttered office. "Make yourself at home," said Katz, turning to leave. "I'll be back in a minute with a couple of bottles of cold water."

Hart had arrived at El Mirage Flight Test Facility from the sprawling Marine Corps Base at Twenty-nine Palms, California, with the mission of acquiring Unmanned Aerial Vehicles—UAVs—for use by the Threat

Mitigation Special Unit. Newman had gotten authority to use the small, remotely operated aircraft for intelligence gathering and for weapons delivery.

There wasn't much to see at El Mirage—several small hangars, a large structure with a sign that declared: "Assembly and Tech Support," and a long runway across the dry salt lake. Off in the distance, through shimmering waves of heat, Hart could see some observation towers and radars—but little else. The whole place was run by the Aeronautical Systems division of San Diego-based General Atomics, the company that built the Predator UAV.

Newman had sent Hart to El Mirage with the mission of selecting ten of the latest, quietest versions of the Predator—equipped with a range of sensors—and with rails for Hellfire missiles. Both he and Hart had used Predators—and the smaller Marine Corps' Pioneer UAV in Iraq—and knew how valuable they could be in combat.

Hart had already arranged for the delivery of several dozen smaller UAVs—with names like Raven, Dragon Eye, Hunter, Shadow, and Gnat—but he also needed the Predators—not just for their longer range and loiter time, but because they were the smallest UAVs with a combat-proven capability for delivering lethal ordnance.

The number Hart dialed rang twice and a voice answered, "Staff Sergeant McKay. Can I help you?"

"This is Lieutenant Colonel Hart. Is General Newman there?"

"Yes, sir. Wait one."

A moment later Hart heard Pete Newman's slightly garbled voice: "Go ahead, Dan, what's up?"

After Hart explained that their Predator order had been superceded, Newman said, "Here's what we're going to do. You identify four of 'em with the capabilities we need. Send me the registration numbers of the equipment we want and I'll call General Grisham. I'll see if he can get the Pentagon to relent. Meanwhile, see if you can order a few more of the Army 'Hunter' UAVs, equipped to fire Viper Strike munitions, and have all that stuff delivered to Twenty-nine Palms. We need to get our troops out there to start training with this gear ASAP. It looks like we're going to get committed a lot sooner than I expected."

Hart had built a six-week training plan for the Special Unit Teams and wanted time to supervise and evaluate their preparations for the difficult and dangerous missions ahead. "How soon?" he asked with some concern.

Newman paused and then said, "Very soon."

Hampton Inn
Miami, FL
Friday, 26 October 2007
2105 Hours Local

Neither Rachel Newman nor Amos Skillings had thought it would take so long to drive the 1,258 miles to Key West, Florida. The exorbitant price of gasoline and diesel fuel had cut the number of cars and trucks on Interstate 95 to just those who had to travel—but clearly there were still a lot of people with a purpose on the road. Despite the reduced traffic volume, they had encountered numerous unforeseen delays.

Many gas stations were simply closed—with signs announcing: "No Gas." They had taken to buying diesel fuel at truck stops—though they were often limited to no more than ten gallons at $7.50 or more a gallon.

Every hundred miles or so—and as they crossed each state border—there were roadblocks where heavily armed state police and National Guardsmen in full "battle rattle" checked licenses and vehicle registrations. At some checkpoints they had been forced to open the hood and all their doors and exit the Suburban while dogs "sniffed" the contents and officers with mirrors peered beneath the vehicle.

They had spent Wednesday night in Fayetteville, North Carolina, at Fort Bragg, in the Army guesthouse. Thursday morning, while Rachel and her children were eating breakfast, Skillings asked some of the soldiers for advice on alternative routes, and they recommended that it would be faster to use old U.S. Route 1, Route 301, or even local or state highways that more or less paralleled the interstate. Rachel agreed, and the sergeant major sent her husband a message on his D-DACT, informing him of the change in itinerary.

They managed to make 510 miles on Thursday—more than twice the distance they'd covered on Wednesday—and they stayed overnight at the Army guesthouse at Fort Stewart, outside Savannah, Georgia. While Rachel and the children frolicked in the swimming pool, Skillings found a gym and got in a good workout.

This morning they had gotten under way at 0830—right after Skillings had returned from the Post Exchange gas station proudly proclaiming that, "as a good Recon Marine," he had made two important "finds"—twenty gallons of diesel fuel and a handful of new children's DVDs to entertain James and Lizzie on the portable player on the backseat.

After more than twelve hours on the road, they finally got back on the interstate on the outskirts of Miami. By the time they saw the sign for the Hampton Inn up ahead, everyone was ready to stop for the day.

Thankfully, there were two rooms left, and they checked in, also grateful that the motel clerk told them that a restaurant was still open across the street. "A lot of restaurants closed this week," he said. "They've run out of supplies. I guess the delivery trucks aren't getting through fast enough." He also gave them the name of a gas station that had diesel within a few blocks of the motel. Skillings made a mental note to get as much fuel as they could early in the morning.

By the time they finished eating and returned to the motel, it was nine o'clock. Young James asked if he could go swimming, but Rachel was too tired to go with him, so she said, "Not tonight, honey. It's getting late, and we have to get up early."

"But, Mom, I slept in the car nearly all day."

"All day? Really? It seemed to me that you were awake most of the time and teasing your sister. Besides, I didn't sleep in the car and I'm beat."

"If it's all right with you, Mrs. Newman," Skillings said while pushing the elevator button with the tip of his crutch, "I'm going to the health club next to the pool. I can keep an eye on James."

"Yeah, Mom . . . besides, each of our rooms has two beds in 'em. You and Lizzie can go right to bed, and I'll stay in Sergeant Major Skillings's room like I did last night. That way I won't bother you and Lizzie when I get done swimming and get ready for bed."

"That's OK with me, ma'am," said Skillings. "I can put up with his snoring," he added, grinning broadly at the boy.

"All right . . ." Rachel laughed. "I'm too tired to argue. But James, make sure you mind your manners, don't be a pest, and don't stay up too late."

Jimmy ran to his mother's room to get his swimming trunks and his clothes for the next day, while Skillings changed into a sweatshirt and an old pair of Recon swim trunks. For the next thirty minutes the boy swam while Skillings worked out intensively with weights and a rowing machine, all the while favoring his injured left ankle. Ordinarily he'd have gone for a jog or used the treadmill, but the crutches had forced him into a different routine.

As he exercised, Skillings alternated his attention between James, swimming in the pool on the other side of the glass partition, and the wall-mounted television set tuned to the evening news. Several of the stories dealt with problems caused by shortages, looting, and mass flight from America's largest cities. Other reports focused on the worsening crisis in the Middle East and terrorists threatening to use nuclear weapons against the U.S.

Tiring of the bad news before exhausting his body, Skillings grabbed his crutches, hobbled out to the swimming pool, loosened the Velcro straps, took off the removable cast, and slipped into the water. As he flexed his damaged ankle, Jimmy swam up and stood beside him.

"How many laps?" Skillings asked him.

"I don't know . . . I didn't keep count," the boy replied, out of breath.

"Sounds like your daddy. He just keeps going and going—until his body says, 'That's enough for now, man.' I've never known him to count laps either—whether it's when he swims, or when he runs. His body knows when it's time to quit. Trouble is, *he* doesn't know when to quit. The man never gives up."

"Yeah, my mom kids him a lot. She calls him 'Gung Ho Newman' when he's like that," Jimmy said. "Sometimes I don't know if she's serious or kidding, y'know, Sergeant Major?"

Skillings grinned. "A lot of Marines get accused of being 'gung ho,' " he said self-consciously. Then he reached over and tousled the boy's hair. "And by the way—my friends call me Amos. I know your folks have taught you how to be polite to grown-ups, but I'd like it if you and your sister called me Amos . . . after all, you guys are family."

"I wish we *were* family," Jimmy said. "I wish my dad was more like you."

"What do you mean?" Skillings asked.

"Well . . . you take time to understand me. Like when Mom was too tired to let me go swimming, you let me come with you. You're always looking out for me—you made sure I got a little extra to eat yesterday . . . you let me ride up front with you while you were driving . . . and you listen to me when I talk to you—I wish my dad was more like you."

"Whoa . . . wait a minute, son," Skillings said. "What makes you think that your dad isn't interested in you? He is. I know, because he's always talking about you and your sister. When we're away on duty, he can't wait to get back to you guys."

"I don't think that's really true, sir. Even when he's home, my dad doesn't take much interest in me, or ask about the things I like. For instance, he never comes to see me play basketball. And when I ran the one-hundred-yard-dash in track last year, I broke the school record, but he wasn't there," the boy said with a heavy sigh.

"I'm sure that if you put your mind to it, you'll be able to think of some times that he *was* there to see you play . . ."

"Not many."

"Well, son," Skillings said, "it's tough to understand, but your daddy is a very special man. And special men like him have to be shared. My own daddy was a lot like that. Y'see, my daddy was a preacher. He was a minister of a Baptist church in Alabama. When I was a boy, it seemed to me that I felt left out of his life, just like you. But when I was twelve—"

"—my age," Jimmy interjected, adding, "in a few weeks."

Skillings nodded, and then continued, "When I was twelve, my mom told me, 'Amos, you and your sister and I have a very special man. God has called him to His work. It's not that he doesn't want to make time for us or hurt us. It's just that God only gave us twenty-four hours in the day to do what needs to be done. And because he's doing God's work, God gives us an extra measure of grace to help us when Daddy isn't around.' "

The boy thought for a moment, then said, "Yeah, but my dad isn't doing God's work like your father did; he's just a Marine."

Skillings smiled as the boy realized that what he had just said sounded like an insult. "Well now," said the sergeant major, "let's think about that for a moment. It may be hard to see from your perspective, but there's a lot of God's work that's done every day by people like your dad who serve their country."

"How?" asked James.

"The whole message of the New Testament is about the sacrifice that was made for us—even though we didn't deserve it. Every day, just by serving, soldiers, sailors, airmen, and Marines make sacrifices for each other—for their families—even for people they don't know. They are away from people they love—and very often in harm's way. I've been with your dad and heard him pray for you and your mother and your sister—even though he was the one in great danger. The Marine Corps calls your dad a 'hero' and has given him medals for courage, bravery, and leadership in combat, and for being wounded—but they don't give out citations for the most important quality your dad possesses."

"What's that?" said the boy, truly enthralled. He had never heard anyone talk about his father this way before.

"He's faithful," said Skillings, looking straight at James. "He would have a hard time saying it, but he's faithful because he loves the Lord, he loves you and your mom and your sister—and me—and his country—and he's willing to die for us. He doesn't do what he does for himself, his own promotion or advancement—

he does it for others. That takes a very special kind of unselfish purity—and your dad has it."

"How do you know?" asked James.

"Well, I've known him a lot longer than you have," said Skillings with a smile. Then realizing how late it was getting, he added, "I tell you what, I know some stories about your dad that I bet you don't know. Tomorrow, while we're driving, I'll tell you some of them. We'll have another man-to-man talk like this."

USS San Juan—SSN 751
Vic 0°11 W; 36°16 N
Mediterranean Sea
Saturday, 27 October 2007
0350 Hours Local

The crewmembers of the USS San Juan, SSN 751, like all sailors assigned to Los Angeles class nuclear submarines, were used to getting under way in a hurry—but this had been something of a record. Just forty hours ago the "attack boat" had been on a routine port visit in Cartegena, Spain, when the communications officer awakened the skipper with a Top Secret, Flash message from Submarine Forces Atlantic. The terse orders detached the San Juan from the Enterprise Carrier Battle Group and placed the vessel under the direct operational control of Headquarters, 6th Fleet in Naples, Italy. The message went on to inform that a SEAL team would be flown to the USS Enterprise from Rota, Spain, and directed the submarine to rendezvous with the carrier off the Spanish coast, take the team aboard, and "carry out such other missions as may be directed by the National Command Authority." The San Juan had gotten under way with her full complement of 129 officers and men, less than an hour after the message was received.

Now, the overcrowded submarine was creeping at three knots at a depth of fifty feet, her periscope barely making ripples on the surface of the Mediterranean. Two thousand yards off her bow were two large vessels—apparently tied alongside each other and clearly silhouetted against the lights of Palma, Majorca, five miles to the west.

Peering through the thermal lens on the periscope, Capt. Travis Woods said, "Lieutenant Commander Carter, here, take a look. Those two vessels dead ahead certainly look like your targets."

Carter, the SEAL team commander was already clad in a black wet suit, and he stepped up to the viewing reticle on the periscope. Two days ago he had been training with his team at Dam Neck, Virginia. He and his men had been given three hours' notice to grab their "takedown gear" and inflatable boats and board a USAF C-17 at Oceana Naval Air Station. When they disembarked at Rota, a Navy captain from the Fleet Intelligence Center in Naples had met them and explained their mission.

An unnamed member of Spain's national intelligence service, DINA, had informed the CIA that two of the missing royal Saudi "yachts" were being repainted in a small shipyard in Palma, Majorca. Satellite imagery and high-altitude photo recon missions flown by aircraft from the *Enterprise* had confirmed the ships' locations. Navy P-3s out of Rota had been ordered to shadow the vessels if they left port. Carter's SEAL team was to seize the Saudi boats and capture as many of the crewmen aboard as possible. He was then to sail the two vessels east into international waters so that a four-man Nuclear Incident Tiger Team could be lowered by helo-hoist onto the captured ships to disarm any nuclear weapons. He'd also been told, "Take as many prisoners as possible and hold them for interrogation."

It had taken the C-2 "COD" two flights to move

Carter's team and their gear from Rota to the *Enterprise*. The small-boat transfer at sea from the carrier to the *San Juan* had been an adventure in seamanship—especially the part where his SEALs had to scramble up the wet, sloping side of the submarine from a pitching launch. By the time they had hauled their rubber boats and tactical gear through the sub's partially opened torpedo loading hatch, they were exhausted.

Now, as Carter stared at the shapes through the periscope and occasionally glanced down at a set of photos in his hand, Captain Woods checked for any electronic emissions coming from the two vessels dead ahead. "The scanner isn't picking up any radar from either boat," he said.

Carter grunted, "Good. Maybe they're all asleep." Finally he said to the captain, "Well, they certainly look like the shapes of the *Nile Princess* and the *Jarad Jal*. They seem to be pretty much identical though I can't tell the paint scheme or make out the names; can you?"

The skipper stepped back up to the viewing reticle and after flipping several switches on the periscope handles said, "The one on the left is *Ocean Queen* and the one on the right is . . . *Sweet Wanderer*."

"Bingo!" said Carter. "Jarad Jal is Arabic for 'Sweet Wanderer.' These are our targets!"

By 0410 Captain Woods had maneuvered the *San Juan* until she was eight hundred yards due east and directly downwind of the two targets. He slowly brought her up until the dark hull of the submarine was dead stopped, barely above the surface of the Mediterranean. As soon as they got the word to "go," Carter and his SEALs raced to silently drag their two inflatable boats up through the forward torpedo loading hatch and inflate each IBS from an air hose running from the conning tower.

Ten minutes later the two black rubber craft, carrying seven SEALs each, pushed away from the submarine. Carter had estimated that paddling into the wind it would take them a half hour to reach and board their objectives. His estimate was off by five minutes.

At 0455 Carter's rubber boat pulled up to the stern of the vessel on the right-hand side. Through his night vision goggles he could see the name: *Sweet Wanderer*. More importantly, he could also see that there was no one on deck. Using a rubber-dampered magnet, he "tethered" his IBS to the hull and then hurled a foam-padded grappling hook up over the rail, hearing nothing but a dull "thud" as it caught. Instantly, three more hooks were in the air—and fifteen seconds later all seven SEALs were on the deck of the ship, and fanning out, their 9x19 mm, H&K MPSD3s submachine guns at the ready.

Aboard the nearby *Ocean Queen* it went equally well. Master Chief Edmund Shultz and his boat team boarded their target vessel at the same time and manner as Carter's and encountered no one until they got to the bridge. There, Shultz startled a man whom he later described as a "military aged male of Middle Eastern appearance" and shot him dead with a single shot when the young man reached for a pistol in his belt. The slight "cough" from the integral sound suppressor of his MPSD3 didn't even carry across to the next vessel—just forty feet away—where Carter's boat team was having the same kind of success.

It was all over in less than fifteen minutes. Shortly after Shultz shouted across to his team commander, "All clear," Carter sent a message to the submarine—and a long list of other recipients from Naples, Italy, to SOCO HQ in Tampa, Florida, to Washington, D.C.

BOTH TARGETS SECURED. TWO EN DEAD. EIGHT EN CAPTURED, THREE WOUNDED. NO US CASUALTIES. NO NUKE WEAPS FOUND ABOARD.

★

Lieutenant Commander Carter's initial message was read with both euphoria and dismay at the Pentagon—joy that no SEALs had been hurt or killed but frustration that no nuclear weapons had been found on either vessel. When the NMCC Duty Officer called the SecDef on his secure line to report the results of the mission, it was about a half hour before midnight in Washington.

Despite the hour, Powers immediately responded, "Send the commander of the SEAL team and the *San Juan* an 'atta boy' from me, and have them sail the two ships into our side of the Naval Station at Rota, in broad daylight. I want to find out if anyone squawks."

"Will do, sir. Anything else?"

"Yes," replied the SecDef. "I want to find out the following, ASAP: First, what's the range of the ships with the fuel they have aboard? Second, has any space aboard either vessel been modified to perhaps hide a nuclear weapon at some point in the future? And third, do these boats have nav systems aboard that may have been preprogrammed? If so, to where? Call me back when we get the responses, no matter what time it is."

Shortly before dawn in Washington, the NMCC Operations Duty Officer, Brig. Gen. Tom Simmons, called Powers on his secure phone again.

"Sorry to wake you, Mr. Secretary, but I have the answers to your questions from the SEAL team commander on one of the captured Saudi ships."

"Go ahead," said the SecDef.

Simmons read directly from the D-DACT message he had received from LCDR Carter: "One. Both vessels fully fueled. Estimated range is eighteen thousand miles. Two: Both vessels have recently had identical, watertight, 48" x 40" x 30" lead-encased, stainless-steel boxes installed in their bilges. Lids for boxes with rubber 'O' rings were positioned beneath bilge plates. Boxes are empty. Three. Both vessels have dual, preprogrammable GPS navigation systems. Both vessels' nav systems were programmed for direct rhumb-line route to Caracas, Venezuela. New charts of Caracas harbor are in chart table. Four. New Info. One of the enemy casualties aboard claims he is Russian. He says his name is Felix Kuznetsov, that he is employed by a Filaya Oil Corporation and that his supervisor is an individual named Nikolai Dubzhuko. He denies any knowledge of vessel being stolen or anything about nuclear weapons and insists on being granted access to the nearest Russian diplomatic mission."

"Did he say Caracas?" asked Powers when Simmons finished his report.

"Yes, sir, Caracas."

"OK," said Powers. "Make sure that message is passed to William Goode at the CIA right away."

"Yes, sir," said the general. "Anything else, sir?"

"Yes," responded Powers. "Send that SEAL team commander another 'well done' from me—and when they make it into Rota—have the wounded terrorists treated and then ship 'em all to Gitmo."

"The Russian too?" asked Simmons.

"Yep, the Russian too."

Lourdes Signals Intelligence Facility
Bejucal, Cuba
Saturday, 27 October 2007
0805 Hours Local

As soon as he picked up the phone call from Riyadh via the secure Murmansk-Moscow-Cuba link, Dimitri Komulakov could tell that Nikolai Dubzhuko was in a state of near panic. "General, I believe that two of our prize vessels are in trouble and may have been captured or perhaps even sunk," Dubzhuko sputtered.

"What do you mean?" Komulakov asked, setting

down his coffee cup. "When did you last hear from them?"

"They were supposed to check in at 0800 this morning our time—midnight your time. Neither ship placed that call, and all of our subsequent attempts to contact them have failed."

"When was the last time that you talked with them?"

"We received a routine report at 2200 last night. Both of them had completed their work at the Palma shipyard and were going to head for the Gibraltar Straits this morning at sunrise. They reported clear skies and good weather. We checked a satellite weather image of the weather in the vicinity for the past twelve hours— there was nothing out of the ordinary. The ships simply disappeared, and there were no warnings at all," Dubzhuko said.

"Were you able to track them using GPS and their transponders?"

"We tried that as soon as they didn't report in," Dubzhuko replied. "But neither vessel's transponders show up anymore. They may have sunk."

"If that was the case," Komulakov snarled, "the Emergency Satellite Beacons—called EPRBs—on their lifeboats and automatic life rafts would have gone off and we would know about it."

"We shall continue trying to contact them," said Dubzhuko, trying not to incur the wrath of his employer.

"No, you fool! Stop trying to reach them! If the Americans took over the ships, and you try to call them, they will obviously trace the signals. Do not call them anymore. If it was some kind of anomaly—weather or atmospheric conditions—making it impossible for them to get through to you, they'll call back when they can," Komulakov said. "Contact the other ships and aircraft and tell them I want every one of them to check in *every four hours* instead of twice a day. And tell them all to get to Caracas just as fast as possible. I think we need to move that aircraft with that special cargo sooner than expected."

Operations Directorate, CIA HQ
Langley, VA
Saturday, 27 October 2007
0930 Hours Local

William Goode had arrived at his office shortly after dawn—and found the D-DACT message from Lieutenant Commander Carter and the cover note from Secretary Powers relayed by the NMCC shoved into a folder labeled "Overnight Cables." After a none-too-gentle reminder to the Night Duty Officer that he was to be awakened for anything pertaining to the current crisis, he sat down and reread all of the reports from the SEAL operation. By now there were more than a dozen.

When he finished, Goode poured himself another cup of coffee and placed a secure call to Joseph Blackman of MI6. It took the SIS duty officer less than fifteen minutes to find the British spy, who rang Goode directly, greeting him with, "Good day, William. Working on Saturdays in the 'colonies,' are we? Not good for the golf game, I'm afraid."

Goode smiled in spite of the fact that no one in either country's intelligence services had taken a day off since the Saudi crisis began and said, "I've given up the silly game, Joseph. Got tired of running around looking for that little white ball that just won't stay on the green carpet."

"You didn't call me for tips on putting, old friend," said Blackman, suddenly serious. "Did your Navy lads pick up anything useful from those pirated vessels they clipped last night? Nice piece of work, that."

"A few things. Both vessels had apparently been

modified to hide one or more nuclear weapons, but there were no nukes aboard either one."

"Too bad about that," Blackman replied, meaning it. "Did any of the pirates survive the experience to tell of buried treasures?"

"There are a couple of very interesting bits of information. According to the on-scene Navy commander, one of the thugs is a Russian who claims he works for Filaya Oil and that his boss is one Nikolai Dubzhuko. Sound familiar?"

"Well, that's very interesting," said Blackman. "I just got off the phone with one of those bright young GCHQ-NSA youngsters over at Menwith Hill. He called to tell me that there was a noticeable big spike in HF and satellite voice and data traffic coming from the Filaya building in Riyadh—and then about an hour ago, the place went mute."

Goode said, "And this means . . ."

"Don't know for certain," responded Blackman. "There was apparently a big flurry of traffic starting shortly after your SEALs seized those boats off Palma, right up until an hour or so ago, and then it stopped—as though someone pulled the switch. But our boys in Jordan and our 'stay behinds' in Saudi Arabia say that there is still 'noise' coming from the Filaya building. They still believe that there is some kind of land line capability there that we just don't know about. It adds to my belief that one part of the command and control for the Islamic Brotherhood, or whatever they are, is set up there—in the Filaya facilities," Blackman said.

"Hmm . . . interesting. The NRO satellite passes don't show much, and none of our 'air breathers' tell us anything except that there are people inside the building," Goode said.

"Downtown Riyadh is obviously a very dangerous place," Blackman admitted, "but the Aussies have offered to have some of their 'local assets' knock on the door to see who answers."

"Well, that's mighty brave of 'em," Goode replied, "but I'm not sure we want to take any action at the Filaya building until we know where the other end of the phone rings. What was that building used for in the past?"

"It was built in the '80s by the Russians, and they constructed it like a fortress. I believe they used it for one of their consulting firms—pipelines, oil, that sort of thing—as I recall. There's no record of it ever changing ownership, but since May 2005 it's been leased to this 'Filaya' group."

"Does Komulakov have any connection to Filaya other than that trip you briefed me on when you were here in Washington a few days ago?" asked Goode.

"Not that we can confirm. The best connection seems to be this chap Nikolai Dubzhuko who runs everything there—and who apparently was mentioned again this morning by this Russian who was captured by your Navy SEAL on that pirated vessel. He and Komulakov worked together for years in the KGB."

"I still think this thing is being masterminded by Komulakov," said Goode emphatically. "My gut tells me that this guy Dubzhuko is his 'operations chief,' and that Komulakov is running this whole operation for the Iranians from somewhere else. He's too smart to be in Riyadh. Maybe he's in Tehran. Is there an undersea fiber-optic cable across the Persian Gulf between Saudi Arabia and Iran?"

"Yes," replied Blackman. "It runs from Ad Dammam on the Saudi coast to Bandar-E Abbas, Iran. It was put in a few years ago, right after the Saudis authorized the Iranians to start commercial over-flights. And I think it connects Tehran and Riyadh."

"Could the Russians have tapped into that fiber-optic cable?" asked Goode.

"It certainly isn't that hard to do," replied Blackman.

"Well, if that's the case, I think I know of a way that we can turn off Dubzhuko's telephone service. I'll check it out and get back to you before 1800 your time. Thank you for your help, Joseph."

After hanging up with Blackman, Goode called Gen. George Grisham—and found the Chairman of the Joint Chiefs of Staff at his desk. He got right to the point. "George, what do we have in the way of submarine assets in the Persian Gulf?"

Grisham was equally direct. "Why, Bill?" he asked. "I'm still smarting from coming up dry on those two pirated Saudi vessels last night."

"General," Goode replied, "we may not have found any nukes—but it was anything but dry. I need a sub to cut an undersea fiber-optic cable between Iran and Saudi Arabia."

Grisham thought for a moment and then asked, "How quickly do we need this cable cut?"

"The sooner the better," Goode answered. "Hours . . . days . . . certainly not weeks."

"Well, Bill," said Grisham with a sigh, "you get me the rationale for this, and I'll look into the availability of the Navy's 'flying submarine.' It's called the ASDS—shorthand for the Advanced SEAL Delivery System. It's a mini-submarine, sixty-five-feet long, manned by up to six Navy SEALs."

"How quickly can we get one out to the Persian Gulf?" asked Goode.

"The ASDS can be carried in a C-5A or C-17 aircraft atop its specially designed tractor-trailer transport. We can certainly link it up with a sub at Diego Garcia—maybe even Qatar or Bahrain if we handle it all at night," Grisham answered.

"Great!" answered Goode, with far more enthusiasm than Grisham was feeling. "I'll get the paperwork out of here this afternoon."

"What else can I do for you, Bill?" asked Grisham, not wanting Goode to feel like he wasn't being supported.

"Well, you might want to get ready to dispatch some of your special ops teams to intercept the nuclear weapons where they will be loaded up for the attack on the United States," said Goode, knowing that he was tantalizing his old friend.

There was a long pause before Grisham asked simply, "When and where?"

"When, I don't know yet," Goode answered. "But the 'where' is Caracas."

CHAPTER THIRTEEN

Dark Domain

Office of the Director, FBI
Hoover Building, Washington, DC
Saturday, 27 October 2007
1155 Hours Local

Thank you all for joining me on this conference bridge," said FBI Director Bob Coffey into the speaker mounted beside his secure phone. On the call were twenty-one of his SACs—the Special Agents-in-Charge of the FBI's biggest field offices in the U.S. and overseas.

"I know we can do a lot by secure data-link, but I thought that under the circumstances it would be best if we could all brainstorm for a few minutes," added the Director. "I trust you all read the most recent 'CIA Threat-Warn' indicating that the next most likely date for a major attack is Monday, 29 October—the day after tomorrow—and then again on November eleventh."

Several voices said "affirmative" and "roger that."

Coffey continued, "Well, there have been some recent developments that may bear on what the terrorists may be planning. Dave Mendez, in Mexico City, I want you to give us an update on what you have learned from your counterparts about that suspicious yacht and aircraft that the Mexican authorities impounded last night."

"Yes, sir," replied Mendez. "Both the vessel and the aircraft were seized by the *Federales* last night in Puerto Morelos—it's on the tip of the Yucatan Peninsula. The boat—it's a ship, really, 170 feet long and more than four hundred tons—had a fresh paint job and a new name: *Desert Mirage.* The aircraft is a Gulfstream Five. It was seized in a hangar where the insides had been stripped out—and a phony Mexican registration number had been painted on its tail. My liaison here says they traced the engine serials, and the aircraft was sold last year to Prince Al-Habib Rasul, the Saudi who was killed in Paris. They're still checking on the ship."

Coffey then asked, "According to your initial report this morning, the Mexicans arrested five from the boat and three who were working on the aircraft. Will they allow us to extradite them to the U.S.?"

"No, sir," Mendez said emphatically. "I went up the 'Leg-Att' chain to the Minister of Justice and the U.S. Ambassador went directly to the Foreign Ministry, and they told us to pound sand. The Mexicans told us that these eight thugs haven't broken any U.S. laws. When the ambassador told them that 'conspiracy to commit an act of terrorism' is a violation of our law, they said that they don't recognize our 'Patriot Act' and, even if they did, they won't extradite anyone to the U.S. who could face the death penalty."

"Great neighbors," said Coffey, the disgust evident in his voice. "Will they let you have access to them?"

"Not yet," answered the FBI agent in Mexico City. "But my amigo in the MOJ has photos they took inside the ship and the plane—and apparently both had lead boxes installed just like the ones that were in those two ships that the SEALs took down last night in the Med."

"As soon as you get those photos, scan 'em and send everyone on this call 'high-res' JPEG files so we can put out a BOLO and everyone will know what to look for," ordered Coffey.

"Will do," said Mendez. "And there's one more thing, sir. The *Desert Mirage* had filed a 'sail plan'—it's required by the Mexican port authorities—and according to the plan they were headed for Caracas."

"Same for the Gulfstream?" asked Coffey.

"Nope," said Mendez. "It had a flight plan for tomorrow—Sunday—for Jose Marti International in Cuba."

Pennecamp Rest Stop
Highway 1, Key Largo, FL
Saturday, 27 October 2007
1640 Hours Local

The sun was settling toward the horizon as Amos Skillings pulled the Suburban into the visitors center parking lot just south of Key Largo on U.S. Highway 1. They'd been driving since nine that morning and had stopped only once for food and fuel around noon. While Rachel and the children were inside using the restrooms, Skillings sat at a nearby picnic table and checked his D-DACT for e-mail.

There was only one message—from Brig. Gen. Peter Newman, responding to one Skillings had sent him the night before, informing the general of their travel plans. Newman's message was brief: *Amos—Glad things are going well. I expect you'll be in Key West sometime late Saturday. I am grateful for your help. You are the best! Will be at work all Saturday. Call my cell when you get a chance.—Semper Fi, PN*

Newman answered on the second ring with his usual, "Newman," then added, "Nonsecure, go ahead."

"Good afternoon, sir, just checking in," said

Skillings, without giving his name—a habit born of long field experience in hostile climes and places.

Even though Skillings's caller-ID was blocked, Newman recognized the voice and responded, "Hello, Amos, how's it going?"

Though he was sitting at a picnic table outside of Key Largo, watching an older couple walk their dog, the ever-cautious sergeant major responded, "We're taking a 'morale and welfare break' about three hours from our objective."

Having made the long drive to the beach house his wife inherited on Boot Key numerous times, Newman asked, "How are the troops holding up?"

"They're doing fine, sir. I'll take 'em with me on a forced march any day."

The general chuckled and said, "You're probably doing better at this than I do." Then, becoming serious, he asked, "How's the traffic? What are you seeing?"

"The traffic is awful," replied Skillings, frankly. "Lots of security stops—and in between, people are driving like maniacs. They must think that driving faster will help them get in more miles before they run out of gas."

"Have you had any problems getting diesel fuel?" Newman asked.

"Nothing major," Skillings told him. "Thankfully, both your wife and I have the new ration cards, and since we're both entitled to buy ten gallons, we have so far been able to make it between stations that are open. There have been a couple of times when we've had to drive around a good bit to find a station with fuel. But it's going OK."

"Are you having any problems getting food and water?" Newman asked.

"Not much," Skillings said. "But it's because most of them are rationing what little they have left. So when we see a store that still has something on the shelves, we stop and buy some canned food and bottled water. I think we've got about a two—maybe three—weeks' supply in the back of the Suburban."

"Glad to hear it. How's your ankle? Hope you aren't overdoing things. I'm going to need you, so make sure you take care of it."

"I am, sir. Your wife and I are splitting the driving fifty-fifty. It's working out fine," Skillings told Newman.

"Well . . . give it rest for a day or so after you arrive at Rachel's place. Then after you get them settled, I think the best thing would be to have her then take you down to the Naval Air Station. You know the one. I'll arrange for a flight to pick you up. It looks like we're going to get thrown into this mix sooner than I had expected."

After signing off with Newman, the sergeant major hobbled back to the car and took out the Florida highway map that was in the pocket of the driver's side door. When Rachel and the children came bounding out of the visitors center laughing and playing, Skillings had the map spread out on the hood of the Suburban.

"What are you looking for, Amos?" Rachel said, still smiling.

"Just checking the mileage between Boot Key and the Key West Naval Air Station, ma'am," he replied.

Then, suddenly serious she said, "Peter wants you back, doesn't he?"

Skillings looked at the woman whose life he had saved years before in Cyprus and said, "Yes, ma'am. We have work to do."

Presidential Commission Townhouse
5 Jackson Place, Washington, DC
Saturday, 27 October 2007
1700 Hours Local

After signing off with his sergeant major, Newman placed the cell phone back in the clip on his belt and turned back to the work on his desk. He had started the day with a lengthy DIA intelligence briefing at Bolling Air Force Base, followed by several more hours in meetings at the Pentagon. By the time he arrived at his office on the top floor of the Presidential Commission townhouse, the day was almost over.

As Newman entered his secured space he turned on the lights, and then he noticed a Post-it note in the middle of his otherwise uncluttered desk. He walked over, set down his jacket and briefcase, and read the note: *Folder is in the safe.—Major Bowes.*

Maj. Ed Bowes was a Pentagon liaison officer whom Secretary of Defense Dan Powers had assigned to Newman when Skillings was injured. Bowes would stay with the Special Unit for at least a year. "Ed's the kind of guy who can read minds," the SecDef had told Newman when he made the offer. "He's intelligent and resourceful—the kind of guy you need to keep you sane when twenty things are happening at once."

So far, Bowes had proven himself well. Newman had been able to communicate with the major at all times of the day or night, by way of e-mail and IM on his D-DACT unit. Bowes was always available and seemed on top of things. Whenever Newman asked for something, it appeared. When he had questions, there were answers or options almost instantly. Newman also appreciated the way that Bowes—as Dan Powers put it—"can read minds." Even before being asked, Bowes took the initiative and got things lined up, waiting only for his superior's approval.

Newman inserted the major's 3 x 5 yellow Post-it note into the shredder and walked over to the four-drawer, high-security safe in the corner of his office. He punched a six-digit number into the keypad and then pressed his right forefinger against the shiny, reddish-brown rectangle about an inch by three-fourths of an inch in size, on the front face of the top drawer. There was a barely-perceptible *clunk* as the locking mechanism disengaged and Newman opened the safe.

Inside the second drawer was a red-bordered pocket file labeled "Top Secret" with his name on it. Inside were a single sheet of paper and two envelopes. Newman put the envelopes on the top of the safe and read what was typed on the sheet of paper. It was a memo from Maj. Ed Bowes.

Sir:

1. LtCol Hart called from Nellis AFB at 1300. He said to tell you that we will get three "Predators" and five "Hunters," and that the Nellis people have promised the use of a "Global Hawk" as long as you don't use this one like the last one they gave you. Not sure I understand that, but LtCol Hart said you would know what they mean.*

2. At 1410 Senator James Waggoner called and asked, "When will the Special Unit commence operations?" Since he was on a nonsecure line I told him that he would have to call the SecDef with such an inquiry. He said "I'll have your rear end for this," and hung up. Not sure if he meant yours or mine.

3. At 1525 Commissioner Russell Bates arrived and requested the file on Samuel Mubassa. Fifteen minutes later

---

*Refers to *Mission Compromised* by authors where in March 1995 Newman used a Global Hawk with munitions to attack a meeting in Tikrit, Iraq, with Saddam Hussein and Osama bin Laden. The aircraft was lost when the mission was compromised and Newman's aircraft was shot down over Iraq.

he returned the file and told me that he had "updated the location information on Mubassa," and departed at 1550. The Mubassa Target Index is now back in the folder labeled 'Hit Parade' in your safe and I've flagged the info Mr. Bates provided so that you're aware of what's been added.

4. At 1600 the CIA courier delivered the enclosed sealed envelopes from Mr. William Goode. I signed for same.

5. 1630. Am going home to have dinner with my wife. If you need me back here for any reason, please call or send msg on D-DACT.

Very respectfully, E. J. Bowes, Major, US Army

Newman walked back to his desk with the folder and the two envelopes. Both had identical labels: "From: W. P. Goode; To: P. J. Newman."

Inside the first envelope he opened, Newman found $25,000 in U.S. currency. He noticed that all of the bills appeared to have been in circulation for some time. The second envelope contained a blue U.S. passport with Newman's picture, but the name "Peter Oldham" inscribed on the first page. There were also fifty business cards identifying Oldham as the Vice President of "Petro-Research, Inc.," with an Oklahoma City address and phone number; plus three credit cards in the same name, a map of Oklahoma City, and a sheet of paper with a fifteen-line "bio" for Peter Oldham. There was also a handwritten note from Bill Goode: *"Peter, herein, the paperwork you will need for any upcoming travel. Please memorize and destroy the 'legend.' Before you leave on any vacations, be sure to talk to me about local points of interest and accredited tour guides. Sincerely, Bill."*

Newman was still smiling at Goode's note when the secure phone beside his elbow warbled, insisting that it be answered. Picking up the receiver, he heard the *whoosh* and *ping* as the encryption systems synchronized and then said, "Newman."

"Pete, this is George Grisham. Secretary Powers just got off the phone with Senator Waggoner, who is apparently ballistic over the fact that the Threat Mitigation Special Unit has yet to 'whack anyone'—as he put it. The SecDef tried to explain that we're dealing with some fast-moving events here—and the very strong possibility that terrorists are trying to get nuclear weapons into the country at this very moment."

"That's very interesting, General, because Waggoner also called here earlier today—in the clear—and then Commissioner Russell Bates dropped in to 'update'—as he put it—the location information on Samuel Mubassa. He's among the top three on our 'hit parade.' Mubassa's apparently on a protracted, 'UN-sponsored visit' to Caracas, and staying with his friend President Valdez, the thug who's running Venezuela."

"Caracas," said Grisham after a brief pause. And then, almost to himself, he asked, "Why does Caracas keep coming up so often nowadays?"

"Sir?"

"Nothing, Pete. Just thinking out loud." Then he asked, "How soon will you have your 'travel teams' up and ready to go?"

"I just received my personal stuff from Bill Goode, and the 'document specialists' at ISA say that they will have ten more sets here by tomorrow," Newman replied. "That should give us enough to send out a 'Recon & Survey' team as early as Monday. But I'm still not certain where we want to send our first team. Most of the 'targets' found guilty by the Commission seem to be spread all over the Middle East—in Egypt, Sudan, Palestine, South Lebanon, Syria, Iran, and of course, Saudi Arabia."

Grisham was silent for several seconds and then said, "I understand that's where most of them are—but Bill Goode believes that the immediate threat is much closer to home. He's pretty well convinced me and the SecDef that there's a lot going on in Venezuela."

"You mean this guy Mubassa?"

"Not necessarily Mubassa," responded Grisham. "More likely Valdez—or people connected to his regime—perhaps in cooperation with the Iranians. I'm going to talk to the SecDef again here in a little while. In the interim, take a look at how you would move eight or ten of your boys—and some special equipment—to Venezuela."

"If all they will be doing is a site-survey on how to take out Mubassa or a few other individuals, they won't need much equipment," said Newman.

"Well, I'm thinking your boys may have to do some double-duty," Grisham replied. "We're flat running out of Spec Ops units, chasing around after all these missing Saudi ships and aircraft. Three of the four that we've recaptured were apparently headed for Caracas, and all of them had compartments installed to hide nukes—but no nukes. There's no doubt that *something* bad is going on down there."

"How much and what kind of special equipment do they need to take?" asked Newman, taking notes.

"Not completely sure yet," replied Grisham. "I have some guys looking at the availability of portable, Passive Millimeter Wave imaging equipment and some of the new Gamma-Neutron Particle detectors. I'll get the cube and weight of what we're talking about and get back to you after our next meeting with the President. Meanwhile, you get a team ready to head for Caracas. That way we can get Waggoner off our backs *and* have some good people in place just in case Valdez is running a *really* dark domain."

Situation Room
The White House
Washington, DC
Saturday, 27 October 2007
1930 Hours Local

"I know you don't want to leave, Mr. President," said Dan Powers emphatically, "but everyone here is adamant that you and the First Lady at least spend tomorrow night and Monday at one of the relocation sites."

The President looked around the small conference room at the other six members of his "Crisis Core Group"—the small team of advisors he had come to rely on the most as the Saudi crisis wore on. The Vice President, Joint Chiefs Chairman Gen. George Grisham, Secretary of State Helen Luce, Bill Goode from the CIA, National Security Advisor Jeb Stuart, and Bruce Allen, his Chief of Staff, were all nodding their heads in agreement with the Defense Secretary.

"Bill," said the President, turning to Goode, "how serious is this threat that these jihadists will try something Monday?"

"Well, sir, based on all this 'numerology' that appears to fascinate the Islamic radicals, the day after tomorrow is one of those days that adds up to eleven," answered Goode.

"But I thought you said that 11 November is the highest threat day in the near future—and that places like New York City—with eleven letters—are at highest risk," challenged the President.

"That's true," interjected the Vice President, "but why take the chance? The Secret Service can take you out through the tunnel over to Treasury, put you in a low-profile motorcade over to Marine One at Anacostia NAS, and have you at Camp David, Mount Weather, or even down to A. P. Hill inside of forty minutes. Besides," he added with a smile, "somebody other than me needs to inspect some of these 'undisclosed locations.'"

"All right," the President reluctantly agreed. "We'll go to Camp David at ten p.m. tomorrow night—and hope that the press doesn't pick up on it. But if everything stays quiet, I want to be back here at first light on Tuesday morning. Now, before I have to go face the First Lady with this news, give me the latest. How many of those missing Saudi ships and aircraft have we located or captured?"

"Six—four of the yachts, and two planes," the SecDef replied. "All of them were modified to hold nuclear weapons—but there were no weapons aboard."

"That's terrific. Details?" asked the President, looking at the Chairman of the Joint Chiefs.

General Grisham said, "In addition to the two repainted Saudi ships taken by Navy SEALs off the coast of Spain last night, we have a ship and aircraft impounded in Mexico, and about twenty minutes ago I was informed by SOCOM that we got some help from South Africa taking down a Saudi in Johannesburg. Three men of 'Middle Eastern appearance' and a Russian were working on the plane in a hangar. They were all killed in the assault on the plane. No U.S. or South African casualties. At about the same time, we intercepted another Saudi yacht in Lisbon Harbor—once again a SEAL team handled it. There were five terrorists aboard, but this time we lost two men and one SEAL was wounded when those aboard began using grenades in an effort to take out the SEAL team along with themselves. All five terrorists died—one of them was a young woman in her twenties. All of the vessels and aircraft had been repainted and modified with lead-lined steel boxes to accept and conceal a single nuclear weapon. It also appears from the most recent reports that all of them had wiring installed to command detonate the weapon once it was installed."

At this point Bill Goode interjected, "Mr. President, we're also checking on reports of other Saudi ships and aircraft in the Azores, the Canary Islands, Cape Verde, Brazil, Trinidad, Barbados, the British Virgin Islands, Aruba, the Dominican Republic, Venezuela, and Cuba. Of course we're not getting any cooperation at all from those last two."

"Everything seems to be focused on the U.S. East Coast," observed the President.

"Yes, sir," replied Goode. "And I continue to believe that Caracas is the key. The Valdez regime, as you know, has had a growing relationship with Iran and Castro and has become very hostile to us. Unfortunately, we haven't had any decent reporting out of Caracas since they threw out our Military Advisory Group back in 2005."

"What do you make of the Russians who have popped up on these captured Saudi ships and aircraft?" asked the President.

Goode glanced at Powers before answering. The SecDef nodded and the CIA Operations Director continued, "I have to admit that my assessment isn't widely shared in the intelligence community, but I still believe that the Iranians are providing the 'muscle' for this 'Islamic Brotherhood.' But I think that the 'brains' behind it—and the nuclear weapons—are Russian, and most likely controlled by this man Komulakov."

"Where is this guy—and how is he running this operation," asked the President.

Powers took over again where Goode left off. "We think that some of the command and control functions are being handled from Saudi Arabia, and partly from somewhere else, perhaps Tehran," Powers said.

"Saudi Arabia? How?" asked the President.

"Some of it seems to be emanating from a Russian-owned facility in Riyadh."

"Russian . . . ?" the President said, adding, "How do the Russians fit into this?"

"Not the Russian government, sir," Powers said. "We think it's a freelance project, run by this 'retired' KGB general, Komulakov. He apparently doesn't believe that the cold war ever ended."

"If we know where this place in Riyadh is, why don't we just level it?" asked the President.

"Because we're trying to work out a way to flush out the other end of their communications links," Powers said, then added, "but we need a little more time to accomplish that."

"I wonder how much time we have," the President said, almost to himself. Then he stood up from the conference table to stretch his legs, restless from the long day of tense activity dealing with the crisis. After a moment, he sat back down and asked, "So all of the captured vessels and aircraft were modified to hold nuclear weapons, but we haven't found any of the nukes. Where are they?"

Powers paused before responding and then he said very quietly, "We don't know. We've mobilized every available recon flight, UAV, satellite, and twenty-nine Special Operations teams. We have some decent leads on two more of the stolen Saudi aircraft, but nothing right now regarding anymore of the yachts. We're hoping that one of the captured terrorists will spill something during interrogation, but none of the prisoners seem to know anything about the mission except for their limited part in it—and for that they were apparently supposed to get instructions later. We're guessing that they were supposed to get the vessels and aircraft to a secure site—perhaps Caracas—so they could install the weapons next week."

"If there are so many indicators that Venezuela is a problem, should we consider a blockade or some other action?" asked the President.

"George has a warning order out to Atlantic Command, Forces Command, and Southern Command," answered Powers. "With your permission we'll start repositioning forces tonight, but unless we're attacked on Monday, I don't think we should take any overt action against Venezuela yet."

"Go ahead and move whatever's necessary," the President said, "and let's see if we can keep it quiet." Then he asked, "Why do you think next week is the 'crunch point'? What makes you so sure?"

"Well, we're not sure. Right now it's just a hunch—much of it is based on some information from one of Bill Goode's sources," said the SecDef, nodding toward the CIA officer sitting across the table from him. "Bill seems to have a good handle on this number eleven business and why it's so important to the terrorists. If he's right, then George and I figure they'll need several days to a week to install the weapons and then preposition their assets for a major attack."

"When?" asked the President.

"Two weeks from tomorrow—the eleventh of November—the date of 'eleven eleven.' "

Newman Family Vacation Home
Boot Key, FL
Saturday, 27 October 2007
2345 Hours Local

By the time the weary travelers arrived at Blue Waters, the Newman vacation cottage in Boot Key, the children were sound asleep in the backseat. They had hoped to arrive hours earlier, but during their final stretch down the 120-mile-long string of islets, they were confronted by dozens of security stops.

All day the news on the radio had been almost universally ominous. There were reports about curfews in most major cities. Martial law had been declared in New York, Chicago, Atlanta, and Detroit where looting was the worst. When one reporter observed that most federal government offices would be closed on Monday and asked rhetorically, "Who's minding the store?" Rachel snapped the radio off and said in frustration to the now mute instrument, "Peter Newman is!"

Just south of Marathon, they were held up for more than an hour so that a lengthy military convoy, headed south, could pass. A military policeman wearing a flak jacket and Kevlar helmet waved the Suburban and several other cars off the road. Interspersed among the passing camouflage-painted trucks and HETs (Heavy Equipment Transporters) were armored Humvees—with .50 cal. and 240 Golf machine guns mounted and manned in their turrets. Seeing that, Skillings said quietly, "Things are heating up."

"Why do you say that, Amos?" Rachel asked, trying to keep her voice low so they wouldn't wake the children in the backseat.

"That's a Patriot PAC III battery," replied Skillings. "It can be used against an air threat—but its principal purpose is to shoot down enemy missiles."

"Where are they headed?" asked Rachel, suddenly concerned that she was bringing her children closer to trouble rather than further from it, as she had intended.

The Marine sergeant major thought for a moment, then said, "I don't know for sure, ma'am, but I'd guess that they're positioning them at Key West Naval Air Station."

"That's only a few miles from Boot Key," said Rachel, increasingly anxious. "Why would that little base be a target for a nuclear attack?"

"I doubt that it would be, ma'am," said Skillings, trying to reassure her with the truth. "It's more likely that the Patriots are being put at NAS Key West to protect cities in the Southeast U.S. and along the Gulf Coast from air or missile attack from Cuba or somewhere else to our south."

"Where else?" Rachel pressed.

"Don't really know," the sergeant major responded honestly. Then after a moment he said, "Maybe Venezuela."

USS *Jimmy Carter*, SSN-23
60° E, 24° N, Gulf of Oman 482 NM from U.S. Naval
Facility, Bahrain
Sunday, 28 October 2007
0115 Hours Local

Capt. Sanford "Sandy" Heflin had been waiting for almost four months for a mission like this—ever since he and his crew had sailed the SSN-23 from their home port in Bangor, Washington. He had begun to wonder if his highly complex sub, like its namesake, the first nuclear submariner to become president, would be sidelined without ever taking offensive action.

The USS *Jimmy Carter* had been commissioned in February 2005, after all the major offensive action in Operations Enduring Freedom and Iraqi Freedom was already over. Unlike so many other U.S. attack submarines, SSN-23—the third and final in the *Seawolf* class—had never fired any Tomahawk T-LAM cruise missiles at enemy targets.

In two deployments to the Persian Gulf all they had done was sit on the bottom and use their sophisticated monitoring equipment to eavesdrop on other people's communications. But now, if the message he had just received from Washington was any indication, Capt. "Sandy" Heflin finally had a mission that would challenge his superbly trained crew and this magnificent boat.

Heflin read the operative paragraph of the message again:

SSN-23 WILL PROCEED FASTEST COURSE TO US NAV FAC BAHRAIN TO TAKE ABOARD ONE ASDS AND ELEVEN SEALS. WHEN DIRECTED BY CINC FIFTH FLEET, SSN-23 WITH EMBARKED PERSONNEL AND EQUIPMENT WILL CONDUCT COVERT OPERATION TO SEVER UNDERSEA FIBER-OPTIC CABLE CONNECTING AD DAMMAM SAUDI ARABIA TO BANDAR-E ABBAS, IRAN.

Lt. Cmdr. Jack Hughes, his XO, looking over his shoulder said, "This is the kind of mission that the guys back in the '70s and '80s used to pull all the time against the Soviets."

"Yeah," said Heflin, "my first CO used to talk about sneaking into Murmansk even before we had the *Los Angeles* class boats—and tapping the Soviets' old-fashioned 'hardwire core' cables."

"I remember at sub school," added Hughes, "we had briefings on how our subs tapped them even after Moscow installed fiber-optic lines and digital switches carrying five gigabytes per second and as many as 60,000 separate, simultaneous international phone calls. They even got stuff that was being put up on Eutelsat, Intelsat, Inmarsat, Intersputnik, and Orbita satellites."

"I must have missed that class," said Heflin. "How did our subs tap into the fiber-optics without the Soviets finding out?"

"Using the first generation of the equipment that we have aboard," replied Hughes, pleased that he could impress his skipper. "Wizards like John Poindexter developed mathematical data-compression techniques and 'artificial intelligence' routines—and the on-board computers 'learned' which cables carried traffic of strategic or intelligence value. What's always amazed me is how long it took the Sovs to figure out we were there."

"Yeah, but in a way, our guys going into Soviet harbors had some advantages that we're not going to have on this mission," said Captain Heflin.

"How's that?" asked Hughes.

"Well," replied Heflin, "for one thing, places like the Seymorput Naval Yard have scores of nuclear-powered submarines coming, going, berthed, and in dry-docks, so there wasn't—isn't—much chance of the Russians picking up one of our subs with some kind of radiation detection."

"Well, the good news for us," said Hughes, "is that today, less than a fourth of the Russian sub fleet is even operational. When we were going through our 're-fresher training' I read that the hulls of forty-five of their most recent boats are no longer hermetic—if they take them to sea, there's a good chance they'll sink. After the fiasco with the *Kursk,* they found all kinds of problems at Gremikha. Something like fifty of their subs have depleted nuclear fuel and they can't afford to reactivate them. They are now using old nuclear subs and other 'rust buckets' in Murmansk Harbor just to store radioactive waste."

"And I thought that the reason Murmansk harbor didn't freeze over was global warming," Captain Heflin said sardonically.

Hughes, really into his subject, said, "The Russians have dumped entire reactors—at least eighteen of them—into the oceans. The last intelligence report I saw indicated that nearly 20,000 canisters of nuclear waste, hundreds of thousands of gallons of liquid radioactive material . . . and about ten million *curies* worth of spent solid fuel rods are stored on those ships and subs in Murmansk Harbor."

"Yeah, well, we're not going into Murmansk Harbor on this run," said Heflin, tiring of Hughes's encyclopedic recitation. "Let's find out what the Iranians have for an underwater listening capability—and where their Kilo class diesel-electric boats are. I don't want to bump into someone who doesn't like us while we're snipping their clothesline."

"Will do," said the XO, taking notes. "Are we going to have to make any modifications to transport the mini-sub—the ASDS?"

"Good question, XO," said Heflin. "Get off a message to ComSubPac and ask 'em. I know that the ASDS is air-transported mounted on its own trailer rig, but I don't know if we have to make any changes to our hull to accommodate her."

"I know the cable says 'When ordered,' but do you have any guess as to the timetable on this?" asked Hughes.

Heflin stood, looked at his XO, and said, "Given what's going on above the surface right now, I'd say ASAP—if not before."

CHAPTER FOURTEEN

In the Crosshairs

Lourdes Signals Intelligence Facility
Bejucal, Cuba
Monday, 29 October 2007
0757 Hours Local

Dimitri Komulakov looked at the printed copy of the electronic message he had just received from Nikolai Dubzhuko, his operations officer in Riyadh. He set it beside the two transcribed intercepts that had been handed to him a half hour earlier by Col. Mikhail Vushneshko—the commander of the Russian Signals Intelligence unit at Lourdes. None of the news was good.

Both of the transcripts Vushneshko had provided to Komulakov were from phone conversations grabbed out of the airwaves by Russian monitors on Saturday. The first was a cryptic call from Senator James Waggoner's cell phone to a Washington, D.C., telephone number, demanding to know when some kind of "Special Unit" would commence action and threatening to "have" someone's "rear end." Komulakov recognized the crude American slang and dismissed the call as irrelevant.

It was the second transcript that alarmed him—from a call made to Marine General Peter Newman's cell phone from another cell phone in Key West, Florida. The transmission had been monitored from both the Russian Embassy in Washington *and* at the Lourdes site. Of greatest concern to Komulakov was the reference to "troops." It concerned the "retired" KGB officer enough that he'd asked Vushneshko if there were any signs of an American military buildup in Florida. He was only partially reassured by the answer: the Americans were conducting an air-defense exercise at their Naval Air Base, ninety miles to the north.

Having dealt with the intercepts, Komulakov turned back to the most recently encrypted e-mail report he had received from Riyadh. It was increasingly apparent that the carefully concocted plans he had made with Ali Yunesi, the head of the Iranian Intelligence Service, were unraveling. Dubzhuko had now lost contact with four of the Saudi yachts and two of the aircraft that his teams had so carefully captured. He checked his watch—it was nearly eight in the morning in Cuba—just before four in the afternoon in Saudi Arabia. Despite his reluctance to use the Cuba-Murmansk-Moscow-Tehran-Riyadh fiber-optic voice link, he decided that he and his principal deputy simply had to talk. He picked up the phone and said to the operator, "Get Dubzhuko on the line for me." Ten seconds later they were connected.

"So, Comrade Nikolai," he said, "have you been able to regain communications with any of the missing yachts or aircraft yet?"

"No, General," the former KGB colonel replied. "There are still the four ships and two aircraft that have not reestablished communications—and now another vessel that was off the coast of Algeria last night has failed to check in."

"And what are you doing to make sure that this does not continue to happen?" demanded Komulakov. "Are you certain that the crews you dispatched to bring these planes and boats to Caracas have not simply decided that they can make more by selling them than you were paying them, eh?"

"That is most unlikely, General," Dubzhuko responded indignantly. "First, each of the ships and aircraft had at least one of our loyal officers aboard to supervise the delivery to Caracas—and that's where they were to be paid. As you know, the rest of the crews—on the boats and the planes—weren't doing this for the money."

"So what happened to the missing boats and planes?" asked Komulakov.

"I think we should consider the possibility that the Americans or their allies may have taken them."

"I agree," responded Komulakov. "I am surprised that their press organs have not made an announcement to that effect, but we must plan accordingly. We are going to move up the delivery of the weapons. I want to get them to Caracas just as soon as possible. Have you talked to the pilots?"

"Yes, they are two of our best," answered Dubzhuko. "The plane is an Airbus 320 freighter— painted as 'Air France Air Cargo.' Right now it's in a hangar at Bandar Abbas, and the weapons are aboard in their containers. Their flight plan calls for them to refuel in Algeria, overnight in the Canary Islands, and into Caracas the next day."

"Why so many stops?" asked Komulakov.

"For safety margins on fuel, crew rest, and because it is a more normal routing for such an aircraft and so is less likely to attract attention," responded the deputy.

"Very well," said the general. "I shall call our employer and tell him that we are moving the weapons earlier than planned. Yunesi will be concerned. Should he or any of his 'Islamic Brotherhood' contact you, tell them that we are simply trying to make sure that everything is in place for their special day."

Central Police Station
Paddington Green, London
Monday, 29 October 2007
1205 Hours Local

It was raining as the MI6 driver pulled up to the gate labeled "Authorized Personnel Only" at the Paddington Green High Security Police Station. He turned to the man in the backseat and said, "I'll be in the car-park across the street when you come out, sir."

"Very well, Johnson," replied Joseph Blackman, pulling the collar of his trench coat up before exiting into the downpour. "I shouldn't be more than a half hour." The MI6 officer closed the door of the Rover sedan, walked to the small gate through the forty-two-inch high cast-iron fence surrounding the station, showed his ID badge to the blue-uniformed guard just inside the portal, and was admitted into the building.

Rather than take the lift, Blackman strode up one flight of stairs and down the quiet corridor to an office door labeled, "Chief Inspector Evan Hadley, Director, Counter-Terrorism." Not indicated on the sign was another, unmentioned title: Hadley was also the chief liaison between the police and MI5—the British domestic Intelligence Service. Blackman knocked twice on the door, entered an anteroom, and was escorted by a young woman in civilian clothes into Hadley's office.

"Joseph, thank you for coming on such short notice," said Evan Hadley. "You know Michael Stevens of Scotland Yard, yes?"

Blackman and Stevens shook hands and as all three men sat down, Hadley said, "I thought it would be good for the three of us to chat a bit since Stevens and I are getting a good bit of heat from the Home Office about all this 'Islamic Brotherhood' business."

"And unfortunately," Stevens added, "the Yanks aren't being particularly forthcoming. Their Leg-Att—

the FBI agent at their embassy—is fairly new and doesn't quite seem to have figured out the 'Anglo-American Special Relationship.' Evan suggested that since you communicate quite freely with your CIA counterpart—Goode's his name, isn't it?—that you might be able to share some insights with us."

Blackman simply nodded.

"I think," said Hadley, picking up again, "much of the concern at the Home Office began yesterday when the Americans circulated those photographs along with the BOLO of the people they had captured that showed those special containers to hold nuclear weapons installed aboard those stolen Saudi ships and aircraft. Our aviation and Port Security people now want us to inspect every sport plane and fishing boat for similar containers."

Blackman looked at the two men he had known for years and asked, "So you want to know what's going on? Are we a target like the Americans? What should we be anticipating? Right?"

Hadley and Stevens both nodded their heads, then took out pencils and paper to take notes.

"Well, let's all understand something right up front," began Blackman. "What I'm about to share with you is Foreign Intelligence Information—and cannot be sourced back to the SIS or we'll all be in the dock."

"Quite," said Stevens, putting down his pencil.

Blackman continued. "You already know all that's relevant about the American operation that netted the two Saudi yachts off Majorca on Friday night-Saturday morning. Since then their SEALs have taken down another one in Portugal."

"How about aircraft?" Stevens asked.

"One has been impounded in Mexico, and the South African Rangers helped an American Delta Force unit seize another in Johannesburg," Blackman responded. "All of the ships and planes were outfitted to carry nuclear weapons," he added, knowing that this would be a surprise to them, "as was the Saudi vessel seized by our lads from the Special Boat Service early this morning off Sidi-Fredj, Algeria."

At this, Stevens dropped his pen. Hadley's head snapped up and he said, "Algeria, you say. Well, Joseph, kind of Her Majesty's Secret Service to let us in on the fun." He then added dryly, "Would you care to tantalize us with some of the details?"

Blackman smiled and said, "It all happened just before dawn. C said that you would want to be aware."

"To say the least," said Stevens.

"It all came down rather fast," Blackman continued. "After the Americans seized the two vessels off Palma, our GCHQ SigInt site at Gibraltar picked up some unusual emissions from Sidi-Fredj. With the help of the frigate HMS *St. Albans* they pinpointed the source as a two-hundred-foot yacht calling itself *Saladin's Prize*. A quick check with Lloyd's showed that there was no such name in their registry, so yesterday morning we sent a few boys from the Special Reconnaissance Regiment to Sidi-Fredj to check her out."

"Any help from the Algerian authorities?" asked Hadley.

Blackman shook his head. "No. Didn't have time to ask. Our lads reported that the crew of the vessel consisted of five bearded males, four of Middle Eastern appearance, one apparently Slavic-Caucasian. Turns out they were right—he's Russian. They were staying at the El Manar Resort Hotel ashore and taking turns guarding their ship."

"Ah, there you go, 'profiling' again, Joseph. What are we to do with you?" said Stevens in mock disapproval. "What happened next?"

Blackman ignored the jibe and continued, "Last night C authorized the SBS lads to take down the vessel. Simultaneously, they grabbed the three that were ashore, brought them out to the boat, and the whole 'lot and caboodle' are now on the way to Her Majesty's Sovereign Base at Gibraltar. No mess, no fuss. All very tidy."

"Was there a nuclear weapon aboard?" asked Hadley.

"No weapons either," Blackman replied, "just the same kind of lead-lined steel box in the bilge and wiring like the Americans reported in the two that they seized and in the photos they circulated from the one impounded in Mexico."

"I realize this is a bit off my turf, as it were," interjected Hadley, "but is the Foreign Office aware that we are about to have a pirated Saudi vessel pull into Gibraltar?"

"Not sure," answered Blackman. "But just as I left to come over here, C was chatting with the PM on the phone, so I assume that the Foreign Office will be in the loop on that matter very soon, if not already."

"Any indication where this vessel was headed before our chaps so rudely took it away from them?" asked Stevens.

"Apparently the ship's navigation system was programmed for a straight run through to Caracas, Venezuela," answered the MI6 officer.

"One last question, Joseph," said Hadley. "What do you plan to do with these five 'pirates' you have apprehended?"

"Why, Evan," said Blackman with just the hint of a smile, "I thought that they would be welcome at a detention facility with a great reputation for discretion—and getting good results from interrogations. How about your place *here*?"

"Well, I've no problem taking in these jihadist thugs, holding them incommunicado under our 'Special Powers' laws, and 'sweating' them a bit," replied Hadley. "It's the Russian I'm concerned about. Moscow is sure to raise a stink when they find out. Anyway, what the devil are the Huskies doing in this mess? Given their problems in Chechnya, I'd have thought they would be with us on this one."

"Can't tell you what the Russians are doing in all of this—yet," replied Blackman. "But C wants to find out, so yesterday we asked for a little help from 'our friends'—to paraphrase John Lennon, or was it Paul McCartney? I actually can't remember."

"Our friends?" Stevens asked. "What friends?"

Blackman looked his Scotland Yard counterpart in the eye and said, "The Norwegians."

São Pedro Airport
St. Vicente Island, Cape Verde Islands
Monday, 29 October 2007
1315 Hours Local

Pilot Is'haaq Al Kabil keyed the microphone switch on the control yoke of the Boeing 737 and in perfect English said, "Dakar Flight Control, this is Air Afrique Cargo Flight Juliet Six One One Seven in transit to Cape Verde Islands, level at thirty-one thousand, squawking one three two five."

"Go ahead, Six One One Seven, we have you," replied the air traffic controller outside the capital of Senegal, two hundred miles east and six miles below.

"Roger, Dakar," replied Al Kabil. "Request permission to make an in-flight change from the flight plan we filed before leaving Freetown, Sierra Leone."

"State your request, Six One One Seven."

"Roger, Dakar, we're experiencing an intermittent cabin pressurization warning indication. Request permission to descend to twenty-one thousand and land at São Pedro Airport on St. Vicente Island instead of Santa Maria International Airport on Sal Island."

"Wait, out," responded the controller. Then thirty seconds later, he came back and said, "Juliet Six One One Seven, this is Dakar. Change approved. Descend to two-one-thousand. Contact São Pedro tower on one-twenty-six-point five. Good day."

Kabil acknowledged receiving the approval and smiled as he approached the ten tiny islets of the Cape Verde chain. He had been told by the Russian sleeping in the back of the aircraft that the plane's new paint job was less likely to attract attention at São Pedro than at the much busier International Airport.

Forty minutes later, and fifty nautical miles from his destination, São Pedro Approach gave Juliet Six One One Seven instructions to land on runway zero two, right. "Roger, One One Seven, turning right ten degrees, switching to ILS," Kabil said as he switched off the autopilot and tuned the radio beacon to the assigned frequency. He then turned to his copilot and said in Arabic, "Descend to seven thousand feet and reduce airspeed from 320 to 240 knots."

A few minutes later, as the twin dormant volcanic peaks on opposite ends of the island appeared through a brief rain squall, his copilot said, "Airspeed two forty, altitude seven thousand."

Al Kabil reached forward on the console between the two men, extended the flaps on the 737 to the first position, took the controls from his copilot—and made a perfect approach. He only needed to check the Glide Slope indicator once as they made their descent to the runway.

Eight nautical miles from the airport, Kabil fully extended the flaps and increased power as the big panels extended behind the wing increased the "drag" by acting like a brake. When the airspeed indicator showed 160 knots he flipped the round wheel-shaped lever on the front panel down, and the landing gear extended and locked.

There was a barely perceptible jolt as the big plane touched down with its nose wheel on the centerline of the tarmac. Kabil smoothly shifted the throttles to reverse thrust, flipped a switch to elevate the "air brake" panels on tops of the wings, and applied pressure to the tips of the rudder pedals, braking the 737 to stop 2,000 feet from the end of the runway. As he taxied toward the "air freight" FBO at the far end of the airport, his copilot said, "Nice landing, Is'haaq" in Arabic.

"Thank you," said Kabil, then he added, "but it should have been a good landing, Jabbar. I have logged almost three hundred hours in this very airplane."

It was not a boast. Kabil had been a pilot in the Royal Saudi Air Force and had been the chief pilot for the owner of this 737, Prince Muneer al-Taif, for more than four years. And unlike nearly all of the other Saudi aircraft and vessels that had been commandeered by the "Islamic Brotherhood," this one had been easy to acquire.

On the tenth of October, Kabil had flown Prince Muneer and one of his young European concubines to the Seychelles for a "holiday." Late on the afternoon of the fourteenth, when the prince learned of the "coup" in Saudi Arabia, he arrived planeside in a panic, demanding that Kabil fly him immediately to Egypt.

The chief pilot took off as ordered, but the prince and his Dutch girlfriend never arrived in Cairo. Four hours into the flight, Kabil put the plane on autopilot, went to the ornate stateroom in the middle of the jet, and, using a .25 cal. pistol, shot the prince and his blonde once each in the head. When he landed in Khartoum, members of the "brotherhood" met the plane, removed the bodies, and secreted the plane in a rented hangar. Kabil had spent the next two weeks waiting for orders while his "colleagues" installed their "special equipment."

Now, with the aircraft parked, Kabil walked back to

the master bedroom where he had murdered the owner and his girlfriend and examined the lead-lined stainless steel box that had replaced the bloodstained bed. He looked at the empty container and the wire harness running from it and whispered, as though talking to a small child, "It will not be long now. Soon we will bring a fiery vengeance upon the infidels. Praise be to Allah."

HQ, 5th Fleet
U.S. Naval Facility, Bahrain
Monday, 29 October 2007
2050 Hours Local

The USS *Jimmy Carter* surfaced and entered port as soon as it was dark. Capt. "Sandy" Heflin, the sub's Operations Officer, and two of his "Communications Spooks" had come ashore immediately for briefings by the 5th Fleet staff and a man from the CIA introduced simply as "Herb." He'd left his XO and the chief of the boat to supervise the installation of special fittings that were being welded to his sub's hull so they could transport their "special cargo" to their "mission area."

As Heflin arrived at the Fleet Support Activity landing, he got his first look at the ASDS—Advanced SEAL Delivery System—that would sever the undersea Iran-Saudi Arabia fiber-optic telephone cable—once his submarine found it. The mini-sub and its accompanying six-man SEAL team were on the big concrete pier as Heflin and his team disembarked from a launch dispatched by the admiral.

The sixty-five-foot-long ASDS had been flown from Groton, Connecticut—directly to Bahrain—inside a USAF C-17. Transporting it three miles from the U.S. military side of the Bahrain airport to the U.S. Navy's Fleet Support pier without "tipping our hand" had been an issue of great debate on the 5th Fleet staff. Finally, a

Navy master chief said, "Let's just cover the thing with a tarpaulin and haul it down the highway. None of the jihadi agents are going to know what it is. Hey, most of *you people* don't even know what it looks like."

By the time Heflin, his officers, and the SEAL detachment leader, Lt. Paul Van Hooser, were seated in the admirals conference room, listening to "Herb" and others describe their mission, the mini-sub, nicknamed the *Minnow,* was being lifted by crane from its specially built transport carriage and lowered into the warm waters of the Persian Gulf. Rather than risk damage by towing it out to the sub, the ASDS, powered by its internal 67-hp electric motor, made its own way the eight hundred yards to where the *Jimmy Carter* was riding quietly at a mooring.

"The ASDS weighs fifty-five tons dry—but it has neutral buoyancy in the water," said a U.S. Navy commander, standing at the front of the room next to a PowerPoint display of the mini-sub. As the image on the screen changed to a computer-assisted design of the ASDS mounted aft of the *Jimmy Carter*'s sail, he continued, "As long as you do not exceed twenty knots, we believe that the fittings we're installing should be adequate to withstand the force of the water pressing against the hull of either vessel."

Only slightly mollified by that information—and the fact that the commander was wearing the gold dolphins of the submarine service—Heflin asked, "What's this going to do to my depth and diving capabilities? And how about noise?"

"We have all the tables worked out and will provide the depth-dive tables to you on a CD and on paper before you leave, Captain," answered the commander. "There is some good news on noise signature for the ASDS. It's been equipped with new, composite material, anti-cavitation screws—so when you detach the mini-sub it will be almost as quiet as you are."

When the engineering experts finished, the "intel-types" took over. Heflin noticed that the Fleet Intelligence officers all deferred to "Herb" on this part of the brief. The CIA officer concluded his presentation by restating what to Heflin was the obvious, "Once you have used your onboard sensors to determine the proper cable that needs to be cut, get the most accurate fix you can on the location. You'll be on the Iranian side of the Persian Gulf, out of the shipping lanes, but it's important that you aren't detected when you come up to detach the ASDS."

"How long will it take you to cut this cable?" Heflin asked Van Hooser.

"It depends on our visibility at depth," the SEAL officer responded. "Looking at the charts, it appears that we'll be at about five hundred feet. If the water is clear and we don't have any problems, we could be done in less than an hour."

"And then we surface to take the *Minnow* back aboard?" asked Heflin.

"That's the idea," responded Herb.

"Easy for you to say," responded Heflin. "What's the latest on mines and the Iranian Kilo subs? I'd hate to have to deal with either one while we're trying to take Lieutenant Van Hooser's SEALs and their sexy little machine back aboard."

"Herb" said nothing and looked instead at the senior Fleet Intelligence officer who looked uncomfortably at Heflin and said, "I'm sorry to say, Captain, that we don't know about mines, and two of the Iranians' subs seem to be unaccounted for."

Narvik-Andoya Science Facility
Tromsö, Norway
Monday, 29 October 2007
2300 Hours Local

It was pitch black, icy cold, and the Aurora Borealis—
the northern lights—were shimmering in the air as the
C-130 turned on its lights, five miles from the end of the
frozen runway, ten degrees north of the Arctic Circle. It
would soon be *moerketiden* in northern Norway—the
two-month period when the sun doesn't rise above the
horizon. Standing beside the tiny control tower, Maj.
Carl Arvildsun, Royal Norwegian Army, clapped his
hands together to stay warm—and wondered why he
had volunteered for this mission.

Though he could see little beyond the dim lights of
the runway, the Norwegian officer knew that he was
standing in a level basin surrounded by terrain that had
been shaped by huge glaciers that had also gouged out
Arctic fjords and left monumental rock formations. Not
far from the airfield was the ancient town of Tromsö,
settled by farmers and fishermen during the Viking era.
Some of that early identity had been preserved—there
were still a number of sod-roofed cottages and ornate
wooden buildings in the town of three thousand people.
Occasionally, small herds of reindeer could be seen at
the edge of the town, pawing through the snow, searching for hidden moss or buried grass.

In the Tromsö town square there was a statue hon-
oring Roald Amundsen, the pioneer Arctic and Antarc-
tic explorer who died in a plane crash while searching
for a missing Italian adventurer. In another nearby park
there was a memorial to the valor of eleven Norwegian
resistance fighters who were captured, brutally interrogated, and then killed by German occupation troops
during World War II. One of them had been Arvildsun's
uncle.

The base—where the Norwegian major now awaited the approaching C-130—had been built by the British, used by the Americans during the Cold War, and now served both the Royal Norwegian Air Force and the Norwegian Weather Service. From here and the Naval Station at Narvik, 120 miles to the south, scientific rockets were routinely launched into the Arctic skies to study everything from wind patterns aloft, to the Aurora Borealis, to the earth's magnetic field.

Yet, even with all this activity, Arvildsun knew that the four engines of the Royal Norwegian Air Force C-130, approaching from the west on the Atlantic air current, would arouse interest as it passed over the town in the dead of night. He hoped that the plane—and its contents—would be far away before anyone came to the base to make inquiries.

The large propeller-driven aircraft touched down and taxied the last two hundred meters of its trip from Scotland on packed snow and ice that had yet to be scraped from the tarmac. After coming to a stop near the austere terminal, the pilot shut down three of the engines, leaving one running to keep the fuel, hydraulic fluid, oil—and the aircraft's cabin—heated.

Arvildsun waited for the clamshell doors at the rear of the nearly one-hundred-foot-long aircraft to open before moving toward the cargo bay. As he walked, his breath made small clouds of steam in the dark air.

When he approached the cargo ramp he could hear men with British accents inside the aircraft shouting out instructions for care in unloading the payload. Arvildsun turned back to the flight line technician who had guided the big plane to its parking spot with lighted orange cones and said to him in Norwegian, "Thank you for your help. You need to go back inside the terminal now."

The young enlisted soldier obeyed, and as soon as he was gone, Arvildsun took out a flashlight and pointed it toward the four large, seven-ton military trucks that had been parked for more than three hours beside a nearby hangar. He flashed the light twice, and the trucks, their mottled black and white winter camouflage barely visible in the gloom, pulled up to the rear of the C-130. Moments later a forklift appeared as if from nowhere and began removing the palletized cargo from the plane's cavernous cargo bay—and placing it on three of the trucks.

The entire transfer took less than fifteen minutes. When the first three trucks were loaded with crates of gear, nine men disembarked from the aircraft and boarded the heated compartment in the rear of the fourth truck. Once again the Norwegian major took out his flashlight—this time using it to blink a signal to the pilot. Nine minutes later the C-130 was racing back down the runway, clawing its way into the Arctic night. By then, Arvildsun, driving his Norwegian Army Land Rover, was leading his little convoy of four trucks off the base and onto the highway, east toward Skibotn. Seated beside him was Maj. Trevor Watts of the Special Reconnaissance Regiment.

As the procession passed through the sentry post, Watts observed, "Nice piece of work, Major. Not a single word spoken on a radio or phone to tip 'Ivan' off that we're coming."

"Thank you," said Arvildsun. He then asked, "Can you tell me how long this mission will last? I was only told that you were to set up mobile electronic equipment to monitor Russian communications. But I was not told how long you would be here. I have enough food and fuel positioned for ten men, for a month. Will that be enough?"

Watts looked at his Norwegian counterpart in the dim light of the instrument panel as they rolled down the dark highway and said, "If we haven't figured out what role the Russians are playing in this 'Islamic Brotherhood' business by then, it probably won't make any difference anyway."

Hotel El Centro
Downtown Caracas, Venezuela
Monday, 29 October 2007
2345 Hours Local

Newman was the last to arrive. Traveling as "Peter Oldham," he had taken American Airlines Flight 2133 from Miami at 1930, landing at Simon Bolivar International Airport, fourteen miles west of the Venezuelan capital at 2230—a two-hour flight that showed as three because Caracas is one time zone east of Florida. Now, seated in the lobby of the aging Hotel El Centro with his two "colleagues" from "Petro-Research," Newman was perspiring in the tropical heat. Over the heads of the three men, ancient ceiling fans struggled to move the heavy, humid, slightly cooled air. But at just twelve degrees north of the equator, the hotel's vintage air conditioner was fighting a losing battle.

Army Master Sergeant Robert Nievos, sitting across from "Oldham" in an overstuffed leather chair, had arrived on a morning flight from Mexico City. He had been the first to arrive at the "Three Star" El Centro, on the corner of *Sur 6 y Oeste 6*, one block west of Plaza Bolívar. The CIA station had chosen the hotel for its proximity to the national capitol building.

Nievos's appearance—short, trim, and wiry, with a pencil-thin mustache and hair pulled back in a short ponytail—belied that he was really a veteran Delta Force team leader. The passport in Roberto's pocket was from Argentina, where he had lived for a time as a child—the son of an American diplomat.

The third man, Senior Chief Manuel Suazo, was a U.S. Navy SEAL. But his well-manicured beard and tailored tropical suit served to disguise his exceptional physique and his real line of work. Suazo had arrived in Caracas on a mid-afternoon flight from Bogota.

Though Suazo was also using his real name, he was traveling on a Spanish passport.

Newman/Oldham looked around the dark wood-paneled lobby searching for their "contact" who was supposed to have been there to meet them a quarter hour ago. In one corner was a young couple, apparently on a romantic getaway or their honeymoon. They were so wrapped up in each other that they were oblivious to the others in the room. At another cluster of chairs, two middle-aged couples were conversing quietly in German—obviously tourists. But at a third table, in the far corner, sat a man in the shadows reading a newspaper.

"That guy has been here all evening," said Nievos. "He was here when I came down for dinner and he was still there when I left for the airport to pick you up. I've been watching him since we sat down and he's not packing heat, so he's not a cop. Since nobody at the front desk pays any attention to him, my guess is that he's just a 'watcher' for the Valdez regime—put here to call in anything unusual on the cell phone he's carrying on his belt."

"Do you suppose he's 'made' us?" asked Newman.

"Doubt it," replied Suazo. "All three of us have good 'paper' that shows we work for Petro-Research—and with oil prices the way they are, this town is crawling with people from every country on the planet in every aspect of the oil business."

As the Navy SEAL was talking, a man who looked to be in his fifties entered the front door of the hotel. He was wearing glasses, a rumpled seersucker suit and had what appeared to be several large sheets of paper rolled up under his arm.

"Well, well, here's our man," said Nievos quietly to Newman and Suazo. "Let me do the 'meet and greet' since I'm the guy who supposedly knows him."

Rising from his chair, Nievos shouted out in fluent Spanish, "Eduardo—over here." He then made a beeline for the man in seersucker, gave him a big *abrazzo*, kissed him on both cheeks, put his arm around his shoulder, and guided the new arrival toward the chairs where Newman and Suazo were now standing. Newman noticed that everyone in the room had glanced up at the minor commotion—and just as quickly, ignored it. The whole scene was so perfectly "normal" that it immediately relieved any suspicion that the four men could be up to anything untoward or nefarious.

"Eduardo, this is Peter Oldham and Manuel Suazo," said Nievos, introducing them effusively as they shook hands with the newcomer. "Peter is from our Oklahoma City Office and 'Manny' is from Houston," the Delta Force NCO continued enthusiastically. "I've told them all about you. Now, what do you have for us?"

As they sat, "Eduardo" placed the papers he had been carrying on the low table centered among the four chairs and unrolled the sheets with a flourish, saying loudly enough for the "watcher" to overhear, "As you asked, Señor Oldham, these charts show the current oil and gas leases throughout the country. I have marked out the available concessions and the areas where we can apply for permits to explore. As you know, most of the proven reserves are in the area around Lake Maracaibo, but I am convinced that with the new equipment you are bringing in, we will succeed in finding more elsewhere."

Once again, Newman was impressed with the "tradecraft" of his colleagues. Bill Goode had told him that his "man in Caracas" was a first-rate field operative, and the unassuming, bespectacled "Eduardo" was already living up to the advance praise. He had just established for anyone who was listening a superb rationale for the gamma-wave/neutron particle detectors and the bulky "Backscatter" PMMW equipment that was en route to Caracas. Only a uniquely trained eye would know that the equipment wasn't used for oil exploration.

Then, as the men bent over the papers spread out on the low table, appearing to study the charts, Eduardo said to Newman, "Do you know when the specialized exploration equipment will arrive, Mr. Oldham? I must make arrangements at customs."

"Here is the bill of lading," Newman replied, handing Eduardo a sheet of paper that he took from his pocket. "As you see, the equipment is in two containers on an Evergreen containership due in tomorrow from Houston."

"Very well," the CIA man said with a smile. "Now, before you retire for the evening, you must accompany me to one of the most beautiful sites in Caracas, the fountain in the Plaza de Bolívar. It is just across the hotel courtyard."

The four of them walked leisurely through the lobby and across the plaza to stand in front of the fountain. Eduardo, positioned between Newman and the two Special Operations men, raised his arms expansively and gestured toward the spraying water, saying loudly, "There is no more beautiful sight in all Caracas." Then, much more quietly he added, ". . . and no better place to talk without the fear of eavesdroppers. Even if someone is hitting us with a parabolic dish or directional mike, the sound of the water masks our conversation. If you keep facing the fountain the cameras will not be able to read our lips."

Suazo smiled and said, "Well done."

Newman, seeming to admire the sculptured man on horseback rising out of the rushing water, asked the CIA operative, "You know that we have two missions?"

"Yes," responded Eduardo, "I was contacted directly by Deputy Director Goode and told that you are here to set up the search for nuclear weapons and to 'deal' with El Presidente's friend, Samuel Mubassa. My instructions are to help you with both. Do we have anything more about when and how the nuclear weapons are to be delivered? That part of the mission is the most difficult."

"Roberto is coordinating that task," said Newman, nodding to Nievos. "We're supposed to receive any new information via D-DACT—and you should be getting the same word, directly from Bill Goode at Langley. We may have new information in the morning."

Eduardo nodded and replied, "The more we know about how the nukes are being delivered here, the more effective we will be in using this special equipment to keep track of them." Then, turning to the Navy SEAL, he said, "So Manuel, I take it you are here to eliminate the Samuel Mubassa problem."

"Not exactly," answered Suazo. "I'm here to eliminate Samuel Mubassa."

The man in the seersucker suit nodded and said with a slight bow, "I stand corrected. Will you need any special equipment?"

"No thanks, Eduardo. My 'hunting rifle' is a Barrett .50 cal. Model 82A3 with ten-round magazine and Leopold ten-power scope. It'll be in one of the containers that arrive tomorrow from Houston. But I could use some help getting this guy Mubassa's schedule down."

"That should not be a major problem," said Eduardo. "He is very close to President Valdez and staying at *El Presidente's* guesthouse. I have a very good source who can tell us nearly every movement that Mubassa makes with Valdez at least twenty-four hours in advance."

At this point Newman interrupted and asked, "Can your source find out if Valdez knows about the shipment of nuclear weapons?"

"Perhaps," responded Eduardo. "He is very good."

"Do you trust him?" asked the Marine.

"Of course I trust him, Mr. Oldham," responded Eduardo, looking offended. "He is my older brother."

Residence of Senator James Waggoner
Old Dominion Drive, Belle View, VA
Monday, 29 October 2007
2355 Hours Local

The phone rang only twice before the "senior senator" picked it up and said, "Hello."

"It's Alan Michaels. Senator, you asked me to call when we put the City Edition of the paper 'to bed.' Well, it's rolling off the press and the story is top right, above the fold."

"Good work, son," said the Chairman of the Senate Intelligence Committee to the young *Washington Post* reporter. "I trust you kept my name out of it?"

"Of course, Senator," replied Michaels. "I'll read the lead 'graph' if you want."

"Go ahead," said Waggoner, reaching for his "nightcap"—three fingers of expensive bourbon in a water glass.

"The headline reads, 'White House Allows Terrorist to Escape,' " began Michaels. When Waggoner only grunted, the *Post* reporter continued. " 'Samuel Mubassa, suspected of being the principal funding source behind the Islamic Brotherhood terrorist organization, has been allowed to flee to Venezuela. Intelligence sources have told the *Washington Post* that Mubassa, who allegedly made hundreds of millions of dollars in the United Nations' corrupt Oil for Food program, is now being protected by the Valdez regime in Caracas. Congressional critics say that this is simply the latest in a string of colossal failures by this administration to take appropriate action against terrorists who now threaten the U.S. with nuclear weapons.' "

When Michaels stopped to take a breath, Waggoner interrupted, "That's just fine, son. I'll read the rest in the morning. But tell me, did you put in there somewhere that the administration is 'covering up' the threat of nuclear terrorism?"

"Absolutely," said the young reporter, thinking of Woodward and Bernstein and how nice it would be to win a Pulitzer Prize for investigative journalism. "You didn't give me very much about who is covering up what—so I'd like to talk to you some more tomorrow about that. Can we meet somewhere?"

"Shoot, son," said Waggoner, "I'm not going to start meeting you in parking garages like that sissy FBI 'Deep Throat' fella . . ."

"Mark Felt," interrupted Michaels, trying to be helpful.

"Whatever," said Waggoner. "That's not what I'm about. I'm trying to keep the innocent citizens of this country from being attacked by bloodthirsty killers. The American people need to know that people like Mubassa are financing nuclear murder—and the White House is covering up the magnitude of his crimes."

"Well, for Wednesday's edition can I get more from you on who at the White House is involved in this cover-up—and what should be done about it? Are we talking impeachment here?" asked the reporter.

"I'll think about it," answered Waggoner, curtly. "Don't call me. I'll call you. Good work—and good night."

CHAPTER FIFTEEN

Running Away

Press Room
The White House
Washington, DC
Tuesday, 30 October 2007
0815 Hours Local

Good morning, ladies and gentlemen," said the President as he walked into the White House Press Room. He and the First Lady had returned to the White House from Camp David shortly after dawn, and, for a change, no one in the media even knew he had been gone.

The nine members of the Fourth Estate, four cameramen, and two producers who were present when the President unexpectedly entered the Press Room, literally fell over themselves in their surprise at seeing the Commander in Chief. In nearly seven full years in office he had made only eight such unannounced visits to meet with members of the White House press corps—and it was usually during a holiday period when the "second string" was on duty.

Although this Tuesday morning was not a holiday, most of the "A-List" faces and names from the print and broadcast media had still found reasons to leave

Washington as rumors circulated that the "Islamic Brotherhood" planned an attack on the nation's capital.

"Mr. President," shouted one of the print reporters, "are we on the record?"

"Sure," said the Chief Executive, adding, "although I warn you in advance that I only have a few minutes— and you might ask me some questions that I just won't answer for security reasons. But you may quote me. Next question."

By now the only two TV news crews present had established connections with their networks, and both producers were whispering into their headsets trying to convince their respective news assignment desks that they should cut away from scheduled programming and go live from the White House.

"Mr. President, have you seen this morning's *Washington Post* article that says your administration allowed a terrorist to escape?" asked one of the producers.

"I read two things every morning," replied the President with a smile, "*The Washington Post* and the Holy Bible—so that way I know what both sides are up to."

"What do you have to say about allegations that your administration is covering up imminent threats of nuclear terrorism?"

"Well here I am," he said, still with a bit of a wry smile. "I wouldn't be standing here if we were busy covering anything up about an imminent nuclear threat."

"Let me put it differently," said a young wire service reporter. "Are we at risk from terrorists using nuclear weapons in this country?"

The President paused a moment, then said, "A group claiming to be the 'Islamic Brotherhood' transmitted such a threat on a videotape several days ago. It was similar to a threat that the same group issued shortly after the attack on Saudi Arabia. The group insists that we release the terrorists detained at Guantanamo and that we—along with every other Western country—withdraw all of our people from what they call 'Islamic lands.' We will not make concessions to terrorists. And if they—or anyone else—attacks the United States, there will be a swift, sure, and overwhelming response."

Now the remaining reporters were clamoring to get their questions answered. One of them asked, "What do you say to the calls from some in Congress for a preemptive nuclear attack on Iran?"

Once again the Chief Executive chose his words carefully as he said, "I'm not going to forecast or foreclose any of our options to protect the American people." He then added, "However, I do want to note that those who seek freedom and justice can find no better friend than the American people. And those who choose to threaten harm to the American people will find no greater enemy than our Armed Forces."

"Sir, in this morning's *Washington Post,* an anonymous Congressional source says that U.S. and British Special Forces have already captured more than half a dozen ships and airplanes headed for the United States with nuclear weapons aboard. Can you confirm or deny this report?"

"No!" said the President bluntly.

"No, what, sir?" persisted the young reporter.

"I answered your question," said the Chief Executive. "But let me remind all the anonymous sources out there—whoever they are—that this administration will pursue and prosecute any and all who violate the law by disclosing classified information."

"So you're saying it's true?"

"I said nothing of the sort, John," said the President, using the reporter's first name. "I simply stated a fact about those who break the law during this state of emergency—or anytime."

Now, another reporter tried a different tack on the same theme: "Mr. President, if there is a real nuclear threat, is your administration considering any mandatory evacuations like when a hurricane threatens the East Coast?"

"Well, as everyone knows, we're already experiencing serious disruptions as a result of what's happened in Saudi Arabia. Many people have, for their own reasons, chosen to leave some of our biggest cities. The Department of Homeland Security is already administering over fourteen thousand shelters around the country—most of them in schools that have been closed for over two weeks now. We will continue to open more emergency shelters as the need arises—particularly as the weather gets colder. But I don't believe that the nation's interests will be well served by a government-directed dislocation of millions more of our citizens from their homes and places of work."

"Then what should people do?" asked the only woman reporter present.

The President looked at her and said, "I know that these are difficult times. But I also know that we are a brave and resilient people. Rather than flee in the face of threats from those who hate us for who we are, I urge that the American people respond with courage, perseverance, and prayer. I know that all three work."

Then, as others shouted more questions to him, the President turned from the podium, made a small wave to the reporters, cameramen, and technicians, and said, "Thank you for your time this morning. God bless you and your families." With that, he walked out of the room.

Lourdes Signals Intelligence Facility
Bejucal, Cuba
Tuesday, 30 October 2007
0955 Hours Local

Dimitri Komulakov had watched nearly all of the President's impromptu press conference live, on the satellite TV in his command center, buried thirty meters deep in Cuban limestone. He had been half listening to the pirated signal of an American satellite broadcast while drafting a lengthy message to his employer in Tehran when the morning news was interrupted by the live feed from the White House.

He watched the Q & A with the American President followed by several minutes of commentary and criticism from an obviously unprepared anchor in Atlanta. Komulakov quickly tired of the editorial and told one of his communications technicians, "Silence that noise, but make sure you record what's being said and any re-broadcasts. Get Riyadh on the secure link, now." It was not a request. Less than a minute later, Colonel Dubzhuko was on the line.

"Well, Nikolai," began Komulakov, sounding remarkably calm, "we now know what happened to the missing Saudi ships and aircraft!"

"We do?" said the former KGB officer in Riyadh.

"They have been captured or sunk by the Americans and the British," said the Russian general.

"How do you know?" asked the stunned subordinate.

"The American President as much as said so—just minutes ago. I saw it live on their television."

"But . . ." sputtered Dubzhuko, ". . . how do you know he is not lying?" The anxiety was evident in his voice.

"I do not believe he was lying, Nikolai—and neither will our client," said Komulakov, "and that means we may have some serious problems. How many ships and airplanes have failed to check in as required?"

"When the last reports came in two hours ago, we received no signals from five of the vessels and three of the aircraft," answered Dubzhuko.

"And were all of them fitted to receive the weapons?"

"Yes, as you directed, Comrade General," responded Dubzhuko, attempting to deflect any criticism.

"We must assume that at least some of these planes and boats have been captured intact—and that the American and British intelligence authorities have figured out what the lead-lined boxes and wiring are for," said Komulakov. "I think we should also expect that some of our crews have been captured and are now being interrogated and telling all that they know."

"They may have captured some of our people, but nobody knows the full plan, General. For example, no one except our client, you, and I know that there were to be eleven ships and eleven aircraft equipped to carry the nuclear devices. And you and I are the only ones who know that we are being paid by Tehran."

"Hopefully that is correct, Nikolai, but everyone aboard knew that the aircraft and vessels were to be delivered to Caracas—and when. And all of our comrades—the Russians and Ukrainians—had identity papers showing that they worked for Filaya in Riyadh—and that you are their employer."

A sudden sense of dread suddenly enveloped the "retired" KGB colonel. Dubzhuko didn't even know for certain where his commander was, but the Americans could right now be targeting the Filaya compound where *he* was sitting. "What should we do?" asked Dubzhuko.

Komulakov couldn't care less about what ultimately happened to his deputy—but he still needed him to finish the operation. He thought for a moment then said,

"First, when is the aircraft with the nuclear devices due in Caracas?"

"Tonight," replied Dubzhuko.

"Good," answered the general. "And are the technicians already in place in Caracas?"

"Two are in place in Venezuela and the other three are with the weapons on the plane. You have their identifiers and contact information in my last message," answered the loyal but very concerned subordinate, who then added, "but what about *me*—and the rest of us here at the Filaya building?"

"Stop worrying," ordered Komulakov. "Ali Yunesi contracted us to convey eleven nuclear weapons to Venezuela—and the means of delivering them to American cities. Right now we have ten weapons on the way to Caracas—and we still have six captured Saudi ships and eight aircraft—plenty of backup—which is what we intended. The Iranians need not know that we are one weapon short. I have made arrangements to have another artillery warhead delivered to Iran from our stocks in the Ukraine for the Shabaz missile that they are so excited about. I am sending three more technicians with the PAL codes to install it for them. What else is there to be worried about?"

"*Worried* about?" Dubzhuko practically shouted. "What about *me*?" he repeated. "If the Americans have figured out that this operation is being run from this building, they will surely target it!"

"Calm down, Nikolai," Komulakov said. "I have made alternative plans for you as well. We have another site in Riyadh, on Al Kadif Road. The sign on the gate is for 'Persian Gulf Exports.' It is somewhat smaller, but it is the tallest building in the neighborhood and, like the Filaya building, it is connected to the Iran-Saudi Arabia undersea fiber-optic cable."

"I remember the site, General," replied Dubzhuko. "I was the one who leased it and installed our equipment, but it is not as secure as this installation—and the generators are not as large."

"It will have to suffice, Nikolai," answered Komu-lakov. "Go over there and make sure it has not been taken over by our 'Islamic allies' and report back to me."

Hotel El Centro
Downtown Caracas, Venezuela
Tuesday, 30 October 2007
1430 Hours Local

By the time Newman arrived at his hotel, his shirt was once again soaked with perspiration. He had been out with "Eduardo" since dawn, reconnoitering places to carry out his dual missions: emplacing surveillance to detect nuclear weapons—*and* planning the "execution" of Samuel Mubassa—as directed by the Commission on Threat Mitigation. Either of the two assignments would be a handful for any Special Ops unit commander, but Newman was dealing with both.

Now, as the fetid, smog-laden tropical air of Caracas neared the high-temperature point of the day, much of the activity on the streets had come to a halt as Venezue-lans sought shade or air conditioning for their midday siesta. Because a "gringo" walking around on the streets at this time of day would be easier for the Venezuelan security services to track, Newman had told his two American colleagues, Army First Sergeant Roberto Nievos and Navy SEAL "Manny" Suazo, to meet him at the El Centro at 1430, to review their plans.

As he turned the key and opened the door of his hotel room, Newman noticed that the tiny piece of toothpick that he had placed in the jamb, just above the bottom hinge, had been displaced. It did not surprise him. He expected that the enormous Valdez secret police opera-tion would be going through his room in his absence.

What did surprise him was the wiry frame of Nievos standing in the sitting room of the small suite with a finger pressed to his lips—a silent warning to say nothing.

Newman entered, closed the door and only then did he notice Suazo, poised behind the door, ready to strike, had Newman been one of the Valdez security thugs. Nievos motioned Newman to come with him and then pointed up to the small chandelier over their heads. The Marine peered closely at the light fixture and then noticed the tiny, omni-directional microphone hidden within it. Nievos then handed Newman a handwritten note: *"I swept the room. That's the only one I've found, but we should go out on the balcony to talk."*

Newman nodded and the three men walked out onto the third-floor balcony. Once the door was closed, Nievos said quietly, "I 'swept' your room yesterday. That mike was not active, but it is now."

"I wonder if the Valdez people have 'made' me," said Newman in equally low tones.

"Doubtful," responded Nievos, "but we've got to find a place where we can talk. We're OK out here right now because I've swept it—and there is enough street noise to cover us for a few minutes—but we've got to find a secure place for planning these operations."

"I agree," Newman replied, "I'll have Eduardo see if he can find us a vacant warehouse."

"Ask him if he can find one on the coast, between here and the airport," said Suazo, "just in case we need to leave in a hurry."

"I'll ask him this afternoon," said Newman. Then turning back to Nievos, he asked, "Did you find any good locations for installing the detection equipment we're bringing in?"

"Some," replied the DELTA Force operator. "There are very good places at the airport and the Central Port here in Caracas. But tomorrow I need to get up to Lago de Maracaibo. It's a much bigger and busier port—and if they bring the stuff in there, we're going to have a real challenge."

"We need more people, ASAP," said Newman—as much to himself as the others.

"Yes, sir, we do," said the SEAL sniper. "I don't need a whole lot of people standing around me when I pull the trigger, but I'm going to need a few experienced guys for security, a couple of 'distractors,' and of course some guys who know how to drive."

"How many altogether, Manny?" Newman asked.

"I can pull it off with seven more—I'd like to have ten if Washington doesn't squawk," answered Suazo.

"How about you, Roberto? Have you figured out how we're going to be able to snatch those nuclear weapons?"

The Delta Force NCO shrugged and said, "It's really hard to tell right now, General. According to the D-DACT message I received this morning, they are sending nine 'techs' to set up the surveillance and detection equipment. If we're going to be here for more than a few days, we're going to need as many as twenty-seven 'shooters' who can be trained to stand watches on the gear—and still have a reasonable force to deal with whoever is escorting the nukes when we find them."

"So, round numbers—thirty more men from our 'Special Unit' down here ASAP?" asked Newman.

Both men nodded and then Nievos added, "Make it thirty-one, General. We ought to ask Washington to send down somebody who really has his act together to ride herd on this lash-up. You need a good sergeant major to help keep all these balls in the air."

Newman smiled, and as they turned to reenter the suite he said, "I already know just the man we need."

Blue Waters Retreat
Boot Key, FL
Tuesday, 30 October 2007
1700 Hours Local

Young James Newman was sitting on a beach chair staring out to where the waters of the Atlantic met the Caribbean when Sgt. Maj. Amos Skillings hobbled up behind the boy in his new, high-tech "walking cast." Earlier in the day a medical officer at the Key West Naval Air Station hospital had fitted him with the device that resembled a modern ski boot.

"Isn't that a fantastic sight?" Skillings asked him.

The boy nodded but didn't speak.

As the big Marine sergeant major drew closer he could see that the youngster's eyes were wet, as if he'd been crying. "How long have you been sitting here, James?"

The boy shrugged, and still he said nothing.

Skillings eased his big muscular frame onto the wooden chair beside the one James was perched on and waited for the boy to speak as the setting sun turned the glassy ocean into millions of refracted prisms of light.

Finally James shifted his weight and said quietly, "You're going away, too, aren't you?"

Immediately Skillings knew what was troubling his friend's son. "Yes, James . . . your dad sent me a message today before I went to the hospital. I'm going to go back on duty. It's my job."

"How come everyone always leaves me—just when I get used to having them be with me? It's not fair. It's the same as Dad. Why does *he* have to go away *all* the time? He never wants to be with me."

"That's not true, son," Skillings told the boy, putting a hand on his shoulder. "It's just that your daddy has a lot of people who depend on him right now—just like I told you when we were driving down here—don't you remember?"

"I remember—but I'm not sure that it's true," James said. "If my dad really loved me, he'd stay home more."

"Let me tell you about your dad, son. I know him better than just about anyone, except your mom, and I know that he'd do almost anything to be with you if he could."

"But he never even tells me where he goes. He says that he has to go away, and then he's gone for a long time and Mom makes us pray for him to get home safely, and one night when I heard her crying, I asked her why and she said she was worried about Dad," the boy said in a rush, his eyes welling up again.

Skillings listened to the outburst, then put his hand back on the boy's shoulder and said quietly, "You worry about your dad too, don't you, James?"

The boy stifled a sob and said, "Yes . . ." then he quickly added, "but it's mean for him to never be around and make Mom cry. It's just not fair. The other day you said he was a hero. Is that what heroes do?"

"Well . . . the Peter Newman that I know isn't mean or unfair," said the sergeant major. "And as for what heroes do . . . heroes are people who do things for others at great personal risk—and expect nothing in return. Real heroes—like your dad—are selfless. That means they think of other people first and themselves last. Do you understand what I'm saying, James?"

The boy nodded and said, "I think so."

"Good," said Skillings, "because this is a very grown-up idea—and it's important because nowadays the word *hero* is misused a lot. The athlete who just set a new sports record isn't a hero."

"You mean like last night when we were watching the football game on TV and they said that guy who caught the pass in the last second of the game was a hero?" asked James.

"Exactly right. That's not a hero," continued the Marine. "Neither is that guy who just climbed Mt. Everest alone. Those fellows may be tough or brave—but they aren't heroes because what they did benefits only themselves in fame or fortune. Like I told you, real heroes are those who put themselves in danger to help others—not themselves—like firemen who rush into burning buildings to rescue someone. And whether they succeed or fail, real heroes inspire others to do better by their example . . . to do right . . . to try harder."

"Why do they say my dad is a hero?"

"Because he is, and has been ever since I first met him. Many years ago, during the first Gulf War—long before you were born—I was with your dad in Kafji, when the Iraqis invaded Kuwait and crossed into Saudi Arabia. He hid our Recon Team in the ceilings and attics of abandoned buildings for days while Saddam's army hunted for us. Even when enemy soldiers were in the same building we were hiding in, your dad called in naval gunfire and air strikes to keep them pinned down. If he hadn't done that, the Iraqis might have broken through and overrun the Marine battalion right down the road."

"Wow," said the boy, wide-eyed. "I've never heard him talk about anything like that."

"And you probably won't," Skillings said, "because like most real heroes, your dad is humble. Real heroes don't brag about what they have done."

"What else have you seen my dad do?" asked James, now thoroughly engrossed in what Skillings was telling him.

"Well, during the first part of Operation Iraqi Freedom, your dad commanded a Regimental Combat Team and I was his sergeant major. When we were fighting to take a town called Salman Pak, a Marine CH-46 helicopter landed in an intersection to evacuate some of our wounded. The helo came under fire from a large group of foreign terrorists who had been hiding there. Your dad saw what was happening and ordered our little command group—just three Humvees—to race into position between the helicopter and the enemy. If he hadn't done that, everyone on that helicopter probably would have been killed."

"Were you scared?" asked the boy.

The Marine sergeant major nodded, thinking back to the desperate engagement in April of 2003—the .50 cal. machine guns and MK 19 grenade launcher hammering away at the black-clad figures charging down the street behind volleys of RPG and AK-47 fire. He could still see Col. Peter Newman crouched down behind the fender of their damaged vehicle, firing his Benelli shotgun at the fanatics as they closed in. Skillings finally responded quietly, "Yes James, I was scared. And so was everyone with us. I know where I'm going . . . and why I'm going there . . . and I'm ready when the Lord calls me, but none of us wants to die or get hurt. It was your dad's courage that helped the rest of us to be brave."

The boy seemed awed by the account, and his spirits had brightened considerably. He was silent for awhile and then asked, "When do you have to go?"

"Tomorrow," Skillings responded. He had been informed via his D-DACT that a chopper would pick him up at Key West Naval Air Station on Wednesday, after dark. But he told James a shorter version of the truth: "I have a ride picking me up tomorrow night at the Key West Naval Base."

"Can we hang out together and do some more fishing until you have to go?" the boy asked Skillings.

"Yeah . . . I'd like that," the Marine said with a broad grin. "But right now, why don't we go back inside the house and surprise your mom and Elizabeth by cooking up a couple of those flounders you caught today. You *do* cook, don't you?"

"Uh . . . not really," the boy admitted.

"Well, son, it's time to learn. And you'll have the pleasure of learning how to cook flounder fillet from the master. C'mon, let's go inside."

USS *Jimmy Carter*—SSN-23
7 Nautical miles West of Bandar-E Burshehr, Iran
Wednesday, 31 October 2007
0055 Hours Local

It had taken Capt. Sanford "Sandy" Heflin three hours longer than expected to locate exactly the right fiber-optic cable lying on the Persian Gulf seabed. His "Comm-Spooks"—the communications intelligence specialists in the back of his sub—had to sort through traffic on five different cable sets. They had to differentiate among offshore oil rig links, Iranian Navy comms, and even some old metal-core cable dating back to the era of the Shah. And while they were running their algorithms and parsing through their arcane data, he had other problems up in the sub's conning space.

First, Heflin's sonar operators kept hearing "ghosts"—reflected noise off the sea floor or the nearby shore. Three times in the course of as many hours, the computers running the vessel's passive sonar mistook the underwater echoes for the slowly turning screws of one of the Iranian Navy's Russian-built Kilo class diesel-electric submarines. Then, there was the dreadful sound of something scraping by the starboard side of the *Jimmy Carter*'s hull as the sub crept at two knots through what some feared was a minefield.

Once the "Comm Spooks" were certain that they had located the Iran-Saudi Arabia undersea fiber-optic cable, Heflin took a fix on their position—accurate to within less than one meter—and deployed a "shot buoy" to mark the spot. As the forty-eight-inch-long metal cylinder dropped straight below the *Carter* and lodged in the mud beside the black-rubber-coated fiber-optic cable, a second class petty officer peering into a computer screen said, "Bingo."

Exactly sixty seconds later, the top of the "shot buoy" canister popped open and a small float the size of a golf ball began to ascend toward the surface, three hundred feet above. By the time the rubber sphere was bobbing on the choppy white caps of the Persian Gulf, the argon gas inside it had expanded until the float was the size of a soccer ball. Trailing below it was a tiny luminescent monofilament tether, leading back down to the canister on the sea bottom.

Once the fiber-optic cable had been "tagged" and the tethered buoy had reached the surface, Sandy Heflin turned to Lt. Paul Van Hooser, the SEAL detachment leader, and said, "X marks the spot. It's up to you guys to cut it."

Heflin then ordered the Officer of the Deck to ascend and "deploy sensors."

The big submarine slowly rose directly over the shot canister to periscope depth and checked first for radar or other electronic emissions on the surface. When the "scanner" failed to detect anything other than an air-search radar, routine CB-frequency broadcasts, cell phones, and a government-run radio station—all of it ashore—Heflin did a careful 360-degree visual "thermal" search with the periscope. It also came up negative. Only then did he order the sub to surface—just out of the water enough for the six SEALs to scramble out of the sail onto the barely awash deck of the submarine and into their ASDS. As soon as they were sealed inside the *Minnow,* two of the "mother-sub" crewmen released the four clamps holding the mini-sub in place.

As SSN-23 very slowly submerged once again to periscope depth, the mini-sub floated free. In a matter of seconds, the SEALs had engaged the *Minnow*'s battery-powered electric motor and the tiny vessel quickly disappeared beneath the dark, choppy waters of the Persian Gulf.

Heflin watched through the periscope as the ASDS submerged, then turned to his XO and said quietly, "Unless there is some kind of emergency, the next sound we hear should be Van Hooser's wire cutters. It's Halloween, but I've got to tell you, this is more fun than cutting Mrs. Murphy's clothesline."

Filaya Petroleum Building
14 Al-Aqsa Street
Riyadh, Saudi Arabia
Wednesday, 31 October 2007
0115 Hours Local

By the time Nikolai Dubzhuko made his way back to the Filaya Petroleum facility, it was well past midnight and he was in very poor humor. His disposition was not improved when the watch officer told him that General Komulakov wanted him to call immediately on the secure-voice circuit. Dubzhuko simply threw up his hands and said, "What now?"

"Where have you been, Nikolai?" demanded Komulakov when the connection was established. "You were supposed to have checked in over an hour ago!"

"Where have I *been*?" Dubzhuko protested. "Seven hours ago you told me to go 'check out' our alternate Riyadh command center in the Persian Gulf Exports building over on Al Kadif Road. I just got back! We were ambushed three times by our 'allies,' Comrade Komulakov. Bands of young men wearing *gutras* over their faces and brandishing AK-47s are all over the place. You may remember Riyadh as an ornate symbol of Saudi conspicuous consumption, but that's not what it is anymore. Today it's a stinking, litter-strewn cesspool. Looted buildings are everywhere."

For a change, Komulakov did not react angrily to his subordinate's complaints. Instead he said, "I am glad you made it back safely, Nikolai. Tell me, what shape is the other site in now?"

"I took eleven men in three vehicles," said Dubzhuko. "We had to fight our way over—and coming back after dark was even worse. In addition to the American and British aircraft that are flying overhead constantly, there is much looting. The gate was still secure and only a few of the Persian Gulf Exports building's windows have been shot out. There is no serious damage. I checked out the generators, lights, air conditioners, the satellite communications equipment hidden in the vault on the roof, and the fiber-optic connections hidden in the basement. It won't be as comfortable as this facility, but everything works."

"Good," said the general, anxious to move on to things more important to him than Dubzhuko's safety or comfort. "Now, I want you to contact the aircraft with the nuclear weapons aboard and delay its arrival in Caracas by twenty-four hours."

"It is impossible!" replied Dubzhuko. "The plane is already en route over the Atlantic—and it is due to land in Caracas in less than three hours. Even if we could contact the aircraft and order it to turn back, to do so would create all kinds of questions from the international authorities. Why? What is the problem?"

"The American press organs are now full of stories about Caracas. Apparently there is some terrorist who is wanted by the Americans who has taken refuge there. That means that they will have stepped up surveillance in Caracas—and I do not want to take a chance that they would accidentally discover the weapons while they are looking for this terrorist."

"Who is the terrorist?" asked Dubzhuko.

"A man named Samuel Mubassa."

"Who's he?"

"He's a petty, corrupt UN bureaucrat from Nigeria," Komulakov replied. "I knew him years ago—and never suspected he would amount to anything. But he is now apparently in Caracas—because he's friendly with Valdez. I'm very concerned that his presence there will likely jeopardize our shipment and installation of the weapons."

"Comrade General," Dubzhuko said, trying to persuade his superior. "We *cannot* postpone this delivery. The best we can hope to do is to see if our technicians can hold the weapons for forty-eight hours longer than we planned at the airport warehouse facility. But I remind you, Comrade General, those arrangements were made directly with Valdez by our Iranian employers."

"Yes, yes, Nikolai, I know all that," Komulakov responded irritably.

Nonetheless, Dubzhuko persisted. "Any delay is likely to cause problems for our technicians. They need time to move the weapons from the airport warehouse to the Saudi ships. Even with the aircraft, installing the weapons correctly, checking the wiring, setting the PAL codes—all of that takes time. If this man Mubassa is a problem, I can have our advance team in Caracas eliminate the problem—and the Americans will go away and we can get on with our business."

"Eliminate the problem?" queried Komulakov.

"Kill him," replied Dubzhuko. "If you like, I can have Major Argozvek—our head of security for the Caracas operation—simply kill Mubassa."

The "former" KGB general actually smiled though Dubzhuko couldn't see it. Komulakov then said, "You know, Nikolai, there are some days when I just really like the way you think. Your idea is *brilliant*. Killing Mubassa would—"

The rest of the sentence disappeared, overwhelmed by the piercing shriek of electronic feedback as the remote control arm on the ASDS *Minnow* severed the Iran-Saudi Arabia undersea fiber-optic cable.

In Riyadh, when the shrieking feedback was gone, Dubzhuko heard nothing over the now dead line, but he kept repeating, "Hello . . . Hello . . . ?"

At the Lourdes, Cuba, Signals Intelligence site, Komulakov said, "Dubzhuko . . . Nikolai, are you there? Can you hear me?"

❂

Aboard the tiny ASDS that its crew affectionately dubbed the *Minnow*, Lt. Paul Van Hooser turned slightly in the cramped confines of the mini-sub "cockpit" and said to his crew, "Mission accomplished." He received a thumbs-up from the wetsuit-clad crewman standing next to him.

Yet, Lieutenant Van Hooser could not know that by succeeding in his mission, he had helped sow the seeds of failure for another.

CHAPTER SIXTEEN

Stay of Execution

CJR Warehouse
867 Avenida Maiquetia, Caracas, Venezuela
Wednesday, 31 October 2007
2100 Hours Local

Come in, Roberto, the air conditioning here is better than at our hotel," said Newman as SFC Robert Nievos arrived at the small suite of offices attached to the 35,000-square-foot concrete-block warehouse.

"Nice digs," said Nievos, looking around as he entered the room. He joined Newman, Eduardo Roca, and Navy SEAL Manuel Suazo in the comfortable climate-controlled space. "I had no trouble finding it with the address you sent to my D-DACT," added the Delta Force NCO. "My question is—how did *you* find it so quickly? This place looks brand new."

"It is," interjected Eduardo. "You are the first tenants. Mr. Oldham said you wanted a warehouse near the water, between the airport and the city. Here we are."

"So how *did* you find this place so fast, Eduardo, and what do the initials 'CJR' on the sign outside stand for?" Newman asked.

The Venezuelan, still wearing the same rumpled seersucker suit—or at least one identical to the suit he had been wearing every day since the Americans arrived—smiled and said, "This building is owned by my uncle Carlos Juan Roca—thus the initials."

"Well, it's perfect," said Newman/Oldham. "Plenty of high-bay space for the equipment that will be trucked in tomorrow morning on flatbeds from the port, drive-in roll-up doors, good area for billeting our troops when they arrive, indoor plumbing. . . ."

"And a nice flat roof where we can set up some of our miniature satellite antennas without attracting a lot of attention," added Suazo.

"Robert, pull up a seat," said Newman, gesturing to one of the folding chairs arrayed around the portable tables that Eduardo had acquired somewhere. "We were just about to review where we stand on Manny's part of the operation when you arrived. I also want to get your report on how things look at the big port at Lago de Maracaibo."

"Yes, sir," replied Nievos, "but before we start, has this place been swept?"

"Just this room," said Newman. "Manny did it himself with his miniature scanner."

"Sir, if you don't mind. . . ." began Nievos, who then turned to Eduardo and said, "Mr. Roca, if you would please excuse us, we gringos need a few minutes alone."

Eduardo, giving no indication of offense, shrugged and said, "Of course," and arose immediately. As he walked toward the door he added, "I shall be outside, savoring the night air. Please just switch the 'authorized personnel' door light off and on a couple times and I shall return."

As soon as the door closed behind the Venezuelan, Nievos turned to Newman and said, "Forgive me for being rude to our host, General, but are we absolutely sure we can trust this guy? He knows everything about our plans—and is about to find out more."

"No apology necessary. I had the same question—and so did Manny. While you were on your trip to Lago de Maracaibo, I sent a D-DACT message to the CIA's Deputy of Operations, Bill Goode. His response was that he had entrusted Eduardo with his life in the past, and we could too." Newman did not repeat the final words in Goode's message: *Eduardo and his family are also members of the Fellowship of Believers. They live under the same sign of the icthus as Samir and Eli Yusef Habib—and are just as faithful.*

"Well that's reassuring," said Nievos. "Shall I call him back?"

Newman nodded and the Delta Force NCO went to the doorway and flipped the light switch off and on. A minute later, Eduardo was seated at the table with the three Americans and as engaged as though he had never left.

By the time the meeting adjourned an hour later, the four men had a plan of action for accomplishing the dual missions they'd been assigned: carrying out the "sentence" on Samuel Mubassa and emplacing the detectors and surveillance equipment necessary to find any nuclear weapons being delivered or moved through Caracas en route to the United States.

Suazo, the Navy SEAL sniper and one of Eduardo's cousins, had spent the day reconnoitering places that offered a "clear shot" at Samuel Mubassa. They had finally determined that the best opportunity would be on Saturday, November 3rd when Mubassa and Valdez, the Venezuelan president, arrived at the *Museo de Arte España* to dedicate a new display of Early Spanish and Amerindian artifacts uncovered at a dig in the Kanuku Mountains. Later that evening at a lavish dinner in his honor, Samuel Mubassa was expected to announce that his fleet of supertankers had been contracted to carry Venezuelan crude oil to China, rather than the United States. Suazo had reserved rooms in three different hotels—all three of them offering clear shots at the various venues where Mubassa was scheduled to appear.

"Won't the police and security people be all over those hotels while Valdez is in the area?" asked Newman.

"Not these hotels," answered Suazo. "The firing positions I've chosen are all more than eight hundred meters from where Valdez and Mubassa will be in the open. The Valdez security goons—like most others—consider a 'long shot' being five hundred yards—six hundred at the most." The sniper added with a smile, "That's almost too close for my Barrett."

Newman nodded and said. "That's good, Manny." Then turning to Nievos, he asked, "How was the port at Lago de Maracaibo?"

"All I can tell you, sir, if the nukes come in there by ship, we're going to have a devil of a time finding 'em," said the Delta Force Operator. "I counted ninety-seven ships in the port and anchored out—everything from super-tankers to oil-rig service vessels to big pleasure yachts. It's one of the busiest seaports I've seen in a long time."

"Any *good* news in what you saw?" asked the Marine brigadier.

"Yes, sir, only three major highways in and out of the port area. If the people in Washington deliver enough gamma ray/neutron particle detectors and 'Backscatter' equipment, we can cover these major routes. But our best hope is if the nukes are delivered through the airport up the road from right here."

"How about if we had a sub parked at the entrance of the Lago de Maracaibo harbor to monitor what's coming and going?" asked Newman.

Nievos smiled and said, "That's why you're a general and I'm a sergeant first class. As long as the nukes haven't already been delivered, a sub would be perfect. Will they do that for us?"

"Don't know until we ask," said Newman, "but I think it's time 'us settlers' called in the cavalry. Everything you both have asked for is in my D-DACT. I'll transmit it on the way back to our hotel and see what they say. Anything else before we wrap up?"

"Si, Señor Oldham," said Eduardo. "Tomorrow is going to be a very busy day. First, the containers of equipment that you ordered will clear customs tonight and be delivered here very early tomorrow morning on flatbed trucks from the container-port, escorted by one of my very reliable associates. Does one of you wish to be here to supervise?"

"I should stay here for that," said Nievos. "Who's escorting the shipment?"

"Edgar, one of my sons," answered Eduardo as though it was the most natural thing in the world to have a son putting his life at risk to help the Americans. He then continued, "If I understood everything correctly, several more of your colleagues will also be arriving here on flights into the airport tomorrow. I can arrange to have them discreetly picked up at the airport and brought here if you wish."

"They are coming on many different flights," said Newman. "How would you do that?"

"Just tell your men to go to the sign that says 'Valet Car Service' outside the 'Arrivals' level and look for the white Chevrolet vans with the number seven on the side. The drivers will only pick up people who say that they are with Petro-Research. When the driver asks who they work for, they must say 'Peter Oldham,' or they will not get picked up. It is only a ten-minute trip from here."

"OK, who are these drivers?" asked Newman.

"My sons Emilio and Estaban," responded Eduardo. "It also occurs to me," said the Venezuelan, "that by tomorrow night you will have many men here. I'm sure you have thought of this, but would you like to have folding cots delivered and plywood partitions erected in part of the warehouse space for their billeting?"

"That would make things a whole lot more comfortable for the troops," injected Suazo.

"Very well, I will have my son Enrique take care of that. Now, what are they going to eat?"

"MREs—Meals Ready to Eat. We have military rations in the containers that arrive early tomorrow morning," explained Newman, amazed at Eduardo's logistical acumen.

"Ahh, Señor Oldham, I am sure that these MREs—as you call them—are very good, but wouldn't your men rather have real food, prepared by magnificent cooks?"

"And who would prepare all these meals, Eduardo?" asked Newman with a faint smile.

"Why, my two very talented and devoted daughters, Esther and Emelda," said Eduardo, proudly.

"Very well," said Newman, agreeing to the arrangements. As Newman and Suazo prepared to leave, Eduardo walked them to the door, saying, "If you will ride with Manuel, Mr. Oldham, I shall stay here to show Roberto around."

As Suazo went to get the car, Newman stood beside the man in the rumpled seersucker suit and said, "Level with me, Eduardo. What's your motive for doing all this? I've already seen your expense reports. You're only charging for your actual costs, so you're not doing it for the money."

The diminutive man in the shabby suit peered directly at Newman through the thick lenses of his glasses and said, "No, it is not for the money, Señor Oldham. My family was originally from Cuba. My father fought with The Brigade against Castro. He was captured at the Bay of Pigs. After he got out of Castro's prison, he took our family to Nicaragua. Somoza threw him into jail in 1978, and when the Sandinistas came to power, they also imprisoned him. He later fought with the Nicaraguan resistance. I served in his column. When he was badly wounded in Nuevo Segovia, I carried him on my back to Honduras where an American Army doctor saved his life. We then moved here to Venezuela. Now once again, tyranny threatens my family—this time from the despot, Valdez."

Newman nodded, "Your family has suffered a lot, Eduardo."

"My father taught his children—as I have taught mine—that America is the greatest, freest country on earth. America is now threatened—and so is Venezuela. My hope is that we can help each other during this time of great peril."

As the two men stood by the door, Eduardo held up a tiny metal fish between the thumb and forefinger of his left hand and said, "I understand you have one of these too, Mr. Oldham."

Newman reached into his pocket and held out an identical silver icthus, symbol of the ancient church. Eduardo nodded and said, *"Muy bien. Buenas noches, señor Oldham. Vaya con Dios."*

Simon Bolivar International Airport
Caracas, Venezuela
Thursday, 01 November 2007
0015 Hours Local

The Airbus 320 with "Air France Air Cargo" emblazoned on its sides made a perfect landing on runway Two-Four-Left. When it reached the last high-speed taxiway, it turned left and rolled to the military area on the south side of the airport. A blue Toyota van with flashing lights raced out to the taxiway, circled in front of the Airbus, and signaled the pilot to follow him between rows of brand new twin-engine, MiG-29 and SU-

34 MKI, dual-role, all-weather jet aircraft—the best export models made in the Russian Federation.

The van led the "cargo" aircraft to a gentle stop—not at the airfreight terminal, but in front of one of the largest hangars at the airport. A nine-foot chain-link fence with coils of razor wire at the top surrounded the rear and sides of the facility, and signs every fifty yards warned, *Ninguna violación*—"No Trespassing." Painted over the doorway of the hangar was the new symbol of the Venezuelan Air Force—a Blue Falcon atop a gold-bordered, red star. But below this was inscribed, *Fuerza-De la Defensa De Bolivaria*—Bolivarian Defense Force—the "Regional Military Alliance" that Horatio Valdez had created with Fidel Castro's encouragement as a means of "confronting the imperialist aggressors."

As soon as the Russian pilot "chopped" the engines on the Airbus, men wearing Venezuelan Air Force uniforms hooked a "tug" to the front landing gear assembly while others opened the large hangar doors at the nose of the aircraft. When the doors rolled wide enough for the wings to clear, the plane was towed into the cavernous building.

Less than ten minutes after touching down, the Airbus was inside the hangar and the doors were again closed. Outside on the tarmac, six armed men were posted in front of the huge rolling doors. A dozen more patrolled the chain-link enclosure.

Inside, a rolling stairway was pushed up beside the forward hatch on the left side of the Airbus, and a tall, well-built man with close-cropped, light brown hair and fair skin mounted the steps, pushed the handle release, and opened the hatch. Standing just inside the aircraft portal were two armed men, both with folding stock AKM submachine guns at the ready.

Instead of reacting with anxiety or anger at the sight of the weapons, Maj. Gregor Argozvek, formerly of the

Russian Military Intelligence Service—the GRU, stepped into the aircraft and waved dismissively at the armed men. Speaking in Russian he said, "You would shoot your commander? Lower your weapons."

They complied instantly and the major then spoke to the balding, heavyset individual standing behind the armed men. "So, Dr. Zhdanov, you are finally here."

"Yes," the older man replied.

"I hope you brought your ten toys and your hired help," said Argozvek. "We have work to do."

The older man nodded and said, "Everything is in order. Do you want to remove them now? I was hoping we would not have to start until tomorrow. We have been traveling for too long. I do not want my technicians working with these devices until they have had some rest."

"All of that has been arranged, Doctor," Argozvek replied. "One of my men is at the bottom of the stairs. He will take you and your 'specialists' to a van, which will drive you to your billet—the officer's quarters, over there . . ." he said, pointing toward the east. "You will rest there until morning. At noon you and I will sit down and work out a schedule for installing the devices in their carriers." Then the agile Russian officer leaned forward toward the physicist's face, sniffed once, and said in a quiet snarl, "Have you been drinking, Oleg Zhdanov?"

The scientist shrugged and looked at the major through bloodshot eyes and said, "Just a little vodka. It helps my airsickness."

Argozvek leaned forward and whispered in his ear, "No more vodka, Zhdanov. That is why you lost your job at the Zlatoust 36 research facility in Trekhgorny. *This* job is your only future. If you aren't sober by noon tomorrow, you not only will not be paid; I will kill you myself."

The Russian scientist swallowed hard and stepped back, staring in silence at the grim-faced officer. It was not the prospect of being shot that penetrated his alcoholic haze—it was the possibility of not getting paid. He and the young woman he had taken as his mistress had already made plans for how to spend the two million U.S. dollars he was getting for this job. Zhdanov finally said, "I will be ready for work in the morning. What will you do with the devices tonight? They are in the baggage compartment, directly below our feet."

"They are in their shipping containers, yes?" asked Argozvek.

"Of course," answered Zhdanov, "and our tools and test equipment are all packed with them."

"Good," said the Russian major. "My men will take care of removing the weapons and the equipment. One of my men is a former artillery officer—and two of your assistants are already here. They will supervise the offload. We will store the weapons here until they are installed in the planes and ships that will carry them to their destinations."

"Yes, yes," said the scientist.

Argozvek continued, "Make sure you take all your personal effects with you. This airplane will be leaving as soon as everything is out of it. Tomorrow, the 'carrier' planes will start to arrive. We will bring them one at a time into this hangar so that you and your technicians can install the devices in them. After you have finished with the planes, we shall take the remaining weapons to the port and install them in the *ships* that will carry them to their targets."

"Very well," said the scientist. He turned back into the cabin, passed the major's instructions to the two technicians who had accompanied him in the plane, picked up a beat-up old leather suitcase, and started to make his way down the stairs behind the major. When he got to the bottom of the steps, he asked Argozvek, "Are you sure that the weapons will be safe here?"

The military intelligence officer looked at the doughy, overweight scientist and replied, "The weapons are as safe here as they were in mother Russia."

"Yes, yes," replied the scientist, shuffling toward the van. "That's what I was afraid of. If they were so safe in mother Russia, how could they be here in Venezuela?"

○

Ten minutes later, Dr. Zhdanov was inside his room at the Bachelor Officers Quarters. The billet reminded him of the American motel that he had stayed in years before when he had lectured at a disarmament conference in Washington, sponsored by the Union of Concerned Scientists. Back then he had been an up-and-coming—and trusted—young physicist at the Ministry of Defense Weapons Design Bureau. He was an expert on Permissive Action Links, the "fail-safe" PAL codes that allow only an authorized person to arm a nuclear weapon.

As soon as he locked his door, Zhdanov placed his battered leather suitcase on the bed, opened it, and removed a bottle of vodka, along with the cell phone that he had purchased from a black market vendor before leaving Moscow weeks ago. After taking a long swig from the half-empty bottle, he fumbled around in his bag, groping for the correct wall-socket adapter for the telephone's charging unit. Failing to find it, he sat down on the bed and then, after another drink, dialed a number at the Gorky Research Center east of Moscow.

Zhdanov swallowed three more long draughts from the bottle of clear liquid before the call went through. When the line answered at the other end, a young female voice said simply, "Hello," in Russian.

"Alexandra, it is Oleg," slurred the scientist.

"I am glad you called," she said. "It is nearly eight in the morning here, I was just leaving to go to the laboratory. Where are you now? I haven't heard from you for days, and I was worried."

"I am where it is very warm," responded Zhdanov. "You remember, the place I told you about before I left you, my little fox."

"You are in Caracas? I am glad that you are warm; it is very cold here."

Even in his stupor, Zhdanov was aghast at the naïve security breach—yet he then compounded it by saying, "My pet, you must not mention where I am or what I am doing to anyone, especially over the phone. It is impossible to know who is listening."

The two lovers chatted for another ten minutes before Zhdanov, groggy from the effects of the alcohol and fatigue, finally passed out, fully clothed, on the bed. His cell phone, still connected to the ITT International Service Connection tower northwest of the airport, remained beside him on the bed, broadcasting the sound of his heavy snoring until the battery died a quarter hour later.

Oval Office
The White House
Washington, DC
Thursday, 01 November 2007
0955 Hours Local

"I'm just not prepared to launch a preemptive strike on Iran," said the President, walking to his desk and pulling out the chair to sit down. In his hand he was holding three large 11 x 14-inch photographs of an Iranian *Shabaz* ballistic missile on a launch pad. He had just walked into the Oval Office from the morning meeting in the Situation Room and had reconvened his closest advisors in the privacy of his own office. Standing in front of the desk were the Vice President; Helen

Luce, his Secretary of State; SecDef Dan Powers; Joint Chiefs Chairman Gen. George Grisham; Bill Goode, the CIA's Operations Director; and "Jeb" Stuart, his National Security Advisor.

The President put on his reading glasses and, peering at the photos now spread out in front of him, said, "Bill, tell me again what we're looking at here."

Goode walked around the desk and stood beside the President and said, "These are all images taken from a Global Hawk early this morning from an altitude of 85,000 feet over the Iranian Rocket Research Facility east of Eshfahan. The first one shows seventeen technicians working on the rocket—which has no nose cone installed. In the second, taken thirty-nine minutes later, the top of the missile is covered by a canopy. And then, in the third, taken almost two hours after the first— that's this photo with the strange-looking truck pulled up to the bunker about a hundred yards from the missile—there are six white-garbed technicians maneuvering a canvas-covered object out of the van and onto a wheeled cart."

"And why is this so significant?" asked the Commander in Chief.

"Well, sir," Goode answered, "the number of technicians, the 'masking' of the nose-cone area of the missile and the concealed object being removed from the truck tell our imagery interpreters that they are preparing to install a nuclear, chemical, or biological warhead on the missile. We've never seen any activity like this before at this facility."

"Why are they doing this in broad daylight? They must be aware of our satellites," said the President.

"Yes, sir, they are," Goode answered. "The Iranians seem to have timed this activity for two times a day— about two hours each—when we *don't* have a satellite overhead. That's why we're trying to keep a Global Hawk up over Iran. The UAV that took these shots was launched out of Diego Garcia last night. The 'Hawks' are 'stealthy' enough that the Iranians can't pick them up on radar or hear them on the ground. Unless they happen to catch its silhouette cutting across the sun, they will never even know it's up there."

"But even if a nuclear warhead is being loaded on this missile, it doesn't have the range to make it here, right?" asked the President.

"That's correct, sir," interjected Grisham. "But it has enough range to put all of our forces in Iraq, Kuwait, the Persian Gulf, even most of those in Afghanistan, at risk of a nuclear attack."

The President sighed and said, "How much advance notice will we have of this thing getting ready to launch?"

"Once they clear the launch pad," responded Goode, "it could be airborne in as little as thirty minutes to an hour."

"Does that give us the time we need to launch a strike and prevent the missile from getting off the ground?"

"It would be a very close thing, Mr. President," Grisham replied. "We would have to see the awnings coming down and launch immediately from Balad—near Baghdad, Ali Al Salim Air Base, in Kuwait, or from the Carrier Battle Group in the north Persian Gulf. There are no other bases close enough to make it to Eshfahan in time."

"And once it's off the ground, we can't stop it?"

"That depends on where it's heading," said Powers. "If it is aimed at our naval forces in the Gulf, our Aegis systems can engage it as it comes in. In Kuwait, we have the Patriot PAC IIIs that can bring it down. But we don't have anything in Iraq capable of hitting it."

"If these pictures were taken this morning, how long before they could have a nuclear weapon on this missile, ready to fire?" asked the President.

"Our S&T experts estimate that if it's a nuclear warhead, because they have never done this before, they will need another five to perhaps ten days to position the payload, check the wiring, run diagnostic tests, and make any last-minute fixes. We'll likely see a crane brought out to the missile and even more technicians," Goode replied.

"So the bottom line is that we probably have some time," said the President, sounding somewhat relieved. When no one demurred, he continued, "So if a nuclear warhead is placed on that Iranian missile, does anyone care to speculate as to what the target might be?"

The CIA Operations Chief, who was still standing beside the President, looked up at Powers, then Grisham. The Defense Secretary nodded and said, "Bill . . ."

Goode took a deep breath and said quietly, "It's most likely Tel Aviv. All of the rhetoric coming from the mosques includes Tel Aviv in the list of American and European cities where the 'infidels' are to be 'struck with fire from the heavens' by the Islamic Brotherhood."

"Why Tel Aviv?" asked the Commander in Chief. "The Israelis moved their seat of government to Jerusalem years ago."

"Because," Goode responded, "the radical imams, mullahs, and ayatollahs also know about the biblical prophecy that the temple will be rebuilt in Jerusalem. They want to avoid inflicting any damage to the Dome of the Rock or the Al Aqsa Mosque that would offer a pretext for such an event."

There was a moment of silence in the room and then the President said, "Have we told the Israelis about this yet?"

"No, sir," said Powers. "I wanted to make sure you saw this before we shared it with anyone else. Second, we need to make sure that the British are brought in next—because they have troops on the ground in Iraq and ships out in the Gulf that are vulnerable. But I'm also concerned that the Israelis might just launch a preemptive strike of their own once we tell them about it or show 'em these pictures."

"Wouldn't that solve our problem?" said the President.

For the first time since they had walked into the room, the Secretary of State spoke up. "No, Mr. President," she said. "It'll make things much worse if the Israelis launch a preemptive strike."

"Why, Helen?" challenged the Commander in Chief. "When they took out the Osirik reactor in Iraq back in 1981, everyone screamed at them—but were quietly glad they did it."

"That's true, Mr. President," answered the Secretary of State. "But back then they used aircraft and conventional bombs. This time they'll use Jericho missiles, with nuclear warheads."

Lourdes Signals Intelligence Facility
Bejucal, Cuba
Thursday, 1 November 2007
1200 Hours Local

"I am sorry, sir," said the commander of the Lourdes Signals Intelligence unit, "we cannot reestablish the link. And if we continue to try and make more inquiries, we risk inviting the attention of hostile intelligence services."

Gen. Dimitri Komulakov looked at his watch. It had been nearly sixteen hours since his communications with Nikolai Dubzhuko—his deputy in Riyadh—had been cut. None of his attempts at using the Cuba-Murmansk-Moscow-Tehran-Riyadh link for either voice or data transmission were working. He had every one of his communications specialists working on the problem—plus some he had "borrowed" from the regular Signals Intelligence garrison.

"Has anyone found out what caused us to lose contact?" asked Komulakov.

"Not yet, General," said the commander of the Lourdes facility. "We do know that your undersea link between here and Murmansk is still working. And you are still able to route some traffic between Murmansk and Moscow. According to the technicians in Moscow, they can still send and receive tones between Moscow and Tehran on your circuit at a very reduced baud rate. Unfortunately, there is no data exchange whatsoever on the link between Tehran and Riyadh."

"What the devil does all that mean, Mikhail Vushneshko?" asked Komulakov impatiently.

"There is a short circuit—perhaps a damaged electronic switch, maybe a cut in the fiber-optic cable. Or it could mean that the equipment has been corrupted by some computer virus in your system. The problem seems to be between Tehran and Riyadh, but it has affected your whole communications network," the colonel responded.

"Well, can it be fixed?" asked the general.

"Oh yes," answered Vushneshko, "but first we would have to find where the damage has occurred. And since it appears that this is not in Russia, we would have to make further inquiries with local telecommunications authorities in Tehran and in Riyadh."

"That's out of the question, Mikhail," said Komulakov abruptly. "I do not want the Iranians to know I am here—and there are no 'authorities' as you put it—in Riyadh. They are all dead."

"Yes, General," said the colonel, anxious to end this unpleasant exchange. "Is there anything else I can do to help you?"

Komulakov thought for a moment and then said, "Is

there any other way for me to send and receive encrypted voice and data communications between here and Tehran and here and Riyadh without using my emergency satellite system?"

Vushneshko thought about it for several seconds and then said, "The problem is your encryption system. You have been communicating over a discrete channel that has now been interrupted. We can't risk compromising our national circuits if your system has a virus in it. I can route your communications between here and Murmansk on a backup fiber-optic line. But in Murmansk, they will have to route your signals to Riyadh and Tehran using a commercial telecommunications satellite."

"What's wrong with that?" asked Komulakov, not fully comprehending all that the younger intelligence officer was saying.

"Well," replied the colonel, "if an unfriendly intelligence service is paying attention, they can intercept the satellite transmissions between Murmansk and Riyadh and Murmansk and Tehran."

"But it will all be encrypted, and it will appear to them as though these are calls between Murmansk and parties in Riyadh and Tehran," said Komulakov.

"That is true, General," said Vushneshko. "But if they have enough time, the Americans and the British have the means of breaking the encryption. That is why the direct fiber-optic connection was so desirable. They wouldn't even know how to look for it."

"How long would it take them to break the encryption systems that my people are using here and in Riyadh and Tehran?"

Vushneshko pondered the question for a moment then said, "With the software you are using, they might be able to 'break' it in a week or two with their supercomputers."

"Two weeks?" said Komulakov, smiling. "That's all I need. Can you get all of this set up?"

"Yes," said the colonel, pleased that he was being helpful. "I will need the codec information for the computers in Riyadh and Tehran, the telephone numbers for their secure instruments, and of course an account number for billing the commercial satellite service. It should only take a few hours—perhaps overnight."

"I shall have all of that information brought to your office immediately," said Komulakov. "Is that all?"

"Just one reminder," said Vushneshko. "Riyadh and Tehran will have to rely completely on satellite communications. As soon as they come up on this new circuit, they must assume that the Americans will very quickly be aware of their locations—even though it may take them some time to figure out what is being said."

"I understand, Vushneshko," said Komulakov, smiling again, "but even if the Americans are listening in, they will not know that I am here in Cuba, correct?"

"That is correct, Comrade General, but they will probably also know you are not in Murmansk. No one in their right mind spends the winter up there."

CJR Warehouse
867 Avenida Maiquetia, Caracas, Venezuela
Thursday, 1 November 2007
2100 Hours Local

"Well I'm impressed," said Sgt. Maj. Amos Skillings as Brig. Gen. Peter Newman walked him around the warehouse that was now becoming crowded with equipment and personnel.

"I'm impressed too," said Newman, pointing to the "ski boot" on Skillings's left leg. "Are you sure that you're not doing more damage than good with that so-called walking cast?"

"No, sir. Doc said it might be uncomfortable for a few days, but I haven't had any swelling; and other than the need to take it off every time I go through airport security, it really isn't that much of a hassle."

The two men made their way back to the office that served as their command post. Newman gestured toward one of the folding chairs, saying, "I'm glad you arrived when you did. I was about to leave for my hotel for the night. Tell me about your trip down here."

Skillings, dressed in jeans and a green cotton polo shirt, took a long drink from the bottle of water he had been carrying and said, "Mrs. Newman dropped me at the Key West Naval Air Station 'pax' terminal at 1930, and Maj. Ed Bowes was already there with a fellow from Langley. They arranged for a large conference room upstairs, and over the next eight hours or so we 'processed' thirty other SEALs, Marine Force Recon, and 'D-Boys' with new passports and all the appropriate stamps, pocket litter, and plane tickets."

"How did they get all that stuff done so fast?" asked Newman.

"The guy from Langley said he worked for Mr. Goode. I've never seen anything like it," answered Skillings. "It would have made a good counterfeiter proud. As soon as everyone had their paperwork in order, we split up into three groups and boarded two Navy C-9s and a DEA Gulfstream. One of the C-9s dropped off at Miami, Atlanta, Newark, and Chicago. The second one did drops at Houston, Dallas/Fort Worth, Phoenix, and Los Angeles."

"How did you get here so quickly? There are only a dozen or so who have made it in," said Newman.

"The plan called for us all to take different flights into Caracas. I rode the Gulfstream straight to the DEA base in Panama and took a quick van ride to the commercial side of the field where I caught an Avianca flight in here an hour later. When I got to the Caracas airport, I just went to the valet car service sign and told the guy in the white number seven van that I worked for Mr. Oldham—and here I am."

"You catch any heat on the way?"

"No, sir," said Skillings with a smile. "You see, my passport says that I am from Grenada and serving as an observer for the Human Rights Commission of the OAS."

Newman chuckled and said, "Well, Mr. Human Rights Observer, do you have any questions about the rather complicated missions we have here?"

"Not yet, sir. I want to get to know the men a little bit better as they make it in here tonight. I met most of them while we were doing the processing back at Key West, but it's tough to get a feel for what a guy is really like in that kind of controlled chaos. I also want Sergeant First Class Nievos to explain that detection and surveillance equipment he has out there, and I'd like to spend some time talking to Chief Suazo and the guys he brought in for taking out that Mubassa character. Let me have until tomorrow morning, and I'll have a lot of questions."

"OK," said Newman, rising to leave. "I'll be back here shortly after 0900. I have a breakfast meeting about oil exploration at the hotel with our host, 'Eduardo' Roca. It was one of his sons who picked you up at the airport. Use the D-DACT for any messages. I'm pretty sure all the hotel phone lines are tapped."

"Aye aye, sir," replied the sergeant major who then snapped his fingers and said, "Messages . . . hold one, sir." Reaching into his duffel bag, Skillings pulled out an envelope and handed it to Newman, adding, "This is from James. He asked me to give it to you. I told him not to write your name on it—that's why the envelope is blank."

As the sergeant major busied himself with his gear, Newman opened the envelope. Inside was a single sheet of paper with James's boyish attempt at good penmanship:

Dear Dad,
   You're my hero. I miss you. So does Mom and Lizzie.
   Hope to see you soon.
Love, James

CHAPTER SEVENTEEN

Running Out of Time

Lourdes Signals Intelligence Facility
Bejucal, Cuba
Friday, 02 November 2007
0745 Hours Local

Dimitri Komulakov learned about the bomb in the Times Square Station of the New York subway system the same way the rest of America did—from FOX News. For more than forty hours, ever since his communications had suddenly gone down, he had been watching the American cable news channels for any word about what was happening in the Middle East—and anything that might give him a clue as to what his deputy, Col. Nikolai Dubzhuko, was doing in Riyadh. All that Komulakov knew, thanks to the ingenuity of Col. Mikhail Vushneshko, the commanding officer of the Russian Signals Intelligence garrison at Lourdes, was that Dubzhuko was still alive. Vushneshko had confirmed that—by having an intelligence officer at the Russian embassy in Tehran make a brief call to Dubzhuko's commercial satellite phone, saying only, "We are trying to reestablish communications."

For the better part of two days Komulakov had been watching news broadcasts and wire service reports focused on events in the United States—the flight from American cities, the disruption and looting, food and fuel shortages, and reports of "leaks" from Congressional sources about how the American President was "covering up" the severity of the terrorist threat. At one point, while Vushneshko had been working on reestablishing the secure communications link with Riyadh, Komulakov had told him, "It's a good thing the Americans have a Congress to leak information, otherwise we wouldn't know anything about what is going on."

But now, with a report of a bomb in New York City, the retired KGB general was frantic to find out how this event had occurred. Bombing the New York transit system had not been on his list of "planned events." He watched the television only long enough to determine that the bomb had been a small conventional device before rushing to the command center, screaming for Vushneshko. "I have waited long enough! You must find some way for me to communicate secure with Riyadh," Komulakov demanded.

To avoid a scene in the presence of others, Vushneshko escorted the general into an adjoining room filled to the ceiling with racks of electronic equipment. Two technicians wearing headphones were there, working with a maze of colored wires.

"Sir, we have been working nonstop ever since your communications link went down," Vushneshko replied patiently. "We have just established a connection, but it is a very fragile link, and it takes much longer for the signal to get from here to Riyadh and back than it did before. The processors must encrypt the signal here, carry your voice or data from here on an undersea fiberoptic cable to the hub at Murmansk, send it up to a commercial satellite, then back down from the satellite and through the decryption at the other end. There is almost a four-second delay."

Komulakov didn't even hesitate. "That will have to do. Connect me immediately to Dubzhuko in Riyadh."

"By voice or data?" asked the communications intelligence officer.

"Voice," replied the general. "I shall take the call at my desk in the command center."

Less than a minute later, Komulakov finally heard Dubzhuko's familiar Ukrainian accent for the first time since Wednesday.

"Nikolai, can you hear me?" the general shouted into the phone.

At this, Colonel Vushneshko leaned over Komulakov's shoulder and said quietly, "General, it is not necessary to raise your voice. The extra volume simply distorts the signal even more."

Komulakov nodded and said, "Yes, thank you, Mikhail Vushneshko, I understand," although he really didn't. Then, at a slightly reduced timbre he said again into the phone, "Nikolai, are you there?"

"Yes, I hear you," replied the garbled voice from Riyadh, replying to Komulakov's first question asked five seconds earlier.

"Ahh, good," said Komulakov, reassured that his exquisitely planned operation was no longer completely unraveling.

"Nikolai, what is this about a bomb going off in the New York subway system?"

There was a long pause before Dubzhuko's voice came through the warble and electronic static on the line: "What bomb in the New York subway?"

"The American news organs are carrying the story," Komulakov said, his voice rising again. "They are saying that a group calling itself the 'Islamic Brotherhood in America' did it."

"I know nothing about it."

"Very well, Nikolai," said Komulakov. "Give me a

status report. Where are our special weapons?" he demanded.

"They are in Caracas, at the airport, as our 'client' previously arranged," came the reply several seconds later.

"Did you instruct our people to delay the installation?"

"Yes," Dubzhuko answered. "I talked personally to Major Argozvek, and he will not start putting the weapons in the captured Saudi planes and ships until tomorrow. But that does not make our employer happy. I also told Argozvek to take care of the Muba—"

"Nikolai," interrupted Komulakov impatiently, "just give me the information I need. How many of the 'carrier' vessels and planes have arrived in Caracas?"

"Five of the aircraft are there already. Only three of the ships have made it in, however."

"Where are the rest of them?"

There was a longer than normal delay as Dubzhuko checked his own data. He then replied: "We have a 737 in the Cape Verde Islands, a Gulfstream in Rio de Janeiro, and an Airbus in Dakar, Senegal. One of the boats is in Aruba, and there is another at the Venezuelan port at Maracaibo."

"Where are the rest of the ships and aircraft?" asked Komulakov.

"I do not know," responded Dubzhuko. "I think we have to assume that they have been captured or sunk by the Americans and their allies. As you told me before we lost communications, they appear to be aware of what's going on and had already—"

"Please, Nikolai," interrupted Komulakov again, "I do not need to be reminded. I want you to send me the list of those whom we have assigned to each ship and aircraft, their communication identifiers, and GPS coordinates in your next report. Have you heard from our employer?"

"Yes!" the colonel in Riyadh responded with agitation. "I tried to tell you, Ali Yunesi is not happy about the delay in installing the weapons. When we lost communications, he sent two dozen of his people here—to Riyadh—to find out why he had not been receiving reports. They arrived this morning and have set up in a looted office building across the street. They have their own communications equipment."

Komulakov's anxiety shot up once again. "Are they using radios?"

"Yes, radios and satellite telephones."

"Are they encrypted?"

"No. They are broadcasting in the clear, using some kind of code from their Quran."

"Are you sure that they are from Yunesi?" asked Komulakov.

"Yes," answered Dubzhuko. "The senior one here was with Yunesi when we met with him in Tehran. He insisted that I talk directly with Yunesi on their equipment to receive instructions about getting one of their people out of the American detention center in Cuba. I told him it was out of the question—that it was too dangerous for me to use their communications equipment to talk to anyone, but they are coming back over here in an hour."

Komulakov thought for a moment. He couldn't care less what ultimately happened to his deputy, but he needed him to stay alive until at least the eleventh of November. He said, "I cannot talk to Yunesi directly on this circuit about the operation because he does not have our encryption. It was all right before because we were connected entirely by fiber optic. I will make a very brief call to him from here and tell him to communicate through the people he has in Riyadh and that they should pass any information to me through you. But to avoid compromising your location, you should not talk to Yunesi from there. Are you still at the Filaya

Petroleum site or did you move to the 'Persian Gulf Exports' facility over on Al Kadif Road?"

"We are still at Filaya. After we lost communications, I decided to stay here until we could reestablish a connection."

"It is good that you stayed there, Nikolai, but if you have Iranians broadcasting via radio from across the street, we must assume that the Americans or the British will very quickly discover them. I think we must expect that they will *attack* that site. You should try to spend your nights over at Al Kadif Road. That is when the Americans and British are most likely to attack."

"I will do so, but what do I tell the Iranians?" asked Dubzhuko.

"Just tell them that I have ordered you to set up an alternate communications site and leave some people behind each night so that they believe you will be back."

"But if the Americans attack this site, our people left here could get killed," protested Dubzhuko.

"Yes, that is true," replied Komulakov. "And that would be a shame. Make sure you take our best men with you."

Simon Bolivar International Airport
Caracas, Venezuela
Friday, 02 November 2007
0945 Hours Local

"Whoa, what's this?" said Robert Nievos, as the tiny earpiece began to screech in his right ear. He quickly reached for the instrument positioned beside him on the floor of the white van and turned down the volume.

Sgt. Maj. Amos Skillings, in the front passenger seat, turned around and said to the Delta Force Sergeant First

Class, "Man, I heard that squeal all the way up here. Is that thing working or is it on the fritz?"

"I think it's working," Nievos replied, fiddling with the dials on the neutron particle/gamma radiation detector. "I did everything the techs back at the warehouse told me to do. I don't understand why we would be getting a false reading out of it," he added. Nievos then began reading the instructions that had been e-mailed into his D-DACT.

Emilio Roca, driving the white airport shuttle van with the big numeral 7 on its sides, turned to Skillings and said, "Do you want me to turn around and go back to the warehouse so that you can get another instrument to test? It is only ten minutes from here."

"Let's do that," said Nievos, shutting off the device and turning it back on again, in accord with the "troubleshooting" instructions.

"That works for me," said Skillings. "No one is going to think it strange that an airport shuttle is coming and going on the airport perimeter road."

Emilio made a wide 180-degree turn at the next intersection. As they returned the way they had come, Skillings, watching his comrade from the front seat, asked, "What's it doing now?"

"It seems to be fine," answered Nievos. Then suddenly, as they passed a high chain-link fence topped with razor wire and *Ninguna violación* signs every fifty feet, the machine screeched again. "Ah-h," groaned the Delta Force operator from the rear of the van, "there it goes again."

Then, just as abruptly, the noise faded and stopped.

"Maybe it isn't broken," Skillings said, looking back at the large hangar inside the chain-link fence they had just passed. "Isn't this the same spot where it screeched the last time?"

Nievos looked up through the tinted window and

said, "I don't know, I was so busy reading the instructions on our device I didn't notice."

"Shall I turn around again?" asked Emilio, slowing the van.

"No," answered Skillings. "If we turn around again in such a short distance, we may attract more attention than we want. Every tenth light pole along this section of road has a camera mounted on it. And there are armed soldiers standing guard around that hangar behind us. Let's assume that we are being watched and go back to the warehouse, pick up a new instrument, and take another 'test drive.' "

Minutes later Emilio pulled the van up to a gate in the masonry wall beside a sign in both Spanish and English: "CJR Warehouse No. 7."

A tall, muscular man wearing a Guayabera that bulged over his right hip stepped out of the guardhouse beside the gate, looked into the van, said, "*Un momento,*" and returned to the enclosure to open the gate. Emilio pulled through, drove around to the rear of the warehouse, and stopped the van in front of one of the four large roll-up doors. A few seconds later the door opened and the van pulled into the warehouse.

Inside, there was a beehive of activity. Beneath bright industrial lights suspended from the ceiling, dozens of well-built men were unloading equipment from two large sea-van containers. The beards on some, mustaches on others, and the long hair on most belied their real occupation. On one of the plywood partitions that had been erected to subdivide the cavernous space, rows of weapons, body armor, and helmets hung from hooks. Beneath them on the concrete floor were metal cans of ammunition and loaded magazines appropriate to each weapon. Along another wall, technicians were working on equipment that had been arrayed on folding tables converted into test benches. Lined up against three of the four roll-up doors were three Chevrolet Suburbans and, behind them, three Ford Excursions, all with tinted windows and all rented by Eduardo Roca. The side and rear doors of the vehicles were all open, and armorers were securing flexible ballistic blankets to the interiors using strips of Velcro.

While Emilio turned the van around, Nievos and Skillings—in his "ski-boot" walking cast—carried the apparently defective detector to one of the technicians. He listened to their complaint, agreed to check it over, guided them to a large Pelican case, and said, "Try this one. I just ran a diagnostic test on it, and it's working perfectly."

"Good," said Skillings, "you can ride along with us to make sure it really is working properly—and make sure that we're not committing any 'operator error.' "

While helping carry the new neutron-gamma detector to the van, the tech said, "If that's what you want, Sergeant Major, but I want you to know, I'm a civilian tech-rep—not one of you guys. I won't be any help if you get into trouble out there."

"Don't worry, young fellow," said Skillings with a smile, as the door opened in front of them and Emilio nosed the van back out into the bright sunlight, "if anybody starts shooting, Sergeant First Class Nievos and I will take care of 'em."

The young technician, seated in the back beside Nievos and his equipment, wasn't reassured. As the van pulled out of the warehouse compound onto the highway and headed back toward the airport, he said, "But you have your leg in a cast."

"Right," said Skillings, "but I don't shoot with my left foot—only my right."

This silenced the young specialist for several minutes until the new machine began to screech. Nievos looked at the tech, who immediately pushed a button on the console of the device. Peering at a small display screen on the top of the instrument, the specialist said,

"There's nothing wrong with this sensor; it's getting a positive reading from a radioactive source."

Skillings and Nievos looked first at each other, then out the window at where they were. Skillings grabbed his D-DACT off his belt, hit the GPS function key, then the "Save" button, and suddenly said, "Emilio, don't slow down! Four men carrying weapons just came out of the hangar and jumped in that military vehicle!"

All but invisible behind the dark tinted glass of the van, the three Americans watched out the rear window as the green vehicle raced up to a gate. One of the blue-clad occupants jumped out, fiddled with a lock, swung the gate open, and then closed it as the Brazilian-built military vehicle pulled through. The green truck stopped only long enough to pick up the gate-man and then pulled out onto the highway—and began following them, about a half mile behind the white van. Nievos, seeing the truck gathering speed, said, "Uh oh, looks like we have company."

Skillings had already grabbed his D-DACT and was busily tapping out a brief message on his keypad:

SKILLINGS TO NEWMAN. DET NINE PURSUED BY 4
ARMED PERS IN VENZ MIL VEH. HOSTILE INTENT UNK.
PREP QRF FOR POSS ACTION.
GPS LOC ON BFT.

He quickly scanned through what he had written on the tiny screen and hit the red, "Emergency X-MIT" button.

Less than two seconds later, the message popped up on a laptop computer screen in the CJR Warehouse office, prompting the young Army "battle captain" to turn around and say, "General Newman, Sergeant Major Skillings may need some backup."

Newman arose immediately from his "desk"—another of the folding tables that Eduardo had obtained, and where he and Lt. Col. Dan Hart had been sitting with Chief Manuel Suazo, the Navy SEAL sniper, going over the final plan for the "hit" on Mubassa the following day. Hart had arrived earlier that morning on a flight from Toronto, using a Canadian passport.

Standing over the watch officer's shoulder, Newman quickly read Skillings's message, then said, "Switch to the Blue Force Tracker display and show me where they are."

Using the computer's mouse, the captain moved the cursor over an icon labeled "BFT" and clicked once. Instantly the screen shifted from text to a map, displaying the area around Caracas. Four tiny blue circles were blinking on the map, showing the GPS designators of Newman's units. Three of them were stationary: a "6," at the location of the CJR warehouse and a "2" and an "8" in downtown Caracas—the over-watch scouts Suazo had positioned for the hit on Mubassa. The fourth blue circle—with a "9" in its center—was moving along the airport perimeter road.

"There he is," said Newman, pointing to the flashing "9." Turning to Hart, he said, "Dan, take two of your five-man QRF teams and move out in two of the Suburbans. Get on the same road that Sergeant Major Skillings is on and follow a mile or so behind whoever is tailing Skillings and Nievos. If they need help, take care of it. If you have to engage, do not return here; go to the alternate location up the road toward Maracaibo. Stay in touch with him and me on your D-DACT. Make sure your GPS transponder is on so I can track you from here."

"Aye aye, sir," responded Hart, hastily putting on his Guayabera to conceal the H&K Mk 23 Mod 0.45 cal. pistol hanging from his hip and the much smaller M11 9mm suspended in a shoulder holster beneath his left armpit. As he buttoned his loose-fitting shirt, Hart grabbed what looked to be a garage door opener suspended by Velcro near the doorway into the warehouse and pressed it once. A large bell mounted in the ceiling of the warehouse rang loudly for about three seconds, and a bright red light centered over the roll-up doors began to blink. In the warehouse, twenty men stopped what they were doing, moved to the wall where the weapons were hung, grabbed their gear, and hastily assembled by the rows of vehicles.

Meanwhile farther up the highway the occupants of the white van were preparing to be stopped by the green vehicle that was rapidly closing the distance behind them. Skillings typed another brief message into his D-DACT, sent it, and then ordered Emilio, "Head straight for the International Departures level at the main terminal. Don't speed up. Don't slow down unless they make us pull over. If they do, just tell them you are taking me to the airport for a flight."

Less than five minutes after Skillings transmitted the first message from his D-DACT, Hart had briefed the ten men who would be accompanying him, and two of the Suburbans had pulled out of the roll-up doors at the CJR warehouse and were heading up the highway. Seconds after they were in the open, a new blue designator—a circle with a "Q" in the center—popped up on the laptop screen in Newman's "office."

In the backseat of the white van, Nievos and the young tech-rep had shut off the neutron-gamma detector and stowed it in its Pelican case. When the green vehicle closed to a distance of less than thirty meters behind them and matched their speed at fifty kilometers per hour, Nievos reached up under Emilio's seat, pulled out a small black nylon fabric briefcase, placed it on the floor between his legs, and unzipped it. Without looking down he withdrew an H&K M5KA4 submachine gun and three extra 15-round magazines. As the young tech-rep watched with growing anxiety, the Delta Force commando calmly cocked the weapon and then jammed it and the magazines down into the pocket on the back of Emilio's seat.

The white van, still shadowed by the green military vehicle, pulled onto the Departures ramp and Emilio turned to Skillings and said, "Which airline?"

The Marine answered, "LACSA—Costa Rican Airlines."

As Emilio halted amidst cars, taxicabs, and hotel vans full of departing travelers, the green military truck pulled around to block the van from pulling out. Three men wearing blue Venezuelan Air Force uniforms and brandishing brand new AK-47s jumped from the truck and surrounded the van. On the curb, passengers scurried away to avoid what clearly looked like a dangerous situation.

Immediately after the crowd had scattered, a tall, well-built, fair-skinned man wearing sunglasses, a Guayabera, and dark trousers emerged from the front passenger seat of the truck. Skillings noticed that he was wearing military-style boots—and that there was a bulge beneath the man's left armpit.

The fair-haired man walked coolly up to Emilio's window and said in heavily accented Spanish, "Why were you driving on the road past the military side of the airport?"

"I was taking a shortcut because we needed to catch a flight," said Emilio.

"What flight are you trying to catch?"

"LACSA Flight 921 to San Jose, Costa Rica," answered Skillings in English.

The man standing outside Emilio's window took off his sunglasses, revealing blue eyes and said, "Who are you?" in heavily accented English.

"I am Amos Skillings, and I am going to miss my flight. Who are you to delay me?"

"Who I am is of no consequence to you, Amos Skillings. Get out of the van."

While Skillings did as ordered, the tall man with the blue eyes and Slavic features came around the front of the van and said in Spanish to one of the uniformed men carrying an AK-47, "Go inside to the LACSA counter and see if an Amos Skillings has a reservation on flight number 921." He then turned to the Marine sergeant major who was now standing outside the van and demanded, "Let me see your passport."

Skillings reached in the pocket of his shirt, pulled out the passport, and handed it to him. The younger man flipped it open, looked at the photograph inside the front page, then up at the Marine and said, "So what business brings you to Venezuela from Grenada, Mr. Skillings?"

"I am with the OAS Human Rights Commission—and as you can see from my passport—I have a diplomatic carte blanche," replied Skillings, in what he hoped sounded like a Caribbean-British accent. He then continued, looking the taller man right in the eye, "And I can assure you, sir, unless you release me immediately to proceed to my flight, I shall report to the Commission that the government of Venezuela is using Russians to illegally detain injured diplomatic personnel. Now I must insist on seeing your identification."

For the first time since the inquisition began, the imperious fair-haired man seemed to be uncertain. He reached in his hip pocket and withdrew a Venezuelan National Police Identity wallet and flipped it open briefly. Skillings ignored the gold badge that would have attracted most people's eye and read the name and title beneath the photograph: *Mayor Gregor Argozvek, Consejero Especial De la Seguridad* before the leather case slapped closed.

At this moment, the armed man who had been sent into the airport returned and whispered something into the major's ear. Neither of them, nor the other two armed, uniformed men standing guard outside the white van, paid any attention to the two Chevrolet Suburbans with the tinted windows that pulled up about thirty feet behind them. The Russian turned back to the Marine and said, "Well, Mr. Skillings, it appears that you do indeed have a reservation on LACSA Flight 921. Where is your luggage?"

The large side door of the van slid open and Nievos handed Skillings the black fabric briefcase—that had moments ago held a submachine gun—and the hard plastic Pelican case previously containing the radiation detector. The major moved toward the open door and asked Nievos in English, "Who are you?"

"Roberto Nievos," the Delta Force operator responded in Spanish with perfect Venezuelan inflection. "We came to help him because he injured his leg."

The Russian peered at the two men in the back of the van, then at Emilio in the driver's seat and grunted. He then waved to the three uniformed, armed men and motioned them toward the military vehicle. As they slung their weapons over their shoulders and started to return to their truck, the major handed Skillings his passport and said, "You may go."

The Marine nodded, picked up the briefcase, and started hobbling toward the terminal. Nievos jumped out of the back of the van, grabbed the Pelican case and started after Skillings, shouting to Emilio, "I'll help him get checked in and then meet you on the Arrivals level where you usually pick up your passengers."

After watching Skillings and Nievos enter the terminal and the van depart, the Russian got back in the military truck and it drove away, headed for the airport exit. The two large American SUVs waited for thirty seconds after the green vehicle was out of sight, then departed for the exit ramp as well.

As they entered the terminal, Skillings and Nievos, never exchanging so much as a glance or a word, separated immediately. To anyone watching them on a security camera positioned inside the building, it would appear as though the two men did not know each other. The Marine proceeded directly to the LACSA counter and Nievos, lugging the large Pelican case, followed the signs toward Baggage Claim. He took an escalator down one level, passed the baggage carousels, waded through the crowd, and walked to the same exit portal he had used just four days earlier.

Before stepping outside, Nievos confirmed that the white van with the big number seven on the side was beneath the "Valet Car Service" sign. After checking to make sure that the green military vehicle was nowhere in sight, he walked out of the terminal and straight to the van. Four minutes later, Skillings exited the same door and followed the same path to the vehicle, this time entering the large, sliding side door.

As Skillings slid the door closed, Emilio put the transmission in gear and immediately drove off. The young tech-rep who had said nothing through this whole experience looked absolutely stunned. As Emilio guided the van into the traffic flow on the airport exit road toward Caracas, the specialist finally found his voice. "How did you *do* that?" he asked Nievos and Skillings.

The sergeant major looked at the young man and said, "Do what?"

"How did you get a reservation on a flight to Costa Rica? How did you get back here?"

Skillings chuckled and said, "As soon as I saw them following us I sent General Newman an emergency message on my D-DACT. I then sent a second message to Major Bowes, back in Washington, asking him to make me a reservation on the next flight out of Caracas to any other country in the western hemisphere. He made the reservation on the LACSA flight and sent the information back to my D-DACT. It arrived just before we got stopped by our Russian friend."

"What if they check to see if you boarded your flight?" asked the tech.

"The young woman at the counter was very sympathetic that my injured leg was much too painful for me to fly and refunded the cost of the e-ticket. We agreed that I would make another reservation next week."

"Where are we going now?" the technician asked, still looking apprehensive.

"We're going back to the warehouse to send a very interesting report to Washington," answered Nievos.

"Good," said the young man, looking relieved. "I really have to pee."

Oval Office
The White House
Washington, DC
Friday, 02 November 2007
1930 Hours Local

"In the last twelve hours we have had bombs go off on trains in Manhattan, Atlanta, and Chicago and a bus in Los Angeles—and a group claiming to be the 'Islamic Brotherhood in America' has claimed credit," said the President, clearly showing the strain of the continuing crisis. He was seated to the right of the fireplace, and in an identical chair to his left was the Vice President.

The split oak logs burning on the grate behind them were fast turning to embers as the Commander in Chief continued, "Dan, you say these new attacks here aren't connected to what's going on in Saudi Arabia. That just doesn't make sense to me. And with more than thirty dead Americans and nearly a hundred injured, I don't believe that, given the earlier threats from this 'Islamic Brotherhood' outfit, our citizens will see them as unconnected events."

"Sir, right now, everything the FBI, ATF, and our EOD personnel have learned about these attacks indicates that all four were different types of explosives," replied the SecDef, seated beside Gen. George Grisham, on the couch to the right of the President. He continued, "New York, Chicago, and Atlanta were apparently suicide bombers. In Los Angeles it was probably a timed device left on a bus."

"That's correct, Mr. President," interjected Sarah Dornin, the Homeland Security Secretary. She was seated beside Secretary of State Helen Luce on the couch opposite Powers and Grisham. National Security Advisor Jeb Stuart, Chief of Staff Bruce Allen, and Bill Goode had pulled up chairs with their backs to the rain beating on the dark windows behind the President's desk. Secretary Dornin continued, "It's going to take law enforcement forensic teams days, if not weeks, to sort through the evidence and figure out who did this, but everything we know about these four transit system bombings indicates that they're the work of 'independent operators' who are simply trying to take advantage of the current situation."

"How do we conclude that?" asked the President.

"Well, first, there's the timing," answered the DHS Secretary. "The Times Square blast was first, at 0729. The Atlanta attack, on the MARTA train to the airport, wasn't until almost noon our time. The blast at the elevated train station on Randolph Street in downtown Chicago occurred at 4:05 p.m. our time—3:05 Chicago time. And the one on the bus in LA didn't happen until a little over an hour ago—about 3:15 in California. They weren't coordinated by time, type of explosive, or even effectiveness. The one in LA went off on an empty bus. Those aren't the signs of a well-planned, coordinated attack."

"Well, in New York and Atlanta, the news media are reporting that they have claims that this is the work of the 'Islamic Brotherhood in America.' That sounds co-ordinated to me," said the President.

"Well, sir, we also have a similar claim delivered to a TV station on Chicago that they have not aired," answered Dornin. "But the FBI believes that Atlanta, Chicago, and LA are 'copycats.' "

"Copycats?" the President repeated. "Who were they copying?"

"Probably the bomber in New York. But the only thing that they have in common is that each was an exploding homegrown bomb. The New York bomb was the most sophisticated; the bomber in Atlanta used a black powder pipe bomb, and the 'claim of responsibility' note spells America with a 'k'—and the one in Chicago did so as well. The bomb in LA was not much more than a 'Molotov cocktail' with a primitive timing device. This is further reason for us to conclude that all four events are independent of one another—probably the work of radical Islamic clerics in each of these cities who have been talking about this kind of action for years. We think that when the radicals in Atlanta, Chicago, and Los Angeles heard about New York, they just called up some of the kids they had trained to die and sent off the first available volunteer in each case."

"Any sign that they are taking orders from leaders outside the country?" asked the President.

"Inspiration, yes; direction, no," Dornin replied. "There are undoubtedly 'sleeper-cells' operating here that we don't know about yet, but all the ones we have broken up so far have been operating independently, much like a franchise operation. It's been that way pretty much since after 9/11. The radical imams preach hatred and how to die the 'right' way in their local, radical mosques. They recruit a few young men—sometimes even young women—and send these 'volunteers' off for training in Pakistan, Syria, or Iran. When these 'warriors' come home, the local imams just wait for what they think is an opportune moment for these kids to become martyrs in their jihad."

The President was silent for a few moments pondering this information. To the others in the room it seemed as though George Washington was looking down on their meeting from the Gilbert Stuart portrait above the mantle. The current Commander in Chief then said quietly, "I think it's important that I visit each of these sites—at least New York, Chicago, and Atlanta—tomorrow."

"Well, sir, if you do, we've got to make these trips fast—in and out—no prior announcement other than to local law enforcement through the Secret Service," said the SecDef. When the President didn't respond, Powers continued, "We've got to be in very close contact with you tomorrow. That's easy on *Air Force One,* but with all that we've learned today, we may need your authorization for certain operations."

"Give me the gist, Dan," said the President.

Powers nodded and said, "Today we got the first real intelligence breaks since this crisis began, Mr. President, and I think we now have at least some definitive proof that the Iranians are behind this 'Islamic Brotherhood' organization and that the Russians—or at least some Russians—are helping them. I think it would help if Bill Goode summarized all that we have learned in the last few hours."

The President nodded and said, "OK, Bill, give us the executive summary."

The CIA's Operations Director had left Langley at 3:00 p.m. for the Pentagon and then the 4:30 p.m. National Security Council meeting in the Situation Room. He had now been away from his office for over four and one-half hours. Yet, every few minutes throughout the afternoon and evening he'd been receiving updates from the CIA's Operations Center via the D-DACT he now carried with him constantly.

Goode began, "Mr. President, let me try to go through this chronologically. On Monday night, at our request, a British communications intercept unit, with the help of Norwegian Intelligence, established a mobile monitoring site near Grense Jacobselv, on the Varanger Fjord—it's about eighty miles west of Murmansk. They began intercepting Russian military, intelligence, and commercial satellite communications on Tuesday."

"Why didn't we do that with one of our subs?" asked the Commander in Chief, looking at Gen. George Grisham.

"Because we couldn't get one there fast enough, Mr. President," responded the Chairman of the Joint Chiefs.

The President nodded and Goode continued, "Late Tuesday—actually it was early Wednesday morning in the Persian Gulf—a U.S. Navy Special Operations unit severed a fiber-optic cable between Tehran and Riyadh. This time we used two subs, Mr. President—the USS *Jimmy Carter* and a mini-sub with SEALs aboard. We cut this communications link in an effort to disrupt what we believed were instructions flowing from Tehran to Riyadh."

"Did all this stuff work?" asked the President.

"Not the way we expected," admitted Goode. "Early Thursday morning, the Norwegian intercept site monitored a commercial telephone call to the Gorky Nuclear Weapons Research Facility outside of Moscow. Dr. Oleg Zhdanov—using a GSM/GDSM cell phone—had placed the call from Caracas. Back in the '80s Zhdanov used to be a deputy director at Gorky, and he's an expert on nuclear PAL codes."

"What's he doing in Venezuela?" asked the Commander in Chief.

"We don't know yet," said Goode. "But we're pretty sure he isn't on a winter holiday. According to an old defector debrief done in 2005, Zhdanov was spotted in Tehran and then at the Iranian Nuclear Research Facil-

ity in Tabriz—in the company of Gen. Dimitri Komulakov."

"Isn't this the fellow mentioned in one of your reports several days ago?" asked the President.

"Yes, sir, but now there's more," replied Goode.
"Early this morning, shortly after the New York subway
bombing, the Norway intercept site began monitoring
encrypted voice and then data traffic on a dedicated
commercial satellite downlink in Murmansk. A company called Filaya Petroleum Services—a Russian-Saudi
joint venture headed by Dimitri Komulakov—leased this
dedicated channel yesterday on the Eurosat system.

"He's a busy fellow, and he may be bad," said the
President, "but I don't see how this proves anything
about the current situation."

"Well, sir, the British GCHQ site in Jordan and their
'stay behinds' in the Saudi capital have been monitoring
communications in and out of the Filaya Oil complex in
Riyadh since this all started on October fourteenth. According to GCHQ, the traffic in and out of the Filaya
building dropped off immediately after the fiber-optic
cable was severed on Wednesday. Yesterday, they
started monitoring all kinds of communications—in the
clear—being broadcast by radio in Farsi—from a building *across the street* from the Filaya complex. Then suddenly this morning, the Filaya building emissions picked
back up again—simultaneous with the new traffic being
picked up off the Murmansk satellite hub. Shortly afterward, one of our NSA satellites monitored a very
brief sat-phone call in the clear to a commercial phone
number in Tehran. NSA believes that the voices on the
call are Ali Yunesi, head of Iranian intelligence—and
Dimitri Komulakov."

The President, grappling with the arcane language of
Signals Intelligence, asked, "But what do these pieces in
the puzzle show us, Bill?"

"By themselves, an incomplete picture," admitted

Goode. "But they tie in with other things we have learned. On every one of the pirated Saudi ships and planes that have been captured or detained, there has been at least one Russian crewman in addition to the 'Islamic Brotherhood' types aboard. All these vessels and aircraft have been modified to carry a nuclear weapon—and all were supposed to be heading for Caracas. A Russian captured by the British when they took down that pirated Saudi vessel off Algeria has admitted that he was recruited by Komulakov's principal deputy, Nikolai Dubzhuko—the man who seems to be running the show from the Filaya building in Riyadh."

"Well, isn't it time we took out this Filaya building in Riyadh?" asked the President, turning to his Secretary of Defense.

"Perhaps, sir," responded Powers, "but there's one more crucial piece of intelligence."

Goode continued. "While we were dealing with the bombings here in the U.S. this morning, one of Gen. Peter Newman's Special Ops teams—in Caracas on another mission—discovered a significant source of radiation in a military hangar at the Simon Bolivar airport. One of the members of this team, a Marine sergeant major named Skillings, also made a positive ID on a person we've seen before, a Russian GRU major named Gregor Argozvek. According to our data, Argozvek worked with Komulakov when he was the KGB *Rezident* at the United Nations."

"What's the source of the radiation? Is it a nuclear weapon or *weapons?*" asked the President.

Before Goode could answer, the President turned to the SecDef and said, "Dan, earlier you told me that you thought this Komulakov person was working for or with the Iranians. Is he doing this from Caracas?"

"We don't know the answer to those questions yet, Mr. President," answered Powers. "But if you're going to be traveling tomorrow, I'd like to have your authority to carry out the following operations if we find it opportune: First, to take out the Filaya site in Riyadh—and this newest 'Islamic Brotherhood' place across the street. Second, we're positioning the USS *Dallas* off Caracas and the USS *Virginia* at the mouth of the Gulf of Maracaibo. If they make a positive ID on any of these pirated Saudi vessels coming or going out of those ports, I want the subs to sink 'em. Third, I'd like to have your permission to take Newman off his primary mission and to give him the task of finding out what's causing the radiation in that warehouse."

The President paused for a moment before answering, then asked, "How would you 'take out' the Filaya site, Dan?"

Powers turned to Grisham, who said, "We'll leave it up to CENTCOM, but when I talked to them about options they said they'd likely use JDAMs from B-52s out of Diego Garcia. That gives us the advantage of accuracy and a good 'stand off' safety margin if someone has figured out how to use the SAMs that the Saudis left behind."

"OK, do it, when you're ready," said the President. "On your second recommendation, is there any way for the subs to tell the vessels to stop and see if they will surrender?"

"Sir, we thought of that," said the SecDef. "But Admiral Coolidge at SubLant was quick to remind us that the men on those captured Saudi yachts are suicidal fanatics. If they have nuclear weapons aboard, we stand to lose a submarine and crew if the 'jihadis' aboard those ships get a warning."

Again the President contemplated the consequences of his decision and then said, "Go ahead and give that order. Let's reduce this one to writing though, Dan, just in case the captains of those submarines have to respond to criticism from some quarter later on. If anyone is going to take the heat for this, let it be me."

The SecDef nodded. "I'll have a National Security Decision Memorandum over to Jeb tonight for your signature, Mr. President." Powers paused a moment and then said, "How about General Newman, sir?"

"Isn't Newman in Caracas to carry out an . . . ah . . . an assignment for the Commission on Threat Mitigation?" the President asked euphemistically.

Powers almost said the word *assassination,* but then thought better of it and replied simply, "Yes, sir."

"If we pull him off his primary mission, we're going to get blasted by Senator Waggoner and his allies in Congress—especially after the bombings here today," said the President.

"Well, if there are nuclear weapons in that hangar, this is certainly 'threat mitigation' if there ever was such a thing," said Powers. "How about we ask General Newman if he and his teams can do both—as long as the missions don't conflict with one another?"

"You're a hard man, Dan Powers," said the President with a humorless smile. "OK, go ahead, as long as Newman's missions don't 'conflict,' as you put it."

Air Force One
35,000 Ft Over Cleveland, OH
Saturday, 03 November 2007
0915 Hours Local

The President walked back into the Staff Quarters of the big Boeing 747 as soon as he finished reading the morning intelligence brief. They had left Andrews Air Force Base for New York at 0545, and he hadn't had a free moment until they took off for Chicago. Frank Kilgannon, Secretary of the Treasury; Energy Secretary Sam Browning; Sarah Dornin, Secretary of Homeland Security; Chief of Staff Bruce Allen; and National Security Advisor Jeb Stuart arose as he approached the table where they had been huddled around mugs of hot coffee.

"Your remarks to the 'First Responders' and the families of those killed and injured in the Times Square attack were right on the mark, Mr. President," Dornin volunteered.

"Thank you, Sarah," he replied. "I just wish we could offer more than promises that this will stop." He motioned for them to sit down, slid into a chair himself, and said, "I just read the FBI assessment that the New York, Chicago, and Atlanta attacks were all 'home grown' suicide bombers. If they're right, at least two of these kids were born here in America, grew up among us, and still came to hate us enough to kill themselves trying to kill other Americans. The press will probably have that from Senator Waggoner before we get to Chicago. Any thoughts on what this means?"

Sarah Dornin said, "Well, sir, we've got to find some way to stop these radical imams from spewing this hatred. Encouraging young people to build bombs, put them in backpacks, and blow themselves up isn't religious speech protected by the First Amendment."

"I agree with Sarah," said Kilgannon. "And these attacks are likely to hit the financial markets even harder than what's already happened because it's an attack on us by our own people. Even without using a nuke the Islamic Brotherhood has severely crippled the U.S. financial markets. The stock markets, commodity exchanges, and many other institutions are still closed. We've never experienced anything like it—it's been the longest bank holiday in American history—worse than anything, even the 'Crash of '29.' "

"Until yesterday's attacks, I thought maybe we had turned the corner, that things were going to start to improve," said the President.

The Treasury Secretary shook his head gloomily and said, "Some of the banks, credit unions, and savings and loan institutions with solid reserves tried to open for just a couple hours a day. But there was such a run as customers tried to withdraw all their cash, they had to shut the doors. It's pretty grim news all around. While you were talking to the families of the injured, I was listening to the guys from the NYSE and NASDQ. They aren't anxious to reopen anytime soon. I think we're going to find the same thing when we talk to the people from the Commodities Exchange when we get to Chicago."

The President looked at Sam Browning, his Secretary of Energy, and said, "Sam, can I tell the American people that they are going to be able to heat their homes this winter?"

"I hope so, sir," said Browning. "Our first two fully operational coal-conversion plants in southern Virginia and West Virginia will come on line at the end of the month. Every nuclear plant is now at peak electrical production and our 'soybeans and corn to diesel' program will be fully implemented by the end of December. On the downside, because of energy shortages and rationing most businesses are operating on less than 25 percent of employees—at least that's how many have been showing up in East and West coastal cities. The figure's a little better, about 50 to 75 percent in the Midwest. No one knows for sure if gas is being priced at some amount that reflects any business or industry standards. Nothing's logical. The price of gas is 'whatever traffic will bear,' and people seem to be willing to pay whatever it takes to get some fuel."

"The economy won't start to improve until we can get the price of gasoline back within reason," interjected Frank Kilgannon. "And now with this attack on mass-transit, even fewer people will be willing to take a train or bus to get to work."

"The problem is bigger than just rationing or lack of fuel," responded Browning. "Since the banks are shut down, no retailer wants to take a credit card because they can't be sure of ever getting paid. With ATMs shut down and pumps that won't take a credit card, there are increasing reports of an underground 'barter economy'—people offering possessions or services in exchange for fuel. That means no sales taxes are being collected."

The President looked around the table and said, "You guys are giving it to me straight, without spin, and I appreciate that. I don't think we ought to sugarcoat things for the American people. But we've been through worse times as a country, and I'm convinced that we can weather this storm as well."

Before the Commander in Chief could continue, his Air Force aide entered the staff space and said, "Excuse me, Mr. President. You have a call from Senator James Waggoner."

The President grimaced and turned toward the others in the room and smiled. "I just said things could be worse. I guess they just got that way."

He took the call in his private quarters. "Hello, James . . ."

"Mr. President," Waggoner said, "I hope that when you get to Chicago you are more forceful about shutting down these radical mosques and Islamic centers than you were in New York a few hours ago."

"Well, thank you for your advice, Senator," said the President. "I can assure you that I am using all the authorities afforded me under the Constitution to protect our citizens and their rights."

"Rights?" said Waggoner. "These terrorists have no right to blow up innocent civilians and threaten us with nuclear blackmail! We need a firm hand at the helm, Mr. President. You and I see the same intelligence. You and I both know the Iranians are behind all this. They're the ones inspiring these radical mullahs or ayatollahs or whatever they call themselves here in the

United States. It's time to cut off the head so that the rest of the snake dies."

"Well, Senator, there is something else that you and I both know," interrupted the President. "This is an open, nonsecure phone circuit that can be monitored by too many people for me to discuss these matters further with you. Thank you for your call. I hope we can talk more when I return to Washington. If you need to talk to me sooner, please use the secure voice instrument in the SSCI secure space. Good-bye."

With that, the President hung up the phone. As he returned to the staff compartment he said, "I sure hope our party can field a serious candidate for the 2008 election. Senator Waggoner already has his campaign slogan."

"What's that?" asked Bruce Allen.

"It's time to cut off the head so that the rest of the snake dies."

CHAPTER EIGHTEEN

Blame America First

CJR Warehouse
867 Avenida Maiquetia, Caracas, Venezuela
Saturday, 03 November 2007
0930 Hours Local

Dan, I don't know quite what to make of it," said Brig. Gen. Peter Newman to Lt. Col. Dan Hart. He was staring at the computer screen, rereading the lengthy Operations Order that he had received by encrypted e-mail from the Chairman of the Joint Chiefs of Staff a half hour ago. "This op order clearly states that we are now 'Operational Control of Special Operations Command'—but that as a 'Special Unit' we will continue to receive 'tasking' from and 'report to' the JCS. How can we be under the Op Con to SOCOM and still take orders from and report directly to the Joint Chiefs?"

"I agree, it doesn't fit any task organization or chain of command that I've ever seen, sir," said Hart, looking over his shoulder. "I think it's because of that paragraph in the 'Coordinating Instructions' where it refers to our 'Initial Primary Mission.' My guess is that back in Washington they're worried about us not carrying out the 'Threat Mitigation mission, given all the political fallout from yesterday's transit system attacks."

"Brother, do I regret the decision I made not to bring any portable printers on this mission," said Newman, scrolling back through the text on the screen. "I want to make sure that we're both reading this the same way. You're saying that we're to carry out the Mubassa tasking *and* find out what's causing the radiation in that hangar—as long as the two missions don't conflict?"

"Yes, sir," said Hart.

"Well that's how I see it too," said Newman, shaking his head, "but I don't see how they *don't* conflict. What time is Mubassa supposed to show up at that museum?"

"At noon, sir," replied Hart. "Chief Suazo and his people left here last night at 2100 to get in position. They're reporting in every hour by D-DACT."

"Well if that goes down as planned, as soon as the hit on Mubassa happens, Valdez will turn this country inside out trying to catch the perpetrators. And that's going to make getting into that hangar where the radiation is coming from a whole lot harder than it is already."

"There's no doubt about that, sir," said Hart. "I talked at length with Eduardo about it. He thinks that he can get two, maybe three, of our people onto the military side of the base. He's rounding up the appropriate uniforms and IDs, and I've picked our three best Spanish speakers to try just walking in the front door, but Eduardo won't have any of that stuff ready until tomorrow at the earliest."

"What did Sergeant First Class Nievos say this morning after the recon he conducted last night?" asked Newman.

"The chain-link fence is alarmed with both seismic and laser sensors. He said the lasers around the perimeter of the building can be seen very clearly with NVGs. There are cameras mounted all over the place, and at night at least a dozen armed guards and two dogs patrol the back and sides of the structure. He also suspects that just inside the perimeter fence there may be anti-personnel mines planted since the guards avoid the area. At one point a guard dog slipped its collar and went over to the fence to pee, and the dog handler hid behind one of the concrete revetments until the dog came back."

Newman chuckled, shook his head, looked at his watch, and said, "A little over two hours before Mubassa shows up in the scope of Chief Suazo's .50 cal. sniper rifle. According to everything in this op order, by that time they'll have two attack subs off the Venezuelan coast, an F-16 squadron with tankers at Roosevelt Roads, Puerto Rico, and the *Eisenhower* Carrier Battle Group headed into the Caribbean. Sure would hate to waste all that firepower just because we 'needed' to take out this guy Mubassa."

"What are you going to do?" asked Hart.

"I'm going to do something that's very uncharacteristic," said Newman. "I'm going to send a message to Washington and see if *they* will make the call on this one."

USS *Dallas*, SSN 700
67° W 11° N, Approx 25nm N of Caracas
Saturday, 03 November 2007
1130 Hours Local

Capt. Ross Conner was justifiably proud of his crew. Just forty-seven hours and 1,600 miles ago the USS *Dallas* had been in port at Hamilton, Bermuda, awaiting the arrival of a SEAL team that was flying in from Dam Neck, Virginia. Now the fast attack sub was hovering at a depth of two hundred feet, just twenty-five miles due north of the Venezuelan coastal city of La Guaira, the main port for nearby Caracas. The high-speed run the

Dallas had made south, down the Atlantic Basin, across the Milwaukee Depth, and through the narrow Canal de la Mona, between Puerto Rico and Santo Domingo, had been one for the record books.

After checking their location one final time on the paper chart and the electronic display above the chart table, Conner looked up and said, "Well, we did it. We're where we're supposed to be. XO, pass a 'Bravo Zulu' to everyone."

"Will do, sir," replied Lt. Cmdr. Mike O'Malley, the executive officer of the boat. "But before I pass that word, you better take a look at the new op order. As soon as we put out the trailing wire antenna, we took in a message from SubLant with a 'Shoot to Kill' order for any of the Saudi boats that they have been looking for."

Conner looked up from the chart at his XO and asked, "Is that just for us, or is it for everyone?"

"It's for everyone—aircraft as well. They even sent it to the P-3 detachment they moved to Guantanamo," answered O'Malley, handing the captain the printout.

Conner bent over the chart table and read the operative paragraph ordering all ships and aircraft to "sink without warning" any pirated Saudi vessels that were "located on the high seas in international waters."

"Well, in my twenty years in the Navy, that's the first time I've seen that written down. I sure hope that the guys running this show have told everyone else where *we* are. I sure don't want to take a hit from someone else's weapon," said Conner, handing the op order back to O'Malley.

"Yes, sir," said the XO. "Theoretically, no other 'friendlies' are supposed to be in our 'operating box.' The *Virginia*'s position is off Maracaibo. I'm having the chief plot her operating area on the display. The boundary between us and them is 69 degrees west."

"I'm trying to remember the original op order that we got before leaving Bermuda," said Conner. "Does

Virginia have a sixteen-man SEAL team, aboard as well?"

"Yes, sir," replied O'Malley, "they picked theirs up at Key West."

"Man, she must have been hauling through the Yucatan Channel and across the Cayman Ridge to get on station that fast," said Conner.

"Yes, sir," agreed O'Malley. "And that's no pleasure cruise. There are all kinds of seamounts, uncharted wrecks, and things to bump into to be going fast on that course."

"Well," Conner shrugged, "they wanted us in position— and we're here. Do they have any satellite imagery for us on any of our targets?"

O'Malley consulted the printout of the message he had just received from SubLant and said, "The imagery is coming in on Norfolk's noon 'data dump,' but according to the info here, three of the pirated Saudi vessels are tied up at the Venezuelan Navy pier in La Guaira at berths 23, 24, and 25. There is a large container ship beside them at berth 20. There are a total of twenty-two vessels in port. Most of them are commercial container and bulk cargo ships, one inter-island cruise ship, and a ferry that comes and goes every eight hours between La Guaira and Isla de Margarita."

"Enough of the tour guide stuff, O'Malley," said the captain good naturedly. "Have any of the Venezuelan Navy vessels moved since the last satellite pass? And where are the other Saudi boats?"

O'Malley pointed back at the printout and said, "Three Venezuelan frigates are still at Maracaibo, there's one here, and two at Puerto La Cruz. Two patrol boats remain in port at La Guaira, two at Cumana, two more are tied up at Maracaibo. Both of their subs are in port—one at Punta Fijo, the other one at Cumana. In addition to the three Saudi vessels up above us at La Guaira, there is one pier-side at Maracaibo and another—

a big one, almost 230 feet—en route in this direction from Aruba."

"Headed this way, and not toward Maracaibo?" asked Conner. "I wonder why? Maracaibo is a lot closer to Aruba than Caracas."

"According to that long message we received in Bermuda, the intel boys believe that the nuclear weapons are in Caracas and are probably going to be loaded aboard ships here in La Guaira. There's nothing here to change that assessment," answered the XO, scanning the message again.

"What's it say about the big vessel headed here from Aruba?" asked the skipper. "Do they have an ETA?"

O'Malley read out loud, "She was built in Italy, twin screws, supposed to have a crew of thirty-five, draws eighteen feet, and has a max speed of thirty knots. She was named *Arabian Star* but has been renamed *Scimitar*—blue hull, white superstructure, helo deck on fantail. The vessel is—or was—owned by Sheikh Abdullah al-Aziz, a cousin of the Saudi Interior Minister. Sheikh Aziz was killed in Riyadh. If she holds current course and speed, the *Scimitar*'s ETA at La Guaira is 2100 local this evening."

"Since we have to take her in international waters, she should be coming this way at about 1930 or so," said Conner, doing the math in his head. "And that means we had better be ready an hour or so before that to send her to the bottom."

Room 1527, Tanausu Tower Hotel
Avenida Las Acacias
Caracas, Venezuela
Saturday, 03 November 2007
1150 Hours Local

It was a very long shot. Master Chief Manuel Suazo had estimated it by eyeball to be 1,300 yards. The laser rangefinder had confirmed that it was actually 1,293.2 yards when he conducted his final recon twenty-four hours ago. The SEAL sniper took another look through the Leupold 10X scope atop his Barrett M82A3 .50 cal., rolled onto his side, and stretched his shoulders and neck.

"What do you think, Chief?" First Class Petty Officer Tony Avila asked his brother SEAL as he lowered his binoculars.

"I think you guys have been living pretty high on the hog for too long in this hotel suite and it's time you went back to work, that's what I think," said Suazo with a grin. "What are you seeing over there, Sanchez?"

Danny Sanchez, a Delta Force staff sergeant, was posted on the north-facing windows of the luxurious suite. Like Suazo and Avila, he too was positioned six feet back inside the room, looking out over the balcony toward *Boulevard Sabana Grande*. "Nothing yet," Sanchez replied, "but it looks like the motorcade might be on time. There's no more civilian traffic on the boulevard, and I've seen two sets of motorcycle cops going the wrong way up the highway."

"OK," said Suazo, "let's get ready. Everybody put your earplugs in. Pam, everything quiet out in the hallway?"

"Yep," said a female voice from the main entryway of the suite. Pamela Browne, one of the two females "on loan" from the CIA Operations Directorate, had checked into the suite three days ago with Sanchez. When Suazo had arrived last night, she had pitched in with the men to turn the luxury suite into a sniper's nest.

Six feet back from the sliding glass doors on the west side of the suite, the four of them had labored to construct a prone firing position high enough for Suazo to fire through the open door and over the balcony railing from deep inside the room. First, they placed four wooden chairs facing inward, atop the suite's dining room table, and then put one of the double bed innerspring mattresses on top of the chair seats. Using bed and chair pillows, Suazo then made a stable position on the mattress for the front bipod and customized rear monopod of the .50 cal. sniper rifle. From his position, six feet above the floor, Suazo had a clear shot 1,300 yards to the west—all the way to the front door of the museum in the *Parque Los Caobos*.

As Suazo rolled back into position, Sanchez said, "Here comes the motorcade. You'll see it in a few seconds moving from your right to your left. There are four motorcycles out in front, followed by two SUVs with guns sticking out the side and rear windows, then two black Mercedes, then two more SUVs."

A moment later, Avila said quietly, "I've got 'em. They just entered the tunnel beneath the *Plaza Venezuela* . . . now they're coming out . . . moving onto the *Avenida Real Quebrada Honda* . . . just as Eduardo's brother said they would." Then, a second later, he added, "There's no wind, Chief. All the flags between here and there are hanging limp."

Suazo never acknowledged or looked to verify the information being passed to him. He and Avila had worked together in Afghanistan and Iraq, and the sniper trusted his spotter implicitly. The chief had carefully memorized the route that Eduardo had given them, and trying to follow the moving motorcade on his scope would do nothing to improve his shot.

"The motorcade is now making the left turn at the mosque, and slowing down," said Avila. Then, a few seconds later, he continued. "The security goons are running beside the second Mercedes, that's the target car . . . helicopter making another pass . . . the cops are pushing the crowd back along the street in front of the museum. . . ."

Suazo, lying totally still on the mattress, could finally

see the cars moving into his field of vision from left to right on the scope. All he needed now was for the car with Mubassa in it to stop where it was supposed to—and for his "target" to hold still for two seconds after exiting the vehicle.

As the second Mercedes came to a halt, he placed the crosshairs directly on the rear door, put his right fore-finger on the trigger, took a deep breath, and slowly started to expel it as he waited for the door to open.

At that moment, Suazo's D-DACT began to vibrate on Pam Browne's hip. The chief had handed it to her when he had climbed up on top of the mattress and told her to hold it "until I finish my work."

She snatched it off her belt, looked through the peep-hole to confirm that the corridor outside the door was still empty, and glanced down at the message on the screen: NEWMAN TO SUAZO. MISSION CAN-CELLED BY WASHINGTON. RTB ASAP. REPEAT, MISSION CANCELLED, RTB. Stunned by the direc-tive, she hit the key labeled ACK—acknowledging re-ceipt of the message—and turned to tell Suazo.

In the scope, Suazo saw the head and shoulders of President Valdez as he exited on the far side of the Mer-cedes. Then, a plainclothes security man opened the rear door and Mubassa emerged smiling and waving to the crowd. With the crosshairs square in the middle of the Nigerian's corpulent mid-section, the SEAL sniper began a slow, steady squeeze on the trigger.

Suddenly, a bright flash all but obscured Mubassa, and then an instant later, a second explosion seemed to detonate on top of the Mercedes. Peering through the scope, Suazo relaxed his trigger finger and muttered, "What the—"

"Grenades," said Avila, calmly, never taking his binoculars off the target. "Looks like Mubassa and Valdez are both down."

A brief moment later, the sound of the two explosions carried down the *Rio Guaire* into the hotel suite. Suazo, still looking through the scope at the pandemonium in front of the museum, said, "It looks like someone just did our job for us."

"You better read this, Chief," said Browne, handing Suazo his D-DACT.

The Navy sniper quickly read the message from Newman, saw that Browne had already acknowledged receipt, shrugged, and said, "Let's get out of here."

"Plan A or Plan B, Chief?" asked Avila.

"Plan A—just as if we had done the job," replied Suazo, removing the magazine from the Barrett, clearing the round out of the chamber, and climbing down from his perch. "We were expecting a lockdown—and there surely will be one after *that*. Sanchez, you and Browne are on Canadian passports. Take the Metro as planned to the *Propatria* Terminal at the end of the line. Send a D-DACT to the warehouse when you're ready for pick-up. One of Eduardo's sons will swing by every hour in one of their white airport vans starting at 1500. Avila and I will take the rental car and drive back to the warehouse on the *Autopista*."

In ten minutes, the four of them had their individual weapons stowed, the hotel suite back in presentable condition, the Barrett stripped down to four component parts and hidden in Suazo's luggage, and were preparing to leave the room. As Sanchez and Avila made one last sweep through the room, Browne asked, "OK, Chief . . . who did it?"

Suazo, mindful of the D-DACT message that had come in just as he was preparing to end Mubassa's life, looked at her and said, "I don't know, but you can bet we're going to get blamed for it."

CJR Warehouse
867 Avenida Maiquetia, Caracas, Venezuela
Saturday, 03 November 2007
1235 Hours Local

"General Newman, sir, there's a secure sat-phone call for you from the NMCC," said the Army warrant officer manning the communications in the warehouse office. The Marine brigadier got up from the table where he, Lt. Col. Dan Hart, and SFC Nievos had been trying to piece together what was happening fifteen kilometers away in downtown Caracas from Chief Suazo's brief D-DACT messages and the local newscasts.

He took the handset from the warrant officer's outstretched hand, pushed the button on the side of the device, waited for the electronic "handshake" of the encryption systems, and said, "Newman here."

"Stand by for the Chairman of the Joint Chiefs," said the caller.

The next voice Newman heard was that of Gen. George Grisham: "Pete, what's going on down there? Didn't you receive our message calling off the operation on Mubassa?"

"It wasn't us, General," said Newman. "We received your message at 1158 local, transmitted a 'Stop Order' immediately, and then somebody else did a hit of their own. Master Chief Suazo saw it happen through his sniper-scope. Apparently two grenades were thrown from the crowd."

There was a long pause, and for several seconds Newman wasn't sure he'd been heard. Then Grisham said, "Roger that. I'm sure this is going to make things very complicated down there, but everything that we have points to Venezuela as the place where all these pirated Saudi ships and planes are being assembled."

"Is there anymore intel on the hangar where we think the radiation is coming from?" asked Newman. "Has

Langley been able to dig up any blueprints or design info?"

"No, Pete, the Agency has been so busy chasing after Saudi boats and planes that all they've been able to tell us is that the hangar was erected in 2006 by a Brazilian contractor for the Venezuelan Air Force," replied Grisham.

"Anything new on the Saudi ships and aircraft?" Newman asked.

"Yes," replied Grisham. "The NRO now agrees with Bill Goode at Langley that three of the pirated Saudi vessels are in port there in La Guaira, one is in Maracaibo, and there is one en route to La Guaira from Aruba, due to make port there tonight. The first satellite pass early this morning clearly shows five civil aircraft parked on the apron, interspersed among the Venezuelan military's new MiG 29s and SU-34s. Bill Goode believes that these civil aircraft are pirated Saudi planes; NRO isn't so sure."

"Well, I know you want confirmation, General," said Newman, "but I can tell you, it was already a tough go just getting onto the military side of the airfield, and it's going to be a whole lot tougher after this. I'm just hoping that they don't round up any of my people or the locals working with us in the manhunt. According to the news reports, martial law has been declared and a curfew is being imposed at sunset."

"Have you got anybody at the La Guaira port facility?" asked Grisham.

"Not now," Newman responded. "We did a recon there earlier in the week, but we don't have any of our people there now—only a security man who is on the payroll of our 'local' named Roca. And he has to report in by phone."

"Does this Roca fellow have any of his people who can get inside or even near the hangar?"

"No, sir," replied Newman. "All we have for surveillance over the hangar are the two small, radio-remote cameras that SFC Nievos put in place last night. One camera covers the gate to the airport perimeter road, and the other one gives us a view of the apron on the north side of the hangar—where the MiGs and SU-34s are. I don't want to sound like I'm getting cold feet, but between you and me, General, the fifty-three men and two women I have here aren't enough people to take care of both the aircraft *and* the ships in the port."

Grisham was silent for a moment. Newman was right. All he had available to him in Caracas were the Army JSOC, Marine Recon, Navy SEAL and CIA specialists who had been sent to Venezuela for the original Threat Mitigation mission. The Chairman then replied, "Don't worry about trying to take out any of those Saudi vessels; the Navy is going to handle that end of things." He then added, "But it would be helpful if we can get the word immediately if any of those ships get under way."

"I'll do what I can, General, but the way things are shaping up, even though the port is only a few klicks from here, it's likely going to be tomorrow before I can get any of our people into position to observe what's happening there," Newman replied.

"Is the local news saying whether Valdez is dead or alive?" asked Grisham. "Our ambassador was apparently there on the steps of the museum and was slightly wounded by shrapnel from one of the blasts. We're not getting much from the embassy."

"The news reports here say that *El Presidente* was wounded during a CIA assassination attempt and was rushed into surgery at the University Hospital—right across the river from where he was hit."

"Any signs that this might be part of a coup?" asked Grisham.

"Nothing yet," replied Newman. "One of our teams is trying to make it back here on the Metro system—

which they've reported is still running. The other team is coming back here by car, and they sent a D-DACT message as they passed the National Guard headquarters southwest of central Caracas, reporting that there were no visible troop movements. But it's only been a half hour since the attack."

"OK . . . good report, Pete. I'm going to tell the SecDef that I've ordered you guys to terminate your original mission, to button up for right now until the situation settles down, and then to go after whatever is in that hangar as soon as possible."

"Roger that, sir," Newman replied, then added, "One last question, General. Do we have anything firm on how long we have?"

Grisham paused before answering, then he said quietly, "*Firm,* no. There are a lot of indications that there's a major attack being planned for the very near future. Bill Goode is convinced that it's going to be the eleventh of November—Veterans' Day. If he's right, and the nuclear weapons are to be loaded on pirated Saudi planes and ships in Caracas, the perpetrators would have to deploy the vessels from there sometime on the fifth or sixth at the latest to meet that schedule. The aircraft wouldn't have to leave there until sometime on the eleventh."

"Then we have some time to figure out how this is going to go down from this end," Newman said hopefully.

"Perhaps—as long as we're reading the tea leaves the right way," responded Grisham. "We're running a 'rational model' analysis on this. As you know, Pete, that only works until our adversary starts behaving *irrationally.* But either way, the scenario tells us that our window of greatest vulnerability begins as soon as a pirated Saudi ship or plane slips out of Caracas, evades detection, and makes it out to sea or into the air. That's why we've concluded that we need to take care of the 'bomb carriers' as far from here, away from there, and as soon as possible. The 'gamers' tell us that we only win when we 'play on the road.' We 'lose' when it's a 'home game.' "

"And that's where we get the date of the fifth or sixth of November to get these guys?" asked Newman.

"Right," said Grisham. "The 'gamers' say that the 'red cell' odds of 'winning'—meaning they succeed in detonating one or more nuclear devices in U.S. territory—begin to increase significantly on the fifth and approach 95 percent by midnight your time on the sixth—and that those percentages happen if they succeed in getting *any* of their assets out of Caracas and on their way toward us. And as usual, our odds of winning also improve every time we get inside the red cell 'decision loop' by disrupting their plan."

"Roger that," said Newman. "Anything else, sir?"

"Not right now," Grisham replied. "I'll call you back if there are any changes coming out of our next meeting at the White House."

When the JCS Chairman signed off, Newman handed the handset back to the watch officer and turned to Hart, who asked, "How much time do we have, sir?"

Newman looked up at his deputy and said, "We have forty-eight hours to start taking their pieces off the board."

Lourdes Signals Intelligence Facility
Bejucal, Cuba
Saturday, 03 November 2007
1240 Hours Local

Gen. Dimitri Komulakov was standing in the Lourdes command center about to take a sip of coffee when one of the young FAPSI technicians got up and switched the channel on the large Sony television receiver at the front of the room. As Komulakov brought the mug to his lips, a BBC "news reader" said, ". . . and we'll have more from Caracas on the attempted assassination of Venezuelan President Horatio Valdez in just a moment, but first, Nigel Meacham, our correspondent in Washington, has reaction from the American administration. . . ."

Most of the hot liquid ended up on Komulakov's shirt and trousers as he roared, "Get Dubzhuko on the secure voice circuit! Now!"

As he waited for the call to be put through, the general stood and watched the remainder of the BBC report—while holding the wet shirt away from his scalded stomach. The reporter in the U.S. said, ". . . and in her statement, Secretary of State Helen Luce says that Washington had nothing to do with the assassination attempt on President Horatio Valdez. Yet U.S. congressional sources have already confirmed that the administration recently officially sanctioned assassinations in a secret codicil, and Mr. Valdez has said repeatedly that the Americans were out to get him. At the same time, no one at the State Department would respond to questions about the death of highly respected United Nations Assistant Secretary Samuel Mubassa, but one of our sources in the American Congress has told us that, and I'm quoting here, 'Mubassa was the real target.' And that, if true, only adds to the confusion and mystery of the assassination attempt. This is Nigel Meacham for the BBC in Washington. Back to you, Francis."

Komulakov was shaking his head, stunned at what this event might mean for his carefully planned operation. He recalled his earlier conversation when Dubzhuko had suggested having Maj. Gregor Argozvek—their man in Caracas—take care of the Mubassa problem, but their conversation had been cut off before Komulakov could sanction it. And in the aftermath, he had forgotten about it. Now it was too late to undo the major's bungling effort.

One of the communications specialists approached him, pointed to a handset connected to the console, and said, "Sir, we have the secure circuit established. Just pick up right here."

As the phone rang in Riyadh, Col. Nikolai Dubzhuko put down the latest encrypted e-mail from Major Argozvek. The former GRU officer's brief missive to Dubzhuko in Riyadh had described the operation against Mubassa as a "success with unfortunate side effects," noting that President Valdez had been "slightly wounded when one of the two grenades was thrown too far." By way of explanation, Argozvek went on to note that "this is the kind of problem we always have when we have to rely upon clumsy natives to do our work for us."

When Komulakov heard Dubzhuko answer the phone, he immediately began to bellow, "Have you heard from Argozvek about this assassination attempt against President Valdez? What's going to happen to our schedule? Does he know if the Americans really were behind this? Is the Caracas—" Then, over-modulated by the excessive volume, the fragile secure-voice connection between Cuba and Saudi Arabia abruptly shut down.

In Riyadh, Colonel Dubzhuko looked at the secure telephone that had just gone dead in his hand and returned the handset to its cradle—knowing that Komulakov would call back. Though the call had been prematurely terminated, Dubzhuko had heard enough to realize that Komulakov was unaware that the grenade attack in Caracas was really Argozvek's ill-conceived and poorly executed effort to kill *Mubassa*. He decided then and there that what Komulakov didn't know now could all be explained later over a bottle of good vodka. After all, everyone was sure to blame the Americans.

Venezuelan Air Force Hangar 3
Simon Bolivar International Airport
Caracas, Venezuela
Saturday, 03 November 2005
1515 Hours Local

"We cannot wait until dark, Doctor Zhdanov. You must finish installing the weapon in that aircraft this afternoon," said Maj. Gregor Argozvek. The former GRU officer was sitting at his desk in the office adjacent to the huge hangar. Through the glass partition that separated the air-conditioned office from the hangar bay, a half-dozen technicians could be seen poring over a blue and white Boeing 737.

"But it is too hot," complained the Russian nuclear weapons expert.

"I don't care how hot you are; you must finish installing the weapon in that aircraft this afternoon," demanded the former GRU major, pointing at the 737 through the window. "You only have two aircraft completed. As soon as the weapon is installed in this plane, we must get down to the port and install weapons in the three ships that are already there—before the others arrive. Then we will come back here and complete the remaining aircraft. Stop complaining—you are being well paid."

"You fool," the Russian scientist snarled. "It is not a matter of comfort! It is too hot and humid *for the device*—for doing this kind of work under such conditions. These are old artillery rounds. They have not been well maintained. The tritium triggers must all be replaced. This is work that is normally done in a carefully controlled environment. It cannot be done properly under these conditions."

Argozvek loathed the scientist for his superior attitude and lack of self-discipline. The GRU officer didn't have the foggiest idea what a tritium trigger was—but he was smart enough to know that he was ignorant on such matters and to not continue arguing about them. He also knew that he needed the older man's expertise to finish arming and loading the nuclear weapons. The major decided to try a different approach. "Please, Oleg Zhdanov, come, sit down. Let me get you a cold drink," he said, rising and going to the small Chinese-made refrigerator and bringing back a bottle of chilled water.

Zhdanov had hoped for something more substantial but took the water nonetheless, and after several long draughts finally muttered, "Thank you."

"You are welcome, Doctor Zhdanov," the GRU officer replied formally. Then Argozvek continued in a very quiet, almost conspiratorial tone, "We have a serious problem. You have seen the tall Iranian who has been here every day?"

"Yes, of course, he is Manucher Rashimani," replied Zhdanov. "He has been looking over my shoulder all afternoon. He doesn't say much. I do not think he is much of a scientist."

"He's not," answered Argozvek. "He works for their intelligence service. He is in charge of 'discipline' for the pilots who will fly these planes and for the crews of the boats. He told me an hour ago that the Iranians believe that the grenade attack that wounded the Venezuelan president at noon today may be part of an American coup attempt. They want all of the weapons installed on the boats and planes just as soon as possible. If we cannot get it all done in the next two days, they may cancel the whole operation and not pay us."

Only part of what Argozvek had just said was the truth. The part about not getting paid was a fabrication—

but it had the desired effect. Zhdanov sat upright in his chair and looked the major in the eye, trying to ascertain the validity of what he had just been told. He then said, "How much does the Iranian know about these weapons?"

"I don't think he knows very much. Why?" asked the GRU officer.

"Listen to me carefully, Gregor Argozvek," said Zhdanov quietly. "It is not the installation in the planes that is taking so much time. My technicians and I have made six of the weapons ready for use. It has taken longer than expected because these warheads have not been properly maintained since they were 'removed' from the Ukrainian stockpiles. Still, I am certain that those six will detonate. The other four probably will not—unless we complete the replacement of the tritium gas triggers and certain other components. We will practically have to rebuild every one."

"How long will it take you to complete the 'rebuilding' of the other four?" asked Argozvek.

"I will need at least four more days, because the same technicians who refurbish the warheads must also install the weapons in the aircraft," Zhdanov replied.

"Can some of our other people help you do the installations?"

"Not unless you want to take the chance of being vaporized because someone does the wiring wrong," answered the scientist.

Argozvek shook his head at the prospect, paused a moment, and then asked, "If you put all your people to work on the 737 out there in the hangar, how long would it take to complete the installation and wiring?"

Zhdanov shrugged, looked at his watch, and said, "We can probably be finished with it tonight."

"Good," the GRU officer said. "As soon as you are finished with the 737, we will take the other three rebuilt warheads over to the port at La Guaira and install them in the three ships that are already there. Take a fourth warhead—one of the ones you have not yet rebuilt—just in case Rashimani insists on putting one in a container on the ship that is tied up next to the Saudi vessels."

"But it very likely will not go off, and even if it does, it will not have its full yield," protested the scientist.

"So be it," said Argozvek. "Rashimani told me that Tehran may want to put a warhead with a timing device on board that containership that is headed for Galveston in two days. Can you rig one with a timing device and put it in a container tomorrow?"

"I suppose so," answered the scientist. "The ships will be easier to rig since we have more space in which to work and run the wiring. We can probably have all three ships and one in a container completely finished in twenty-four to thirty-six hours."

"That will reassure our 'client' who is so worried about getting them back out to sea," said the major, smiling now. He then added, "Then, after the ships depart, we will come back here and you can complete the work on the other four warheads."

"How many more ships and planes are coming in?" asked Zhdanov.

"There are two more ships en route and three more aircraft."

"What are you going to put in *them*?" asked the scientist.

Argozvek smiled again and said, "Some of them will be used as 'decoys' for the attack on the eleventh and one of them will be our ride out of here on the night of the tenth."

Zhdanov thought about that for a moment and said, "That is probably a good idea—so long as we do not get on the wrong ship or airplane."

Qom Al-Mashhad Mosque
Tehran, Iran
Sunday, 04 November 2007
0730 Hours Local

"Why is it not going as planned, Ali Yunesi?" asked the Ayatollah Ali Hussein-Khamenehi, as the two men walked quietly through a back corridor of the ornate mosque. Behind them were two dozen bodyguards—six from Yunesi's secret police and intelligence service—the *Vezarat-e Ettelaat va Amniat-e Keshvar*—VEVAK, and eighteen from the security detail that protected Hussein-Khamenehi, Iran's "Spiritual Guide"—the *real power* in Tehran.

The two men had delayed their departure from morning prayers to talk without the benefit or distraction of others in the government. Yunesi knew that his job might well be on the line, depending on what Hussein-Khamenehi told the Supreme Council later that morning.

"All is not going perfectly, Ali Hussein, but then no plan ever does," began Yunesi, "yet most of it has gone very well thus far. The American puppets have been removed from Riyadh, the 'Islamic Brotherhood' has declared that all infidels must depart the 'Land of the Prophet,' and the Westerners are now fleeing all over the region. The Great Satan has been crippled by the loss of oil, and they are increasingly bedeviled by internal disarray. Witness how they reacted to four puny bombs on their trains."

"But the uprisings you promised in Iraq, Kuwait, the Emirates, and Egypt have not occurred," responded the Supreme Leader.

"Not yet," answered Yunesi. "But after they see the devastating 'fire from the heavens' brought down on the Zionist pigs in Tel Aviv and the American infidels on the eleventh of their month of November, there will be many uprisings."

"Will the missile be ready by then?" asked Ali Hussein.

"Yes, and so will the other weapons, I assure you," responded the intelligence chieftain. "I personally spoke with our scientists from Tabriz who are working with the Russians to install the warhead on the missile, and they assure me that it will all be ready one week from today."

"And what of the weapons in Venezuela?" asked the Supreme Guide. "Is our friend Valdez going to survive this American coup attempt?"

Ali Yunesi nodded and said, "I spoke with Manucher Rashimani in Caracas yesterday and again last night. He assures me that President Valdez is going to fully recover and will not be overthrown. Rashimani also promised that the Russian warheads will all be installed in time. They have three of the Monarchist airplanes ready. Today they will install warheads on three of the ships—and another with a timing device in a container that will be placed aboard a containership headed for the port of Galveston."

"Do you still trust the Russians you hired to help with this task?" asked the Supreme Leader. "You know that they have never believed in the jihad. They only help because we promised to abandon our spiritual allies in Chechnya—and for the money, of course."

"Do I trust them—no," replied Yunesi. "But they are useful. A year from now, after the Caliphate has been proclaimed, we can resume support for our Chechnyan brothers, and there will be no way for anyone to stop us. We will have our own nuclear weapons by then and will no longer need the Russians. The Europeans will not be able to cope with the mass uprisings inspired by the 'Islamic Brotherhood' movement, and Moscow will also have to withdraw their forces from all Islamic territory."

"You paint a very optimistic picture, Ali Yunesi," said Iran's Spiritual Guide, stopping his measured pace through the mosque. Behind the two men, their body-guards also halted, a respectful thirty feet away. Hussein-Khamenehi, running his fingers through his beard, then said quietly to the Iranian intelligence chief, "I hope that you are correct. But you must take care that you do not forget things here at home in your zeal for spreading Islam elsewhere. Tomorrow you must come before the Council and explain why the students in Qum, Esfahan, and even here in Tehran have not embraced this turn of events. Surely you have seen the protests. Yesterday al Jazeera broadcast pictures of some of our citizens demonstrating and waving American flags."

For the first time since his Operation Dawah began, Yunesi felt a rush of fear in his gut. If he lost the confidence of the nation's Spiritual Guide and the Supreme Council, he could end up like so many of the people that his own VEVAK agents had dragged off the streets—to a dungeon or worse. He inclined his head toward his superior and said, "The CIA is instigating these protests just as they tried to kill the Venezuelan president yesterday. I will reassure the Council tomorrow that the protest ringleaders in Iran will be found, apprehended, and punished."

"Very well," said Hussein-Khamenehi, as he turned toward his bodyguards. But then he abruptly stopped and said quietly, "And after the fire from the heavens rains down on the Zionists and the Americans on the eleventh, what will become of this Russian Komulakov and his lackey in Riyadh?"

"I assure you that they both will be eliminated, Ali Hussein," replied Yunesi. "I have placed four of our best men beside Komulakov. Though I cannot communicate with them directly, they know what to do. As for his assistant in Riyadh, I have dispatched twenty-four equally dedicated soldiers there—and they too will act when the time is right."

"Good," replied the Spiritual Guide. "It would not be good for it to become known that we had to rely on infidels to carry out this jihad."

São Pedro Airport
St. Vicente Island, Cape Verde Islands
Sunday, 04 November 2007
1915 Hours Local

"We have been given the go-ahead to proceed to Caracas," announced Oleg Solomatin, as pilot Is'haaq Al Kabil opened the door of his cheap hotel room, less than a mile from the São Pedro Airport.

The Saudi pilot grunted and said, "Finally. I thought we were going to stay on the miserable, infidel-infested island forever. I shall get the others and meet you at the hangar."

A half hour later the entire four-man crew—the two Saudi pilots, the Algerian flight engineer, and the Russian—were assembled at the hangar where their 737 had been sequestered since the 29th of October. They had not been idle in the days since arriving.

The pirated Saudi plane had landed in the Cape Verde Islands as Air Afrique Cargo Flight Juliet Six One One Seven. But now it had yet another new paint job and registration number—the second since being stolen from its murdered owner. The fuselage was now emblazoned with the words *International Air Express* and its tail adorned with the company logo—a winged package and the initials IAE. Just forward of the horizontal stabilizer was the plane's "new" Argentine registration designator: LV-TRK—a designator that corresponded to another Boeing 737 parked in a "boneyard" west of Buenos Aires.

Kabil ordered the tanks topped off for the five-hour flight to Caracas, filed a flight plan that would have them arrive in Venezuela at 2230, and conducted a careful preflight inspection. Satisfied, he watched two young men from the fixed base operation hook up a tug and a tow-bar to the 737's nose wheel. They were brothers and had assisted the crew in repainting the aircraft. The two affable young men had worked diligently, and though they thought it unusual to change an aircraft's "tail number," they had apparently accepted Kabil's explanation that the plane had been sold to a new owner.

Solomatin wasn't convinced. On the night of 3 November, the Russian had been drinking in a bar near the airport when the two brothers entered and sat down with him. From their conversation it was apparent that the young men had questions about why a luxury jet had been converted into a cargo hauler. The next day, Solomatin told Kabil, and after discussing the matter they decided that the brothers were a liability.

As soon as the two completed the hook-up, Kabil called the young men over to the portable stairway and presented each with an envelope containing five hundred dollars in U.S. currency and a bottle of expensive brandy—a beverage Solomatin had noticed that they preferred. "We want to show our appreciation for your good work," Kabil told them. "Please enjoy what is in the bottle—perhaps you should have a toast when we take off."

The brothers were enthusiastic in their gratitude for the generous payment—and for the libation. As Kabil mounted the stairs they smiled broadly and saluted. Once the door was closed, one brother pushed the stairway back while the other mounted the tug, started the engine, and expertly backed the large aircraft out of the hangar and well out onto the apron, leaving plenty of room for it to turn.

In the cockpit, Kabil and his copilot completed the pre-takeoff checklist and fired the APU. Then as the twin GE jet engines began to spool up, they watched the two brothers open the bottle, take generous swigs, and then stand at mock attention, smiling and saluting their bene-factors as the aircraft slowly began to pull toward the taxiway.

"How much longer?" the copilot asked as he looked down from the flight deck at the two men on the ground.

"They will be dizzy in a couple of minutes," Kabil re-sponded. "By the time we are rolling down the runway, they will feel nauseous. They will lose consciousness after we are airborne, and be dead by the time we reach ten thousand feet."

"What if the authorities inquire about their deaths?" asked the copilot.

"I doubt that they will think to look for Ricin in the alcohol," answered Kabil without a hint of remorse. "If they do, they will notice the American currency and the fact that the brandy was made in America, and they will blame the Americans. But their deaths mean nothing. We have a great assignment in the jihad—delivering Allah's wrath on the American crusaders. If they remained alive they could have interfered with our mission."

The copilot shrugged and said, "Well, those two will not be talking about what they saw in the hangar."

As he pressed the left pedal hard, turning the 737 onto the runway, Kabil replied, "Thanks be to Allah."

CHAPTER NINETEEN

Approaching Fail-Safe

CJR Warehouse
867 Avenida Maiquetia, Caracas, Venezuela
Sunday, 04 November 2007
1930 Hours Local

Dan, do you think you can remain in position overnight tonight despite the curfew?" Newman asked. He was standing at the satellite radio inside his warehouse office/command post talking to Lt. Col. Dan Hart, and Sgt. Maj. Amos Skillings was standing beside him. Both men were wearing T-shirts and jeans. Neither had left the building for more than twenty-four hours.

There was a quiet *whoosh* and a *ping* as the encryption relay engaged and the two Marines could hear the fatigue in Hart's voice as he answered Newman's question. "Staying here isn't the problem. Eduardo has us in a perfect location. We have a visual on the Venezuelan Navy pier and the three Saudi boats, but we're no longer getting a reading on one of the nukes. Chief Suazo needs to talk to the tech-rep for the 'Backscatter' gear."

"Roger that," said Newman, as Skillings headed across the warehouse to find the needed expert.

Hart, Suazo, eight "techno-operators," and Emilio

Roca had departed the warehouse in a Suburban and a rented panel truck that morning as soon as the curfew lifted. Estaban Roca had escorted an identical "expedition" headed by Sergeant First Class Nievos to a nondescript building adjacent to the airport perimeter road, about nine hundred yards from the Venezuelan Air Force hangar. The Suburbans were loaded with personnel and weapons, and the panel trucks had been jammed full of electronic equipment: a Passive Millimeter Wave imaging device, neutron particle/gamma wave radiation detectors, cameras, and communications gear.

By 0800 both teams were in position. Hart and Suazo, the Navy SEAL sniper, had set up their observation post in the third-story offices of one of Eduardo's family businesses just outside the main entrance of the La Guaira Port complex. Less than an hour after Hart had his equipment up and running, a convoy of Venezuelan military trucks arrived at the gate outside their window. The young Army sergeant operating the PMMW scanner was stunned to see what appeared to be heavy artillery rounds—one each in the back of four of the trucks. He immediately summoned Hart, who verified that these were four of the 152mm nuclear artillery warheads for which they had been searching. Newman had forwarded Hart's report directly to the NMCC—marked "Flash—Nuke Warn—For The Chairman JCS."

Skillings entered the office/command post with the civilian tech-rep and put him on the radio with Hart and Suazo at the La Guaira OP. The Navy chief described their problem: "This morning when they passed the PMMW scanner we could see the images of the weapons inside the trucks—and the radiation detectors also went off. Since then we've watched them unloading heavy boxes from four of the trucks. They have put one on each of the Saudi ships—and we think the fourth one was placed inside a sea-land container on the pier, but it's hard to tell. How close do we have to be to use the PMMW device and the neutron particle/gamma radiation detectors?"

The tech-rep sounded like he was reading a manual when he answered Hart's question. "The PMMW scanner has to be within ten meters of the target in order to measure reflections from natural background radiation. That way you can get a clear 3-D image that looks like an X-ray—or an ultrasound. The neutron/gamma detectors will give you a reading out to about seventy-five to one hundred meters. The radiation sensor uses a crystalline material called cadmium zinc telluride—or CZT—which is similar to the silicon used in a computer chip. The sensor gives detailed spectroscopic information within limits of performance set by the size and quality of its crystal—"

"Whoa," Skillings interrupted, "the chief doesn't need to *build* the thing, he just needs to know how close he needs to be to get a reading."

"Uh . . . pardon me, Sergeant Major," the technician replied sheepishly. He then asked over the radio, "Did I answer your question, Chief?"

"Well, if we can find a way to drive the PMMW scanner out onto that pier, will it give us a clear enough image to confirm that the warheads have been placed on those ships and inside one of the containers being loaded on that merchant ship?" inquired the Navy SEAL.

"Yes, but you'd have to be moving very slowly, otherwise the image will be too blurry to make out," answered the tech. "Why can't you just do it with one of the neutron/gamma detectors?"

"We can," answered Suazo, "but one of the four warheads that we imaged gave us a much lower reading on the radiation detectors than the other three—even though they all looked the same on the PMMW image."

The civilian tech-rep thought for a moment and then

responded, "My guess is that the one that gave you a low reading may have had more lead shielding than the others or it may not have the same amount of nuclear material as the other three. That would probably mean a lower yield on detonation. Did they all look the same on the PMMW image when they were parked outside your OP?"

"Yes," answered Suazo, "each warhead was in a separate truck and they were all packed the same way. In fact, all the trucks carrying weapons even had the same number of armed personnel with them."

"Well, you don't need the PMMW to tell which is which," said the expert. "If you need to know which one is the 'low yield' warhead, just run the radiation 'sniffer' past each ship and container. If you're close to the same distance from each of them, the one with the low yield will give you the lowest reading."

"Roger that," answered the chief. "Thanks for the info. Lieutenant Colonel Hart wants to talk to General Newman."

The tech-rep handed the handset back to the general as Dan Hart said, "If Emilio can arrange to get the Suburban out onto the pier, do you want us to try to figure out where that low-yield weapon is getting loaded, sir?"

"I don't know that it matters enough to put you and your team at risk, Dan," said Newman. "What matters most is knowing when those three boats and that container leave port. Unfortunately, our satellite coverage down here is very intermittent, so right now you and Chief Suazo at La Guaira and Sergeant First Class Nievos at the airport are the best 'Early Warning Systems' we have for a nuclear attack on the U.S."

Lourdes Signals Intelligence Facility
Bejucal, Cuba
Sunday, 4 November 2007
2000 Hours Local

"General, Moscow Centre has just ordered me to inform you that we are now picking up a significant increase in the amount of encrypted U.S. military communications. Much of it is emanating from places we would expect during a crisis—Washington, the American East Coast military installations, Key West, Guantanamo, and their fleet units in the Caribbean. But now, a good bit of it is new—coming from Venezuela, in and around Caracas," said Colonel Vushneshko. The commanding officer of the Russian Signals Intelligence garrison at Lourdes was standing in the doorway of Dimitri Komulakov's "VIP quarters," holding a printed cable in his hand.

"Come in, Mikhail," said the "retired" KGB general. The two men entered the room, and Komulakov closed the door, motioning to a chair at the small table where a laptop computer was open. "So what does this mean?" asked the older man.

"We're not sure," answered Vushneshko. "As you know, the Lourdes facility is within the 'footprint' of their East Coast military and government data and voice communications satellites. Unfortunately, all of their communications are encrypted so we don't know what is being sent or received, but the increase in the volume of traffic is what brought this to our attention."

"How long has this been going on?" asked the general.

"Well, it has been going up and down ever since the attack in Saudi Arabia last month, but it spiked again several days ago—and now there is a fairly constant stream of traffic that seems to be flowing in and out of Caracas."

"Can we tell if this is related to the attempt to assassinate President Valdez?" Komulakov asked.

"Well, it certainly increased after that happened," responded Vushneshko. "It was after the 'coup attempt' that our embassy SIGINT site in Caracas began to detect American tactical military communications in and around the city."

Komulakov's eyes widened. "You say *tactical* communications—from American military units?"

"Well again, we do not know whether they are military units or not," answered the GRU Signals Intelligence officer. "All we know for certain is that encrypted communications streams are emanating from short- and mid-range equipment in and around Caracas—and that this equipment is normally associated with the American military, usually at the brigade or division level."

"Has Moscow notified the Valdez government of this development?" asked Komulakov.

"Not yet," said Vushneshko. "We have the usual problem. If we tell Valdez about the American tactical intercepts that we are picking up from our embassy, he will realize that we're also able to monitor his military's communications. Moscow does not want him to know that."

"Humph," Komulakov grunted. "Sometimes we are too cautious for our own good. I must tell my deputy in Riyadh about this. The whole operation in Caracas could be in jeopardy."

Vushneshko was concerned and said so. "General, I do not know all of what you and our government are doing in Caracas—nor do I need to—but it is very important that neither the Venezuelans nor the Americans become aware that we are intercepting these signals."

"Yes, yes, of course," the Russian general replied, rising from the table. "Now, let us go to the command center, so that I can talk on the secure voice circuit with Dubzhuko in Riyadh."

Five minutes later, Komulakov was holding a telephone to his ear at a command center console trying to hear his deputy through the warble and electronic static of their tenuous fiber-optic satellite connection through Murmansk. "Why are you still at the Filaya location, Nikolai?" the general asked, speaking very slowly.

"Because the Iranians who came here several days ago insisted on yet another late-night meeting. It is now after five in the morning and we just finished," Dubzhuko replied after a four-second delay.

"What did they want?"

"Apparently Ali Yunesi is now insisting on knowing every detail of what is going on in Caracas," the voice in Riyadh replied. "As I indicated in my last report, they insisted that one of the warheads be loaded on a containership. I have instructed Major Argozvek to inform me the minute the three Saudi vessels and the containership leave La Guaira—so that I can tell our 'allies' encamped across the street. Were you aware that there is an Iranian—Manucher Rashimani—with Argozvek in Caracas?"

"He is with the Iranian Intelligence Service at their embassy," Komulakov answered. "He is the one who made the arrangements with Valdez for the warheads to be delivered and stored in Caracas. I have only met with him once. You should alert Argozvek that Rashimani is not to be trusted. You also must inform him that I have just learned that there may be American military or intelligence units operating in Caracas."

Again there was a protracted delay before Dubzhuko replied, "Are you sure? How do you know?"

Komulakov, struggling to keep his voice reasonably modulated, responded, "Do not be concerned with how I know; just make sure you inform Argozvek."

"The reason I am asking," Dubzhuko said, "is because the Iranians told me tonight that if anything interferes with the warheads being 'delivered' on the eleventh of November, we will not be paid. As you know, this was not part of our agreement. I have not told any—"

Dubzhuko was cut off in midsentence. Komulakov, believing that it was yet another "anomaly" in their communications, slammed the phone down and yelled, "Mikhail Vushneshko, my line is dead."

Filaya Petroleum Building
14 Al-Aqsa Street
Riyadh, Saudi Arabia
Monday 05 November 2007
0515 Hours Local

Nikolai Dubzhuko never knew what hit him. As he talked on the phone with Dimitri Komulakov, neither he nor any of his men were even aware of the two B-52H bombers racing at 530 knots toward Riyadh at 60,000 feet. Twenty miles south of the Saudi capital the aircraft dropped down to 45,000 feet and at fourteen miles out, each B-52 released sixteen MK-84, 2,000-pound, JDAM-equipped, high-explosive bombs. As the GPS-guided weapons struck the Filaya Petroleum building—and the building across Al-Aqsa Street where the two dozen Iranians were just going to sleep following their late-night meeting—the two B-52s were already climbing again and heading toward their tanker, orbiting over the Indian Ocean. By the time the bombers landed at their base, 3,400 miles to the southeast on the tiny island base at Diego Garcia, it would be almost noon in Riyadh.

The blast and concussion of the thirty-two warheads detonating almost simultaneously flattened the entire Filaya complex as well as the structure across the street. Burning diesel fuel from ruptured underground storage tanks for the generators created a bright orange fire and an enormous plume of black smoke over the rubble. Within a half mile of the targets, every window that had not already been broken by marauding crowds incited by the "Islamic Brotherhood" was shattered. A mile away at the British Embassy "Annex," two SIS "stay behinds," who had been told to take shelter in the basement of their building, returned to their rooftop OP and reported on their satellite radio: "Bombs appear to be on target. No further electronic emissions from target area. Will report BDA after first light."

Lourdes Signals Intelligence Facility
Bejucal, Cuba
Monday, 5 November 2007
0705 Hours Local

"I am sorry to disturb you, General," said Maj. Viktor Sakharovsky, over the telephone.

"What is it?" a tired and irritable Komulakov asked the young *Spetznatz* officer. He had returned to his quarters less than an hour ago to rest after spending most of the night waiting for Colonel Vushneshko's technicians to reestablish communications with Nikolai Dubzhuko in Riyadh.

Sakharovsky continued, "I am in the command center where they are monitoring the American morning news broadcasts. I think we now know why you lost communications with Colonel Dubzhuko."

"What are they saying?" asked the general, suddenly alert.

"According to their television news, the Americans bombed Riyadh last night."

Two minutes later, the unshaven and rumpled Komulakov was in the command center. He had obviously fallen asleep in his clothes. On one of the large television screens a correspondent standing in front of the

Pentagon was just completing his report: ". . . though officials here are being tight-lipped about what actually transpired in Riyadh, our Congressional source says that last night's air raid against the Saudi capital was—quote—'a waste of good bombs and likely caused massive civilian casualties'—unquote. This critic of the administration went on to say that—and again I'm quoting here—'This White House can't even hit the right country. They should be going after Tehran.' But the Pentagon and White House are still offering no comment. John, back to you in Atlanta."

The Russian general turned to Sakharovsky and said, "Do we have anything from Moscow Centre yet on what was hit in Riyadh?"

"Yes, sir," replied the major somberly. "Right after I saw the first report on this, I called the imagery analysts at Centre on one of Colonel Vushneshko's dedicated circuits. They say that the city block where the Filaya complex was located is nothing but smoking rubble and bomb craters."

Komulakov looked stunned. Still, he couldn't care less what happened to Dubzhuko or the others who had been with them. If they were all dead it would mean fewer people to pay at the end of the operation. But there was a practical consideration for wishing that Dubzhuko were still alive: without the Riyadh command center to coordinate things and relay orders, Komulakov would have to take over that responsibility himself—or risk not being paid. Leaning toward Sakharovsky's ear so that others would not hear, he said, "Dubzhuko is undoubtedly dead. We're going to have to take over running this operation."

Now it was the major's turn to be surprised. "General, we can't do that from *here*," he said. "Moscow will never allow us to communicate with all of the units involved in this operation from the Lourdes facility. The Americans would pick up on the signals immediately.

That is why we were relaying everything through Riyadh."

Komulakov thought for a moment then said, "Yes . . . you're right, Viktor. We will have to go to Caracas."

The major gave a shrug of resignation and asked, "How will we get there? Do you want me to arrange for a commercial flight?"

Again the Russian general paused and then said, "No. One of the captured Saudi aircraft arrived last night in Caracas from the Cape Verde Islands." Then, consulting notes that he pulled from his pocket, Komulakov continued, "According to the last message I received from Dubzhuko, it is a 737, marked "International Air Express" with Argentine registration designator: LV-TRK. Contact Major Argozvek on his commercial satellite phone and have him send it here, to Jose Marti International Airport."

CJR Warehouse
867 Avenida Maiquetia, Caracas, Venezuela
Monday, 05 November 2007
2300 Hours Local

"It looks like they're preparing to get under way, sir," said Lt. Col. Dan Hart. "I was going to send this by D-DACT, but I figured a call would be better."

Standing at the secure Sat-Com terminal in his command post, Brig. Gen. Peter Newman chewed on his lower lip for a moment and then said, "Roger that, Dan. Can you tell us which one is headed out first?"

Hart, standing at the darkened window of his observation post overlooking the La Guaira Port facility and peering through a long-range night vision scope, replied, "They seem to be getting ready to leave in the order in which they're berthed. A pilot boat has just pulled up next to the one that had the name *Desert Wind* on it until they painted over it just after dark. The crew has thrown off the lines, and I can see her exhaust. My guess is that the next one out will be *Nile Princess*—but they've painted over that name as well. Because of the way they are berthed, we can't tell if the third one—*Iridescent*—has had her name painted over."

"Roger that, Dan," responded Newman. "Anything happening with the containership on the other side of the pier?"

"Wait one, while I move the scope," Hart replied. Then a few seconds later he was back. "Affirmative. They have rolled the gangway back and she also has a pilot boat alongside. Looks like she may be joining this parade. Maybe they're all going to sortie together in some kind of convoy."

"OK," said Newman, "let me send this off to the JCS and I'll get back to you."

Newman passed the handset back to the communicator on watch and turned to locate Sergeant Major Skillings. He was already sitting at the laptop computer, drafting the communiqué to General Grisham.

"In our last message at 2000, we informed them that we were unable to confirm that a nuclear weapon had been loaded on the containership," said Skillings. "Do you want me to reiterate that here?"

"Yeah, you better, Sergeant Major, just in case somebody missed that fact when they were sending the data on to the subs offshore. But don't make it sound like we're unsure that it *is* on board."

"Do you want me to tell 'em that we'll send a message as each ship clears the breakwater?"

"Good idea, Amos," said the Marine brigadier. "I must be getting tired. I should have thought of that."

"Not to worry, General. You don't have to think. You have a Marine sergeant major here to do that stuff for you," Skillings said with a grin. "Here you go, sir, take a look at this before I transmit it."

Newman looked over his sergeant major's shoulder, read the message marked "FLASH" precedence, followed by the words: "NUKE-WARN." After scanning down the text, he said, "Send it. I'll bet we'll have a call from the NMCC within five minutes. I'm going to get a cup of coffee. Do you want one?"

Skillings moved the cursor over the words SEND ENCRYPTED, clicked the mouse, and looked up at his boss with a broad smile and said, "The stuff in that coffee pot is a biohazard material concocted by some civilian tech-dweeb. My body is a temple of the Holy Spirit; I wouldn't abuse it that way."

Newman smiled and shook his head and went out into the warehouse carrying his canteen cup. He wasn't gone a minute before the secure Sat-Com phone warbled for attention. The duty communicator picked up the receiver, said, "JTF Seventy-seven," listened for a moment, then said, "Roger, wait one." The young NCO then turned to Skillings and said, "Sergeant Major, there's a guy on here who says he's George Grisham and he wants to talk to General Newman."

Skillings jumped up from the table, grabbed the handset, cupped the mouthpiece in the palm of his hand, and said, "It's a good thing that you're not a Marine or I'd have you busted a rank—that's *General* Grisham to you—the Chairman of the Joint Chiefs of Staff! Now go get General Newman." He then put the receiver up to his ear and said, "Sergeant Major Skillings, sir. General Newman will be right back."

"Amos, how are you? Is your ankle healing?" asked Grisham, with real concern evident in his voice. Years before, Skillings had served with Grisham and, at one point, had been the head of his personal security detail.

"Just about ready for my PFT, General," the sergeant major replied.

"How is Pete doing, Amos? Level with me," said the Chairman.

"He's tired, frustrated—hoping we can end this thing down here before these warheads get anywhere close to home," answered Skillings honestly.

"How are the troops holding up?"

"They're good soldiers, sailors, and Marines, General," the sergeant major replied. "They know how important this mission is—even the civilians we have down here are 'with it.' The hardest part for everyone is the waiting. Like you used to remind us, sir, 'War is 95 percent tedium and 5 percent stark terror.' It still is." Then as Newman reentered the office/command post, Skillings said, "Here's General Newman, sir."

Newman set down his canteen cup full of steaming black liquid and took the receiver. Grisham said, "The sergeant major is probably doing more than he should on that broken ankle, Pete. Tell him if he does anymore damage to it down there I'm going to have him court-martialed for destruction of government property."

"Will do," said Newman, glancing over at Skillings. Then he added, "But I know that's not why you called, sir."

"No, you're right. I just wanted to bring you up to speed on the latest intelligence we have and what we're going to be doing about those Saudi ships that are leaving La Guaira, so there are no surprises."

"Yes, sir," said Newman, sitting down and tucking the handset between his shoulder and his ear so he could take notes on the laptop for briefing his team leaders after the call.

"First, Bill Goode now says that he's confident that there are no more than ten nuclear warheads in Caracas. He comes to that number from several days' worth of intercepts from a SIGINT site in Norway, some Brit and Australian 'stay-behinds' in Riyadh, and comms that we're picking up between Tehran and Caracas."

"Well if he's right, then there are only six left—because four of them are apparently on those three Saudi vessels and that containership pulling out of La Guaira," interjected Newman.

"I want to come back to the containership in a moment, but let me finish with the latest intel," Grisham responded. "According to Goode, this GRU major— Gregor Argozvek—that Sergeant Major Skillings ran into a few days back is in charge of handing over the warheads. The 'mad scientist,' Oleg Zhdanov, is responsible for arming the warheads, and the guy in charge of delivering the warheads to the U.S. is Manucher Rashimani, an intelligence officer assigned to the VEVAK office at the Iranian Embassy. We sent you the latest photos of all three in the last 'data dump.' Bill also says that everything happening there is being done with the knowledge and support of the Venezuelan regime."

"Nice division of labor," noted Newman. "And that all fits with what we can see here. Dan Hart observed three males matching the descriptions of Argozvek, Zhdanov, and Rashimani earlier today at the port while the weapons were being loaded on the Saudi vessels. We know that Argozvek works out of hangar 3 at Simon Bolivar Airport, and Sergeant First Class Nievos is fairly certain that he has seen Zhdanov and Rashimani there too. Do we have any idea where this whole thing is being run from? Is it Tehran, here in Caracas—or is this whole thing on 'autopilot' like 9/11 once the orders were given?"

"Good question—and we still don't know the answer," Grisham replied. "We took out what we thought was their command and control node in Riyadh very early this morning, but that doesn't seem to have stopped things. Goode and the British are convinced that the whole operation is being run from Cuba by Dimitri Komulakov, but the rest of the intelligence community is split between thinking it's Tehran or believing that it's all being conducted from a checklist—'autopilot' as you put it—that was devised weeks or even months ago."

"So where do we go from here, sir?" asked Newman. "I still have my OP at the port and another one about a kilometer from the hangar at Simon Bolivar. Because of the security clampdown, we haven't been able to get anyone on the military side of the field yet, though Roca—our 'local'—thinks we may be able to do that by tomorrow."

Grisham was silent for a moment, then said, "I was going to put this in a message to you, but this is probably faster. At midnight here in Washington, the President is going to notify the UN and every diplomatic mission that any nonmilitary vessel transporting a weapon of mass destruction and headed toward the United States will be sunk on the high seas. If the three Saudi ships don't turn around within an hour, they will be sunk at 0600 Zulu."

"What about the containership? As I understand it from the 'local' with Dan Hart, it's headed for Galveston. Is that ship going to be allowed to proceed?" asked Newman.

"Well, because it's Chinese-owned and we can't *confirm* that the container with the nuke was put aboard, the plan is to interdict and search it before it can pose a danger to the U.S. mainland," answered the Chairman.

Newman reacted as though he had been punched. After a long pause he said, "We tried to get the sensors onto the pier and just couldn't pull it off. We're 99 percent certain that there's a nuke aboard that ship. If it turns out that it does have a weapon aboard that kills Americans, I don't know how anyone here is going to be able to live with themselves."

Grisham listened and then said thoughtfully, "Don't dwell on it, Pete. That ship isn't going to get anywhere close to the U.S. We'll let the Coast Guard and the Navy

handle the stuff at sea. You focus on the remaining warheads that are likely in that hangar. No one can do that
any better than you and your men. We wouldn't even
know what to be looking for if it weren't for you and
your teams."

USS _Dallas_, SSN 700
67° W 11° N, Approx 28nm N of La Guaira, Venezuela
Tuesday, 06 November 2007
0230 Hours Local

"Let's take another look at what else is up there before the shooting starts," said Capt. Ross Conner, moving from the plotting table to the starboard search
periscope. With the submarine barely moving at three
knots, the Type-18 mast barely made a ripple as it
broke the surface of the Caribbean. Its tiny sensors immediately detected the navigational radars of the three
Saudi vessels and the containership that were approaching the submerged submarine from the south.
Inside the conning space there was only silence as the
new data appeared on the targeting display over the
chart table.

"Down 'scope," said Conner. "Let's take another
look through the attack 'scope, I don't want these guys
too close to us when we put a fish into them—and I sure
don't want to take out that merchantman by mistake."
Conner did a 360° sweep of the horizon with the Type-2
attack 'scope, its aperture wide open to take in as much
light as possible. He then focused in on the approaching
vessels and said, "XO, start the tape."

Lt. Cmdr. Mike O'Malley, the executive officer of the
boat, said, "Starting tape," as he punched a button on
the console above his head, engaging a digital "black
box" that would make a recording of all the submarine's sensors, weapons systems, navigational data—and

all that was said and seen by the officers jammed into the submarine's conning space.

"Let's go through that checklist you came up with one last time, XO," said Conner, as much for his own benefit as for the history that was being documented. "We have a presidential directive to engage these three Saudi vessels designated as targets Alpha, Bravo, and Charlie that intelligence indicates are transporting nuclear weapons. . . ."

"Check," replied the XO.

"It is now 0635 Zulu, and the target vessels have not complied with the NOTAM broadcast at 0500 Zulu to return to port."

"Check."

"Targets Alpha, Bravo, and Charlie have been positively identified by our TB-16D passive towed array sonar and confirmed on the AN/BQQ-5D sonar array."

"Check."

"The targets are at ranges between three and five miles, approaching from right to left at eighteen knots, and we have their acoustic signatures on the WLR-9 Intercept receiver and have validated the information on the AN/BSY-1."

"Check."

"The weapons officer confirms that we have four Mark-48 ADCAP torpedoes loaded in the forward tubes set for wire-guided targeting and hull-contact detonation."

"Check."

"There is no other known shipping within range of our torpedoes, other than a single merchantman that is not to be engaged."

"Check."

"Well," said Conner, "this is why we get 'sub pay.' Let's go to work. Bring up the attack 'scope so we can see what's happening up there."

As the port side periscope slid up to his eye level,

Conner leaned into the eyepieces and adjusted the focus with a flick of his wrist.

"Confirm range to Target Alpha," he said.

"Five thousand one hundred and four yards," said the XO, looking up at the display from the fire control computer.

As the submarine commander rotated the periscope to the right he said, "Range to Target Bravo . . . ."

"Six thousand one hundred and sixty yards."

Shifting his feet, Conner turned the periscope further to the right and said, "Range to Target 3 . . . ."

"Seven thousand five hundred and sixty yards," said the XO.

"All right, people, listen up," said Conner. "We're going to engage the furthest target first, then the middle target, and then the one closest to us. That way there will be less warning for the forward two vessels. Weapons officer, do you have that firing solution?"

"Yes, sir, tube number one set to engage Target Charlie," the weapons officer responded.

"Very well," said Conner looking into the 'scope. "Fire one."

There was a hiss of compressed air as the nineteen-foot-long, 3,400-pound torpedo shot out of its tube and started racing at thirty-five knots toward its preprogrammed target. As the pump jet drove the sleek cylinder through the water, a tiny wire played out behind it, giving Conner the ability to control the torpedo's guidance system.

With his eyes still pressed against the 'scope, Conner said, "Time to impact?"

The weapons officer, staring at the display above his head, said, "Two minutes, thirty-two seconds . . . thirty-one . . . thirty. . . ."

Conner, doing the math in his head, waited for twenty-five seconds and said, "Fire two."

Once again there was the muted hiss of air from the

bow of the sub as a second torpedo launched. On the fire control computer display, a second track appeared, headed toward a triangle with the letter "B" in its center.

"Time to impact, two minutes," volunteered the weapons officer.

Conner waited twenty seconds then repeated the ritual, sending a third MK-48 wire-guided torpedo toward Target Alpha—the closest of the three pirated Saudi vessels.

"Time to impact—one minute forty seconds," said the weapons officer, now watching the three tracks closing on their targets.

Without taking his eyes away from the periscope, Conner said, "XO, place all sonars in 'stand-by' mode and pass the word for everyone to open their mouths and clear their ears if any of those nukes go off."

Then, watching through the 'scope, Conner saw a tremendous explosion as the 650-pound warhead of the first torpedo found its mark in the side of the furthest Saudi ship. "Scratch one," said Conner. Two seconds later there were two more flashes as the second and third MK-48 ADCAPs detonated almost simultaneously. Then, just moments later, a sound—like an enormous hammer striking the hull of the submarine—signaled the first hit. This underwater concussion was followed by two more—each successively louder—and then silence.

Conner, still peering through the periscope, said, "Turn the sonars back on and give me what the TB-16 is picking up over the speaker."

Lieutenant Commander O'Malley reached up and punched some switches, and the speaker above their heads came alive with what sounded like metal being torn and loud cracking and snapping noises—all being picked up by the passive towed array trailing behind and slightly above the *Dallas*.

"I'm not hearing the merchantman," said the weapons officer to no one in particular.

Still peering through the periscope, Conner said,

"She's at a dead stop, about a mile behind where Target Charlie once was. She has her searchlights on. Bring up the search 'scope and see if she's transmitting."

"Yep," said O'Malley, "she's up on channel sixteen—and probably a dozen other frequencies yelling 'Mayday' in four different languages."

"Any of 'em Arabic?" asked Conner.

The XO looked over at his skipper, not certain if he was kidding, and said, "Our ROE doesn't specify what we're to do about picking up survivors. What do you want to do, Skipper?"

Conner shook his head and said, "I don't think there will be any survivors; all three boats broke up and went down really fast. We'll wait 'til that containership clears the area, and if it's before dawn we'll creep on over to where they went down and take a look. That's more than they would have done for us."

"Roger that," said the XO. "Where do you want to go between now and then, Skipper?"

"Take her down to two hundred feet where the water is colder, set a course of two-niner-five at five knots, and let's see if we can locate that big Saudi ship that was supposed to be heading to La Guaira from Aruba. We still have one fish in tube number four, and I hate pulling those things back inside."

Lourdes Signals Intelligence Facility
Bejucal, Cuba
Wednesday, 07 November 2007
1900 Hours Local

For the third time in as many days, Dimitri Komulakov was ready to depart Lourdes for Jose Marti International Airport, just six miles north of where he had been encamped at the Lourdes SIGINT facility. His plan to leave on Tuesday had been quashed by an inability to get clearance from the Cuban government to land the Argentine-registered 737 at the airport serving Havana. Then on Wednesday, after Col. Mikhail Vushneshko had intervened with his Cuban counterparts, the flight was scrubbed because of the international outcry over the mysterious sinking of three vessels, thirty miles off the coast of Venezuela.

. Komulakov had watched the coverage from the "comfort" of Vushneshko's command center and had quickly concluded that it was the work of American submarines. According to the news reports, the captain of a merchant ship that had just left the Venezuelan port of La Guaira had observed the explosions and searched for survivors. Apparently, none were found.

Now, as Komulakov awaited the arrival of the Zil sedan and the two military trucks that would transport him and his small party to the airport, he was increasingly concerned that the whole venture was coming apart. He turned to Major Sakharovsky, the *Spetznatz* officer who would be accompanying him on the flight to Caracas, and asked, "How many are going with us, Viktor?"

"Well, it was only supposed to be just eight of us— you, me, and six of my best men," replied the younger officer, "but now the four Iranians insist on coming along."

The anxiety showed on Komulakov's face. "How did they even know we were leaving?"

"I don't know, General, but it has been common knowledge here among Colonel Vushneshko's people for several days now. The senior Iranian of the four who have been with us, Assad Bashayan, told me a few minutes ago that he must report to Manucher Rashimani in Caracas. He also said that I should tell you that this Rashimani person is looking forward to seeing Ardon Najm again."

Now Komulakov was truly alarmed. Ardon Najm—

Arabic for "Bronze Star"—was the code name he had been given more than two years ago by Ali Yunesi, the head of Iranian intelligence, for their private communications. "How has this Bashayan been communicating with Rashimani in Caracas? Have they been using commercial telephones? If they have, the Americans will undoubtedly know we are coming."

Sakharovsky tried to allay the general's concerns. "I have talked to Bashayan, the leader of the four Iranians, many times since we have been here. He is an educated and reasonable man. After the incident with the Cubans shortly after we arrived here, he completely understood."

"You are naïve, Viktor Sakharovsky," said Komulakov in a fatherly tone. "We cannot trust any of these people—and they do not trust us. Do not forget the lessons of Afghanistan when you were a young officer. These Islamic fanatics will offer you a drink of water with one hand and cut your throat with the other."

Sakharovsky shrugged and said, "I will remind Bashayan again about making sure that all communications must go through us."

As the two were talking, one of the Lourdes Signals Intelligence technicians approached them and said, "Excuse me, General, but your transportation is here, and Colonel Vushneshko is waiting outside to say goodbye." The two officers walked outside into the humidity. Now that the sun was setting it had cooled somewhat. The commander of the FAPSI installation was standing beside the black Zil sedan, holding the door.

"Travel safely, General," said the Russian colonel, trying not to let his joy at Komulakov's departure seem obvious.

"Ahh, Mikhail Vushneshko," said Komulakov, "your smile betrays you. We have been a burden. I shall send a report to Moscow Centre telling them that you have been a gracious host."

"Thank you, General," said Vushneshko, saluting the senior officer as he entered the backseat of the car. "I hope the rest of your mission is a success."

As the car pulled away from the command center, Komulakov looked back to make sure that the trucks were following them toward the main gate of the complex. He then turned to Sakharovsky in the seat beside him and asked, "Do you have your personal weapon with you?"

"Yes, General, it is right here," he replied, patting what looked like a laptop computer case on the floor between his feet.

"Good," said Komulakov. "Keep it handy. If any of the Iranians try anything, kill them all."

CJR Warehouse
867 Avenida Maiquetia, Caracas, Venezuela
Thursday, 08 November 2007
1930 Hours Local

"NMCC on the secure sat-phone for you, sir," said the Army captain manning the communications suite. Newman got up from the table where he, Lt. Col. Dan Hart, Sgt. Maj. Amos Skillings, Master Chief Manuel Suazo, and SFC Roberto Nievos, as well as Eduardo Roca, had been poring over a detailed layout of the Simon Bolivar International Airport.

Newman pressed the rubber-covered button on the side of the handset, paused while the encryption software engaged, and then said, "This is Peter Newman. Go ahead."

"Pete, this is George Grisham. Bill Goode is here and has some very recent intel. Rather than have me relay, let me put Bill on."

"Roger that, sir," said Newman.

There was a brief pause, then Newman heard the familiar voice of the older man he had first met more than a dozen years before in the midst of a dangerous mission in the Middle East: "Pete, let me get right to the point because I'm sure you're very busy," said Goode. "We just got an NSA intercept of a conversation between a fellow named Assad Bashayan in Cuba and a man named Manucher Rashimani in Caracas. They were talking 'in the clear' in Farsi about a flight that's taking place tonight from Jose Marti in Havana and Simon Bolivar in Caracas. They made reference to a VIP on the flight that they referred to as Ardon Najm—that's Arabic for 'Bronze Star.' "

"I copy that," said Newman, taking notes on the laptop.

"Is there any way that you can have someone observe who gets off that airplane?" asked Goode. "I am convinced that this 'Bronze Star' person is very important to the attack we're expecting here in the States."

"Well, sir, after almost a week of trying, thanks to your friend Eduardo Roca, we finally have a 'local' inside the military side of the airbase," Newman answered. "He's a nephew of Eduardo's and he's in the Venezuelan Air Force Security Police. He was reassigned to the detachment guarding the military side of Simon Bolivar yesterday and started duty there today. We also have our OP, but that's pretty far away from the hangar where everything seems to be taking place."

"I know there's a significant element of risk involved, but if you can get word to Eduardo's relative, the aircraft carrying this 'Bronze Star' person has filed a flight plan to land at Simon Bolivar tonight at 2200 your time. The pilot is named Is'haaq Al Kabil, and the aircraft is a Boeing 737 with Argentine registry, LV-TRK. It's painted to look like an International Air Express freighter."

"I'll get right on this," said Newman. "We don't have much time. Do you have any idea who this 'Bronze Star' guy really is?"

There was a long pause, then Goode responded, "It's just my hunch. Not very many people here agree, but I think it's Dimitri Komulakov—and I believe he has been running the nuclear weapons part of this whole thing for the Iranians all along."

CHAPTER TWENTY

Veterans' Day

Venezuelan Air Force Hangar 3
Simon Bolivar International Airport
Caracas, Venezuela
Friday, 09 November 2007
0030 Hours Local

Don't tell me that it cannot be done!" Komulakov snarled at Zhdanov. The Russian nuclear weapons expert recoiled in terror, fearing he was about to be struck. Furious, the ex-KGB general continued, "You must make the rest of these warheads ready, or none of us will be paid!"

"Sir, please hear me out on this," said Maj. Gregor Argozvek, intervening between Komulakov and the shaken scientist. When the enraged general paused in his tirade, Argozvek looked around the room to make sure that the door to his adjoining office in the hangar was closed. When he was sure that only Komulakov, Zhdanov, and Major Sakharovsky could hear what he was about to say, he continued: "The Iranians are not aware that two of the six remaining warheads have not yet been repaired—nor do they need to know."

"What do you mean, 'the Iranians are not aware'?" demanded Komulakov. "Hasn't this Manucher

Rashimani been watching everything that has been going on here?"

"It is true that he has been here a great deal, General," replied Argozvek, "but he does not know enough about the warheads to know whether one will detonate and another will not. The warhead we put on the containership headed for Galveston was one of those that Dr. Zhdanov had not yet repaired. Rashimani was with us that whole time, and he said nothing."

"But when I arrived here two hours ago from Cuba," interjected Komulakov, in a calmer voice, "the first thing Rashimani said to me was that we must have all of the remaining weapons ready to go by midnight tomorrow night."

"Yes, sir," said Argozvek, nodding his head, "that is because Rashimani's only job is to make sure that the pilots of the planes and the crews of the ships carrying the warheads know where they are to go when they leave here early on the morning of the eleventh—and that they know how to detonate the weapons. I provided all of this information to Colonel Dubzhuko several days ago."

"Well, since Dubzhuko is dead, tell *me* what you told him," said Komulakov.

Argozvek nodded and continued, "There is not much else. We have eight aircraft and six warheads here. Doctor Zhdanov has replaced the tritium triggers in five of the six weapons. Those five with the new components will certainly detonate. The other one probably will not. We have neither the parts nor the time to refurbish it, but none of the Iranians or the jihadis know this. They think all the weapons will work."

Komulakov looked at the slovenly scientist and said, "Is that correct, Zhdanov?"

The weapons expert meekly nodded and said, "Yes."

"Has Rashimani told you his plan?" asked Komulakov, turning back to the GRU major.

"Here is what he has told me," answered Argozvek, consulting notes that he removed from his pocket. "By 2100 tomorrow night he expects warheads to be installed in six of the aircraft: the two Airbuses, both 737s, a Gulfstream, and the Hawker. All eight of the aircraft are to be fully fueled and out on the apron by 2200. Each aircraft will be crewed by two of what he calls their 'martyrs': a pilot and a copilot. At his command, they will depart individually for their target cities in the United States with instructions to arrive over their target cities at 0700."

"This is not what we originally planned many months ago in Tehran," said Komulakov, awed by the audacity of the plot. "We were going to pre-position the planes in Mexico, Canada, and the Caribbean islands and attack from many different directions. Did Rashimani say how he expects these 'martyrs' to penetrate the American air defenses?"

"No," replied Argozvek, putting away his notes, "but I did hear him tell several of the pilots yesterday, 'If Colombian infidels can fly planeloads of drugs into America, then Islamic warriors should be able to deliver Allah's cleansing fire the same way.' "

National Military Command Center
The Pentagon, Arlington, VA
Friday, 09 November 2007
0700 Hours Local

"Pete, we're sending you the latest imagery from the most recent satellite pass. The folks at NRO agree that those eight commercial aircraft outside hangar 3 on the military side of Simon Bolivar Airfield are very likely all repainted, stolen Saudi planes. We've looked at the options here and believe that if at all possible, they need to be taken out down there before they ever get off the ground," said Gen. George Grisham over the speaker hooked into the secure voice circuit. The Chairman of the Joint Chiefs of Staff, Secretary of Defense Dan Powers, and the CIA's Bill Goode were sitting at a conference table in the NMCC, deep beneath the Pentagon's A-Ring. In Caracas, Brig. Gen. Peter Newman, Lt. Col. Dan Hart, Sgt. Maj. Amos Skillings, and the team leaders for Newman's little task force were jammed into the office of the CJR Warehouse. Grisham continued, "We're pretty sure that we have all bases covered on the threat from any remaining Saudi ships. Last night at 1800, the USS *Virginia* sank a pirated Saudi vessel headed out of Maracaibo, and then about three hours later the *Dallas* dropped one trying to make it into La Guaira from Aruba."

"Well, sir," said Newman, "if that means I can pull my five-man OP back from over-watch at the port, it'll give me a few more 'bullet throwers' if we have to shoot our way into that hangar at Simon Bolivar."

"Go ahead and pull 'em back, then," said Grisham. "What else do you need that we can send your way?"

Newman realized that if his task force were going to have to blast their way into the military side of the airport, destroy eight aircraft, and perhaps seize an unknown number of nuclear weapons, this was likely his last chance to get additional assets. He looked down at his notes and said, "I know it's a long shot, but can we get any fixed-wing close-air support?"

"Are you talking about an air strike on Caracas?" the SecDef asked. "You saw the Presidential Guidance on this, Pete. He doesn't want to start a war with Venezuela—he just wants to keep those pirated Saudi airplanes from getting to American cities. Everybody here knows that the easiest thing to do would be to bomb the beans out of that hangar and those Saudi airplanes. Unfortunately, we can't do that without also hitting Valdez's Air Force—and if there really are nuclear warheads in that hangar or aboard those Saudi aircraft, we'll spread radioactive waste all over the place—and catch unmitigated grief from the rest of the world for decades."

Newman shrugged and plunged on. "Sir, I'm not suggesting a 'Rolling Thunder' air raid on Caracas, but if my guys can't find a way to just sneak into the military side of the airport and take out those planes, I'm going to need more support than I've got. Our recon team and the 'local' we've got inside confirm the presence of eleven Russian, twenty-five Middle Eastern, and as many as fifty Venezuelan MAMs in and around that hangar and those airplanes. All I have is fifty-three 'shooters,' Mr. Secretary. We're going to try to slip in there tomorrow night and do this as quietly as possible, and slip back out again. Our egress plan is to have the SEALs from the *Dallas* and the *Virginia* extract us off the beach. But if there's a gunfight, I'll need some help or we're going to have a lot of dead soldiers, sailors, and Marines."

In the NMCC, the Secretary of Defense and the Chairman of the Joint Chiefs looked at each other. Finally Grisham spoke. "You're right, Pete. At the very least, you're going to need something 'on call.' We'll kick this around with the chiefs here in 'the tank' later this morning and get you some kind of fire support."

CJR Warehouse
867 Avenida Maiquetia, Caracas, Venezuela
Friday, 09 November 2007
1600 Hours Local

"I think we've got it, sir," said Lt. Col. Dan Hart as he, Sergeant First Class Robert Nievos, and Eduardo Roca walked into the warehouse office/command post.

Both Brigadier General Newman and Sgt. Maj. Amos Skillings looked up from the satellite imagery that they had been poring over. Newman said, "Got what, Dan?"

"I think Eduardo and SFC Nievos have found a way for us to get as many as forty of our men into the airport without any problem. I don't know why we didn't think of it before."

"I'm willing to look at any good ideas right now," Newman responded. "Amos and I have been working on the back end of this problem: how to get fifty-three U.S. military personnel, two CIA females, and six American civilian tech-reps from the airport four miles down the road to the beach, link up with thirty-two Navy SEALs, paddle out to two U.S. submarines, and get clear of this place before Valdez and his band of merry minions catch us. What's your idea?"

"Starting tomorrow morning—so it's not too obvious— we send forty of our 'operators' to the domestic terminal at the airport with their bags packed—just like any other departing passengers," said Hart. "They buy tickets for flights that depart from Concourse B—those are the commuter airlines. They go through security, then downstairs like they're going to board the little bus that takes them over to the B Concourse—only the shuttle bus they take drops them off at the old Avianca Airlines hangar, here . . ." Hart said, pointing to the satellite imagery on the table. "By 1700 or so, we'll have forty men inside the airport security perimeter—granted, on the civilian side of the field—but they'll be almost directly across the runway from hangar 3."

"Who's driving the bus that takes our guys from the main terminal to the Avianca hangar instead of Concourse B?" asked Newman.

Hart smiled and said, "Who else? The Roca family has the contract for the airport shuttle buses—including the one that shuttles between the terminal and the concourses. They aren't allowed over on the military side of the field. That's why we didn't think of it before."

"How do our guys get their weapons?" asked Skillings. "They sure can't take 'em through security—and forty unarmed guys, no matter how tough they are, won't be much help taking down the aircraft on the other side of the field tomorrow night."

"Right, Sergeant Major," Nievos replied. "Eduardo, tell 'em about the Avianca hangar."

Roca shrugged his seersucker shoulders and said, "Well, I just rented the Avianca hangar this afternoon to use for maintaining my shuttle buses. It has been empty for about six months—ever since Valdez stepped up his support for the FARC terrorists and the government in Bogota responded by cutting their flights. First thing tomorrow morning, my sons must move much equipment in large, heavy boxes into the hangar. If you pack the weapons in plywood boxes tonight, they will be there waiting as your men filter into the Avianca hangar during the day tomorrow."

"I'm impressed so far," said Newman. "But tomorrow night, how do these forty men get across to the military side of the field if your shuttle buses can't cross over to that side."

Hart, smiling, said, "Remember Eduardo's nephew—the one in the Venezuelan Air Force Security Police?"

"Yeah," said Newman.

"Well, his new job at the air base is driving those blue Air Force buses—the ones that are permitted to go anywhere on the field," replied Hart. "Tomorrow night, at the designated time, he takes one of the blue buses, drives around to the Avianca hangar, picks up our forty guys, and brings them right to the front door of hangar 3!"

Newman shook his head, marveling at the simplicity of the plan. He turned to Skillings and said, "That blue bus solves another problem for us: how to get all of our guys from the airport to the beach to link up with the SEALs from the *Dallas* and *Virginia*. The blue bus, plus the Suburbans, should give us enough mobility to do it all in one move."

"Yes, sir," said the sergeant major. "About the only thing we haven't licked is how to keep local military reinforcements from getting to hangar 3 from their barracks to the south of the flight line once the shooting starts."

Hart agreed. "That is a problem. You only have thirteen men—and two women, I guess—for a security element, command and control, and a base of fire along the back gate behind the hangar. We need to find some way to keep reinforcements from getting to hangar 3 for ten or fifteen minutes while we take out the Saudi planes, find any nukes that are lying around, police up our brass, and skedaddle for the subs."

Newman's head snapped back. "The subs . . . that's it!"

"What's *it*, sir?" said Skillings.

"The subs—that's where we're going to get our fire support," said Newman. "Sergeant Major, draft a message for the Chairman of the Joint Chiefs of Staff and tell him we need four Tomahawk TLAM-Cs 'on call' for tomorrow night. Give him the ten-digit GPS coordinates for the Venezuelan Air Force barracks building and the electrical distribution transformers at the far end of the airport."

Home of Samir Habib
Anah, Iraq
Saturday, 10 November 2007
0515 Hours Local

"You are up early this morning," said Samir Habib to his father. Both men were wearing traditional Arab robes to lessen the predawn chill along the northern Euphrates. The songbirds in the palms and olive trees were chirping and trilling.

"Yes, my son," said Eli Yusef Habib. Then the old man added, "I had a dream . . . and could not go back to sleep. So I arose to pray and read the Scriptures."

Samir knew that when his father had a dream it was not the trivial nocturnal occurrence that most people experience. His father's dreams often had "significance." Eli Yusef was a devout man and had lived a long life of faith. And sometimes his dreams were an extension of that "life of faith" experience. "Can you tell me about your dream?" Samir asked his father.

"It was very strange," Eli Yusef began. "It was about our friend Peter Newman and his friend—the black man."

"Sergeant Skillings?" Samir prompted.

"Yes, Amos Skillings."

"What were they doing?"

The old man sat in his carved wooden chair and placed his hands in his lap atop his open Bible. "Peter and Amos were together, and they were battling a great enemy—an evil one that they had fought before. This evil one is intent on starting a great fire that will consume the innocent and the guilty alike. It was a great and terrible battle, with many soldiers on both sides." Eli Yusef paused, as if to give his son time to visualize the dream.

"Go on, Father," Samir urged.

"Peter and Sergeant Skillings have swords, and Sergeant Amos Skillings is able to fly over the heads of the enemy and attack them with his sword, while they try to kill him. He is always able to elude their weapons," said the elder Habib.

Samir's thoughts were distracted by the dream. *Dreams are so strange,* he thought. *In our dreams we never question how it is that someone can fly.*

His father continued his narrative. "But then, just as the evil ones are being vanquished, Amos Skillings has a choice—he can flee or confront the leader of the evil ones. He chooses confrontation—even though he knows it will mean his death. The evil one is slain, but the fire he has started is now raging. To save the innocent, Amos Skillings throws himself into the fire—and is consumed by it."

Samir shivered in the early morning mist and didn't realize that it was a reflex of hearing what his father described. He licked his lips and sat down in a nearby chair as Eli Yusef continued.

"But Peter's friend seems to be dead only momentarily," Eli Yusef said. "After he is killed and lies lifeless for a brief time, he gets up—restored to life. And looking around, I see that all of Peter's enemies are gone, and he stands alone with his men. And then, Amos Skillings stands alone but surrounded by legions of people who want to thank him for his valor in the battle and for saving their lives. But he seems not to notice these people. Instead, he flies into the sky again—only this time he flies up and up, until we can no longer see him. And then I woke up."

"What do you suppose it means, Father?" Samir asked.

The old man smiled and shrugged. "Sometimes a dream is just a dream," he said.

"And yet, sometimes God speaks to you through such dreams. Has God spoken to you about *this* dream?"

"Not yet, my son," Eli Yusef replied. "If there is a message, He will tell me."

Samir said nothing, but then he asked, "Did this 'evil one' in your dream have a face, Father?"

The old man thought for a moment and then said, "Yes, my son, it was the same man that our friend Peter Newman confronted many years ago, over on the Syrian border. He was a Russian, I believe. I can still see his face."

"He has a name too, Father," said Samir. "Dimitri Komulakov. Perhaps I should call our friend William Goode."

"This is the word that God gave me," Eli Yusef said, flipping the pages in his well-worn Bible. He read:

All who rage against you will surely be ashamed and disgraced; those who oppose you will be as nothing and perish. Though you search for your enemies, you will not find them. Those who wage war against you will be as nothing at all. For I am the Lord, your God, who takes hold of your right hand and says to you, "Do not fear; I will help you."

"Has God given you any specific message besides what this Scripture passage says?" Samir asked his father.

The older man shook his head. "I cannot think of any. If it is important, God will speak. It will be good if I listen for His voice. But I think it would be wise for you to call our fellow believer, William Goode, as you suggest. Meanwhile, I shall pray for our friends, Peter and Amos, and ask God to protect them."

Venezuelan Air Force Hangar 3
Simon Bolivar International Airport
Caracas, Venezuela
Saturday, 10 November 2007
0700 Hours Local

"Have you made our reservations for a flight out of this tropical hell, Viktor?" asked Komulakov, turning toward the *Spetznatz* officer. The "retired" KGB general and Majors Argozvek and Sakharovsky were standing inside the office adjacent to hangar 3, watching through the glass partition as a pirated Saudi Lear jet with its "new" registry designator—TI-PQG, appropriated from a Costa Rican charter jet—was pushed from the hangar into the gray, early light of dawn.

"Yes, General," replied Sakharovsky. "As you directed, you are booked on the 0600 flight to Paris tomorrow morning as Vladimir Zhivkov. I am going to Cape Town, South Africa, via São Paulo, and Major Argozvek has booked himself on the morning flight to Rio de Janiero."

"Well done," said Komulakov to Sakharovsky. Then, turning to the taller GRU major, he asked, "Which two of those eight aircraft out there do not have warheads in them, Gregor Argozvek?"

"That one—that's being pushed out right now," replied Argozvek, pointing at the plane visible through the glass, "and the other Lear. But the pilots say they would be very happy to fly their airplanes into buildings in Miami and Atlanta."

Komulakov shook his head in disgust and asked, "Is everything else in order?"

"Yes, General. As soon as that aircraft is fueled," Argozvek said, "we will have completed all of our tasks. Dr. Zhdanov is now packing up all of his equipment. He will be flying out at 0200 to Buenos Aires."

"Where is the old fool going from there?" asked Komulakov.

"I do not know, sir, but he has given me the number for a bank account in Luxemburg in which he asks that you make his final payment."

"Humph," Komulakov grunted. "Before I can pay anyone else, the Iranians must make their final deposit. Where is Manucher Rashimani? I must talk to him about that. Before these eight aircraft take off, the Iranians are supposed to make a wire transfer into a numbered account in Switzerland. What time is the first one of these suicide flights scheduled to depart?"

Argozvek withdrew two sheets of paper from his pocket and said, "Rashimani is briefing the 'martyr pilots' on their routes and targets in the International Air Express 737 that you arrived on. It's out there on the apron, among the MiGs." Then, handing his employer one of two sheets of paper and consulting the other, he said, "This is the list you asked me to prepare. According to Rashimani, the first plane to leave is the Airbus 319 with the Panamanian registry HP-5691JMC. It departs at 0030 tonight, headed for Los Angeles. The second one to go is a Gulfstream, with Cayman Islands registry VPC-LG. It leaves here at 0100 in the morning and its target is Chicago. The third one is a Gulfstream—"

"That is enough, Gregor Argozvek," commanded the general. "I have the list. I couldn't care less what time the rest of these suicidal fanatics are taking off or over what American city they plan to immolate themselves. The only thing that matters is what time the first one is scheduled to depart. You say twelve-thirty tonight. Before then, Ali Yunesi must make a deposit."

"Or what?" said Argozvek, looking directly at his superior. "What if they do not pay? How are we going to stop them or force the Iranians to pay?"

Komulakov was not used to having his orders or judgment questioned—particularly by a relatively junior officer. Normally he would have exploded in rage—or worse, acted on it—when confronted with such impertinence. Instead, his face twisted into a cruel smile and he said, "If I do not have notice that payment has been received before the first aircraft takes off, Ali Yunesi in Tehran will be informed by Manucher Rashimani, or that other goon who came with me from Cuba, Assad Bashayan, that the American Embassy in Caracas will have this list within the hour. Then his 'martyrs' will find out what the Iraqi Air Force learned too late about how good American pilots are at shooting—how do they say it?—'fish in a barrel.' "

National Military Command Center
The Pentagon, Arlington, VA
Saturday, 10 November 2007
0900 Hours Local

"Happy Marine Corps Birthday, Pete," said Gen. George Grisham over the secure phone link.

"Thanks, General, and the same to you," Newman replied. "I'd forgotten that the Corps is 232 years old today—but today I feel every one of them."

"I have no doubt that you're tired, Pete," the Chairman of the Joint Chiefs replied, "but I do have a nice birthday present for you."

"What's that, sir?" said Newman, standing at the folding table in his office/command post, looking into the now nearly empty warehouse that had been such a beehive of activity for so many days.

"I just saved 15 percent on my car insurance," Grisham said, trying to ease the tension. Then he continued. "The President just approved the use of as many Tomahawk TLAM-Cs as you want tonight. The only restrictions are that you may target only military personnel or installations and must try to avoid hitting those nuclear warheads, to avoid spreading radioactive waste. I've just sent the alert order to both the *Dallas* and the *Virginia*."

Newman smiled for the first time in nearly twenty-four hours, then asked, "You said 'only military targets,' but can we still take out the airport electrical grid? We'll do a lot better tonight with the NVGs if we're the only ones who can see in the dark."

"Roger that," said Grisham.

"Great," said Newman. "I'll send in the coordinates of twenty preplanned targets and we'll only use the ones we need. The barracks and the electrical transformers will be targets 1 and 2. They will have to be hit first—and simultaneously. We'll use that as the signal to kick off the attack. Since I can't communicate directly with the subs, how do you want me to call for the Tomahawks?"

"Use your D-DACT as primary, secure Sat-Com voice as backup. We'll have both of them constantly monitored here until we get the word that you have everyone safely out to the subs," Grisham replied.

"Did anyone come up with what we're supposed to do with these nukes if we find them on the aircraft?" asked Newman. "I really only have four guys with me who know anything about how to disarm a Soviet-era 152mm nuclear artillery round—Dan Hart, two of the SEALs, and Sergeant Major Skillings. They have briefed everyone else on how to do it, but I don't want to hang my hat on their crash course on nuclear weapons assembly and disassembly."

Grisham didn't reply immediately but then said, "The Navy isn't happy about this answer, but the specialists here and at Los Alamos we consulted agreed that the best thing you can do is to bring them with you to the beach where the SEAL teams will have 'experts' who will disable them and bring 'em out to the subs. We all agree that you can't leave them behind."

Newman shrugged and said, "Roger that."

"You have anymore questions, Pete?" asked Grisham.

"No sir, everything else here is just about ready," Newman replied. "This place is just about empty except for the teams going with Skillings and me in the Suburbans. The weapons and ordnance for forty 'shooters' got delivered to the Avianca hangar about an hour ago, and thirteen of our guys are already there. If all goes as planned from here on out, this whole thing will go down at 2300 tonight—and by midnight we'll be on our way to the subs."

"Well done, Pete," said Grisham. Then he added,

"Hold on a second. Bill Goode is here with a message to pass on from a mutual friend."

"Pete, I just heard from Samir Habib," said the CIA Ops Deputy. "He said his father had *discerned*—that was the word he used—that Dimitri Komulakov is somewhere near you. Were you able to see who got off that flight last night from Cuba?"

"No, sir," Newman replied, "we didn't want to get caught by any of the Valdez goons looking for curfew violators."

"Well, the timing of this call from Samir is very interesting," said Goode. "Last night the mobile Sig-Int site in Norway that has been monitoring the Murmansk satellite hub said that the channel they thought was Komulakov's has gone cold."

"I'm not sure what to make of that, Bill," replied Newman. "But you know even better than I how very often Eli Yusef has been right. He has a very special gift."

"Yes, he does, Pete," replied the old CIA operative. "Just thought I'd pass it along. So be careful," said Goode, making the decision not to tell Newman that Eli Yusef had also "discerned" that Amos Skillings would be killed.

USS *Dallas*, SSN 700
67°08' W 11°40' N, Approx 409nm N of Maiquetia,
Venezuela
Saturday, 10 November 2007
2251 Hours Local

"Bring up the search 'scope one last time," said Capt. Ross Conner, moving from the plotting table to the starboard search periscope. He held the 'scope up only long enough to have it "sniff" for electronic emissions and then dropped it again.

"Nothing but the radars at the airport and the directional beacon from our SEAL team on the beach," said O'Malley, the XO.

"Roger that," said Conner. "We've got a good fix on our position?"

"Right where we're supposed to be," said the navigator.

"Man, we're a lot closer to the beach than I'd like to be for launching a Tomahawk," said Conner, looking at the electronic display above the chart table. On it were displayed twenty triangles, numbered one through twenty—all of them targets that Brig. Gen. Peter Newman had sent to the NMCC five hours ago from his D-DACT.

"We didn't have much choice, Skipper," said the XO. "It was either shoot from close in or make our SEAL team have to 'hump it' thirty miles to the beach."

Conner nodded and said, "Target 1 programmed into the TLAM-C in tube number one?"

"Roger," replied the weapons officer, double-checking his data.

Conner glanced up at the digital clock, slaved to the Naval Observatory in Washington, and said, "Prepare to launch Tomahawk from tube number one."

Five seconds later at precisely 2256 local, he said, "Fire one," and there was a now familiar rush of compressed air as an eighteen-foot-long, 3,200-pound Tomahawk missile was ejected from the number one torpedo tube. The smooth cylinder, containing more than 1,500 parts, sped straight out for fifty meters, suddenly turned up toward the surface, and shot out of the water. As it broke the surface of the Caribbean, the missile jettisoned its protective capsule, two wings flipped out, and a solid-fuel rocket booster ignited with a bright flare that lit up the surface of the sea. The Tomahawk's inner guidance controls sent the missile into the air in a high arc, and then—when the solid-fuel was spent—a turbofan engine leveled the missile in the air, pushing it at 550 miles per hour over the surface of the water toward Target 1—the Venezuelan Air Force barracks building at Simon Bolivar Airport, forty-two miles inland.

Seconds later, four miles to the west, an identical missile was launched from the USS *Virginia,* aimed at Newman's Target 2—the Simon Bolivar Airport electrical distribution grid. Both missiles leveled off, just feet above the water, practically invisible on radar as they sped toward the destinations programmed into their GPS memories. Both missiles climbed slightly as they crossed the white sand beach and then, less than a mile out, dived neatly into their targets. The Tomahawk launched from the USS *Dallas,* still nearly full of fuel, struck the barracks building just above the second floor of the four-story structure. Three seconds later, the one fired by the USS *Virginia* flew at full speed through the large, twelve-foot-square, top-left skylight of the Electrical Distribution Facility. The two buildings were blown apart by the explosions. As the lights went out throughout the airport, fire engulfed both buildings.

Venezuelan Air Force Annex
Simon Bolivar International Airport
Caracas, Venezuela
Saturday, 10 November 2007
2300 Hours Local

As the lights went out and the horrendous roar of the two, near-simultaneous Tomahawk explosions echoed across the airport, a blue Venezuelan Air Force bus pulled up in front of hangar 3. Men wearing NVGs, Kevlar helmets, and body armor poured out of the bus from every exit, assembled immediately into teams of five, and fanned out, racing for the eight commercial jets parked amidst the MiGs and other military aircraft.

Seconds later, when terrified men raced out of the

darkened hangar 3, they were immediately cut down by fire from a 240-G machine gun, positioned to the south of the structure. From his OP atop a building five hundred yards down the road, Master Chief Manuel Suazo, peering through the night scope mounted atop his Barrett .50 cal. sniper rifle, began dropping anyone who made a move toward the search teams headed for the aircraft flight line. Two of the first to die were Russian majors Gregor Argozvek and Viktor Sakharovsky when they ran out of the hangar.

One minute and ten seconds after the two cruise missiles impacted, Newman's "Mobile Command Group," mounted in five Suburbans, pulled up the perimeter road to a spot fifty meters short of the back gate behind hangar 3. A Delta Force commando jumped out of the lead vehicle, deployed an AT-4 anti-tank weapon, fired it, and blew away the metal gate. Leaving two Suburbans as a security element, Newman raced through the open portal with the other three vehicles to pick up any warheads found by the forty troopers searching the civil aircraft on the tarmac.

Sgt. Maj. Amos Skillings, driving Newman's Suburban, pulled up parallel with the front of the hangar. The large aircraft portal was still closed, but from inside the building they could hear the sounds of a pitched battle. Suddenly, Sergeant First Class Nievos came reeling out the front personnel door of the large hangar, dragging another wounded commando, his own MP5 hanging limply from his right hand. Newman turned to Skillings and said, "I'll be right back," and jumped out of the vehicle.

Skillings, seeing his commander running toward the wounded troopers, turned to the men in the backseat and yelled, "Go with him! Cover him! Tell Briggs, driving that Suburban behind me, to pull up and pick up the wounded!"

As the five men piled out of the side and rear doors of the vehicle to follow Newman, Skillings flipped his

NVGs back down and caught a glimpse of a heavyset man running toward a Boeing 737, parked about fifty meters away—on the side of the apron that had not yet been covered by one of the five-man search teams.

He tried calling on the handheld radio beside him, but the radio net was jammed with teams talking to one another. As he watched, the heavyset man reached the portable stairs beside the 737, looked around furtively, and scurried up the flight of steps.

Spotting two other soldiers dragging one of their wounded comrades toward the Suburban, Skillings shouted out, "Take the wounded to the vehicle behind this one! The general is over there." Then pointing toward the 737 off to the right, he shouted, "Tell General Newman I'm going to grab a team and check out that aircraft over there. . . ."

With that, the Marine sergeant major threw the Suburban into gear and raced out onto the tarmac, weaving in and out of the parked aircraft, looking for anyone not otherwise occupied. Suddenly, over the din of the firing, he heard the sound of a jet engine starting.

He looked toward the 737 that had originally caught his attention and realized too late that there were two heads in the cockpit, barely visible through his NVGs. He stopped looking for help and spun the wheel, turning the Suburban toward the big Boeing aircraft, intending to slam the vehicle into the nose wheel and prevent it from taking off.

Suddenly, thirty yards short of the aircraft, an RPG round, fired from one of the sandbagged revetments surrounding hangar 3, slammed into the right rear of the Suburban, spinning the vehicle out of control and igniting the nearly full gas tank. Grabbing his MP5 off the seat, Skillings rolled out of the burning SUV and onto the tarmac.

Lying prone on the black macadam, Skillings realized that he had lost his NVGs. But in the light of the fire behind him he could see a man at the top of the portable stairs struggling to try to close the main passenger hatch.

Skillings rolled, put the MP5 to his shoulder, tried to release the safety, and found that he could not. Holding the weapon up so that he could examine it in the light of the flames, he saw that the receiver was full of holes—shrapnel from the RPG. That's when he noticed the blood on his dark skin. He rolled again, looking where he had been, and saw a puddle of his own blood.

As the wounded Marine started to feel around his body, trying to find the source of the hemorrhage, the heavyset man raced down the portable stairs to release the brake holding the movable steps against the 737. Forcing himself to his feet, Skillings drew his 9mm Beretta and stumbled toward the aircraft, as the heavyset man raced back up the stairs.

Skillings got to the bottom of the steps as the man reached the top. The Marine pistol expert paused, fired once, and charged up the steps as the large figure fell back inside the cabin.

With his "ski boot" foot cast making a clumping noise on the metal steps, the wounded American hauled himself to the top of the stairs and into the cabin. Immediately, a burst of fire from the cockpit struck him in the left side, and he fell on top of the heavyset man whom he had just shot. As Skillings lost consciousness, he realized that the man beneath him was Dimitri Komulakov.

Neither the Russian nor the American Marine heard Is'haaq Al Kabil, in the left seat of the cockpit, say in Arabic, "Good shooting, Jabbar. Now go push the stairs back from the door so we can depart and carry out our mission for Allah."

❂

As the copilot returned to his seat and strapped in, Kabil spooled up the 737's two GE turbofan engines, deftly turned the aircraft to avoid the burning Suburban and becoming entangled in the portable stairs, and spun again to get on the taxiway. At the last minute he flicked on his landing lights to align the plane with the narrow, darkened tarmac, turned the light off again, and then, pushing the throttles to their stops, did the unthinkable—took off on the taxiway.

In front of hangar 3, Newman heard the sound of the aircraft screaming down the dark taxiway, turned to Pamela Browne, one of the CIA women he had pressed into service as a communicator, and said, "Call Search Team 1 and see if they got the tail number of the aircraft. We've got to let Washington know one got away. Then see if you can raise Sergeant Major Skillings on the radio."

Three minutes later, as Newman and Lt. Col. Dan Hart were taking a "head count," supervising the loading of five 152mm nuclear warheads in the back of the Suburbans, and directing the placement of the wounded in the blue bus, Browne interrupted to say, "Lt. Jim Curry with Team 1 reports that the aircraft that got off is a Boeing 737 with 'International Air Express' markings and registration designator: LV-TRK. He thinks Skillings may have gotten aboard. He doesn't answer on the radio."

"Dan, send off that airplane info immediately to SOCOM and the JCS on your D-DACT," ordered Newman. Then, turning to Browne, he said, "See if you can raise Skillings on his D-DACT. If he's still alive, I want to communicate with him about our options for bringing down that aircraft without losing him."

"Roger that, General. I'll get right on it," said Browne.

Newman turned back to Hart and said, "Do we have everyone?"

"Yes, sir," Hart responded. "We have two dead and

nine wounded though. It may slow us down when we get to the beach. I'll notify the SEALs."

"Do we have all the seized weapons loaded?" Newman asked.

"Yes, sir."

"Any 'High Value' detainees we should take with us?"

"No," said Hart. "There are several dead Russians inside the hangar and a few more outside. All of the pilots of the commercial planes were in their cockpits, and they're all dead—except for the one or two that got away. And there are six dead guys in the hangar who are Iranian. I have their passports."

"Good work, Dan," said Newman. "Let's get out of here. We're going to have to double up—that's my Suburban burning out there on the tarmac. As soon as the last vehicle is a klick down the road, I'll send a D-DACT to the JCS to alert the subs we're coming and tell 'em to give us another Tomahawk on Target 3—this hangar."

Twenty-five minutes later the little convoy of Suburbans and a blue bus pulled up on the Maiquetia beach and were greeted by thirty-two heavily armed U.S. Navy SEALs. Newman looked at his watch. It was exactly twelve-thirty in the morning on 11 November. Veterans' Day, 2007.

Aboard "International Air Express" Boeing 737, LV-TRK
35nm E of Boot Key, Florida,
Sunday, 11 November 2007
0200 Hours Local

Is'haaq Al Kabil was a self-destructive, homicidal terrorist. But he was also a very good pilot. For more than three hours he had been pushing the rugged Boeing 737 and its twin GE turbofan engines to their limit. Kabil kept the airplane—made to fly economically at 25,000 feet or more—at no more than 200 feet and no less than 450 knots as he screamed northwest toward his target: Dallas, Texas. Flying the straightest possible route, he'd had to pull up to get over the rugged spine of Cuba. Now, as he neared the Florida Keys, after nearly 1,200 miles of low-altitude flight, he felt the need to relieve himself. He pulled up to 250 feet, put the aircraft on autopilot, told Jabbar to be attentive to the controls and the altitude, and opened the cockpit door.

Barely glancing down at the dead American lying atop the dead Russian, he stepped over the bodies, opened the door to the head, and, from force of habit, closed the door behind himself. As he did so, Amos Skillings stirred.

As he became conscious, the Marine sergeant major realized that he was gravely injured. Each breath produced a bubbling sensation in his left lung, and he could taste blood in his mouth. His left arm was numb, and he had no sensation in his fingers. But with a massive effort he could still move his right arm and hand and soon found the Beretta 9mm pistol he had fallen on when he was shot.

As he grasped the butt of the weapon, he heard the snap of the lock as Kabil opened the door to the head. For a split second, the grievously wounded Marine considered "playing possum" in hopes that Kabil would pass by, but then reasoned he did not know how much life he had left. With a superhuman effort, Skillings rolled left, onto his painfully shattered ribcage, raised his arm, pointed the pistol at the wide-eyed pilot, and pulled the trigger.

Kabil was dead before he hit the carpeted floor of the aircraft. And somehow, Skillings managed to climb over his inert form and make his way to the cockpit where Jabbar was frantically trying to extricate himself from his harness and reach a switch taped to the top of the instrument panel in front of the vacant command pilot's seat.

Despite his wounds and loss of blood, Skillings quickly deduced that this switch was very likely connected to a nuclear warhead somewhere in the aircraft. Even though the copilot was his only chance for a safe landing, the sergeant major didn't hesitate. He raised the pistol and fired again. As Jabbar slumped back into his seat, Skillings crawled forward to see if he could figure out where they were.

As he painfully worked himself into the vacant pilot's seat, dragging his "ski-boot" walking cast over the center console, Skillings examined the instrument panel, searching for familiar instruments known to every military man with years of experience around aircraft—the altimeter, air speed indicator, the GPS. First he found the altimeter and shook his head to clear his vision—until he realized that it really was reading 200 feet!

In a few seconds he found the GPS and was able to discern that they were nearing the Florida Keys. He immediately thought of Rachel, James, and Lizzie Newman somewhere down there—and he thought about the fact that he was riding at the controls of a nuclear weapon that could go off at anytime. He desperately wondered why the aircraft had not been shot down—and then realized that it must be too low to have been picked up on radar.

After several moments of frustration, he found the IFF transponder and flicked it on, knowing that this would make the aircraft instantly visible to radar intercept operators. Finally, he located the autopilot.

For several seconds he contemplated how to turn off the autopilot switch with his right hand and still maintain control of the aircraft without being able to use his left arm. Finally, he made a lunge with his right hand, flicked off the autopilot, and grabbed the yoke, pulling back on it with all the strength he had left.

The nose of the big airplane pitched up and the altimeter began to spin like a clock on adrenaline. Unable to use the rudder pedals, he turned the wheel to the left and felt the G-force pushing him into the seat. As he tried desperately to steer the guided bomb away from the chain of tiny islands below, he could feel the blood draining from his head—and blackness enveloping him.

Blue Waters Retreat
Boot Key, FL
Sunday, 11 November 2007
0205 Hours Local

Rachel Newman had tossed and turned for three hours after going to bed but had been unable to sleep. Finally, frustrated at whatever it was that was keeping her awake, she got up, put on a robe, and quietly opened the front door of the house and sat down on the steps of the deck, facing the Atlantic Ocean.

For several minutes she listened to the gentle surf lapping a few hundred feet away on the shore and enjoyed the light, cool breeze blowing through her hair. *This place is perfect for the children,* she thought. It seemed so safe and peaceful here, and she wished Peter were with them.

After ten minutes or so of reverie, Rachel stood up and turned toward the front door. Suddenly there was a brilliant flash high in the sky behind her, so bright that it cast her shadow on the front of the house. She started to turn to see what it was, but as she did so, she could feel the warmth of the intense light on her face—not painful—more like standing in front of a blazing fireplace.

Rachel suddenly thought, *Terrorists! Nuclear*

weapons! She spun around to run into the house for her children. As she did so, her bare foot caught on the top step and she pitched forward onto the deck, striking her head on the edge of a heavy wooden recliner. In that instant, the bright light, and everything else, went black. Rachel never heard the ominous *thud* that came several seconds later—caused by whatever had made the vivid flash of light, thirty miles to the east.

CHAPTER TWENTY-ONE

Eulogy for a Brother

Oval Office
The White House
Sunday, 11 November 2007
1030 Hours Local

Dan Powers had called the President about the success in Venezuela and the Patriot PAC-III shoot-down east of the Florida Keys even before he and the First Lady had breakfast. The President uttered a grateful, "Thank God," then attended an early morning prayer-and-worship service. He later returned to the White House Situation Room to watch things play out in what he referred to as "the beginning of the end" of the nuclear crisis.

At 1000, Chief of Staff Bruce Allen came to him and said, "Mr. President, it looks like our prayers are answered. SOCOM reports that five nuclear weapons have been captured; that the 'Islamic Brotherhood' has gone off the net in Saudi Arabia. The only new wrinkle in the fabric is the Israelis have just informed us that early this morning they fired five Jericho-III missiles at the Iranian launch site near Tabriz and knocked out an Iranian nuclear-tipped Shahab 3 missile on the launcher. We're asking NRO for verification before we say anything."

The President smiled. "That's great news. Any loose ends?"

"The SecDef reports that we may have to deal with some back-blast—literally—over the weapon that was aboard a pirated Saudi Boeing 737 hit by that Patriot missile over the Gulf. One of our Marines, a Sergeant Major Skillings, is credited for heroically getting on board, taking over the aircraft, and diverting the plane before it could reach U.S. territory," Allen read from a report. "This man is a genuine hero," he added.

"It sounds like it," the President said. "God bless him. That took a lot of guts. Lesser men would have panicked and not kept their wits. There's an awful lot of people on the Gulf Coast who owe that Marine for saving their lives," the President said solemnly.

Bruce Allen handed him a 3 x 5 card. "What's this?" the President asked.

"It's the name and phone number of Sergeant Major Skillings's sister. She's his next of kin, sir."

"Uh . . . yeah . . . thank you." The President took the card, bowed his head, and said reverently almost to himself, "God bless you, Amos Skillings . . . and thank you, on behalf of a grateful nation." Then he looked into the face of his Chief of Staff and said, "I'll call his sister now . . . just excuse me for a few minutes."

"Yes, sir . . . thank you, Mr. President," Allen said as he backed out the door of the Oval Office.

❂

A half hour later the President went before TV cameras in the Rose Garden to give an "all clear" statement. "It is with a heart filled with thanksgiving to Almighty God that I come to you this morning. By now you have heard the reports of the detonation of a nuclear device off the Florida Keys. Let me tell you how that came about," the President told the American people.

"It is because of the personal sacrifice of an African-American Marine sergeant major that no lives were lost—except one. That single fatality was the precious life of Amos Skillings. He was a man of faith, the son of a black preacher, and a career Marine warrior. Sergeant Major Skillings was the brother of Mrs. Luella Banks, whom I had the sad duty to inform that her brother had lost his life as a sacrifice to America this morning," the President said sadly, but proudly.

"Amos Skillings represents everything hopeful about our great country. He also is a model for those who ask cynically, 'Where are today's heroes?' Sgt. Maj. Amos Skillings, USMC, represents the men and women of all the military services who serve quietly and selflessly around the world. They too have many among their ranks who have likewise given the greatest gift a man can give—the sacrifice of their own lives.

"Thanks in great part to Amos Skillings and his fellow warriors, I'm proud to be standing here this morning, and happy to tell you that this terrible crisis is finally over. Those who started it are standing down, and their evil accomplices are either dead or fleeing. The weapons of mass destruction that threatened our cities and homes have been captured. For all you who prayed that God would 'deliver us from evil,' you can be especially grateful to our God for bringing us through. So as we approach the Thanksgiving season, I know that your hearts will be especially overflowing at these wonderful answers to prayer.

"It is also ironic that I'm standing here this morning, and it's a bit odd that events have strangely brought us back to what originally took place on this date nearly a century ago. For you see, today is November eleventh . . . in 1918 this day was called Armistice Day . . . and sometime later it was renamed Veterans' Day. It was a day set aside especially to honor veterans—particularly those veterans who lost their lives, the ultimate sacrifice—in their duty protecting the United States of America. So, the irony today is that it's Veterans' Day once again. And more than ever, as Americans we've been made aware of the significance of those who have sacrificed for us. Today's generation of men and women in the military are still fighting the ongoing battle against tyranny so that the bells of freedom can ring loud and clear not just across this wonderful land but all over the world."

The President paused for only a brief moment, then his gaze wandered across the many faces in front of him, as if to impress upon each person listening the importance of his words. He said, "I want to conclude my remarks today with this reminder: we need to always remember this day of sacrifice and courage. Please bow your head and think for a moment of these brave men and women who serve without protest and who go quietly but steadfastly about their sworn duty to uphold and defend the Constitution of these United States of America. And today, let us take another moment to remember the valiant life and courageous death of a single brave Marine—Sgt. Maj. Amos Skillings."

The President bowed his head, closed his eyes, and there was absolute silence in the Rose Garden, save for the singing of birds nearby. After a moment, he said a quiet "Amen" and turned to walk back into the White House.

Emergency Medicine Clinic
Boot Key, FL
Sunday, 11 November 2007
1040 Hours Local

Rachel Newman had awakened in an ambulance— her head throbbing with dull pain from the fall on the deck of their beach house following the nuclear detonation twenty-five miles out at sea.

The doctor at the nearby emergency medicine clinic

had treated her for a deep laceration on her forehead, carefully sutured the cut with seven stitches, and bandaged her. "But I want you to stay here for another hour or so, to see if you have any other injury that shows up," he had told Rachel.

As she sat in the nearly empty waiting room, her eyes were fixed on the TV set on the wall. Young James and Elizabeth were sitting on chairs beside her. Lizzie was napping, her head in her mother's lap, but James was alert and his attention was riveted to what the President of the United States was saying. And when he mentioned the name of Amos Skillings, they both gasped in shock and looked at each other in disbelief as the President described what had happened.

James recalled memories of the gentle bear of a Marine who had befriended him and told him wonderful stories about his dad. Now his friend Amos was *dead*. The boy, not quite twelve, understood the concept of death but was still too immature to grapple with the emotions of great sadness and grief that accompany such events. He began to cry softly.

Rachel's reaction was more complex. She, too, was moved to tears at the announcement that their friend had been killed in action. She felt a catch in her throat as she remembered him and his selfless love for her family. But in addition to overwhelming grief for Amos, her emotions were also now immediately engaged with another, fearful thought—*Peter!*

She knew that Amos was with Peter; that they were on some kind of mission together, and if he were killed by a devastating nuclear blast, and if Peter were anywhere in the proximity, then he'd also be dead. Her heart began to race in a kind of panic.

The President concluded his brief televised Veterans' Day tribute from the Rose Garden of the White House, but Rachel could watch no longer. She was so overwhelmed with feelings of loss and helplessness that she felt weak and faint. She heard her cell phone chirping. At first she didn't know where it was. Then James reached into his pocket and retrieved it. She remembered; he must have used it to call "911" when he found her unconscious on the beach house deck.

James handed her the phone and she answered it hesitantly, as if she knew immediately that it would be bad news. "Hello?" she said weakly.

"Rachel, this is George Grisham. . . . I've been trying to reach you. I tried calling your vacation home in Boot Key, but there was no answer," he said.

"I . . . uh . . . I'm here," she said, afraid to ask the reason for the call.

"Rachel . . . please stand by . . . I've got someone on the line for you. Hang on."

There were several clicks and electronic sounds as the call was transferred to the cell phone. Her heart quickened when she understood that Peter was alive.

"Hello, Rachel . . . it's me. Are you guys all right?"

"Oh Peter! We are now. . . . We're going to be just fine."

Joint Session of Congress
Washington, DC
Monday, 19 November 2007
1111 Hours Local

Once again the U.S. House and Senate convened together—but this time not in secret. It had taken a week for members of both parties in both houses to convince their leaders that one of their own deserved censure for his actions that had contributed to a national crisis.

After less than forty minutes of debate, there was a call for a vote. "Will the honorable senator from Tennessee please read the resolution as proposed?"

The senator walked to the microphone, addressed the combined assembly of American representatives, and then read from the proposed resolution:

Whereas in a Joint Session of the One Hundred Tenth Congress held this nineteenth day of November 2007, we hereby resolve that this Congress has deliberated on matters pertaining to the Bill known as the "Terrorist Threat Mitigation Act of 2007" and finds that certain provisions of the Act were enacted as the result of affirmations and intelligence that were not provided to the Congress in good faith, and rather, were the result of a criminal conspiracy. It is therefore the resolution of this Body to agree that any and all pending or future actions whether planned or under consideration shall be held in abeyance until a bipartisan commission consisting of representative members of the three branches of government can form a committee of nine members — including three each from the legislative, judicial, and executive branches — to determine whether the organization created by Joint Session and named "The Threat Mitigation Commission" shall continue to exist and function as created.

When it came time for a vote, the resolution passed unanimously, with only two congressmen abstaining and none opposed.

Martyr's Square
Tehran, Iran
Tuesday, 27 November 2007
1900 Hours Local

For more than two weeks, the Iranian people had been hearing on television about what had transpired in their government and how a handful of people had disrupted the affairs of the entire world for a month. It had not taken long for opposition figures in Iran to assume a secular leadership role, assessing blame to those who had gotten caught.

The opposition publicly called for the United Nations to come and help them "root out those who had gone down this road to nuclear disaster." But in New York, the United Nations building was still almost empty; its leaders and administrators had not yet returned to the city since it had been threatened with a nuclear attack. Iranian dissidents committed to democracy provided evidence that the former ayatollah was the one responsible for creating the mythic Islamic Brotherhood and its supposed ties to Muslims worldwide.

The streets were filled with students and other Iranians seeking change in their government, mainly those who had demonstrated in favor of democracy. Yet now they came out by the hundreds of thousands. For days Martyr's Square in Tehran was filled with these joyous celebrants—eventually over a million of them—calling on their government to institute democratic ideals and reforms.

Amazingly, these younger citizens saw beyond the hateful rhetoric of their elders. In Tehran and other Iranian cities they shouted slogans advocating freedom and called for their country to change its policies and direction. People even waved tiny American flags—they just appeared spontaneously midway through the demonstration—and soon everyone wanted one. The emblem once trampled in the gutter or burned in the streets was now symbolic of the future. As one voice, thousands of Iranians yelled, "Freedom now!"

When these events were shown on international television, they sparked similar demonstrations in Baghdad, Beirut, and Amman. Fundamentalist jihadist Islamic leaders shuddered at what they saw. They now knew that they could no longer hold back the floodgates of liberty and democracy.

Newman Residence
Foxhall Road
Monday, 24 December 2007
1805 Hours Local

Six weeks after her reunion with Peter following the Saudi nuclear crisis, Rachel Newman pushed the switch on their family room wall, and the seven-foot-tall Christmas tree that they had just finished decorating flickered on with appropriate "oohs" and "ahs" from the children. Peter stretched his arm up to affix the silver angel onto the tip of the tree and adjusted it so it looked down on them all.

"Well . . . six weeks ago I was afraid that we wouldn't be together for Christmas Eve this year," Rachel said to her husband.

"So was I," he replied soberly. It had been a little more than a month and a half since the nuclear explosion had killed their good friend Amos Skillings but also brought an end to the terrorism and initiated a tentative peace in the Middle East. "We've got a lot to be thankful for this year," Peter added.

"Are you going to read us the Christmas story?" little Elizabeth asked her daddy.

"What a good idea, honey," said Rachel. "Why don't you guys get settled over there on the sofa by the fireplace while I get some cookies and milk for afterward."

As the children scurried over to find the best seat, the telephone rang. Newman was always wary when phone calls came at times like this. He picked up and said, "Hello?"

"Ah . . . my friend Peter," the voice said. "This is Samir Habib, and I wish for your family a blessed Christmas."

Relieved that this wasn't a work-related phone call, Newman replied, "And a merry Christmas to you and your family, Samir. It's so good to hear from you. But it's the middle of the night there in Iraq. Does your family celebrate Christmas Day this early?"

Samir did not respond to the question but asked, "Peter . . . do you recall when I contacted you right after the nuclear disaster off the coast of America?"

"Yes, you called to console me about the death of our friend Amos—and you told me about the strange dream that your father had about him the day before he died. You know what else is odd? I've run into a couple others who told me privately that they had the same dream. I haven't shared this with anyone. . . . I simply don't know what to make of it; do you?"

"That is why I am calling you—in addition to giving you our good wishes for a blessed Christmas, of course. I believe that my father's dream must have been supernatural. Why would several people have the same dream?" Samir asked.

"Yes, I've been wondering the same thing," Peter said. "And for the most part, the details were much the same. It's one thing to dream about a person, or for several people to dream about the same person, but for *all* those people to have the *same* dream—well, the odds of that must be astronomical."

"I have felt the same way," Samir told his friend. "But then yesterday while I was in Baghdad on business, my father was at our family compound in Anah and he called me. He said, 'Will you be coming home soon? I have had a revelation about the meaning of the dream I had about Amos Skillings. It is important.' And so I drove quickly to return to our home."

Peter knew about the deep faith and mystical, prayerful connection that the patriarch of the Habib clan seemed to have. Twice Eli Yusef had been "told by God" to interrupt his life and go to a certain place. Both times it was to save the life of Peter Newman. It didn't take any other convincing for Peter to believe that Eli

Yusef Habib was not just a Christian believer, but that he had a special connection with God.

"What did he tell you about the dream?" Newman asked his friend.

Samir waited for a moment before replying, and then he said, "When I arrived back home, I found my father sitting in his chair . . . his Bible spread out before him on the table . . . and his head was on his chest. He often falls asleep like that. But this time, when I tried to waken him, I could not. My father had gone to heaven."

Peter caught his breath, and his voice had great grief in it when he said, "Oh, Samir . . . I'm sorry . . . I'm truly sorry to hear that your father passed away. Please give our sympathy and condolences to the rest of the family, all right?"

"We are grieving, but we are at peace. Our hearts are reassured that Father has gone to heaven and is with the Lord he has served so faithfully these many years," Samir said quietly.

Rachel came over to stand by her husband when she heard Peter express his sadness and sympathy. He mouthed the words, "Eli Yusef passed away," and she understood.

As he continued talking about details of the funeral to be held the day after Christmas, Samir added, "We are saddened beyond expectations. We knew that my father had not been well the past two months or more, but we had no idea that he would die. Yet, as he has always said, 'My life and times are in God's hand.' We cling to that same assurance."

"I know how you feel, my friend," said Peter. "Rachel and I are still grieving for our friend Amos, and now we'll be grieving for another dear friend. Eli Yusef was a man I loved as much as my own father."

"And you were a son to him, too," Samir said. "He prayed for you every day. I only wish I could have been there when he received his insight regarding the strange dream."

"So you didn't get a chance to hear about his revelation?"

"No . . . and even his notes scribbled in his prayer journal told me nothing. He had simply written down ideas that came to him while reading the Bible, and they were all about the Bible passage he was reading from. Except—" Samir said hesitantly.

"Except for what?" Peter asked.

"He wrote something on the back of an envelope. . . . It was for you."

"For me?"

"Yes, Peter. The note said, 'Tell Peter that his warriors did not find them all.' I do not know what that means—do you?" Samir asked.

The hair on the back of Peter Newman's neck stood up. Eerily the voice of Gen. George Grisham flashed into his mind—he had used precisely the same words when he told Newman that very morning, "Pete . . . I'm sorry to have to tell you that your Special Ops guys didn't find them all—we have intel that says that there's still one or more nuclear weapons out there someplace. And we have no idea where to start looking for them."

EPILOGUE

In the days, weeks, and months following the nuclear crisis, the world seemed to quieten some. Tentative and fledgling efforts toward peace and democracy took root in Iran, just as they had in Iraq—which grew stronger day by day. Under pressure from the United States and Great Britain, the leaders of radical Islam seemed to stop and reassess their strategies. In the West, leaders tried to pick up the pieces after coming so near to Armageddon.

Amos Skillings was honored with a marker and eulogized at Arlington National Cemetery on 15 November 2007, and two months later his sister Luella was invited to the White House where she accepted on behalf of her brother the President's award of the Congressional Medal of Honor. Enlistments in the USMC increased by 17 percent in the six months following his death.

Brig. Gen. Peter Newman was reassigned at his own request to the Marine Corps Combat Training Command at Quantico, Virginia, so he could have more time with his family. In 2012, he will make a decision on whether to run for the U.S. Senate. Peter Newman's son James plans to enroll at the U.S. Naval Academy in 2015.

The President accepted the findings of a bipartisan commission concerning serious problems (including evidence of criminal conduct) on the part of Senator James Waggoner and others, and the Threat Mitigation Commission was finally dismantled and scrapped in June 2008.

Ralph Monroe, in exchange for a promise not to prosecute him, turned over tapes, documents, and other evidence to a Grand Jury convened by the U.S. Attorney for the District of Columbia during his investigation of U.S. Senator James Waggoner for illegally divulging classified information and campaign finance fraud. He also granted extensive interviews to the FBI in their conspiracy case against Waggoner. Monroe later became a highly paid consultant and a Washington lobbyist for a major pharmaceutical firm.

James Waggoner resigned his Senate seat after being indicted on twenty-seven separate criminal and conspiracy charges. After a sixteen-month-long trial Waggoner was sentenced to twenty years in prison. He died in prison after serving three years of his sentence.

William Goode retired from the CIA in June 2008, after locating Dimitri Komulakov's hidden fortune. Goode donated the confiscated funds to the Fellowship of Believers and the "Amos Skillings Scholarship Fund" for the children of military personnel killed in the line of duty.

Samir Habib decided to sell the family business and then have a role in the government of the emerging democratic nation of Iraq. In 2009 he was elected to a seat in the Iraqi Parliament.

Marine Lt. Col. Dan Hart was awarded the Bronze Star for his heroic action in Venezuela in 2007. He was also awarded the Navy-Marine Corps Medal for saving the lives of fellow Special Operations warriors.

Prince Arshad, the only surviving member of the Saud Royal family, completed his education at the U.S.

Naval Academy and after graduating became the king of Saudi Arabia. He now works to establish his country as a new democracy in the Middle East.

Gen. George Grisham retired from the Marine Corps in 2008 and settled in North Carolina, where he practices fly-casting in a local trout stream and is writing his memoirs.

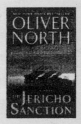